Have you ever heard of Fei Tsui jade? … It's the only
really valuable kind.

Raymond Chandler, *Farewell, My Lovely*

Freddie! Startled, she put her hand up to her necklace. 'Yes ... I suppose ... I never thought ... yes, he'd have loved it – did love it. I think he was here at the end of the war.' And she felt guilty, for it must be – oh, aeons – since she'd thought about Freddie.

'I wonder what he'd make of it all today.' Charles squinted away into the white heat of the square. 'He'd be bored by the politics. Bombs, kidnapping, revolutionary violence, that wasn't exactly his scene.' He grinned. Renato shifted in his seat and an odd, flickering glance passed between the two men.

'I suppose Freddie was more of an aesthete.'

Again the silence became awkward, with Renato fidgeting and then, when the waiter brought the beers, questioning Charles in Italian.

'That whole business fucked me up completely for years.' Charles was looking at her again now. 'I was so angry with Freddie for dying. I hated everything, I hated everyone. Actually, that's what I like about Italy now. Everyone's so fucking angry.'

And his anger still lurked in some deep unconscious crevasse, she thought. She went on playing with her necklace. That phrase of Dorothy's she'd never forgotten: the idealised violator ... loving your abuser ... Freddie 'adoring' Charles and Charles subjugated and yet enthralled and ... perhaps it was wrong, but he'd always have been *gay* (the word you had to use now) anyway and if Freddie had lived it would have worked itself out, come to a natural end; only as it was, death had cut off love or fascination, if that's what it was, while it was still a living thing, so that it was somehow unnaturally mummified ... oh, but perhaps ...

'What a beautiful necklace,' he said.

'I had it in Shanghai.'

Eugene held it out to her. The beads dangled, intensely

green. The smooth rosary of emerald lozenges slid between her fingers. The cold green jade of the necklace, lying coiled like a snake in a drawer all those years.

Eugene had been right, of course, not to believe her, but she'd stuck to her story, hadn't once wavered ... until, that is, the very last time, that last time on the Heath she'd cracked, she was too frightened, she'd held the beads in her coat pocket as she walked towards Eugene, about to call truce, to hand them over ... and then that foolish young policeman had shot him ... It was her fault, she shouldn't have told Murray she was meeting Eugene ... had she wanted him to be killed? ... but no, she'd never dreamed they'd shoot him ... she frowned, impatient now with Charles for having reminded her of ... everything. 'It's supposed to be valuable. It probably isn't, it could be a fake,' and with a laugh, 'I might have to find out soon – Ronnie and I aren't exactly millionaires.'

And they were here in Venice to sell it, but Charles wasn't interested in her necklace. She looked at him as he turned to his lover, and as he lounged back on his little chair she wondered what had happened to the marble ephebe of all those decades ago, and most of all she wondered at how her brief, mad desire for him could have disappeared so completely, how a once-living passion could have turned so completely to dust.

sources

I AM INDEBTED TO Donald Thomas, *An Underworld at War: Spivs, Deserters, Racketeers and Civilians in the Second World War* (London: John Murray, 2003) for information on crime during the war and the austerity period. I am also indebted to Bernard Wasserstein, *Secret War in Shanghai* (London: Profile Books, 1999) and Emily Hahn, *China to Me* (London: Virago, 1978) for material on Shanghai in the 1930s and 1940s; to Graham Macklin, *Very Deeply Dyed in Black: Sir Oswald Mosley and the Resurrection of Fascism after 1945* (London: I.B. Tauris, 2007), Richard Thurlow, *Fascism in Britain: A History 1918–1985* (Oxford: Blackwell, 1987) and Trevor Grundy, *Memoir of a Fascist Childhood* (London: Heinemann, 1998) for information about the fascist movement after 1945; to Ina Zweiniger-Bargielowska, *Austerity in Britain: Rationing, Controls and Consumption 1939–1955* (Oxford University Press, 2000), and Michael Sissons and Philip French, eds, *The Age of Austerity* (Harmondsworth: Penguin, 1963) for information on the austerity period; to Richard Buckle, *The Adventures of a Ballet Critic* (London: Cresset Press, 1953) for material on the world of ballet; to Olive Renier, *Before the Bonfire* (Shipston-on-Stour: P. Drinkwater, 1984) for a wonderful account of the 'Ears of Britain'; and to Caroline Cooper for sharing with me her memories of life in Regent's

Park Road in the late 1940s.

The account by John Gross in Sissons and French assesses the Sidney Stanley affair rather differently from Donald Thomas, who believes it contributed to the turning of the tide against the Attlee government. John Belcher, a junior minister at the Board of Trade at the time, was forced to resign as a result of the scandal. However, there is no suggestion that he had a mistress, fathered an illegitimate child or was blackmailed.

A complete catalogue record for this book can be obtained from
the British Library on request

First published in this edition in 2010 by Serpent's Tail
First published in 2009 by Serpent's Tail,
an imprint of Profile Books Ltd
3A Exmouth House
Pine Street
London EC1R 0JH
website: www.serpentstail.com

ISBN 978 1 84668 692 4

Designed and typeset by Sue Lamble

Printed and bound in Great Britain by CPI Bookmarque Ltd,
Croydon, Surrey

10 9 8 7 6 5 4 3 2 1

FSC

Mixed Sources
Product group from well-managed
forests and other controlled sources
www.fsc.org Cert no. TT-COC-002227
© 1996 Forest Stewardship Council

War Damage

Elizabeth Wilson

Praise for *The Twilight Hour*

'This is an atmospheric book in which foggy, half-ruined London is as much a character as the artists and good-time girls who wander through its pages. It would be selfish to hope for more thrillers from Wilson, who has other intellectual fish to fry, but *The Twilight Hour* is so good that such selfishness is inevitable' *Time Out*

'A vivid portrait of bohemian life in Fitzrovia during the austerity of 1947 and the coldest winter of the twentieth century' *Literary Review*

'A book to read during the heatwave to keep you cool. The observant writing ensures that the iciness of the winter of 1947 rises off the page to nip your fingers ... [An] exciting, quirky story and a gripping evocation of an icy time' *Independent*

'Fantastically atmospheric ... The cinematic quality of the novel, written as if it were a black and white film with the sort of breathy dialogue that reminds you of *Brief Encounter*, is its trump card' *Sunday Express*

'An elegantly nostalgic, noir thriller; brilliantly conjures up the rackety confusion of Cold War London' *Daily Mail*

ELIZABETH WILSON is a researcher and writer best known for her books on feminism and popular culture. She is currently Visiting Professor at the London College of Fashion. Her novel *The Twilight Hour* is also published by Serpent's Tail.

Praise for *War Damage*

o n e

'HOW DID YOU GET A KEY?'

Charles slid his smile sideways, but didn't answer as he unlocked the art annexe door. The neglected appearance of this outbuilding reflected the status of art at the school. Easels and shelves for paint and brushes left little floor space for pupils, since the studio also functioned as an office, and was furnished with a couple of old wooden filing cabinets, a desk, two bentwood chairs, and a sagging antique chaise longue. A door at the back opened onto a darkroom the size of a cupboard, separated from the main room by a flimsy partition.

Charles locked the door again on the inside, leaned back against it and stared at Trevelyan – Harry – whose eyes widened with fear and adoration. Charles knew it would be all right then. 'God!' He took hold of the boy's shoulders, steered him towards the convenient sofa, pushed him down on to it and was about to undo his flies. But then he paused and took Trevelyan's face – so gently – between his hands and kissed him. Charles's heart was beating frantically. He'd thought about this all summer. And the boy wanted him too. He was stiff. Charles was shaking as he undid the heavy flannel and his throbbing prick wrung a groan from his throat. Trevelyan came almost at once with a little strangled whimper.

Charles left a stain on the sofa. He didn't care. He lay back, breathing heavily. But as time passed a fearful lethargy came over him. He smiled at the boy and stroked his hair. But the obsession that had sustained him since the end of last term had leaked away with his sperm and he was left with a feeling of utter emptiness.

Trevelyan was trying to tidy himself up. 'Hadn't we better go? What if Carnforth comes in?'

Charles laughed. 'He won't, will he? Everyone's gone home. That's why I told you to bring your stuff – we don't have to go back to main school.' For the annexe, located at the far end of the playing fields, was near the goods entrance so that it was easy to come and go without being seen. Anyway, no one came down here after school; except, of course, the art master himself. And if Carnforth *had* by an unlucky chance turned up, well ...

'But ...' Trevelyan dimly sensed that there was more to it than that.

'Actually,' drawled Charles, 'Carnforth lent me the key. I told him I wanted to finish my backdrop for the play.'

Trevelyan still looked puzzled.

'He's a fan of the ballet, you see.'

'Oh.'

'He cultivates me.'

Carnforth had lent him the key some time ago, when Charles had genuinely needed to work on the backdrop, but he did not know that Charles had had a copy made.

'What d'you mean?'

Charles gazed at Trevelyan from under his eyelashes. 'My mother's a famous ballet dancer. Didn't you know? Carnforth thinks if he smarms up to me it'll please her.'

Trevelyan's mouth opened. His father, a wealthy Baptist property developer, took a dim view of theatrical performance in any form. But this unexpected information only added to the hideous excitement he'd experienced during the past half hour.

'Yes … darling.' The endearment – daring, unthinkable in this environment – came straight from his mother's world, and the cruelty of it excited him again. He leaned forward and seized the boy quite roughly, pulling his head back and kissing, almost biting, his neck, as he felt for his prick through the coarse flannel of his trousers. The kiss too was unthinkable, almost a kind of blasphemy.

'I'll be so late home.' Trevelyan looked scared now.

'Tell them you had an extra art lesson or something.' But Charles's incipient erection subsided. He was bored again. 'It was an art lesson in a way,' he murmured, and smiled to himself. 'You're right, though. We'd better go.'

'Suppose Mr Carnforth—' and Trevelyan looked round the untidy, battered room. Charles put an arm round the younger boy's shoulders. 'God – you're shivering. Don't worry. I can twist Arthur Carnforth round my little finger. Everything'll be fine.' And he rumpled the boy's hair.

Trevelyan's eyes were as round as saucers. Charles smiled, but didn't enlighten him, other than to murmur languidly something he'd heard Freddie say: 'Love takes the strangest forms.' Trevelyan, of course, had no idea what he was talking about.

Charles locked the annexe and slipped the key into his pocket. They walked to the periphery of the playing fields and through the gate, which gave, unexpectedly, onto the main road. Fortunately Trevelyan lived in the opposite direction from Charles, so they didn't have to travel together. To have to make conversation with Trevelyan would have been unutterably tedious. The younger boy scampered across the road, and Charles waited for the bus to Hampstead underground. Emerging at Camden Town, he still felt listless as he walked up

Parkway, but he rallied slightly as he remembered it was Thursday and Freddie would probably be there when he got home.

And indeed, he was. He'd brought a red-haired woman friend along as well.

t w o

REGINE MILNER'S SUNDAYS were casual affairs. She never tidied up in advance. Newspapers and books lay where they fell; and coats were cast over the banisters or left in a heap on the stairs. Bottles and glasses were marshalled in advance, but she didn't bother with extra ashtrays; canapés appeared, if at all, only after several guests had arrived. Informality was still the order of the day three years after the end of the war. But then, as Freddie said, things were never going to get back to how they'd been before 1939. 'Pre-war' had become merely a sentimental gesture towards a vanished order to which most of Regine's friends hadn't belonged; and bohemian shabbiness – battered antique furniture, Persian rugs unravelling at the edges and balding velvet upholstery – suited this epoch of post-war shortages and making do. And if in the streets and squares of post-war London austerity still dulled the look of everything, in Regine's drawing room the Chinese jars gleamed, the amethyst and sapphire cushions glowed and the crimson walls produced an atmosphere of womb-like warmth in which everyone relaxed.

On this mild autumn day, the first in October, Regine was trying out the new 'separates' idea, teaming a voluminous paisley skirt (made from an old shawl she'd found in the house

– it must have belonged to Lydia) with a garnet sweater, and had tied back her tangle of red hair, so curly it fizzed and frizzed round her face, with a green ribbon. Her black suede court shoes, with their old-fashioned square toes, dated from 1942 and had worn to a shine, but that could be passed off as part of the look. And the good thing about the new long skirts was they hid the parlous state of one's precious silk stockings.

Regine's Sundays had begun almost by accident at the end of 1943. She had left the Vale of Evesham and was back in London where she had a new translating job in Whitehall. Once she and Neville were married, it just naturally came about that they opened the doors of his Hampstead house to wartime London's birds of passage. There were so many people in the war who were lonely and unanchored, separated from spouses, bombed out, home on leave, men and women rushing in and out of the capital or searching for lovers, appearing and disappearing. My sitting room's like Waterloo station, she used to say – and Sunday was the ideal day because then everything was shut and boredom could so easily set in.

Now her Sundays were monthly instead of weekly occasions and she could offer her guests gin and sherry again instead of tea, or those home-made brews – gin distilled from potatoes – or dreadful rum concoctions. Nor did she make such an effort these days to give them all something to eat; the cakes and biscuits made from soya flour and the little canapés with fish paste or even dried scrambled egg had dwindled to a few cheese straws and savoury biscuits.

Yet although she sat carelessly with her feet up on the chaise longue, she was as usual a little nervous as she waited for the first arrivals. You never knew whether four or fourteen guests would turn up, indeed she wondered, as she wondered on the first Sunday of every month, whether *anyone* would.

'Perhaps people don't need my Sundays any more. They'd

nowhere else to go in the war, but now things are looking up – the theatres open again, the lights going on, life's slowly getting back to normal, isn't it, so ...'

Neville had already started on the whisky. Without looking up from the *Sunday Times*, he murmured: 'Kitten – your Sundays are an institution. Our friends *love* coming here.'

Regine stood up and moved restlessly around the drawing room, then sat down again, this time on one of the overstuffed chairs, and looked at her husband, her gaze travelling over the familiar sharp contours of his face, the crimped, receding, mousey hair, and the neat, well-worn suit. None of the arty set's corduroys and tweeds for him; he always looked dapper. From behind his round, steel-framed glasses, his sharp gaze stared out guardedly at the world.

She sometimes felt her gratitude to him for giving her a settled and comfortable life prevented her from knowing him as intimately as she ought, from understanding him as fully as he deserved from a wife. But perhaps he didn't want to be understood, keeping his life in tidy compartments to which only he had the keys.

The door knocker rat-tatted smartly, and she sprang up in relief. But she was disappointed and even irritated to see Muriel and Hilary Jordan on the doorstep. When Regine had first met Hilary during the war, he'd been a cheerily aggressive bohemian with libertarian views, but Muriel had transformed him into a living embodiment of Austerity. Like the Chancellor of the Exchequer, the lantern-jawed Sir Stafford Cripps, Hilary was now an extreme vegetarian who ate only raw food and probably took cold baths. Muriel had strange eyes, like a hawk's, each golden iris encircled by a dark ring. Her hooked nose reinforced the likeness to a censorious bird of prey. She stared at Regine. 'What a wonderful *ensemble*, very Hampstead,' she said. 'How do you do it on the coupons?'

This was an attack, thinly disguised as admiration. Regine had purchased the coupons from her charlady, but why should she feel guilty? Mrs Havelock needed the money and couldn't afford new clothes anyway.

'Oh—' and Muriel made a darting movement, her finger poked at Regine's cheek, 'your lipstick's smudged.'

Regine recoiled in horror, but managed a smile. 'Go and say hallo to Neville, he's holding court in the library.' Though that was hardly an accurate description of Neville behind his newspaper.

'I saw Arthur Carnforth at church this morning,' said Muriel. 'We go to All Saints Margaret Street, you know – very High Church, but I don't like our local vicar … anyway, I said to him, haven't seen you at the Milners' for a long time. He said he might come along.'

Mingled with Regine's dismay at the mention of Arthur Carnforth's name was an awareness, more definite than ever before, that she really disliked Muriel. She said coldly: 'You know quite well he and Neville had a falling out some time ago.' What an interfering, nosy person Muriel was – and the cheek of taking it upon herself to suggest such a thing.

Arthur Carnforth, that grim, awkward man – a failure, a misfit. Regine remembered his clammy handshake, the way he blinked nervously when he talked … Freddie disliked him, although they'd all been friends before the war.

'Yes,' said Muriel, unabashed, 'but Neville was very kind to Arthur when—'

'When he had his breakdown. Yes, I know that.' Regine felt patronised, Muriel's patronising smile infuriated her – as if *she* knew Neville better than his own wife.

Now, though – thank God! – Freddie was in the open doorway. His bulk dominated the crowded little hall. 'Regine! Darling!' As if he hadn't seen her for years, when it was only last Thursday.

Arm in arm they swerved into the drawing room and sat down on Regine's great dark green Victorian chaise longue, the pièce de résistance of the room. Freddie had got hold of it for her. Away with all that frightful Moderne rubbish, he'd boomed, enough of ghastly Syrie Maughan white walls and Omega designs, the nineteenth century knew a thing or two about luxury, the more ornament the better.

'So what did Edith Blake have to say about your latest translation?' he began.

'She liked it. She's given me a book about tenth-century France to work on now.'

'That'll give you something to get your teeth into.'

'It's more likely to break my jaw! I mean, it's nice to have something serious, but the Dark Ages are so depressing.'

'The Dark Ages ... darling, that's what we're having now, isn't it, a post-war Dark Ages.' That was so Freddie – a sombre remark, its sting neutralised by his camp laugh. 'There's something I must talk to you about,' he said, speaking more quietly than usual. 'Not now, but perhaps we could have lunch tomorrow. It's quite important. Someone we used to know—'

But he was interrupted by another knock on the front door.

'Phil will answer it. Go on. Say what you were going to say. Someone?'

Perhaps it was Arthur Carnforth.

'No, darling, this isn't the moment. Tomorrow, when I have you to myself. *Now* I must tell you about my marvellous idea. A new ballet magazine. My photographs will be at the centre of it, of course, but I just *know* there's a demand for new writing, more information, something different from the old dance magazines. *God* knows how I'll scrape the money together.' Freddie passed his hand over his fading blond hair. 'By the way – ' and he leaned forward so that she caught a whiff of eau de cologne, 'Vivienne *is* coming – she'll be here any minute – in fact, I'm going to wait for her outside—' and he sprang to his feet. Then he paused. 'What did you think of her house?'

'It must be dreadfully uncomfortable to live in while it's being restored – but of course it'll be lovely when it's finished. Makes this place seem like a doll's house.'

'They paid nearly eight thousand for it, you know. *Eight thousand*!'

Freddie had taken her to tea with the ballerina the previous Thursday: 'I want my two best girls to get to know each other.' But it hadn't been a success. Vivienne had seemed withdrawn; there'd been little rapport. The only moment of animation had been when her son had turned up as they were all sitting stilted in the middle of her ruin of a house on the canal. The boy had leaned against the door jamb, languidly still and silent so that they'd had to look at him.

'I'm thrilled she's coming. You're marvellous, Freddie.' Vivienne Hallam, or rather Evanskaya – the stage name an adaptation of the mundane Welsh Evans – was certainly a scalp for her salon, as Regine secretly thought of her Sundays, especially as the dancer was quite reclusive, didn't go out much at all. Or so Freddie said.

'I'll wait for her outside,' repeated Freddie. 'She's rather shy, you know.'

Regine strolled away to look for Phil the lodger. Phil was a godsend. Soon he'd be moving around with a tray of drinks, leaving Regine free to devote herself to her guests. And of course it was Phil who'd made sure Cato, their great, bony poodle, was safely shut away upstairs where he couldn't knock over ashtrays with his tail or threateningly rear up on his hind legs in an attempt to hug guests. He'd barked and howled for a bit, but now there was a sulky silence.

By the time Freddie ushered Vivienne Hallam into the drawing room, seven or eight guests had gathered. At this early stage they were bright-eyed with expectancy and a first drink. The space the ballerina's still potent fame created around her brought an almost imperceptible pause as the others recognised her, but too polite to show it, continued their conversations.

She walked as ballerinas did on stage, with feet turned out, like an elegant duck, each step slightly springing. Her son followed behind. Everyone looked at him too.

'My husband sends his apologies – he's on call this weekend.'

Just as well, Regine thought. Freddie said he was the gloomiest man this side of the Iron Curtain.

'This is my son, Charles. I didn't introduce you properly the other day.'

The boy shook hands with Regine and as Freddie settled on the chaise longue between his two 'best girls', Charles perched on the arm at his mother's side.

'Isn't he divinely Caravaggio?' whispered Freddie in Regine's ear; then, aloud, he turned towards Vivienne Hallam and said: 'Now, darling, about my ballet magazine. You see, it would be marvellous, Vivienne, if we could have something about the company in the war. You were *heroic*, your escape from the Nazis in Holland, travelling about all over England through the Blitz, bringing dance to the people, keeping art going through the darkest days – it was so vital for morale. And it *transformed* ballet from a minor specialised art form into what it is today. Thanks to you everyone *loves* ballet.'

Vivienne Hallam smiled, but to Regine her dark eyes seemed full of melancholy. 'I'm not sure John would look at it like that. And it's such a long time ago, Freddie.'

'Rubbish – five years, four years. What are you *talking* about! It will be just the thing for the first issue. You have to support me, darling, this ballet magazine is going to be a huge success. There's an audience out there just waiting to adore you all over again – and with my pictures – and the original sketches for the scenery designs – '

'Won't it cost a lot to produce?' enquired Regine. 'And what about the paper shortage?'

Freddie frowned. 'Oh, my God – *expense*! I'm trying to scrape the capital together at the moment. Any ideas – and offers of help, of course, are welcome.'

'Oh Freddie,' murmured Vivienne, 'I don't know …'

'I'll get the lolly together somehow, don't you worry. But the main thing will be *you*, your public *demands* it, the first issue a special edition dedicated to you: your memories; an interview; and the photographs, of course. You must come and choose for yourself.'

'You've so much energy, Freddie. Where do you get it from?' Vivienne spoke faintly as if exhausted by his enthusiasm. Charles stood up and the dancer glanced after her son as he moved through the room, lifting a glass from Phil's tray en route.

Regine hoped that was all right. 'Is he allowed?'

Vivienne shrugged. 'He's sixteen – nearly. And his father says he has to learn to hold his drink.'

'He's very self-possessed, isn't he.'

'Well, he was in America during the war. John insisted – you know, at the beginning, when we thought the Germans were going to invade. He seemed so much older when he got back. Well, of course he *was* older.' She smiled and Regine thought she looked sadder than ever.

'Didn't you miss him terribly?'

'Terribly.'

'But you were dancing, weren't you, darling. You couldn't have done that if you'd had to look after the boy,' said Freddie.

'He'd have been at school.'

'You couldn't have done it. All that travelling. And you

know he had a wonderful time in New York.'

'Oh, he did. Thanks to those wonderful friends of yours, only ...'

'Exactly. The Denton-Bradshaws will be tremendously useful to him in the future. American connections are so important these days.' Airily Freddie swept Vivienne's maternal guilt away. 'But I must tell you about my *other* plan. I am thinking of organising an exhibition on Diaghilev, and I need your help with that too, darling. If you'll give it your support – your name means so much.'

'A Diaghilev exhibition!' Vivienne Hallam looked more doubtful than ever. 'But how can I help? I didn't know Diaghilev.'

'You can conjure the money out of the ground. All your connections with the ballet world – oh, I know I have connections too, but your name is so much more persuasive – do say you'll help, darling.'

Regine sprang to her feet. 'You should talk to Alan Wentworth. He'd love to do something about Diaghilev on his arts programme.'

'Not *yet*! Oh – I shouldn't have *mentioned* it. It's just a gleam in my eye at the moment. The ballet magazine's the priority, that's the first thing, of course, but then it will be a forum for the discussion of the exhibition, a platform to float it from, it'll be a way of raising more money.'

'You always seem to be broke, Freddie,' said Vivienne plaintively.

'Darling, you know me, I never have a bean – all the family money went on the stately pile and Daddy's gambling debts. And when I do have any it runs through my fingers like water. But this is different – it's not for me, it's for art, it's for the *dance*, darling.'

In search of Alan Wentworth, Regine paused to chat to

Dorothy Redfern, who was discussing the previous evening's performance of *Rosenkavalier* at Covent Garden with one of Neville's colleagues. 'Oh – I didn't know you were there, Dorothy,' cried Regine. 'Didn't you think Elisabeth Schwarzkopf was *marvellous*?'

'We were in the gods, you wouldn't have seen us, Reggie dear. And no – actually I didn't. The voice is wonderful, of course, but I thought her performance was so terribly *arch*.'

'Oh …' Regine, who hadn't great confidence in her own artistic judgements, felt a little downcast.

'And I'm not sure one shouldn't boycott her,' continued Dorothy. 'They say she was a Nazi in the war.'

In so many ways Dorothy always held the high ground, moral as well as aesthetic. She added: 'Of course, it's very hard to know what one would have done. Most people compromise, don't they, when you really come down to it. Except those of us who had no choice.'

Regine found Alan Wentworth in the library. He and Neville were talking to Noel Valentine. Vivienne's son was there too, leafing through a book on Chinese art.

Regine slid her arm through Alan's. 'You're looking well.'

'Not as well and gorgeous as you, Reggie, the Rita Hayworth of Hampstead.'

She laughed off his ponderous flirting. 'Where's Dinah?'

'She's gone to some meeting. The local Labour Party's trying to start a women's peace group, or something. You know – against the atom bomb.'

'Tell her I'll call round one day next week.'

'She's at the Courtauld most days. Come in the evening, when I'm home from work as well.'

He resumed his conversation with the other two. Regine sat on the arm of Charles's chair, looking at the prints with him. 'They're exquisite, aren't they.' The boy nodded, lifting with long fingers the fragile tissue protecting the next plate. 'Your mother tells me you were in New York during the war. That must have been exciting.'

He looked up at her and she saw what Freddie had meant about Caravaggio: the pale skin, so utterly unblemished by adolescent spots; the heavy-lidded glance; the sinuous lips. With a startling throb of desire she imagined those long hands on her body. Senseless French words came into her head: *elle se penchait sur ce corps … le visage exquis d'un éphèbe …*

'I stayed with a rather nice family. They had an apartment on the Upper East Side, *Eleven Hundred Park Avenue, East Eighty-ninth and Park.*' He chanted the address like a spell. 'In the summer we went to their house on Long Island,' he added.

The mysterious names reinforced Regine's vision of an imaginary New York, where all the women looked like the Duchess of Windsor and all the men like Humphrey Bogart. In the American films she'd seen, brash, noisy streets, wise-cracking trilby-hatted men and long-legged showgirls defined the city, but Charles's careless allusions suggested a different Manhattan, of martinis and stilted elegance. 'You are so lucky. I've always wanted to go to New York.'

'It was swell,' he said with an exaggerated American accent. Then in his normal voice: 'It was great fun and rather grand; the house had its own lift and three bathrooms.'

'*Three bathrooms*?'

'They had a daughter my age, Lally. We became great friends. I miss her rather. It was coming home that was the hard part. It's been frightfully difficult getting used to the food.'

What a blasé little tike he was! Speaking of a house with *three bathrooms* as though it were the most normal thing in the world! At the same time his blasé air shaded towards a melancholy that was like his mother's. 'And I suppose there was lashings of food – no rationing. And New York itself? Do tell me about it.'

'I was only eight when I arrived, you know.' He was still turning the pages of the print book. Silence; he wasn't going to say any more.

'I've lived abroad too, in Shanghai, but that was before the war.'

Now he looked interested. 'Shanghai? Freddie was there. Did you know him then? I'm madly interested in China. They're having a revolution.'

'Yes, that's where I first met Freddie – in Shanghai. The thing is – I must go and look after my other guests, but – why don't you come round for tea one afternoon? You could come over after school? I could show you my souvenirs.'

'I'd like that.' He smiled faintly, as if the invitation concealed a vaguely indecent meaning, to which only he had access. Then he began to turn the pages again. She'd been dismissed.

She stood up. 'Alan – go and talk to Freddie. He wants to organise a Diaghilev exhibition.'

The boy joined in again. 'Freddie's potty about Diaghilev. Isn't he the one who was in love with Nijinsky, the famous dancer, who went mad? Freddie told me a fortune teller predicted Diaghilev would die on water, so he never went anywhere by boat. But then eventually he died in Venice, which *is* built on water. And when they lowered the coffin into the grave on the cemetery island there, his two lovers jumped in after it and started to fight each other. Freddie said he'd visited it at the end of the war – I forget the name of the island, but anyway, he said there were flowers by the grave and even a pair of ballet slippers.'

'That's just Freddie's sort of thing,' said Regine, and to Alan: 'You could do a wonderful programme on Diaghilev.'

'That's a good idea.' Noel pricked up his ears. His art gallery specialised in modern and contemporary art, but everything to do with the arts fascinated him.

'Is it?' said Alan.

'Yes,' said Noel. 'Go on. I'll join you in a minute.' He turned back to Neville, with whom he was discussing a forthcoming auction.

'Ian Roxburgh will probably be along later,' said Neville. 'Did you meet him here before? I'd like to know what you think of him. He's been in the Far East, knows a lot about China. Seems to think he could get hold of some vases for me ...'

Noel raised his eyebrows.

'Freddie brought him along originally,' said Regine. 'Earlier this year.' She tried to remember exactly when it had been. These days the two seemed thick as thieves. Of course she wasn't jealous, that would have been absurd, but ... she wasn't crazy about Ian Roxburgh.

Phil came into the library with his drinks tray. 'Cynthia's here,' he murmured to Regine, raised his eyebrows and jerked his head in the direction of the garden.

Regine found Cynthia in a cluster of people, including the Jordans. At her side, shorter than she, stood a sleek, besuited figure.

So Cynthia had finally brought him. Together in public ... that must mean ... was it going to be official? Was he actually going to ...?

She approached them, Cynthia made the introductions and Regine shook hands with Ernie Appleton, as though it were the most usual thing in the world to find a government minister standing on her lawn. Cynthia said: 'We've just dropped in for a moment, we can't stay long.'

But Muriel Jordan began to talk about the Berlin airlift, transparently trying to draw the politician out. He merely smiled enigmatically as she gave him the benefit of her views on the current crisis, but when she moved seamlessly on to the rumours about the Board of Trade Cynthia and her companion moved indoors, and Muriel turned to Regine. 'How extraordinary! You don't mean to tell me—'

Regine looked blankly at the older woman. 'Cynthia works at the Board of Trade too, you know,' she said repressively. 'But what were you saying about the Berlin airlift, Muriel?'

Ignoring the question, Muriel contorted her face into a knowing grimace, literally eagle-eyed. 'Oh, *really*!' she said with laboured theatrical sarcasm. 'Is that what it's called! As if he isn't in enough trouble already.'

Regine had no idea what the last comment meant. 'How long do you think the Berlin airlift can go on?' she persisted rather desperately, longing to be talking to Cynthia. She hated Muriel's endless tedious complaints about everything and her manner of casting blame on all and sundry – and all the time she pretended to be so holy.

In any case, being against the bad news that surged across the papers every day was about as much good as railing against bad weather. The atom bomb was terrifying, but Regine hadn't spent nearly two years in Shanghai for nothing. She knew that with war raging nearby, it was perfectly possible for life to continue in a normal, indeed thrilling way and that if you were dancing on the edge of a volcano it was better not to look down into its fiery heart. 'No one will want to go to war over Berlin,' she said. 'Things are bound to get better soon.'

'You're unbelievably frivolous, Reggie. Talk about *après moi le déluge*!'

Happily Cynthia and her escort re-emerged, accompanied now by Freddie. Regine wondered what on earth Cynthia saw in this paunchy, balding politician. And yet the very fact he was a member of the government lent him an aura ... of sorts. 'We must be off, I'm afraid,' said Cynthia, 'but I'll ring you soon, Reggie.' Ernie Appleton shook hands again. He smiled in a way that made you think he had to smile too often when he didn't feel like it. Freddie walked them to the gate, where they stayed chatting for a moment, and then went back into the house.

Hilary watched Freddie. 'Don't know why you give him house room.'

Regine was used to Hilary's extraordinary rudeness. *That* hadn't changed. He never stinted what he called his honest, forthright and unvarnished views.

'You know perfectly well Freddie is my oldest friend. I've known him since Shanghai. Please don't talk like that about him. He's the kindest person in the world.'

Hilary probably didn't realise how rude he was. Unusually he even apologised. 'Sorry, old girl, didn't mean to offend, but there's no getting away from the fact that moral degeneracy is on the rise. During the war things got completely out of hand – I mean, look at the illegitimacy rates – '

Regine laughed. 'You can hardly blame the Freddies of this world for that!'

'It's no laughing matter, Regine.'

'No.' A different topic was needed. Fortunately Muriel embarked on a new grumble.

'The state of the Heath! That army camp opposite us in East Heath Road – it's an absolute disgrace; the Nissen huts, great slabs of concrete, barbed wire, old tins, broken glass – weeds all over it now, of course, but you can still see it all poking through—'

'And all those new asphalt paths all over the Heath and so much of it still fenced off,' added Hilary. 'Still, at least they didn't put prefabs up all over Parliament Hill Fields. We must be grateful for small mercies, I suppose.'

'They wanted to build permanent housing,' snapped Muriel. 'They've still got their eye on it probably.'

The war was over, yet its effects lingered on, like a hang-over, or, no, a debilitating infection, a sort of malaria of the mind that, once contracted, continued to lurk within the system, never finally cured. But grumbling didn't help and Regine was all for getting completely away from the war. The best medicine, she was sure, was simply to enjoy life as much as one possibly could.

Noel Valentine came out onto the lawn, and she drew him into their conversation. He at least wasn't full of dismal political views. Unlike Hilary, whose sweeping statements brooked no denial, Noel always saw the detail. Detail is everything, he said. That's what's wrong with Arthur Carnforth's painting, he'd once said to Regine. He's not good enough on the detail, fuzzy impressionism just won't do.

Once he and the Jordans were safely talking about the Van Gogh exhibition, Regine returned indoors. She was looking for Charles. I think I've fallen for him, she thought. 'Mad about the boy' – that song Freddie used to sing. But after all, she'd been so good for so long … a fifteen-year-old, well, nearly sixteen; it reminded her of the Colette novel she'd read on the boat home. *Chéri*. Darling.

three

T HE PARTY HAD MOVED into a different phase, her guests gelled in conversational groups. She was free to go in search of the boy. She returned to the library, but Charles was no longer there and she was ambushed by Ian Roxburgh. She hadn't seen him arrive – it certainly hadn't been while she was in the garden – but there he was now, with his ginger hair and neat moustache and the pale, pale blue eyes she found slightly disturbing. He was leaning against the desk next to Neville, who looked a bit squiffy in his armchair.

'I was telling your husband about my contacts in Hong Kong. There's a lot of good stuff coming out of China now. With the civil war it's all chaotic. The communists are winning. Some say there'll be no hope of anything after that, but I don't know … and then there's Formosa … impossible to know, really.' He was looking at her all the time. 'You were with Freddie in Shanghai before the war, weren't you?'

'Yes. I was there for two years.' Ian knew that already, but he always asked about it, as if there was something more he wanted to know.

Neville laughed. 'Oh, tell him the story.' Regine smiled, shook her head. 'You see,' said Neville, 'my wife came from the best society in Dublin and her family had her educated in the best convent in Brussels. I think they hoped she'd become a nun, didn't they, Reg, because there were five sisters, a lot of girls to launch onto the marriage market.'

He knew it embarrassed Regine to talk about her childhood, but seemed to take a malicious delight in her unease. If only when they first met she hadn't told him that yarn about her family in Dublin. But it was much too late – years too late – to contradict him, although these days she stuck to the part that was nearest the truth. 'I was the ugly duckling, red hair, you see, considered rather common.' And she touched her wild halo. She loved her red hair now, the growing up being teased laid to rest, almost, but never quite forgotten.

Neville went on: 'Failing the nunnery, she was to be trained as a teacher and sent out to educate the heathens. But she arrived – you tell him, Reg.'

'Well, I met this wonderful man, at least I thought he was wonderful then – and in a way he was, at first, he was a charmer … anyway, within three weeks we were married. I wired the convent to say I wasn't taking up the post. There was nothing they could do about it. I behaved rather badly,' and she smiled, not truly penitent. 'Still,' she added, 'my husband turned out to be a gambler, and a bit crazy really, so I suppose it served me right. I came back in 1938, when things got really difficult, the situation, I mean, the war, not Eugene. I never heard from him again. He was killed when the Japanese took over.'

'I see.' Ian Roxburgh stared at her as he flipped cigarette ash into the fireplace. 'I envy you. I'd have loved to see Shanghai as it was then. It's too late now, of course.' He looked at her, with curiosity she felt, but there was also something calculating in the insistence of his pale eyes. 'Yes, I can't see you as a teacher.' His speculative glance and foxy half grin remained just this side of suggestive. 'But didn't your family object to your going out there on your own?'

She felt herself blushing. That was the weak link in the
story. Yet it wasn't a crime, was it, to reconstruct a different past
from the one you'd been landed with? To pretend that she'd
come from one of the best families in Dublin, when in fact she
had been the daughter of the cook, well, what harm did it do?
She'd hated the way they'd *pitied* her as her mother took to
drink, but she'd had to be grateful, because they'd paid for the
convent in Brussels. They'd meant it for the best, but she was
sure they'd basked in their own generosity and boasted of their
kindness to their friends. They couldn't have realised – hadn't
had the imagination to understand – that to be banished from
all things familiar had seemed like the end of life itself, with her
mother left in an asylum never to be seen again, while she was
put on a ship to the end of the world, Ostend.

Now, Kathleen, you'll be good, so you will, I know it. The
nuns'll be the making of you, they'll train you up. It's a great
opportunity, darling. But they'd never invited her back for the
holidays. The convent had been her life and it had been
assumed she'd take her vows.

You have no vocation, Kathleen. The Mother Superior's
clear eyes had stared coldly, her words dripped like water on
marble. The fear – she was about to be cast from their doors,
thrown on her own devices, abandoned in the world; and then
the reprieve on account of her gift for languages. There were
Catholic schools in China; you didn't have to be a nun to teach
out there. You could be a lay assistant.

She thought she'd cast it all aside when she'd married.
Kathleen Roisin O'Kelly became first Rosheen Smith and then –
better still, because no longer Irish, but French – Regine. By the
time her passport had expired she was back in England and
about to be married for a second time, so she'd just told them
she'd lost it in the Blitz and got a new one with her new name.
Regine – it was so elegant. But then Neville had started calling

her Reggie, which sounded like some beefy, golf-playing businessman. She'd resented that, but – it's so bloody pretentious,
kitten, he'd said, and shamefaced she'd had to swallow her hurt
and smile at her own pretensions.

Freddie was the only one who knew about her past. I
haven't told Neville, she'd said to Freddie. Neville was rather a
snob, after all. Freddie had winked. Your secret is safe with me,
darling. It was their secret, hers and Freddie's; it was part of their
special relationship.

'Shanghai was just extraordinary.'

'You must come round to dinner,' said Neville, 'we can talk
about it then. But now I want to introduce you to Noel Valentine. He's an art dealer.'

Now she was free to search for Charles again. He was talking
to Dorothy Redfern in the dining room. Dorothy worked with
children and adolescents all the time, so she knew how to draw
them out: all those children so damaged by the war – Jewish
orphans, refugees – and Charles was almost animated now,
talking about the girl, Lally, he'd known in New York. Perhaps
he'd been a bit in love with her.

Freddie surged towards them, heaved himself down on to
a fragile Regency dining chair next to the boy and embarked on
a furious argument with Dorothy about Freud. 'Spewing out
your emotional guts to someone who just sits there and says
damn all! Emotional diarrhoea! Stick to the stiff upper lip, my
boy. Always the wisest course. I mean, what is the use, Dorothy,
if you'll forgive me for saying so, of maundering on about one's
childhood?'

Dorothy took his aggression in good part, hardly bothering
to argue, but that seemed to irritate Freddie almost as much as
the thought of psychoanalysis itself. It was as if he was trying to
goad Dorothy into losing her temper. 'Turning sex into an
illness,' he boomed, 'and criminalising desire.'

This last jibe hit the mark. Dorothy started to speak, but Charles butted in. 'The Denton-Bradshaws and their friends all had – "shrinks", they called them. They talked about it all the time. It was an essential part of living in Manhattan.' Regine was sure he'd said it in an attempt to take the conversation in a different direction. And up to a point he succeeded, for Freddie laughed and said: 'Just as opium was an essential part of living in Shanghai.'

Regine frowned. Surely Charles was too young ... she said quickly: '*I* never set foot in an opium den – I think all that was exaggerated – perhaps the Chinese ...'

'Didn't your—' Freddie broke off, then started again. 'You were more of a cocktail girl, eh? D'you remember the cocktails at the Pacific Cathay, weren't they *marvellous*!'

'Oh, *yes*! Martha and I used often to go for pre-lunch drinks there. That's where we met our admirers. We stayed in the Park Hotel at first and I realised quite soon that Eugene was always in debt – we owed them so much, we couldn't leave. That's where I met Martha Strang, my American journalist friend, she introduced me to the international crowd. She got me a job on the French newspaper. The editor thought my story was amusing, so he sent me to report on a local Catholic school. Soon he had me writing the gossip column – it was all about our social life. I paid off the bill and Martha and I set ourselves up in a cheap flat. I didn't see Eugene for weeks on end. And you turned up, didn't you, Freddie, with that ballet company, and became a sort of impresario for that little theatre, the Far Eastern Grand Opera Company – what a grandiose name! It was such fun.'

The stories of that legendary Shanghai to which Freddie so often treated his friends had quite removed it from the realm of normal morality. 'Living in Shanghai,' he said now, 'was like ... it was like skimming the surface of the black lagoon.' And as Freddie reminisced Regine was seeing again the seething crowds of Chinese workers, coolies, hustlers, and beyond them the shabby, desperate worlds of refugees and emigrés, white Russians, old Bolsheviks, Soviet agents, Germans, Jews, Armenians, British intelligence, American adventurers ... and beyond them again the shadow world of the Green Gang and the warlords and the Kuomintang.

'In a way it wasn't quite real,' said Regine.

Each different world pursued its course parallel and invisible to the others, yet achieved the impossible in bending these parallel lines so that they twisted together at certain points, where the tracks crossed and the points changed. And everyone came to Shanghai sooner or later, so that it was not so much a city as a huge swarming beehive of passions and appetites, plots and conspiracies, a rotting compost heap generating the fermenting gases of every possible human need, desire and transgression.

'So many different worlds,' she said. Regions that became ever more phantasmagoric and obscure, shady realms in which personalities were dissolved and reconstituted and every individual was a master of disguise, identity as fleeting as a fancy dress costume, to be put on and discarded at will. Shanghai was an ever-expanding multiple *scape*, fanning out in all directions. It was a series of interlocking rooms, each leading further into the labyrinth; a Chinese puzzle; a succession of spectacles and transformations, a Japanese lantern show, a pantomime, each scene as fantastical as the previous one, which yet coexisted, impossibly, across the same space.

Freddie told – for the hundredth time – the story of the fake Indian princess and they laughed about the days at the races and their life in the little flat with the bamboo furniture and the green walls painted with parakeets, with Eugene coming and going, no one ever quite knew where to or what he was doing.

'And now here we all are, back in bombed-out London,'

said Charles, then stood up abruptly and left the room. When he returned he looked at Freddie. 'I think Vivienne is ready to go.'

How odd to call his mother by her first name! Regine hastened away to talk to Vivienne before it was too late. How could she have neglected her so! Was it because she felt the tiniest bit of rivalrous resentment at Freddie's other 'best girl'? She hoped not.

Freddie walked the ballerina and her son to the gate and returned, to Regine's surprise, with Edith Blake, the power behind the throne at her publishers, Crispin Drownes. A late arrival, when the others were beginning to drift away, she stood in the doorway looking disconcertingly like Queen Mary the Queen Mother. Regine hoped she wouldn't be bored; only a handful of guests remained for her to talk to. Drownes fils, hovering behind her, was very much her adjutant. About Regine's own age, or – no – a few years younger, probably in his late twenties, William Drownes seemed pleasant and carefree. She knew it was in her interest to be as nice as possible to both of them, for she was serious about her translating and hoped for more work, so she exerted all her charm, settling Edith Blake in a tête à tête with Freddie while William gravitated in the direction of Alan, Noel and Clive, Neville's colleague from the museum.

Freddie was the last to leave, lingering after the others had departed and Phil was unobtrusively gathering up the used glasses and ashtrays. 'One for the road, eh, darling, if you can spare it, that is.' When she'd refilled his glass, he said: 'Please be friends with Vivienne, she needs someone to take her out of herself. That dismal husband of hers ...' His leg jiggled, as it did when he was tense or anxious. 'I don't see so much of her as I used to ... I feel a bit guilty about it to tell you the truth ... and now I hear she's taken up again with bloody Arthur Carnforth.'

'Was that who you wanted to talk about? We haven't seen

him for months – oh, longer than that. After he and Neville quarrelled ...'

'No, it was something else.' Freddie looked suddenly sombre. He straightened his shoulders. 'Anyway, you will make her your friend, won't you, sweetie. Take her out of herself. She just sits moping about in that ruin they've bought. And the boy – he's almost like my nephew – or a godson, y'know. Of course he can't *actually* be my godson, because I'm a Pape like you, but I feel I have a duty of care towards the lad. His father gives him a hard time. Her too. She's not happy.'

Regine laughed. *'Ça se voit.* But I hardly know her.'

'You could get to know her, darling. Your translating isn't exactly full time.'

'I wish translating was better paid.'

'Neville doesn't keep you short, does he? We all know he's a bit of a Scrooge, but ...'

Regine wondered if Freddie had asked her husband for money. He certainly wouldn't get much change out of Neville. There was a little silence. Freddie heaved himself out of the sofa. From the front path, he turned. 'Tomorrow,' he said, 'it's really quite important.'

'Can't you tell me now?'

But Freddie shook his head. 'No, I haven't time, I have to – look, just meet me at – at – oh, I know, that little place behind Harrods, you remember – we won't see anyone we know there – at one.'

Neville was still in the library, half-cut by now. Regine wandered into the kitchen. Phil was at the sink. Cato was frisking around them, mad for attention.

'Don't wash up now. We can leave it for Mrs Havelock in the morning.'

But Phil insisted on doing it there and then. 'You dry the glasses,' he said, a job Regine hated, but he was right, really, it was a waste of the char's time to wash up, when there was so much else to clean and dust and tidy. The house wasn't huge, but there was always so much housework. It never ceased to surprise her. Partly it was due to Neville's Chinese porcelain collection, which the char wasn't supposed to touch, but Regine told her to dust them anyway; for God's sake don't break anything, but if you do, I'll say it was me.

'Freddie was a bit … I dunno, tense, didn't you think? Perhaps it was because the star guest was a bit on edge too. The ballerina.'

'Was she? What d'you mean – on edge?' Regine frowned.

'I don't know … just not very much at home.'

'Oh dear, I was a bad hostess, I neglected her. I think she's shy.'

'Perhaps it's just she looks rather haggard. Not really beautiful, is she. Not what I'd expected. Features too large. Face too pale. But that probably looks good on stage, I suppose. Everything exaggerated.' He paused. 'And then she got stuck with Muriel Jordan. Enough to make anyone depressed. Don't know why you let them keep on coming.'

'How can I stop them? I've known Hilary for ages, before he married her.'

'Neville should put his foot down. She's very right wing – I mean really right wing.'

His vehemence surprised Regine. She laughed. 'Neville and I are not exactly socialists.'

Phil grinned. 'Oh, you, you're beyond politics, Reggie.' He rinsed out the bowl and dried his hands. 'I'm meeting a friend for a drink, but I'll walk Cato first.'

When Neville emerged from the library he called: 'I'm just going out for some cigarettes.'

'Where will you get any at this time of night?'

'It's not ten yet – I'll just make it to the pub before closing.'

He seemed to be gone a long time. When he returned he stood in the hall and said: 'I think it's time we went to bed.'

She knew from the way he said it what to expect. It was always the same. She followed him upstairs.

'You were flirting with Alan Wentworth, weren't you.'

'No I wasn't!' She was genuinely annoyed, although she knew it was only part of the ritual.

'Don't tell lies. The more you lie, the harder the punishment will be.'

Always the same mixture of disbelief, humiliation and the worm of self-abasement.

'You've been disobedient again. Why can't you do as you're told. I'm going to have to teach you a lesson. Bend over the bed.'

'Please – can I take off my skirt first? I don't want to—'

'Bend over the bed. Don't argue with me.'

She knelt. He pushed up her skirt and slowly pulled down her knickers. It was always the same. There was a silence as he looked; at the pink suspenders that held the flesh-coloured stockings, delineating the obscene space between waist and thigh. She waited meekly, wincing inwardly, for the first stroke of the belt across her buttocks, and then gasped and grunted like an animal in the way he liked at the slow, rhythmic thrashing. The musty smell of the eiderdown removed her to some other distant, but familiar place as he talked about punishing her arse.

She heard the belt drop to the floor. He was undoing his flies. And as the bed creaked rhythmically and she surreptitiously moved her hand between her legs, an image of Charles Hallam brought a groan and with it the engulfing, humiliating, shameful waves of orgasmic pleasure.

She thought of the cold stone floor of the convent. You knelt in self-abasement: confession, penitence, expiation.

four

REGINE WAS BRUSHING HER HAIR. She could hear Phil moving his bike in the hall, leaving for work. Someone knocked at the front door. Cato barked and barked as he hurtled out of the kitchen, his claws clattering on the tiled floor. Regine stared at herself in the bedroom mirror, her brush suspended in mid-air as she heard male voices, then resumed, but more slowly, the strokes that tried to tame the stiff, tangled furze. It must be the postman, perhaps with that book William Drownes had promised to send her, except that the promise had been made only yesterday and—

'Regine!' came Phil's voice, quiet but urgent, as though he'd found a deadly snake in the hall. 'Can you come down?'

'I'll be down in a minute,' she called. Damn – she couldn't go down without her make-up. Whatever it was would just have to wait. Seated in front of her looking glass, she smoothed on a mask of foundation. The ritual of adornment momentarily stilled her seething thoughts. She dusted powder and rouge over her pale skin, drew green eye shadow along her lids with a finger, scrubbed the brush across the little palette of mascara to darken her pale lashes, and painted her lips with her favourite dark lipstick, Elizabeth Arden's Redwood. Lastly, a dab of Chypre on her wrists, and she pushed her feet into the shabby black court shoes and ran downstairs.

She knew at once the two dark-clad men who crowded the narrow space were plain-clothes policemen. Thin, gangling Phil wilted alongside the pair.

'Stop it, Cato. *Down*,' she shouted, as Cato attempted oppressively to embrace them, but Cato was not an obedient dog. 'I'm sorry – he's rather excitable.'

'I'm Detective Chief Inspector Plumer and this is Detective Sergeant Murray.'

Something must have happened.

'Mrs Neville Milner? Perhaps we could—' He gestured with the hand that held his hat towards the drawing room.

'Is it my husband? Has there been an accident?'

'There's been an incident on the Heath. We're making enquiries.'

He would be thinking she meant a road accident or a heart attack, but she was wondering if Neville had done something silly. From time to time when unusual luxuries had appeared, especially when rationing was at its height, she'd wondered whether the black market ... Ivor Novello had gone to prison over the petrol ration after all ... and then there was his Chinese collection ... or could he, after all, have been drinking this early in the day and had an accident in the car on the way to work ... why had he taken the car to work anyway, using up all the petrol; he normally took the tube ...

'We've no reason to suppose ... Is Mr Milner about?'

What on earth had Neville done? She showed the two policemen into the drawing room. They sat down. Phil hovered in the doorway. 'D'you need me? I'll be late for work.'

'Just for a few moments, sir. If you wouldn't mind. You are—? You're not Mr Milner, I take it?' The inspector stared at Phil as if his presence required explanation.

'Philip Jones. I'm the lodger.'

'Ah.' The policeman nodded. He sat hunkered forward, twirling his hat between his hands.

'Would you like some coffee?' Regine, still standing, because sitting down was rather painful this morning, felt ridiculous pretending to be a hostess, but anything to ward off what was coming. It must be something serious. Neville must have … perhaps they'd come to arrest him.

'No thank you; please don't trouble yourself. I apologise for disturbing you like this. Please do sit down, Mrs Milner.'

She eased herself carefully onto the chaise longue.

'We're making enquiries about a body that was found late last night. On the Heath.'

'A *body*?'

He pulled a card from an inner jacket pocket. 'We found this in his coat. No wallet – there was nothing else to identify him by.'

Phil had sat down beside her on the chaise and they looked at it together. She'd had the postcards printed with her name, address and telephone number only the other day. A luxury; such things were still hard to come by and she'd had to wait for weeks. She never sent invitations for her Sundays – people just knew about them and came along if they wanted, it was open house – but she'd dashed off a card … she stared at her own hastily scrawled words: 'Do persuade Vivienne H. to come on Sunday, won't you. It would be lovely to see her again.' She'd put the card in an envelope, so there was no address on the other side.

'What on earth was this note I sent Freddie doing in someone else's coat pocket?'

Phil pushed his glasses up his nose. His hand was shaking. He said in that same deadly tone of voice, the voice of someone backing away from a cobra: 'Reggie – they think – that is – it must be Freddie. Isn't that right?' He glanced at the men who sat there, out of place, invaders who had turned this ordinary domestic day into a nightmare.

'That was the assumption – that the deceased is the person addressed on the card,' said the older detective ponderously.

She stared in front of her. 'Freddie – what on earth do you mean? How could ... He was here – just last night.'

'He was here? What time did he leave?' The chief inspector pounced.

The sergeant was watching her too. 'He was a friend – a relative?'

'You don't mean – what are you saying?' Her soft voice was suddenly hoarse.

Phil came to her rescue. 'Mr and Mrs Milner usually have friends round on a Sunday; Mr Buckingham was one of the guests yesterday afternoon.'

'Buckingham's the name, is it?'

'You mean Freddie ...' She stared at them. 'Freddie – on the Heath? What was he doing on the Heath?'

'A close friend, was he, Mrs Milner?'

'Yes, but ...'

'Perhaps you know his next of kin? They'll need to identify him.'

'Identify him? What d'you mean?'

'They mean he's dead, Reggie,' said Phil.

'Freddie – *dead*? That's *impossible*. He can't be! It can't be him!'

The sergeant said: 'We do realise this must be a shock, Mrs Milner.'

'Oh no – that's impossible,' she cried and then, 'was it a heart attack?'

Phil put his hand on her arm, but spoke to the detectives. 'You say his wallet's gone? What happened, was he attacked?'

Attacked! Her heart turned to lead.

'We don't know exactly what happened. It would be most helpful if you could give us a few details about the gentleman, an address, for instance. Or next of kin? Was he married?'

She said slowly: 'He wasn't married.'

'It is important we establish the next of kin.'

'He really had no family. Well ...' Freddie had been at loggerheads with his family ever since she'd known him. His brother had been killed in North Africa ... his mother was dead, she knew that. Anger welled up. 'There's a sister, I think, but they're barely on speaking terms. His friends were much more important. We can – I don't know – do whatever has to be done.'

'It isn't that simple. I am truly sorry, Mrs Milner, but the fact is, he was murdered.'

'Murdered! You didn't say he'd been murdered!' Freddie had kissed her goodbye. 'He was – I was supposed to have lunch with him today.' She shook her head; she was trying to get rid of the thoughts that buzzed furiously inside her skull like bees in a hive. 'What was he doing on the Heath?'

'That's what we'd like to know, Mrs Milner.'

It wasn't one of the places he went to ... but she mustn't let on about that. She had to protect Freddie. There mustn't be a scandal.

There were so many questions. 'When did it happen?' she said, trying to picture it, trying to imagine ...

'We'll know more about that after the post mortem.'

Phil patted her arm and stood up again. 'I'll phone work and tell them I'm delayed.'

'Just one or two questions and then you can be on your way, sir.'

Phil looked down at her. 'I'll stay, shan't I, Reg?'

She stared at him blankly. 'What? Oh ... no ... I'll ring Neville. And Mrs Havelock will be here any minute.'

The inspector said: 'We needn't take long. The main thing at present is identification. We may need you or your husband to identify him, I'm afraid. If we can't trace his family, that is.'

She stared in front of her. She sat still as a stone.

'You're upset. He was a close friend?' The younger policeman leaned towards her.

But she felt no emotion at all. She stared at him blankly as he said: 'We'll probably need to talk to you at greater length later. But there are a few things you could help us with now – what time he left here last night, how he seemed, whether he was alone or accompanied, if he was going home or planned to meet someone.'

Phil pushed his spectacles up his nose and his hair fell over his forehead. 'Freddie left on his own. He was the last to leave. That's right, isn't it, Regine? About eight, I'd say.'

'Was it? Yes, I suppose ...' His bulky figure visible in the beam of light from the front door as he waved from the path, brushing against the overgrown shrubs.

'What about your other visitors? It will assist us if you can tell us who else was here.'

'Other visitors?' Now she was alert. This was a disaster. The police going round to interview all her guests! No one would ever come again! 'Why do you need to know? What have they got to do with it? Anyway, as Phil says, they'd all left before Freddie.'

The two men in their dark, worn suits were impassive. Then the sergeant glanced at his superior and said: 'Perhaps you could give us a list later.'

'I can't even remember exactly who – I mean it's all very informal, people come and go. Isn't that right, Phil.'

'Absolutely.'

The policemen were silent.

Phil blinked at them. 'Whereabouts on the Heath ...?'

'At this stage we can't divulge details.'

'Near here? Hampstead Heath's a big place.'

Why was Phil asking all these questions?

'Indeed it is,' said the inspector. 'You say you know his address. That's the most important thing at the moment.'

'His address? 66 Markham Square, Chelsea.' As soon as she'd said it, she wished she hadn't. But she could hardly have pretended she didn't know.

'Is there anything either of you can recall, anything unusual about your friend's manner, anything he said?'

The inspector's neutrality unnerved her. He was opaque. She glanced at Phil. Eugene used to say, if ever the police call round, say as little as possible. Why had she remembered that? 'We were reminiscing about Shanghai.'

'Shanghai?'

'Freddie and I were there before the war. We were just chatting about old times.'

And then he'd said, I need to talk to you … What had he wanted to talk to her about? She'd never know now.

'Perhaps, sir, now we have an identification and an address … perhaps we can leave it for now – Mrs Milner will need some time to gather her thoughts.' The sergeant looked across at her. He had a kind face, Regine thought.

Phil was frowning. 'Why should there have been anything unusual? Surely it's pretty obvious what happened. You say his wallet was missing, it must have been stolen, mustn't it? I don't suppose whoever it was meant to kill him, but if Freddie tried to fight him off—'

'At this stage that's pure speculation, sir.' The inspector stood up and the sergeant followed suit. 'And as it happens, he was shot. I apologise for having to bring you bad news, Mrs Milner. But you've been most helpful. At least we have an identification now. We may need to talk to you again later, but finding his next of kin is our first priority and you say you can't help us there.'

'He was *shot* – on the Heath?' It was incredible. She swallowed. 'Well, at least it would have been instantaneous.'

The two policemen glanced at each other. They were not going to enlighten her about that. Then: 'You're sure you can't give us an address for any family?'

She hated the way they were going on about the family, the next of kin. Of course he had a family, somewhere, people like Freddie always had hordes of relations, and however hard Freddie had tried to wrench free of their tentacles there were sure to be some waiting to get their hands on … what? He never had any money. But his things, his *bibelots*, his knick-knacks, his baubles; and the house, of course. She already felt immense hostility towards the sister she'd never met.

In the hall the inspector paused once more. 'In the next few days – if we need to telephone you, this is the number on the card I presume.'

She could not bear the fact that they had the right to keep the card – *her* card – the card she'd written to Freddie. She watched them walk away down the path, their dark clothes shabby in the sunlight.

Phil was waiting for her as she shut the front door: 'Are you all right? This is absolutely ghastly. Look – d'you want me to ring work and say … I mean, I don't want to leave you here on your own.'

'I'll be all right, Phil. Honestly. I'm perfectly all right. You go off. Mrs Havelock will be here any minute. And anyway I'll have to ring Neville.'

She was desperate to be alone. She sat numbly in the drawing room. When Cato came nudging and licking and wanting attention she pushed him away. Shot! Freddie had been shot.

She had to phone Neville. The phone was inconveniently in the hall where there was no room for a chair to sit on – Neville's strategy to discourage lengthy calls. It was always irritating; but at least Phil's bike wasn't there now, cluttering up the passage.

She dialled the museum number. When she got through to Neville and told him, there was a prolonged silence at the other end of the line. Then: 'What the *hell* are you talking about? He can't be dead! What on earth was he doing on the Heath? Trolling around?'

'*I* don't know, Neville. He always talks about going down the East End – look, we mustn't let on to the police that he's – you know ...'

'They'll find out, won't they. They'll go sniffing around Markham Square. *God*! The bloody *fool*!' He paused and then spoke more calmly. 'Reg – I'm one of his executors. Hilary Jordan's the other; he's his solicitor. I'll have to ring him. God, this is going to mean so much work. Why the hell did he have to ... We've got a set of keys, haven't we? You'd better get over to the house, Reg, have a look around. See if you can find a will. And anything incriminating.'

She gripped the handset. 'Don't be ridiculous, I can't go to the house, it'll be crawling with detectives. Hilary will have a copy of the will, won't he. And why didn't you tell me you're his executor?'

'For Christ's sake, Reggie, it never arose!'

'And what do you mean – incriminating? Look – can't you come home? You can get away, can't you, tell them what's happened?'

'No, no, I can't do that. I've got an important meeting. I don't want to ... this day of all days—' He left the sentence unfinished. 'God! What on earth made him – the *fool*!'

'You don't sound very upset. Why are you so angry? He

didn't mean to – this didn't happen just to inconvenience you.'

'Of *course* I'm upset. I'm bloody beside myself.'

'The police said we might have to identify the body.'

'I tell you what,' her husband said in a calmer tone of voice, 'I tell you what, I'll meet you at the house. And then we can have lunch or something. But just take the keys and go over to the house now. You'll be able to tell if the police have got there before you. Obviously if they're there, make yourself scarce. But if they're not – well, see what you can find. Actually, the most important thing is his address book. We don't want them knowing all about all his friends – and ours, do we.'

'No!'

'That's the girl, Reg. God, what an awful, rotten thing to happen.' He still didn't actually sound *upset*. 'I'll try to get to the house by twelve.'

She stood in the hall. It was crazy to go over to Freddie's, but Neville was right, it was vital to make sure the police didn't find anything … a sordid scandal would be so dreadful.

She should have insisted on more details. When had Freddie's body been found? Who had found it? She collapsed onto the drawing-room sofa, feeling slightly faint. When Mrs Havelock arrived she found her employer staring into space.

'Whatever is the matter, madam, are you all right?'

'I've had a shock, Mrs Havelock, a friend of mine has – has died. Suddenly.'

'You look quite white. I'll make you a cup of tea.'

'Thank you – yes, a cup of tea … no milk or sugar.'

When Mrs Havelock returned with the tea, Regine said: 'That's so kind. But I'm quite all right, honestly.'

After a while she knew she was sitting there because she didn't want to reach the Markham Square house before Neville. But she could look in at the shops in Knightsbridge on the way, Harrods, Woollands, Harvey Nichols … At the same time she was unbearably restless, filled with a burning desire to get out of the house. She knew she wouldn't be able to sit still or do any work today. She ran upstairs to find a jacket and pulled on the old red leather one. She had to get away before the lugubrious char asked any more questions.

It was another fine day. She registered the blue sky and leaves beginning to turn – orange, yellow. Her high heels rapped against the pavement up the hill to Hampstead underground: banging nails in a coffin.

five

THE KING'S ROAD WAS BUSY with buses and pedestrians, but when she turned into the square, its emptiness seemed eerie, the blank windows seemed to watch her and the sunlight seemed too bright.

No sign of a black police Wolseley. No sign of Neville either. She stared up at the house. Freddie used to congratulate himself on having a house on the sunny side of the square. Now the house was here, but Freddie wasn't. Freddie didn't exist any more.

Thank God, there was the old Bentley sliding into the square and a moment later Neville climbed out and hurried towards her. He put an arm round her and squeezed her shoulders. How relieved she was to have him with her. As she fumbled with the keys, Neville said: 'I couldn't get hold of Hilary. But I don't suppose it matters. We're here now, anyway. There'll be a copy of the will somewhere. Let's hope we find it.'

Regine walked into the long, narrow double drawing room, stood still and looked round. What Freddie had always called his 'tat' was everywhere: Victorian wax fruit in glass domes, odd little genre scene paintings on the walls, a skeleton clock, also encased in glass, boxes stuck all over with shells, a lacquer screen, the petit-point fire screen. The chimney piece was laden with postcards and invitations from people she didn't know, names she didn't recognise, and she inspected them with jealous interest. Freddie had so many different friends, moved in so many different circles.

He was more important to me than I was to him. It was a sad, sour little thought. She felt ashamed of it.

In the bright sunlight the Regency striped wallpaper looked faded, the room was like a theatrical set, and suffocatingly camp. The sense of Freddie's presence was suddenly overwhelming. A lump in her throat; she somehow mustn't cry; not now, not here.

Neville was riffling through the drawers of the desk. 'No will here.' He banged a drawer shut and opened the next.

'Why is Hilary Freddie's executor? He was very nasty about him yesterday. I can't imagine they got on very well.' Regine peered out of the window and then walked slowly round the front part of the room, smoothing the polished wood of a table, touching a glass dome. What had happened? Freddie must have picked someone up; either that or it was a thief, as Phil had suggested. And Neville was right; the police were bound to turn over every aspect of Freddie's life until they solved the crime and there was every reason for them to know as little as possible about all his – their – friends. Everyone had a secret; and Freddie knew – had known – them all.

'No address book either.' There was a note of panic in Neville's voice. 'Business letters and bank statements, there isn't time to read those. But no will and no address book. Keep a look out for the *Polizei*, kitten.'

She moved over to the front window and drew the lace curtain aside. 'But if I see the police it'll be too late to get away.'

'I'm the executor. I have a right to be here. That's what I'll say anyway. Brazen it out.'

The street was empty, uninhabited. Like the house.

She walked away to the back half of the room and glanced at the books along one wall. Ballet books mostly, some photographic volumes, art books, Edmund Dulac's illustrated *Arabian Nights*. Neville came up behind her and took out a volume. 'Crebillon's *Sofa*. High-class pornography.' Then, as a sudden thought hit him: 'Oh God – the studio.'

The large extension at the back of the house had been one of Freddie's reasons for buying the house, or so he'd told her. Seen from the poky back garden it was ugly and disproportionate, but provided room for an adequate studio, with behind it a darkroom and a box room with filing cabinets. Regine switched on the light. The studio was as it should be: the long roll of white paper hanging down from the ceiling, the light reflectors, the tripods, everything was in place.

Neville made straight for the box room, where Freddie had kept the prints in filing cabinets and where the negatives were stored along the shelves, in boxes.

'We'll have to remove them. Can't be too careful.' Neville's clipped, dry words puzzled her. Everything was taking a long time to understand. Then in a different tone of voice he said: 'They're not all here – some of the negatives – and prints. They're missing.' She heard him open and shut the filing cabinet drawers. He came back into the main room.

'Why are you …?'

'For God's sake, kitten, you don't think he confined himself to ballerinas, do you?'

'But no one else has a key,' she said stupidly.

You're the only person I'd trust with a key, darling, I don't want my inquisitive neighbours poking around … in case something happened.

And now 'something' *had* happened.

'Oh yes they have, Reggie. Of course someone else has a key. His own keys weren't found on the body. You said the police found nothing on him except your postcard. Do pull yourself together. Someone's been here. Must have been.' He looked round. 'Could he have kept them somewhere else, hidden them ... *Damn* – we can't stay here indefinitely. There's no time to make a proper search. And there may be all sorts of other things: incriminating love letters, diaries, anything.'

The police were bound to find out about Freddie's private life, unless ... suppose Phil was right and Freddie had been attacked by a thief and things had gone horribly wrong. They'd find something – footprints, a knife, a witness who'd seen something, perhaps a man running from the scene – and there'd be no need to delve into his private life. Oh, how desperately she hoped that was the case.

'It doesn't *look* as if there was a break-in,' said Neville, looking round and speaking more to himself than to Regine. 'Though if they had the keys there wouldn't be a forced entry, but ... look, I'm going to have another poke around in the desk. Why don't you nip upstairs, see if you think anything else has been stolen – any of his precious objects – the clocks are valuable – and didn't he have quite a lot of silver? But that'll be in the basement, I suppose. But anyway, have a look. I'll be just a sec.'

'We shouldn't stay too long, Neville.'

'I *know* that, but I'd like to find his address book. And his diaries. He always boasted about his diaries – said one day he'd publish and be damned. The will's less important. He may not have kept a copy. Hilary'll have one.'

Regine reluctantly climbed the steep staircase to Freddie's bedroom. She'd never been in this room and it felt like an intrusion. Sometimes she'd thought theirs was a love affair without sex, somehow forbidden and romantic. But she'd never been *in love* with Freddie. More like brother and sister, then; but she shook her head irritably. That was sentimental, somehow false.

Perhaps she hadn't known him as well as she'd believed. What Neville had said had shocked her. She hadn't entirely realised ... did he really mean ... and if so ... her thoughts moved on to blackmail, exposures in the papers – even that glamour pose he'd taken of *her* – it didn't bear thinking about.

The bedroom could not have been more different from downstairs; grimly masculine with a mahogany tallboy, ivory-backed brushes, a navy blue silk counterpane, a free-standing cheval glass, no pictures on the dark grey walls.

A portrait photograph of Charles Hallam stood on the chest of drawers.

She stared at it, lost in thought – or non-thought – a kind of formless dread.

She must pull herself together. She looked in each drawer of the chest, one after the other, but found only neat piles of folded garments. In the top drawer of the tallboy was a box full of cuff links, dress shirt studs, and ...

Good God! It was almost an automatic reflex to thrust what she'd found into her bag.

A few moments later she ran down the stairs. 'No diaries, no love letters, no will, no address book, nothing,' she said, sounding as matter of fact as she could. 'Of course, there's no time to look properly.'

He stared about, tense, agitated. Eventually he said: 'Yes, we'd better go.'

The front door clicked shut behind them. They walked away along the west side of the square towards the car, without noticing the figure who watched them from the other end.

In the restaurant she sat down too quickly and winced as her bruised buttocks met the hard little chair. Tears welled up.

'Don't be upset, kitten.' He held her hand across the table.

'Bloody Freddie. It's a nuisance not finding his diaries. God knows what he wrote in them. If the press get hold of them ... perhaps they're libellous, though. Or – perhaps they don't exist. It'd be just like Freddie to make it all up. But the photos. *They* were real, all right. Perhaps he gave them to someone to look after. Though why would he do that? And the address book, that's the worst of all.' He looked at her and softened. 'I know it's ghastly, kitten, of course it is. I'm upset too.'

'He was shot,' she said suddenly.

'*Shot*?' He lit a cigarette. 'Shot? A hold-up – on the Heath? You didn't tell me *that*! Good God.'

The waitress came to take their order. The wine came quickly and Neville poured a glass for her as well as himself. 'You'll feel better when you've drunk some of this.'

Neville mistakenly imagined alcohol always made everyone feel better. Regine never normally drank during the day, but now she gulped it down.

'I'll try to get hold of Hilary again later. He'll have the will at least.' He stared at her with pinpointy eyes through his wire-framed glasses.

'I'm amazed he made a will,' said Regine. 'I can't imagine Freddie being that organised. And I should've thought he'd have been too superstitious.' She suddenly remembered Charles Hallam and what he'd said about Diaghilev never travelling by boat because some fortune teller had predicted he'd die on the water ... and Freddie *had* been superstitious, but he took risks as well ...

They sat hunched close over the shiny American cloth table covering. 'There's so much that doesn't add up about all this,' murmured Neville. 'And there could be the most frightful scandal, that's why we're worried, isn't it. Because we are. We're frightened. We're nervous. It could involve people we know.'

'What on earth are you talking about? You don't think

someone we know might have ... look, the police said his wallet was stolen. And his keys, no doubt. Just a senseless, random attack – almost an accident.'

Neville was silent while the waitress set down their plates of cauliflower soup. 'But what was he doing on the Heath? Well, I can guess. Did he say where he was going? Was he just going home? If it is something more complicated – it'll go on for weeks, months, it'll be in the papers. If it's just some nasty little thief, with any luck it'll go away quite quickly, otherwise ... all the private life stuff will emerge. And that's why we're panicking, isn't it.'

'Panicking ... are we?' The soup was insipid. Regine stirred it round in her plate. She didn't feel like eating. She took another gulp of wine instead. 'You're right. It won't go away.' Freddie was dead. That would never go away.

'If it comes out,' said Neville, 'it won't be a fair trial ... If they get anyone in the first place. They might not even bother much if they work out he was queer. Which of course they will. And even if they do manage to pin it on some oaf, it'll be Freddie in the dock ...'

'Don't, please.'

Neville wiped his mouth with the paper napkin. 'This soup is disgusting.' He lit a cigarette. 'At the very best it'll be a sordid little story – there'll be speculation in the *Sunday Graphic* or the *News of the World* – you know, "a confirmed bachelor, he moved in bohemian circles", making us all look thoroughly *louche* and dubious. They won't like it at the museum.'

'It'll ruin my Sundays.'

How selfish it was of them to have such thoughts!

She thought of how the detectives had wanted to know all about their friends, but the implications of what Neville had just said were too alarming to contemplate.

The blanquette of veal arrived. It resembled a lumpier

version of the cauliflower soup.

'There was something he wanted to talk to me about. I've no idea what it was.'

'Money, I expect.'

'Did he really not have any? His family's frightfully rich.'

They ate stoically in silence. After the half-eaten stew was removed, Neville lit another cigarette as they waited for the crème caramel.

'It must have been a robbery,' said Regine. 'No one who knew Freddie would want to hurt him. He wouldn't harm a fly.'

'I wouldn't be so sure about that.' Neville looked at her. 'You know, actually, Reggie, yesterday evening—' and then he stopped.

'What about yesterday evening?'

'Oh, nothing.'

'He stayed on quite late, after everyone else had gone. And then at the end he seemed in a hurry to leave. He hadn't time to tell me what it was he wanted to talk about. Perhaps he was going to meet someone.'

Neville frowned. 'I don't know. When I think back now, I think he seemed a bit – hysterical. He was over-excited, agitated. That red flush. I think the spring was wound up very tightly.'

Regine had drunk more than she'd eaten and as they left the restaurant she tottered slightly, feeling squiffy. Neville patted her bottom and took hold of her arm. 'Steady the buffs, kitten. Chin up and all that.'

Regine lay on her back in the dark. In the other twin bed Neville snored gently. She opened her eyes and saw the ghosts of furniture with edges smudged in the soft shadows of the room, as a lesser darkness showed through the gap in the curtains.

She'd laughed so much with Freddie, he was such fun, so

naughty. She lay on her back in her twin bed with her eyes wide open and stared at the impossible truth.

Neville hadn't said anything, not really, but ... why *had* he been in such a hurry to rush over to the house? What was it about the photographs?

She'd wanted to go; to say goodbye to Freddie in that preposterous pastiche drawing room, that crazy museum of Victoriana – all that stuff he'd picked up in junk shops and made so fashionable. She remembered feeling tearful, yet comforted for a moment as she'd stood in his drawing room in the morning sunlight. But in retrospect she was uneasy. That room, like a theatrical set, hadn't it been *too much* like Freddie, a façade, just as his bonhomie, his jokes, his darlings, his adorations had been a screen or a mask for something different hidden behind it all?

That was a cruel, disloyal thought. It was unlucky to have bad thoughts about the dead. She crossed herself.

It was no good. She couldn't sleep. She eased her legs to the floor, pulled on her dressing gown and crept down to the kitchen. As she stood waiting for the kettle to boil, she was thinking about the photographs, about Freddie, but also about the Hallam boy. She made a cup of tea and took it up to her study, a little room above the back extension, more a partitioned bit of the half-landing than a proper room. But she liked it. It was her territory in what, after all, was Neville's house, the house he'd lived in with his dead wife, Lydia, killed in the Blitz, Lydia with her twin beds, with her fur coats, still in cold storage at Woollands in Knightsbridge, and most importantly, Lydia with all her money, conveniently bequeathed to Neville so he could buy oriental vases to his heart's delight and keep his second wife in the manner to which she was far from being accustomed.

Freddie had taken a portrait photograph of Lydia. It looked down, with approval Regine couldn't help feeling, on the scenes of sexual discipline her husband staged with Lydia's rival and usurper, wicked Regine. Had Neville spanked Lydia, taken his belt to her backside? She'd never liked to ask and the question itself might well have earned her a well-deserved session with the belt: Neville's words, the ones that excited him, and now they'd got inside her head too.

Freddie hadn't liked Lydia, Regine was sure of that, for he'd told her bitchy anecdotes about the dead wife. She was so utterly middle class, such a social climber, it was quite shaming – and all that money from some dismal patent medicine her grandfather invented. Neville's done *much* better with you, darling.

Freddie knew all about Regine's background. She'd told him about it quite early on in Shanghai. It hadn't seemed such a shameful secret, then. Only later, after she met Neville – or no, it had all begun in the Vale of Evesham where there were men and women, new, glamorous friends she really wanted to impress – had she started to lie …

The stair creaked. Phil stood in the doorway in his shabby plaid dressing gown with its orange cord piping, looking like an under-nourished *Just William* schoolboy. 'Are you all right? I thought I heard something.'

'I couldn't sleep.'

Phil had been semi-billeted on Neville after Lydia was killed. At the end of the war, Neville had talked about giving him notice. His room would have made a better study for her. But she'd grown used to Phil. Neville was out all day and it could be lonely working away at her translations. Phil's different shifts at the library meant he was quite often at home for lunch or morning coffee. She liked that. He was part of the family now.

'Thinking about Freddie?' Phil propped himself against the edge of her desk. 'I couldn't sleep either. It's most unsettling. Ghastly, actually.'

'I made myself a cup of tea. Why don't you have one?'

He shook his head. 'I was thinking: Freddie was in a strange mood on Sunday. D'you think he might have been going to meet someone, you know, a rendezvous?'

'He didn't say anything,' said Regine doubtfully. But then, he wouldn't have.

'Actually, I thought he seemed a bit tense and – I don't know – almost hysterical.'

'You know, Neville said exactly the same thing. That he was very wound up, yes, hysterical.'

Perhaps his change of mood had been due to an encounter during the afternoon; which meant with another member of her little circle. She said: 'Did you notice who he talked to at the party?'

Phil, going round with the drinks tray, was in a position to notice. 'Well,' he said, 'he sat with the dancer to begin with. That cheered him up for a start, I daresay, he was such a big fan, wasn't he. But perhaps I'm making too much of his mood ... Yes, it was just that when he arrived – I answered the door – he seemed ... Anyway, then Alan Wentworth came over and they were talking for quite a while. And then ... oh, I can't really remember. I got caught up with her son for a while. He was asking me about cocktails. He seemed very knowledgeable.'

'Oh! He wouldn't talk much to *me*!'

'I'd better go back to bed. I'm on early shift at the library.' But Phil stayed where he was. 'Reg—'

'Yes?'

'Well, you know I went out after the party – yesterday evening? Actually I think I may have seen Freddie. On Rosslyn Hill. He was with someone. They were quite a way off.'

'Why didn't you say that to the police? You must tell them, Phil. It goes towards the idea he picked someone up, doesn't it. Perhaps then they'll stop being so interested in all our friends.'

'That's worrying you, isn't it.'

'Of course it is!'

'At first I thought it was so obviously an encounter that went wrong. But I've been thinking about it all day. You know, there were some … there really were some tensions around on Sunday; something in the air.'

'But you're saying he was with someone – he must have picked someone up.'

'Not necessarily, it could have been prearranged.' Phil hesitated, went slightly pink. 'The thing is, I can't be sure, but it did look rather like Neville.'

Regine stared at him. Then she laughed. 'But that's impossible. He … we …' They'd been engaging in their version of marital relations in the bedroom.

Then she remembered. Neville *had* gone out, to get some cigarettes. 'Have you said anything to him?'

Phil shook his head. 'I thought you …'

'Yes. Of course.'

She went back to bed and lay for a long time in the dark. And puzzled again, tantalised, over the last thing Freddie had said to her: there was something he had to tell her, and she thought he'd said it was something about someone they knew.

six

RIGHT FROM THE START Plumer was under pressure from Detective Chief Superintendent Blatchford, whose authority extended over the whole of north London, to make a quick arrest. Not only was the London crime wave continuing, the murder rate up, the squad getting nowhere near enough convictions, but a shooting in suburban Hampstead meant things were really out of control, alarm bells ringing all over the show. This was a damn sight worse than a gangland slaying in Soho or down the East End.

At first, Plumer had been full of confidence. It had been an amateurish job. The victim had been shot in the leg and the shoulder before taking the fatal wound in the stomach. Yet the use of a gun at all meant it was unlikely to have been an amateur pick-up, or street thief. So all he and Murray had to do was lean on a few of their contacts. It wouldn't be long before an informer crawled out from the woodwork. It was a typical sordid underworld crime. The difference was the villain had had the cheek to trespass outside the usual stamping grounds. A shooting in Hampstead was a bloody liberty. Plumer remained nonetheless confident that any minute information would be forthcoming and he would have the satisfaction of nailing some small-time Soho gangster, who, even if he hadn't actually murdered Buckingham, was sure to be guilty of other violent crimes and was better removed from circulation, if possible permanently.

Of course there were courtroom pitfalls in cases like this, where the victim was equally undesirable, as vicious as his assailant if not more so. The charge might be reduced to manslaughter if a clever brief got the killer to say he'd been propositioned by a pervert. Why, he might even be acquitted on grounds of self-defence. After all, men like Buckingham had it coming to them. Still, Plumer was optimistic. Judges took a dim view of guns. That sort of thing had to be nipped in the bud and with any luck the murderer would swing.

Yet although Plumer remained convinced the death had all the marks of the underworld he knew so well, he and Murray returned empty-handed from their visits to the usual suspects and their trawls through the drinking clubs and dives of King's Cross and Soho. Nothing. A lurid release from the Scotland Yard press room (CHICAGO COMES TO HAMPSTEAD) not only did not bring the new information hoped for, but, on the contrary, served only to increase public alarm.

Plumer therefore suppressed his intense distaste for everything about the kind of life Buckingham had lived, and accompanied Murray into the murky underworld of male prostitutes, gents' toilets and unnatural acts in which the dead man had, in Plumer's imagination at least, dwelt like some amphibian creature from the black lagoon. Murray put the frighteners on the boys that hung around Piccadilly Circus. There were queer clubs, too, the sort of place a man of Buckingham's type would frequent. Visits to them had been equally useless. The furtive, respectable clients had taken fright and run for the hills; useless, lily-livered pansies.

A few days later, however, Buckingham's wallet was handed in to Hampstead police station. It contained a large sum of money, five pounds, untouched other than by damp from having lain hidden on the Heath.

The detectives sat in Plumer's shabby office, drinking tea.

'That casts some doubt on the robbery theory, doesn't it, sir.'

'I'm not so sure. His keys haven't turned up. Perhaps the idea was to get into the house.' But Plumer knew that didn't hold water. The keys could have been flung away anywhere on the Heath – down a drain, into a pond – they'd never be found. Anyway, no killer with a gun would have baulked at the thought of breaking and entering. Men like that didn't bother with keys.

'We've been to all the Hampstead pubs and nobody saw him. I don't think it was a pick-up.' Murray had a feeling this was going to be his big break. He desperately wanted it to be. 'Could it have been a jealous lover, sir? Someone he knew? Something to do with the guests at the party? We ought at least to check alibis. And his friends could tell us more about the man. Don't you think, sir? And there is that witness in the square – the neighbour we spoke to.'

'The chief isn't keen on harassing high-ups. Not that the Milners and their friends are toffs exactly, but they're the sort that complain. And some of our friends in the vice squad are itching to get involved, to crack down on the queers, but he doesn't want that either. He thinks the vice squad are getting too big for their boots. That's what he thinks. But you're right, this is a murder investigation. All I'm saying is, let's just go very carefully.'

This time the detectives came in the evening. The Milners were due for supper at the Wentworths', who were more or less neighbours since they'd recently bought a cottage at the back of Hampstead High Street. Regine was changing into the black dress she'd bought yesterday from Harrods for the funeral that hadn't yet taken place. It had the full New Look skirt, which, sadly, largely hid her slender ankles and long legs; on the other hand the great bell of material enhanced waist and curves. People didn't wear black to funerals much any more, a black armband was enough and there were still so many of those, but it had felt right. Only full black would do for Freddie and his well-developed sense of drama. It was also too dressed up for an informal supper with the Wentworths, but she couldn't resist, she had to get Dinah's reaction. It was so lovely; such soft wool and sweet little round buttons up the front like black peas or pearls. Neville had said he thought clothes would soon be de-rationed. Then, he suggested, things might at last begin to get back to normal, with people dressing properly again, changing for dinner and so forth. So he approved of the black dress.

Life had to go on. It was important to look your best – and the nuns, after all, had insisted on neatness and the importance of detail, only not, of course, as an expression of the vanity and worldliness they'd tried to crush out of her, with their gibes at her colouring; as if her glaring hair had been inherently sinful in being so bold and so violent.

Black was flattering. But it was also the colour of death and beneath the surface ran death's deep undertow. There was also the nagging worry of what Phil had told her about Neville, how he'd seen Neville and Freddie together on that Sunday night. Almost every evening she'd tried to find out if her husband really had met Freddie, but all she'd discovered was that Neville didn't want to talk about that evening. She hadn't taken note at the time of when he'd gone out and come back. Had the wire-less been on? Had the clock in the hall rung the hour? It was before ten, but *how long before*? She couldn't remember. All she knew was that Neville not only wouldn't talk about it, but became irritable and peevish at the very mention of the murder.

He was going to be even more irritable when the telephone bill came at the end of the month. For she'd spent hours on the phone to Dinah, Cynthia and Dorothy, mulling over the meagre facts, trying to believe it was true.

And into the stream of anxiety and sadness that was there all the time, every so often the thought of Charles Hallam swam through her mind.

On his way home Neville had managed to buy a bottle of gin. He mixed pink gins in Lydia's pre-war cocktail glasses. Rather vulgar and very 1930s, he said, the first time they'd been brought out; but Regine liked them. Each was a different colour, spotted with motes of gold leaf. Neville handed her the blue one. As she took her first sip there was a knock at the front door. Cato barked and pounded through the house.

'Who the hell is that?'

She sprang up. 'I'll answer it.'

The chief inspector loomed up behind his sergeant, who was trying to ward off the dog. 'It's the detectives, Neville,' she called brightly. She led them into the drawing room with a sense of suppressed panic, but she was not too agitated to have a close look at the younger man, who'd hardly registered on his previous visit. He was not so tall, after all, but he was well built, muscular, and he moved with energy. His eager face ran to a point with his keen nose and bright, dark eyes; yet to have described him as resembling a rodent would have given the wrong impression, although his face did have the alert curiosity of a rat or ferret on the qui vive. His curly hair, released from his trilby, seemed full of energy too, and, short as it was, sprang over his forehead.

'I'm so sorry. I've forgotten your name.'

'Murray, Detective Sergeant Paul Murray. And Detective Chief Inspector Plumer.'

Neville had risen to his feet. He was frowning in a failed

attempt at hauteur. 'To what do we owe the pleasure of this visit?' To Regine his words sounded ridiculous. 'A drink? We were just having a cocktail before going out. I hope this won't take too long. We're due to meet some friends.'

Plumer didn't beat about the bush. 'A wallet was handed in to Hampstead police station yesterday. It had been found on the Heath. It contained five pounds, an identity card and a cheque book belonging to Mr Buckingham. This somewhat alters the complexion of the case, as I'm sure you'll appreciate.'

'It was found some way from the scene of the crime,' added Murray. 'We had made a search of the immediate area. The wallet was found in undergrowth much further down the hill.'

'Five pounds? And it wasn't stolen?' Neville stared at the policemen cluttering up his drawing room.

'Surely ...' Regine dreaded what they might say next. 'I thought you said it was just some – some *lout*. That's what you said, wasn't it?'

Plumer looked bleakly across at them. 'No, Mrs Milner, that's not quite what we said, although on the face of it, yes – an encounter, of whatever kind, that went wrong; an attempted robbery, that was a hypothesis. But five pounds is a tidy sum of money. What sort of thief would chuck that away?'

Neville cleared his throat. 'I take it his keys weren't found?'

Plumer smiled thinly. 'No, sir.'

Regine's sense of dread intensified. She picked up her blue and gold glass. It was empty. Wordlessly she handed it to Neville.

'Are you sure you won't join us?'

Plumer shook his head. 'We're interested in what Mr Buckingham may have done after he left your house on the Sunday afternoon or evening.'

'I can't quite see what Sunday afternoon has to do with Freddie being attacked on the Heath.' Neville handed her glass, refilled, to Regine and sat down again, pulling the creases of his trousers.

Sergeant Murray looked at Regine. 'I believe you said he left here on his own. What time would that have been? Can you give me a rough idea?'

Freddie waving from the path, more than several drinks to the good, the light from the door streaming into the darkness.

'About eight? That sort of time. It stays light quite late even now, doesn't it, with double summer time, but it was getting dark – was dark. But I told you the time, didn't I, when you were here before?'

'It was a cocktail party, was it?' put in Plumer.

'Not a party, more informal, friends just drop in if they feel like it.'

'I believe you said you could provide us with a list of the guests?'

She stared, appalled. Her horror must have been obvious, for Murray said gently: 'We do need to know who was here.'

'I can't see how that's relevant.' Neville spoke sharply.

'Well … it's important to try to piece together his movements after he left your house. He left alone – but he could have met up with someone again later.'

Regine glanced at her husband. His face was expressionless.

'What are you implying exactly?' he said with hauteur.

'I'm not implying anything,' said Plumer patiently. 'The body was discovered around 11 p.m. by a man who was walking his dog, and we think the post mortem will show that the deceased hadn't been dead long. So … let's say the attack probably took place around ten. That's not an exact time, of course … but if we assume that's when it happened, around ten o'clock, then that would be roughly two hours after he left here and we need to know what he was doing during those two hours. He didn't say where he was going?'

She frowned, couldn't remember what he'd said, if he'd said anything. She shook her head. 'I thought he was going home. But I don't think he said he was, I just assumed that's where he was going.'

I need to talk to you ... lunch tomorrow ... someone we used to know ...

'But in just two hours, if he left your house at eight, it seems unlikely he went home to Chelsea and then came back up here again.'

'He *could* have.' She said it more for the sake of argument than anything.

'Theoretically, yes, but it seems rather unlikely. He'd have to go more or less straight there and back. What would be the point of going home for twenty minutes or less?' he insisted softly. 'Was he in the habit of having a drink in any of the local public houses? Are there other friends in the area he might have looked in on?'

It was borne in on Regine that she was completely vague about Freddie's other life; picking up men in pubs – or worse. Oh, that would be the worst thing, so terribly sordid ... some common little male prostitute ... She shook her head violently. A curl broke out from the ribbon she'd scraped her hair back with. She put her hand up to smooth it back.

'He'd been drinking at your party?'

She smiled. 'Not to excess.'

Regine was aware the sergeant's attention was directed exclusively at her. He leaned forward. 'Can you tell us a bit more about him? I know this is painful. I realise how difficult this is for you, but – there must have been some reason he was on the Heath two hours after he left your house, mustn't there?'

His eager gaze was tempting. It would be so easy to confide in him. But she mustn't, she mustn't. 'You're just assuming that's what happened.' If she sounded sulky, that was too bad.

They had no right to come poking and prying. 'What would you like to know about him? He was a photographer; and a ballet critic. He wrote about ballet. It was his great passion. He was part of the … the arts, the theatre world, he was great friends, for example, with Vivienne Evanskaya.'

But – oh why had she said that? Now they might want to interview Vivienne. But the sergeant looked blank.

'The prima ballerina,' she said.

'Oh … of course, yes.'

Regine laughed. 'You don't know who I'm talking about?'

Murray went red. 'Of course I've heard of Vivienne Evanskaya, I wasn't expecting her name to crop up, that's all.'

Plumer frowned: 'She was one of the guests, was she? Who else was here that afternoon? We really do need a list of the guests, if you don't mind.'

Neville removed his pipe from his lips and started to gouge out its innards. 'I don't see the necessity for that.'

'Well, it's quite simple, Mr Milner. It's possible one of your guests could tell us something useful, something Mr Buckingham said about where he was going, if he was meeting anyone. Surely you can't have any objection to that?'

The telephone calls had started, of course, as soon as the first reports appeared in the papers. There'd even been an item on the wireless, and on the Wednesday morning after the murder there'd been an obituary in *The Times*. By that time she'd broken the news to everyone she could think of. He had so many other friends she didn't know, but in any case, the news spread like wildfire.

'I can't even remember exactly who was here.' Regine knew she was only playing for time. 'I told you, it's not a formal thing. I never know who's going to turn up. Is it really necessary? A list? It'll be rather upsetting for people …' And she smiled at Murray, hoping he'd tell her it didn't matter, not to bother, but although he smiled back he was adamant.

'He may have said something to someone. You can never tell what's going to be crucial.'

Regine fetched paper from the library. She sat opposite Murray, staring ahead, trying to remember. It was all so pointless and could only do harm.

'The Jordans, Vivienne and her son, Alan Wentworth ...' She was writing as she spoke. 'Noel Valentine looked in, but I don't think he was here that long ... and there was Dorothy Redfern and Edith Blake came later ... with William Drownes ... who else was there, Neville?'

There was one name that must absolutely be suppressed, of course, that of the cabinet minister, so it would be better to leave Cynthia out of it as well. Or would it be better to include her, to stick as closely to the truth as possible?

'That's about it, I think.' She handed Murray the list, and he passed it to Plumer. Plumer looked at it and passed it back. 'I'm afraid we need addresses and telephone numbers as well.'

'Really, Inspector—' protested Neville and looked at his watch, but Regine stood up again. 'I'll have to get my address book from upstairs.'

Murray smiled at Regine. 'Please – don't bother. I can call in tomorrow – when it's convenient.'

But Plumer overrode him. 'We need it now, if you don't mind, Mrs Milner.'

There was something about Plumer's stony deadness that frightened Regine. She fetched her address book and as she started to copy out addresses Plumer was saying: 'We've traced Mr Buckingham's relatives in Yorkshire.'

His words intensified her resentment. 'He didn't get on with his family, didn't have much to do with them at all. And what about the funeral? What's happening about that?' They'd probably want him buried up there, in Yorkshire.

'We haven't released the body yet.'

Regine was aware of Murray watching her. There was something, not intense exactly, but intent, watchful about him. She looked up and caught his gaze, smiled. He smiled back. 'It's all so crazy,' she said softly, 'I can't believe this has happened. And I don't know why you need all this – it won't help.'

'It's important to find out who killed him, don't you think?'

'I suppose so.' But was it? Did she really care if the murderer was caught? Freddie was dead. That was what mattered, the unbearable truth, nothing else seemed that important. In fact, a trial, with all the sordid details leaking out … it was a terrible thought.

Neville stood up. 'I don't wish to be rude,' he said firmly, 'but – we are expected round at our friends'.'

'Of course,' said Plumer, 'just one other thing, though. You see, when we went over to Mr Buckingham's house in Chelsea, we naturally had a word with his neighbours, and one of them said they'd seen a couple leaving the house on Monday; a red-haired lady and a gentleman … Could that have been the two of you, by any chance?'

Sweat broke out under her arms. She felt her face go rigid with dismay. But she looked at Neville and he seemed quite calm.

He puffed at his pipe. 'I can explain, Inspector. I'm Freddie's executor. We thought it would be all right. We wanted to make sure the house was untouched. After all, you'd told my wife his keys were missing, so we naturally assumed whoever killed Freddie must have had his keys as well. Freddie had valuable things, objets d'art, they might have been stolen.'

'How did you gain entry? *You* had a set of keys?'

'Yes – you're not accusing *us* of breaking in, I hope.'

'Perhaps you knew the deceased had other things to hide –

secrets I mean, not works of art or valuables,' said Murray. 'Look, there's no point in beating about the bush. Mr Buckingham wasn't married, was he. Wasn't the marrying type, I suppose. Preferred the company of his own sex.'

So they knew. But of *course* they knew. They'd known all along. Guessed, anyway. 'I suppose you think just because a man likes ballet, he's – he's abnormal in some way,' said Regine.

Paul Murray did have a nice smile. But she must be on her guard, mustn't be led into saying too much. 'We're not here to pass judgement on anyone, that's not our job,' he said, knowing full well this didn't quite reflect his superior's position. 'But if Mr Buckingham was inclined to get involved with other men in a way that put him outside the law, then he was in a vulnerable position, wouldn't you agree. Perhaps he got talking to someone in a pub, they went for a walk on the Heath ... things turned nasty, unexpectedly – I'm more inclined to condemn those who prey on the weaknesses of men like your friend, weaknesses they perhaps can't help, can't do much about – but on the other hand perhaps the obvious scenario isn't the correct one. Is there anything else you know that could help us? You must have gone straight round after we called here on Monday. Why was it so urgent? Did you go round to see if there was anything incriminating you could remove?'

Neville broke the bond between his wife and her interrogator. 'Are you suggesting we went there to *steal* something? To interfere with evidence in some way?'

'I'm not suggesting anything. But you must have had a reason to go there.'

'We told you. I'm the executor. I was hoping to find a copy of the will.' Neville stood up and took a turn around the room, sucking at his pipe. 'However, I didn't. I didn't find his address book either. Also – I haven't had an opportunity to tell you this, kitten – but I've since discovered I may not be his executor after all.' He looked at the detectives. 'According to a will made some years ago, I *was* the executor. Freddie's solicitor is or was another friend of ours, Hilary Jordan. However, when I spoke to Jordan, it turns out he has no copy of the will either. His firm's offices were bombed in 1945 – a V2 – and all their papers and records were destroyed. He told Freddie this some time afterwards, but Freddie didn't produce another copy. Apparently he just said he might make a new will. He never saw fit to mention this to me. I acted in good faith.'

'In that case, we'd better have the keys, hadn't we.'

Regine rebelled at this. 'But he – Freddie – gave me the keys.'

'I'm sorry, Mrs Milner, but this is a murder inquiry. Granted the dead man's house was not the scene of the crime, nonetheless anything there may be relevant. People can't just wander in and out.'

'We have no *locus standi*, kitten,' said Neville drily, aware of Regine's intense resentment. Reluctantly she fetched the keys from the desk drawer and handed them to Murray. His smile seemed intended to reassure, but she only felt angrier, though she said with outward calm: 'If nothing was stolen, that doesn't mean it wasn't someone he'd just met.'

But Plumer said: 'But you've just told us that items may have been stolen. And quite apart from that there may be important evidence in the house. Fingerprints, for example. And even if you were under the impression that you were his executor, Mr Milner, it was hardly within your remit to investigate his home in such haste.'

'I thought it was, Chief Inspector.'

'So you had a look around and didn't find a will or an address book, significant items you expected to be there. Was anything else missing at all? Valuables, for example.'

Regine hesitated. Perhaps it wouldn't hurt to be frank ... up to a point. Neville had said not to mention the photographs, it would only lead to more scandal, but it was obvious they knew about Freddie's private life anyway. She smiled confidingly at Murray. 'You're right to suggest we're worried about his private life being exposed. I so hope it doesn't all have to be dragged through the courts – in the gutter press. But as it happens we do think some of his photographs were missing, personal ones, that is.' As soon as she'd spoken, she regretted it. Neville's face was pinched together in a frown. A bad mistake – she'd let herself be softened by Murray's quiet, sympathetic manner.

He watched her, but it was Plumer who spoke. 'You're sure *you* didn't remove anything incriminating?'

'I suggest you retract that remark,' said Neville.

'This is a murder inquiry, Mr Milner,' repeated Plumer. 'We have to investigate every possibility. So perhaps you could tell us what sort of personal photographs these were.'

'Just photographs of his friends.' Neville was sulky now.

'Friends of the same persuasion as himself, perhaps.'

Regine thought Neville was going to object, but he cleared his throat. 'There's something you should know, although I don't know how significant it is. That evening – the Sunday – I went out later on to get some cigarettes before the pubs closed, and I actually bumped into Freddie. I was a bit surprised – although of course he could easily have been meeting other friends in Hampstead. But I got the feeling he wasn't too pleased to see me. We walked along together for a few minutes, then he turned back towards the tube station, saying he had to get the train home.'

Chief Inspector Plumer stared impassively at Neville. 'What time was this?'

'I'm not sure – before closing time. Before last orders. It just seemed rather odd, that's all.'

'Phil, our lodger, he went out too,' said Regine. 'He went for a drink and then he went to a friend's house. He must have got back here quite late. I don't remember hearing him come in. We must have been asleep.'

'We need to talk to him too, then. Is he at home?'

'He's on late shift at the library. It doesn't shut till eight.'

'Did Mr Buckingham say where he'd been, or where he was going?'

Neville squinted through the smoke from his pipe. 'No. And there's nothing particularly odd about it, really, it was just that he seemed a bit on edge.'

Chief Inspector Plumer stared, but said nothing. A sixty-a-day man, he pulled another cigarette from its Player's packet and lit it off the end of the last. He took a deep lungful and exhaled a plume of smoke. Regine disliked the way he never even bothered to take the cigarette out of his mouth. It sat there between his pale lips until it was just a stub and waggled up and down when he spoke.

Neville repeated himself to cover the silence, 'We chatted for a few moments. He was uneasy, I thought – I got the feeling he wished he hadn't seen me. We walked along in this direction, then he suddenly stopped and said he had to go back to the tube.'

'He was going to meet someone, perhaps?'

Neville shrugged. 'For someone so expansive, Freddie didn't talk much about his private affairs.'

'He led a double life?'

'I didn't say that.'

'You knew Mr Buckingham well.'

Neville sucked at his pipe. 'I knew him well at one time, before the war. Then he went out to the Far East. But we met up again during the war – in fact he introduced the two of us, didn't he, Reg, but now he's really your friend more than mine, wouldn't you say? Was, that is.'

Regine nodded, suddenly feeling tearful again.

'He went off in the direction of the tube? And he said nothing about meeting anyone?'

'No,' said Regine.

'Actually, I don't know for sure about the tube,' said Neville. 'I didn't see which way he went.'

'And your meeting with him was entirely accidental, Mr Milner? You hadn't made a prior arrangement to meet him?'

Neville frowned. 'Of course not, Inspector.'

Plumer turned to Regine. 'Looking back, can you remember anything about his behaviour, his mood, who he talked to, whether there was any indication he might be meeting up with someone again, later in the evening? The party took place in this room, did it?' Plumer looked round as he spoke.

'Here and in the dining room and the library – as it's a double-fronted house people tend to wander from room to room,' said Neville. His mood changed; he became unexpectedly chatty. 'That was one of the reasons for choosing the house in the first place. It's so much better than the normal London terraced house, where you have to live on the vertical. We – that is to say my first wife and I – had been living in Kensington, which I really prefer, as an area, but we were charmed by the layout of this house.'

'Guests don't have to be manoeuvred up and down stairs,' explained Regine.

'So you wouldn't necessarily have noticed any tensions.' There was another little silence.

'Why should there have been *tensions*?'

'No reason,' said Plumer, pleasantly enough.

Murray added: 'On the face of it the most likely thing is your friend met his death at the hands of a stranger. Even though we now know he wasn't robbed. We still think that's the most likely explanation. But we have to look at every angle. We can't rule out the possibility that Mr Buckingham knew whoever killed him. His keys are probably still lying around on the Heath somewhere, but they may have been taken – by someone who wanted to get into his house, and who therefore knew something about him; in other words, it wasn't just a casual encounter.'

'Why not just break into his house, then? Why go to all the trouble of murdering him and stealing his keys?' interrupted Neville.

'Why indeed,' agreed Plumer, 'although having a set of keys would obviously simplify matters, particularly for someone who wasn't a professional thief. But this is pure speculation. No witnesses have come forward, although the alarm was raised not so long after he died. Nor is there a history of attacks on the Heath – the only violence up there in the past year or so was the Jewish group, Group 43, that saw off Oswald Mosley's lot. So you will understand why we have to explore the possibility that some of his – your – friends may have helpful information.'

'But no one who was here that day would have – I mean, the guests who were here that day are my friends, mine and my husband's,' cried Regine. 'And anyway everyone adored Freddie. I can't think of anyone who would have dreamed of hurting him.'

'I said information. I didn't say they'd be suspects. We shall be talking to them, hoping for useful information, but otherwise as a matter of form, you understand, a process of elimination. On the other hand, of course, there's still the firearms factor. That does suggest the underworld. We're continuing our investigations there.'

Regine watched them walk down the path. She shut the door and returned to the drawing room. Neville was cleaning out his pipe.

'Why didn't you tell me you'd met Freddie?'

Neville looked up at her. 'I didn't say anything about it

because he told me he'd met Arthur Carnforth and they'd quarrelled. They met in some low pub in Camden Town and had a
row about Vivienne. It got quite unpleasant, apparently. Arthur
was rather belligerent.'

'Why didn't you tell the police that?'

Neville smiled a funny little thin smile. 'It's old history,
kitten. Water under the bridge.'

'Phil thought he'd seen you with Freddie. I kept trying to
ask you, but you just shut me up every time.'

Neville banged his pipe on the coal scuttle. 'We don't want
it getting around that he'd been with Arthur.'

'Why should it – get around? He wasn't with him when you
met Freddie, was he?'

'No, but ... it might look suspicious. We could be in queer
street ourselves. They know we went to Markham Square – and
it was a bit of a bombshell, when Hilary told me we're not the
executors and there doesn't seem to be a will. I only found out
when I rang him today.' Neville walked up and down and
sucked at his pipe. 'I thought I had to tell them I'd seen Freddie,
but there's no point dragging Arthur into it. And it probably
doesn't mean anything at all.'

'We'd better be going.' But Regine sat down on the sofa and
stared at her thick, bluish glass with its flecks of gold. 'I didn't
realise Freddie ... he did say something a while ago about Arthur
being friendly with Vivienne Hallam these days, but why did he
mind so much he tried to stop it? That seems very strange.'

She stood up and he put his arm round her waist. 'Poor
kitten – it's all so beastly, isn't it.'

She nodded, the lump in her throat threatening yet again.
She'd been tearful on and off all day. She was grateful for
Neville's comforting arm and pressed her head against his
shoulder. But Neville had been out in the darkness too, that
evening. And why had he needed cigarettes so suddenly? He

always kept lots of them all over the house – he'd known how to get them, all through the war, he'd never gone short, he'd positively hoarded them.

seven

THE DETECTIVES DROVE UP TO Jack Straw's Castle, the tavern at the top of the Heath, and settled down over a pint. Plumer had a new packet of Player's Navy Cut. Murray, who'd smoked around ten a day until he came within Plumer's orbit, feared he was fast becoming almost as heavy a smoker as his superior. Lighting up had become automatic. But now he resisted.

'What did you think of the Milners then?'

'I thought they were fairly straight with us,' said Murray. 'She's a real looker, isn't she – very striking. He was a bit prickly, I thought. But I felt they were genuinely upset about it all, her anyway.'

'Why did they dash round to Buckingham's house like a couple of electric rabbits when the gate goes up?'

'To get hold of the will? He's the executor.'

'That's what he *says*. Tearing round like that – it looks suspicious. And now it turns out there isn't a will, and he isn't the executor! Very fishy. Did he just cook up the story as some kind of explanation? And why? What were they bothered about? Possibly they wanted to get their hands on something – incriminating material – the dead man was a criminal himself, remember. Don't ever forget that. Everything about his private life was against the law. There may have been letters – we may get wind of others like him – a whole network of perverts. They may have suppressed all kinds of evidence. Have you thought of that?'

Murray hadn't.

'The dead man was a photographer, wasn't he. Maybe some of the pictures he took weren't just portraits and ballet. The prints we looked through were harmless enough, but that doesn't prove anything. That one in his bedroom, for instance. Now why would a flaming pervert have a photo like that in his bedroom?'

Murray felt he was going red. 'It was just a portrait,' he said. 'You're not suggesting—'

'I'm not suggesting anything. But there is something I don't quite like about it all. A queer's shot dead. His wallet's stolen, only it isn't. The Milners rush round to his house. No signs of disturbance, but no sign of a will either. Photographs missing – and an address book. That says blackmail to me – bearing in mind his private life. Nothing else stolen, so far as we know, although there were plenty of valuables. And what about Milner just happening to meet him by accident? I think he was keeping something back. What was all that about?'

Murray shook his head. 'D'you think he was trying to cast suspicion on someone else? After all, what was he doing wandering about at that time – more or less the time of the murder?'

Plumer nodded. 'We need to find out more about that lot. Where's the list then?'

Murray brought it out, unfolded it and spread it on the low table in front of them. 'I'll check their backgrounds, sir. The name Alan Wentworth strikes a chord. I think he was mixed up in that trial where some commie was up for murder; got off on appeal earlier this year. You remember the case. I'll have a word with a chap I know in Special Branch. I have a feeling the name was Wentworth – bit of a fellow traveller before the war. But there can't be anything suspicious about him now. She's put down here he works for the BBC.'

'All these long-haired, arty Hampstead types, don't trust any of 'em. The BBC's full of pinks and pansies. Keep away from Special Branch too, we don't want them poking their noses in.'

'Yes, sir.' He hesitated. 'They've no reason to, though, have they?'

'I'm just saying, on principle.' As they went down the list, Plumer seemed disappointed that the Milners' guest list wasn't more exciting. 'It's not politics we're interested in, it's blackmail,' he said. 'With a man of this kind, that's what you always want to look out for.'

'But – if you're suggesting the stiff was being blackmailed, shouldn't he have been the killer, not the victim?'

'Perhaps that was the intention. Perhaps someone turned the tables on him. Blackmailers are a nasty breed, very nasty.'

After a further round of bitter, they emerged into the chilly night. Scarves of mist gathered along the trees.

As they drove away Plumer repeated: 'Between ourselves, we've got a problem. The chief isn't keen on having us upset a lot of high-ups, well-known people, not that the Milners and their pals are really well known, not most of them anyway.'

It was the second time Plumer had said that. It was odd. Plumer was not the deferential type. And normally neither was the superintendent. 'The dancer's famous,' he said, stating the obvious.

'Yes, yes, I know that. Covent Garden, part of the war effort, got a gong. But we've got to go carefully. He's like a cat on a hot tin roof over this one. Look – there's a crime wave on, haven't you noticed. And this blighter was shot. Superintendent Blatchford wants it solved double quick, but he doesn't want a lot of scandal about queers and pansies. Member of the underworld, criminal fraternity, that's what we're looking for.'

'We've done what we could in that direction. And the shooting was so amateurish.'

'It's early days, whatever Blatchford says. We'll have to go back and try again. Apply more pressure. And as for amateurish – whoever shot the pansy probably did time in the war, not square bashing. A lot of these young hoodlums have no idea, they are bloody amateurs.' Plumer looked at his companion. 'I know what's on your mind: Rita Hayworth. I'm right, aren't I. And I've nothing against you going and seeing her again. You might get her talking when her husband's not around. See if you can get anything out of her – romance her a bit, if you like. Never hurts to turn on the charm. And she probably knows as much about the dead man as anyone – and what her husband was up to, if anything. Worth a try, you never know. Don't get carried away, mind. Go easy. Always remember these sort of people have a different moral code from ours. We need to talk to the lawyer too. I suppose theoretically he is still an executor.'

'The guest list – shall I follow them up as well?'

The chief inspector dropped Murray at Archway underground station before turning north-east towards his home and his meekly understanding wife in faraway Chingford.

Murray bought an evening paper and tried to read it in the tube going home, but he hadn't got over his astonishment at his boss's words. Romancing Mrs Milner! That Plumer, a model of moral rectitude, should have suggested flirting with a married woman had deeply shocked him. And he couldn't help wondering how Plumer behaved when 'turning on the charm' – if he ever had, which was hard to imagine.

Yet perhaps the older man had more intuition than Murray gave him credit for, because as the train rumbled southwards, Paul Murray could not let go of the mental images of *her*: the white skin against the smooth black material of her dress, the curve of her backside as she'd risen so gracefully from her chair.

His eyes wandered over the sports pages, but he was seeing the way her hands scrunched into her curls and feeling the warmth of her smile and the ingenuous gaze of those wonderful green eyes.

When he came out of Clapham North station the air seemed grimier and the streets dingier. As he walked towards the terraced house he rented with his mother – one in a long, long road of identical Edwardian houses, each façade top-heavy with crude plaster ornamentation – he sank into a mood of glum fatigue, and when he reached home, he found the house shabby and the furnishings sparse after Downshire Hill.

'How the other half lives, Mother,' he said as she set a plate of cottage pie and cabbage in front of him. She did her best with the rations, but what depressed him about their life at home was the acceptance of drabness. The Milners' house had been so bright and colourful, but for him and his mother austerity had little to do with temporary shortages, it was rather the fabric of life itself; austerity was their *lot*, and always had been.

Paul Murray's father had died when he was eight. He'd got a scholarship to a grammar school and his mother had gone out to work as a char to keep him on after fourteen to sit the School Certificate, but the expense had been a tremendous strain. The school had wanted him to stay on even longer and do the Higher Certificate, but that was out of the question.

He'd joined the force as soon as he could after leaving school. At least the police offered a career; it was better than an office job and with more prospects. When war broke out he'd have liked to join up, but there was his mother and little brother to think of. He didn't know how she'd manage if he got killed. So he'd stayed on all through the war. People thought you had it easy back in Blighty. That was a laugh, he thought bitterly. The home front had been far from bloody safe. And as if criminals didn't have to go on being caught even if there was a war on. The amount of crime there'd been in the war; it was unbelievable! The callousness of it sometimes – looters going in after a raid and pulling rings and jewellery off corpses, lifting anything they could lay their hands on, handbags with ration books, absolutely anything. And talk about the black market ... As he sat with his cup of tea and his cigarette at the end of the meal he felt himself descending into a mood of self-pity. If only he had medals and tales of wartime bravery in action with which to dazzle Mrs Milner.

But he pulled himself together. He had been brave in the war. He'd risked death many times. He'd chased gangsters and deserters. He'd saved bomb victims from toppling buildings and chased army deserters from them too. Now he was determined to solve this sinister case, and as he pictured again the overripe body of the masculine-looking man said to be a flamboyant homosexual, he wondered at what Neville Milner had said: that the late Freddie Buckingham was one of his wife's closest friends. How could such a beautiful woman sully herself by friendship with such a character? And how could her husband allow it?

His tea drunk, he left the house again, to telephone his fiancée, Irene, from the box at the end of the road. He'd applied to have a telephone installed in the house, he could afford it now, but there was a lengthy waiting list, even for a policeman, although Plumer had promised to pull some strings.

It would be Irene's birthday soon. He had to think of a present, and of somewhere more exciting to take her than the Gaumont restaurant on the Broadway.

eight

THE CONGREGATION DRIFTED OUT of Brompton Oratory and stood about in twos and threes. One mourner, then a second, walked out to the kerb and scanned the horizon right and left for a taxi.

'I'm going straight back to the museum, kitten. I don't feel like hanging around, toiling over to the Hallams' and then coming back here again, it doesn't make sense and I've missed half a day's work already.'

Regine watched the retreating figure in dapper suit and bowler hat as he made off at a brisk pace. But now Freddie's brother-in-law, who had organised everything, simply drove away with his wife, Freddie's sister, Margaret, in a large black Austin behind the hearse, accompanying Freddie to his final resting place in Brompton Cemetery. The mourners were left rudderless in the Brompton Road.

Regine had wanted to invite friends back to Downshire Hill, but Neville had pointed out that they didn't know Freddie's more famous friends from the world of ballet. Better by far to let Vivienne take charge, even if her house was a bomb site.

John Hallam rounded them up. Regine found herself in a taxi, her thigh squashed against that of Roberto Miletti, the famous male character dancer. Charles sat on the pull-down seat opposite her. He looked out of the window in a silent trance as they drove up Park Lane, still lost, perhaps, in the funeral.

The inspector and his sergeant had stood at the back of the church all through the service in a pretence of respect, when really it was part of the investigation. They were watching, the hypocrites. Regine saw the sergeant smile at her, but ignored it. How dared he intrude on her private thoughts. The solemnity of the requiem mass had not consoled her. On the contrary, the mournful Latin cadences echoing up into the roof to expire in the shadowy vaults had intensified the gloom that suffused the church, and reminded her of the convent.

Roberto Miletti brought her back to the present. 'We should have followed on to the cemetery anyway. That's where the taxi should be taking us, not back to Vivienne's.'

'Freddie *hated* his sister.'

'She looked as if she'd swallowed a toad.'

'Well, she certainly married one.'

The taxi's other occupants seemed pleased to be done with the funeral, to be heading back to life after the baroque darkness of the mass. Soon Roberto Miletti was regaling his companions with filthy anecdotes about Freddie. Regine glanced at Charles as the bitchy comments flew to and fro, but, still staring at the passing traffic, he ignored the ribaldry.

'Rather fun to have a wake in a bomb site,' commented Miletti, looking up at the scaffolded façade as they eased themselves out of the black cab.

'Do come in,' said Charles, fishing his keys from a pocket. 'You just have to think of it as post-war picturesque.'

It was the sort of thing Freddie would have said. In fact, Charles must have got it from Freddie, he couldn't have made it up himself.

Another taxi drew to a halt. Soon there was quite a crowd

in the drawing room, picking their way over the torn-up floor-boards in the dusty hall, standing on the front step and spreading onto the pavement.

There was a camaraderie at such events; nothing like a funeral to reinforce your sense of being alive, as she knew from the war. But today it went beyond that, bordering on hysteria. Vivienne certainly seemed unusually vivacious as she held court on the sofa, while her husband passed among the guests pouring wine into glasses already emptied, and an untidy young maid proffered plates of sandwiches, sausage rolls and cheese straws.

Cynthia Johnson was standing by the window on her own, looking out at the street. Regine touched her arm. 'I need to talk to you.'

The room was packed. Voices brayed to and fro. Knocks and bangs and the rasping sound of wood being sawed came from upstairs where, presumably, the builders were continuing their work, and added to the noise. The two women eased past the jammed bodies and walked out into the street, turning left towards Primrose Hill. Cynthia peered over the bridge. 'You didn't tell me it was on the canal. Won't it be stunning when it's finished. I suppose they're doing it with war damage money.'

They walked on towards Primrose Hill. 'That ballet crowd depresses me,' she said, 'they're so ... artificial.'

'Oh, I think they're fun. And so glamorous.' But Cynthia, she knew, had never liked Freddie. He'd boomed into their little flat at the top of a house near Marble Arch when he came home on leave in 1943. 'It was fun in New Cavendish Street, wasn't it?' said Regine. They'd lived together for less than a year, before Regine had settled for Neville, yet the light-hearted interlude, lost in time, lengthened in retrospect. War had made all pleasures more intense. Less so, perhaps, for Cynthia, who always looked the same in her white blouse and grey flannel suit, with her page-boy hairstyle, horn-rimmed glasses and no make-up. She'd watched in amazement Regine's procession of beaux, with their invitations to dinner, their black-market chocolates and relentless attempts at seduction. Cynthia's life had been so calm, but then, unlike Regine, she hadn't been trying to get over a broken heart.

Now Regine was the respectable married woman and Cynthia the mistress. But it was always the serious ones who fell furthest, who were too innocent, who didn't know how to protect themselves.

'Is that all you wanted to talk to me about – reminisce about the war?'

Regine took her friend's arm as they crossed the road into the park. 'You know the police came to see us. About Freddie. Well, I had to give them a list of all our guests. That Sunday. I tried to ring you the next day, but I couldn't get hold of you.'

'I spent a few days with my parents,' said Cynthia. 'I know you're dreadfully upset about Freddie, darling, and it does seems terrible to lose your life over a stupid theft. Personally I never – of course I only met him a few times really, once or twice at New Cavendish Street and then at your Sundays – I mean – I know he was a great friend of yours, you know I could never quite see what you saw in him. But I came to the funeral to support you.'

'He was such fun.' Regine swallowed the lump in her throat. No tears at the funeral; the mass had been cold and impersonal, and she couldn't cry now, because she had to talk to Cynthia. 'It must have been a robbery, but the police seem to be awfully interested in everyone who was at my Sunday. They know more or less the time it happened, because he was found quite soon. It wasn't much more than about two hours between the time he left us and the time he was killed. For some reason that's made them very interested in our guests that afternoon. They want to know what Freddie was doing during those two hours afterwards too, of course. He was in some pub, I expect, but they say he could have gone round to friends in the area. It could easily have been someone who wasn't there that afternoon, of course. It's ridiculous, actually.'

Cynthia looked no more than mildly interested, suitably serious.

'Don't you see,' said Regine, thinking Cynthia was being quite dense, 'they asked for a list of everyone who was there that Sunday. But of course I didn't mention *him*.' It was ridiculous that Regine somehow couldn't utter Ernie Appleton's name. 'I mean, why did you bring him, why did he agree to come? I still don't understand.'

Cynthia didn't answer. She stared ahead as they walked slowly up the hill. Then she said: 'I'm pregnant.'

'Oh Cynthia! I'm so sorry – do you have an address?'

'I'm having the baby.' Cynthia spoke as if it were the most natural thing in the world, when of course it was impossible. She glanced at Regine and laughed. 'Don't look so horrified! He hasn't any sons, you know. If it's a boy … ' She strode forward. 'I didn't say anything at first. I didn't even *realise* at first. I suppose I just wouldn't face facts. Then when I kept feeling so sick … I told myself it was some sort of bilious attack. But I finally went to the doctor. When he said I was pregnant I nearly fainted. But then I thought it could be the most wonderful thing, you know. And now it's over three months and I'm not feeling sick any more.'

Over three months! Already almost too late … 'It would be the end of his career!' said Regine. The minister had been slightly larger than life yet at the same time smaller than imagined. And just *dull*! What on earth did Cynthia see in him? He'd talked quietly, stayed at Cynthia's side, and most of Regine's friends hadn't recognised him; he wasn't well known, although he was in the cabinet now, just a hard-working ex-union man, slightly bewildered by Regine's more flamboyant coterie, most of whom – apart from Alan Wentworth and the ultra-rightwing Jordans – had little interest in the Labour government and its tribulations.

'He enjoyed the party. He doesn't normally meet people like that. It's good for him to widen his horizons.'

Cynthia must be mad. She was deluded.

Seeing the expression on Regine's face, Cynthia said: 'You don't approve!' She looked boldly, confidently at her friend.

They were passing a park bench. 'Let's sit down here.' Regine carefully arranged her new black dress so as not to crease the skirt. 'It's not that I don't approve, darling, it's … I mean, are you sure he'll … will he …?'

'Come up to scratch? I don't expect him to marry me, you know.' And now there was a hint of defiance. 'Anyway, I haven't told him yet.'

Regine buried her fingers in her hair. 'Mother of God, Cynthia!' There was so much to talk about, so many angles. But first she had to make Cynthia see that lies had already been told, sins of omission, that already the web of deceit was being woven. 'The police don't know about him. I didn't tell them he was there. But I told them you were. I thought the closer I stayed to the truth the better. So they may want to talk to you. I don't know if they'll really interview all the guests – I very much hope they don't, but you have to be ready.'

'Don't be cross.'

'I'm not cross. I'm just worried for you. All I'm saying is, if the police do get in touch with you, you don't have to mention *him*.'

'Of course, I understand, thank you for thinking of it.' But Regine could see that Cynthia wasn't interested in the investigation. 'I'll live quietly in the country. I hate London anyway, all the bomb sites everywhere, one just wants to forget all that.

I'm going to find a little cottage and then the baby will have country air and sunshine and good food.'

'But how will you support yourself? Will he be able to give you anything?'

But watching Cynthia's face, Regine saw it suffused with an unfamiliar happiness. 'I'll manage somehow – I've got a little money of my own, you know. And there are welfare benefits now, aren't there, and the family allowance.'

'That won't get you far.' Regine pictured Cynthia the fallen woman, ostracised in some godforsaken English village.

'I might even go back to the Vale of Evesham.'

'For goodness' sake, Cynthia! Have you forgotten what they were like? They may have welcomed us because of the war effort and all that, but … that was the sort of village where witches were denounced in the seventeenth century – and probably much later. Most of them were pretty narrow-minded. Don't you remember how my awful landlord objected to my wearing trousers! He said it was against the scriptures, he actually quoted the Bible to prove how immoral it was. And the funniest thing of all was, he wouldn't speak to me about it, he took Sergei aside and talked to him!'

The trousers had symbolised what Mr Rawton hadn't consciously known, but which somewhere deep in his psyche he must have sensed: that she and Sergei were lovers.

'But you used to say how idyllic it was, the happiest time of your life, you said,' protested Cynthia.

'It was the war, wasn't it, and they knew we were doing important war work, I mean they were awfully kind and decent on the whole, but now the war's over places like that'll all revert to type.'

'Oh Regine – and I thought you were the adventurous one.'

'My adventures these days are of a different kind.'

'You're happy with Neville.'

'Of course I am! I've been good – oh, for ages. I take my marriage vows very seriously, you know.' What a tactless thing to have said! What about Ernie Appleton's marriage vows?

As if Cynthia read her mind, she responded fiercely: 'So does Ernie, you know. He's devoted to his wife, but their – their love life isn't – his wife doesn't enjoy that side of marriage.'

'Oh Cynthia! They *all* say that!'

'But he loves me too – he says it's like nothing he's ever known. I've opened up whole new worlds to him, he says. You know he left school at thirteen – he's completely self-educated – he'd never been to a theatre.'

Regine hadn't the heart to point out that living in the country with a small baby would hardly favour the further cultural education of the minister. 'He says he can talk about things to me his wife just wouldn't understand.'

Regine experienced a growing irritation; how could Cynthia be so naive! She had got herself into a mess. She was about to walk off a precipice. It was the last thing Regine wanted to have to think about, when Freddie was at the forefront of her mind. 'Cynthia, are you sure? Three months; it's not too late, you know. And will you still find him as interesting when he's out of a job and in disgrace?'

'That might happen anyway. With all this trouble at the Board of Trade, Sidney Stanley and everything, the press are after him like a pack of hounds, it'll probably all come out. In a way – I know this sounds awful – I feel it's a good thing, or no, not that, but at least the cloud has a silver lining, because he's begun to be more open. That's why we came on Sunday. In a funny way it's made him more defiant, less cautious. He's acknowledging me more – throwing caution to the winds.'

That was the most alarming thing Regine had heard so far. The man was going off the rails. God knew what he'd do next. 'Yes – what *about* all this scandal brewing up at the Board of

Trade?' She tried to remember what Alan had said about that, but she hadn't been listening. 'He has enough problems already, surely ...' Then again, sometimes men *did* become more reckless when they were in trouble. 'You know, darling, men are so funny and unpredictable. You must be careful. Are you really sure about the baby? I know it sounds awful, but you have to think of the future.'

'That's exactly what I am thinking of. What you have to understand is we love each other. And he's a wonderful man.'

'I know, darling. I'm sure he is. But he's a politician, isn't he. How would he feel if he had to leave it all?'

'We'll find a way.'

'Well, don't forget – I didn't mention him. If the detectives do come round, you don't have to say anything.'

'Anything?'

'I mean anything about *him*.'

They walked back slowly. Suddenly Cynthia stopped. 'But what would the police want to know? What could they ask me about? If they're interested in all of us it could only be something like if he had a flaming row with someone that afternoon, or made an arrangement to meet someone and I overheard it. I've only ever met him with you. The first time was – d'you remember, he came round to New Cavendish Street with Neville, he was on leave. We all went out to dinner.'

'Oh yes! I'd just had a fling with that RAF chap, the squadron leader, who turned out to be a bit of a cad. Ronnie.' She laughed at the memory.

Two men stood in the distance on the other side of the road. Regine said in a low voice: 'Look, there are the detectives, over there. They're watching us.'

The mourners had congealed into little groups, inside and outside the house, set for the duration. Reminiscences of Freddie had long since morphed into more generalised gossip or even quite mundane discussions of work and above all short-ages, the staple of any conversation these days.

Cynthia went home. Regine wandered through the house and downstairs to a kitchen filled with furniture. French windows opened onto a ledge abutting the canal. Vivienne's son was standing there alone. He was staring into the oily water and smoking a cigarette. As she stepped out onto the ledge, he turned his head. 'Hullo.'

They stood side by side. The boy said: 'You were great friends with Freddie, weren't you.'

'Yes.' It was impossible to gauge what the boy was feeling. She said: 'He was very fond of you, you know.'

Charles smiled faintly. 'What an old rogue he was.'

That was a strange thing for the boy to say, to be sure! She shivered as a chill breeze blew across the stagnant water. 'Did you like the funeral?'

Charles flicked ash off his cigarette into the canal. He shrugged. 'You?'

'I'm a lapsed Catholic.' She searched for the right word. 'I found it oppressive. The requiem mass is so grand, but so imper-sonal. I suppose it's meant to be, meant to set one little death in the context of the eternal.'

'It wasn't really Freddie, was it ... and yet in a way it was.'

He was so cool, so deadpan. She waited in vain for him to say more. Finally: 'I should go,' she said, 'I've done no work today.' She hesitated, then: 'When I said you should come and visit me – I did mean it. Do have tea with me one afternoon. Promise you will.'

That earned her the smile. 'I promise.'

'Next week?'

'I get off school early on Wednesdays.'

'I'll see you on Wednesday then,' she said firmly. And left him there, staring out over the canal.

She went to say goodbye to Vivienne, who was seated now between Roberto Miletti and –

Arthur Carnforth.

Why was Arthur Carnforth smarming all over her? He was listening with an ambiguous expression as Miletti told more of his scurrilous jokes and then started to reminisce about a walking tour in Germany, years ago, before the Nazis came to power, and how Freddie had loved the *Wandervogel* – the youth walking groups – and the nudist bathing at the lakes around Berlin.

Dorothy Redfern was standing behind the sofa, also waiting to say goodbye. She had been staring at Carnforth, but now she smiled, less guarded than usual. 'I used to sunbathe – everyone did, back then – when I was still at school. I had a girlfriend and once we were sunbathing in the nude by the Schlachtensee – I was lying there with my eyes closed and all of a sudden I heard something and opened my eyes to find an enormous stark naked man standing over us. I thought we were going to be raped, but all he said was, "*Sind Sie organisiert?*" – are you organised, are you in a proper nudist group, as good Germans should be, not doing it in an anarchistic way on your own!'

'Freddie thought Germany was wonderful. Until 1933 of course.'

Vivienne glanced up at Carnforth, but Carnforth fidgeted and seemed uncomfortable. 'Freddie didn't really understand,' he muttered.

No one knew what he meant. There was an awkward little silence. Then: 'We need to think of a memorial for him,' said Miletti. 'Sadler's Wells must have a memorial evening to him – that's the only appropriate thing. He would have loved that. And he'll be there in spirit of course. Sitting in the royal box.' Miletti's gestures were exaggerated; he was never off stage.

Carnforth looked round the room. There were fewer guests

than half an hour ago. 'Where's John?'

'He went back to the hospital. He didn't want to disrupt things by saying goodbye, he thought it might make everyone feel they should leave too. But he's so overworked.'

'Oh, but we should get going – leave you in peace.' Miletti stood up.

'No, no, don't go yet! When everyone's gone – that's the worst time.'

'I'll stay,' said Carnforth.

Regine looked at him. The way he'd said it – as if his presence was all that mattered! And he did, she supposed, have a sort of presence, an authority. You couldn't ignore him.

She bent down and kissed Vivienne's cool cheek, not sure it was the right gesture. 'Thank you, Vivienne. I hope – I hope you'll come to my next Sunday. Lots of Freddie's friends will be there.'

'I'll try,' she said coldly. Regine wasn't convinced.

'Shall we walk back up to Hampstead together, it's not very far?' said Dorothy, touching Regine's elbow.

As soon as they were away from the house, Dorothy burst out. 'That dreadful man, Arthur Carnforth!'

They turned into Gloucester Avenue and walked towards Chalk Farm.

'I was surprised to see him,' said Regine. 'He and Freddie didn't get on. Neville's not friends with him any more either. There is something rather unpleasant about him.'

'Poor Vivienne. I've seen her a few times, you know. Dr Bell – Henry, at work, you know – I've been round to see them with him a few times. John Hallam and he were at medical school together.'

'You didn't tell me! You could have brought them to one of my Sundays.'

'Well, but ... I suppose I thought you might be annoyed –

my getting to know her, when I knew you wanted Freddie to introduce you, but – she's such an unhappy woman.'

'Is she depressed? Freddie used to say she never went out.' Regine had suspected that was Freddie's excuse not to bring his 'two best girls' together, but now it seemed the truth might be rather different.

'She's not depressed, that's an illness,' said Dorothy, now speaking in that pompous professional way she had. 'She's unhappily married. It's as simple as that. John fell in love with a dancer, but then he was jealous of her dancing and in the end he made her give it up. When she was Vivienne Evanskaya – when she was a world-famous dancer – she fulfilled herself, her life had meaning. And he was in love with the performer, the magical, elusive butterfly upon the stage. But now she's not a dancer any more. He doesn't find her magical, and she's lost her reason for living.'

'But what about her son? She loves him – you can see she adores him. And she was forty anyway. She'd reached the age to retire – gone past it even.'

'She should never have had a child of course.'

'What do you mean! She worships Charles!' Dorothy was infuriating, always so certain of being right. Psychoanalysts thought they knew everything. But Regine couldn't resist keeping Charles in the conversation, asking: 'What about the boy? You talked to him on Sunday. What did you make of him?' For Charles was Regine's new secret, something to take her mind off the misery of Freddie's death, if only intermittently. How beautiful he was ... the thought of kissing him ... was it wrong ... if her sex life with Neville were normal ...

Dorothy snorted. 'Worships! She sent him off across the Atlantic! Didn't see him for four years! Oh, I know, everyone thought Hitler was going to invade. But ... well, it makes me angry when the parents of the children I see *had* to let their children go, they had no choice, they knew they would never see them again, they didn't abandon them to strangers in order to have a career. And then – like you to some extent, Regine, I have to say – she found or tried to find emotional sustenance in a sterile relationship with Freddie, a homosexual who could give her no real love, a relationship built on denial, a pseudo-relationship. It was a real case of the idealised violator, absolutely.'

'What's that?' The idealised violator; it sounded like one of Dorothy's paradoxes. She always talked about relationships in such a contrary way. Nothing was ever straightforward for Dorothy. Like the detectives, in a way. But then, Dorothy was a sort of detective of the mind.

'The idealised violator is when someone has a bad relationship with someone, an abusive relationship, but yet romanticises it, idealises it; a woman with a husband who beats her – or it could be, say, someone who's kidnapped and falls in love with their captor. Or even the relationship so many Germans had with Hitler.'

'That's absurd, Vivienne and Freddie were such great friends! He didn't *abuse* her!'

'But you know how Freddie used to talk. He "adored" Vivienne. He "adored" *you*. It's all so false. What does adoration mean? People "adore" their gods, their myths, another fantasy, all to make themselves feel better, worshipping a nonexistent entity, an unreal person.'

'That's a bit steep!'

But Dorothy continued obstinately, 'In love with the stage – it's all unreal. The great ballerina, Vivienne Evanskaya, who is she? Not the woman sitting in that bomb site.'

Regine wondered if in rechristening herself, she'd become an unreal person too, but she said tartly: 'I don't know what you think that says about me. I was as close to Freddie as Vivienne – closer, actually. Was that sterile? We just had fun, that's all.'

Dorothy shook her head. 'It's not as simple as that. And look at your marriage.'

'How dare you – there's nothing wrong with my marriage!'

'Well, you haven't any children, have you.'

'Don't judge everyone all the time! You're just like the Catholic Church. No – really; you *are*. Just a different set of rules and dogmas. The only difference with your lot is your poor bloody patients have to pay.' She stalked furiously along, trying to get away from Dorothy.

'Don't tell me you don't pay the Church! Your Church has milked its congregations for centuries.'

'It's not my Church!'

They reached Downshire Hill before they spoke again. 'I'm sorry,' said Dorothy. 'The funeral must have been difficult for you. I know you were genuinely fond of Freddie. I shouldn't have said what I did.'

'It's all right.' Regine was feeling sad and dejected now. 'I did want to talk to you about what happened. About the murder. It was so odd – it wasn't mentioned once. No one talked about it. And yet the police were there, you know. I wanted to warn you about them. They'll want to interview you. They seem to think there may be more to it than a robbery. You see, Freddie left us about eight, and then no one knows what he was doing until he was on the Heath about two hours later. I had to give them a list of who'd been there. I'm so sorry. I felt terrible.'

But Dorothy only said, almost dreamily: 'It's not your fault, Regine. There's no need to feel so guilty all the time. That's another difference between psychoanalysis and catholicism, they try to make you feel guilty, but we aim to lessen the irrational guilt of living.'

The sound of Regine's steps on the front path was the trigger for Cato to begin a hysterical volley of barking and as she entered the house he was there, jumping up, mad with excitement, not to be ignored. Regine pushed him away, but then felt guilty and was about to say sorry and stroke him when the telephone rang. She snatched it up: 'Hampstead 02—'

'Roisin?'

That voice! She gripped the handset. 'Who is this?'

'It's been a long time … ' He paused, tantalising. But she knew; she knew – of course she knew.

She leant against the wall with her eyes shut. Cato whined.

'Aren't you going to say hello?' Oh, the soft, familiar voice with a laugh in it. She felt as if she'd been punched in the stomach; winded. 'A bit of a shock, I suppose, sweetheart. I hope you're not thinking – I hope you don't mind, only I had to look you up, only for old times' sake, you understand. You're living up by Hampstead Heath these days, I believe. We could go for a walk. Could you manage tomorrow? How about meeting up there – by that old house that's all shut up now. Three o'clock? I'll be waiting for you.'

n i n e

A S CHARLES TURNED INTO Regent's Park Road he saw
the bulky black figure ahead of him. The skewed walk, the
hat, the sense of a man determined, yet somehow adrift,
pushing himself along as if against a stiff wind, although the
late afternoon was calm. Arthur Carnforth. Charles stopped
dead, then dawdled along very slowly, desperate not to catch
up with him. But what was the use? They were both going to
end up at home. There was no avoiding him. So he walked fast
until he caught up with the art teacher.

'Mr Carnforth! Sir!'

'Hallam. I'm so pleased to see you. I'm on my way to see
your mother, as you've probably surmised.'

What normal human being would use the word 'surmise'?
And why – why was Carnforth hovering round his mother all
the time?

'Your mother is very keen for you to be confirmed, you
know, Hallam – or Charles, if I may.'

Charles was tempted to retort 'I'm an atheist', but thought
it wiser not to get into an argument. Refuse to engage.

'The spiritual life is so important, don't you think?'

Charles tried to think of a witty answer, but he was too
angry, too appalled. Worried too; school and home were two

separate spheres, to be kept apart at all costs.

'Charles?'

'Yes sir, absolutely.' Charles infused as much insolence into his voice as he could manage, but Carnforth seemed not to notice.

'I do hope we can discuss this, you know. Between pals.'

Pals! But thank God, they'd reached the house.

Every day Vivienne waited for him to come home, every day, curled up on the sofa in the dust-sheeted room, with the Home Service droning in the background. There was usually a tea tray on the floor.

The difference today was the intrusion of Carnforth's great, black bulk. He seated himself in the chair by the window.

But perhaps she'd been waiting for Carnforth too? For with a sickening qualm Charles saw that the art master, despite his ungainliness, was actually quite good-looking. Surely, though, it couldn't possibly be that she … he couldn't even think about it.

'You look tired, darling. Sit down and have a cup of tea. Madge made a special cake for you. She's so good at that eggless sponge.'

'I must have a wash.'

The builders had obviously gone home for the day. Charles passed through the dusty hall, picking his way between the joists where the floorboards had been taken up to get at the dry rot, ran down to the basement and washed at the kitchen sink. He wanted to get away, upstairs to his room, to not think about Carnforth, to not be in the same room as him. But to get up there, you had to climb the ladder where the whole staircase had come down.

There was no looking glass in the kitchen. He ran his hand through his hair. He'd have to go back to the drawing room for a minute, but he wasn't going to stay.

They looked at him. Vivienne wore that tragic face he hated. Even in the few minutes he'd been away, they'd been talking about him, he knew it. Even about him and Freddie, he thought with a shudder. Like ghouls or vampires. Carnforth was a vampire, and he brought the earthy smell of damp plaster and dust from some graveyard. Charles liked the thought of Carnforth hanging about under the yew trees. But how dared he be here, smiling so unctuously and making himself at home. Carnforth as vampire would have amused Freddie. He'd have given that great, filthy laugh of his.

Charles leaned against the door frame in his favourite position. A faint smile twisted his lips at the irony of it – the only person with whom he could possibly have laughed away the menace of Carnforth, talked about the murder, the funeral – *everything* – was Freddie himself. But Freddie had gone. There was only a gaping void beneath the trees, between the gravestones ...

There was always Freddie's red-haired friend, Regine. He could talk to her, perhaps, she'd understand ... she'd invited him round, he'd call on her next week ...

'Do sit down, darling.'

He sat beside his mother on the shrouded sofa and stared at her photograph on the chimney piece. 'Did Freddie take that?'

'Oh *no*, that's by Lenare. That was the year ... you know what I really like about that photograph? *You're* there too. I was already expecting you, although I still wasn't quite sure.'

Charles almost choked on his tea at the curdling embarrassment. 'I should go up and make a start on my prep. I've got loads to do.'

'Oh, darling – you haven't drunk your tea.'

'Honestly, Mama – ' He didn't know what to call her these days – in fact ever since he'd come back from America: Mummy,

Ma, Mother, Mum, *Mom,* they were all childish, and Mama was wrong too, it sounded so affected. He'd have liked to call her Vivienne, but he knew his father wouldn't have that. 'I've so much prep. I've got Greek, Latin, Maths – everything.'

'I'm glad to see you're taking your work so seriously,' said Carnforth. Ugh – that slimy voice of a defrocked clergyman.

'Oh darling, do stay ...'

'No, honestly ...' He escaped and was in the dusty hall again. You could see the laths where the plaster had come off the walls. The whole staircase had been rotten. The workmen's ladder wobbled as he climbed. In his room two flights up, he stared out of the window at the trees. He opened his maths prep, but he wasn't working. His mother thought she knew everything about him: 'We're so close, aren't we', and he remembered when, much younger, he'd sat on her knee and she'd murmured, 'I love you best in the whole wide world.' That was before they'd sent him to America – before the war itself. He'd been too young, then, to ask – even to think – better than Daddy? But he knew the answer to that question now without ever in the end having had to ask it.

Close! He had a horror of her finding out about his other life, his secret world. Every day for weeks he'd sat here and dreamed about Trevelyan, but now it was as if the boy had never existed. He could think only about Freddie and that first time and then there'd been the man in Regent's Park, it had all happened so quickly in the dusk, behind some bushes. It had felt dirty and dangerous. The stranger had sunk to his knees and at the memory of the frightening, frantic haste of his actions, Charles closed his eyes at the throbbing in his groin. But it subsided and there was just the thought of death and Freddie.

It wasn't like being sad or upset. It wasn't like Granny dying, which had been awful mostly because his mother had cried so much – Granny was seventy, after all, and he'd hardly known her. It wasn't like when Goering the cat had died. Freddie's murder was more like when *Goering* had died, and gave him the same feeling as the concentration camps: all of it, hangings, cyanide pills, Goering's broad lips, his fleshy face and ... he even looked slightly like Freddie ... and the heaps of broken bodies piled in heaps like firewood, you couldn't let yourself imagine things like that, you must look away, pretend you hadn't seen, blank out the gas chambers, the walking skeletons and worst of all the obscene, unspeakable tortures. But averting your face was no good. You still saw it all out of the corners of your eyes and felt as if your entrails were being gouged out. And Goering's bland, blind smile.

That Thursday before Freddie died: they'd walked along the road together ... the last time he'd talked to Freddie – the Sunday at Mrs Milner's didn't count with all those other people there. Why don't you walk up the road with me, dear boy?

Freddie had marched along at a terrific pace; looked sideways at him and lightly touched his arm for a moment. 'How's life?'

'The work's all much harder this year.'

'No time for any fun, eh.' Freddie had grinned in a way that had thrilled and repelled. 'It's an open invitation. I'll take you down the East End, meet the sailors. You'd like that, wouldn't you.'

Excitement had clogged Charles's throat. 'You're always trying to lead me astray, Freddie.'

'Well, someone has to do it. Your father isn't going to oblige.'

'It's not his fault.' Obscene of Freddie to join his father and that other utterly secret part of his life all in the same sentence.

'Well – fathers used to take their sons to brothels ... on the continent anyway.'

No going down the East End now. Freddie had had the key

to so many worlds Charles was desperate to know about and now Freddie was dead Charles was terrified he'd never find that key.

'You're such a man of the world,' Charles had mocked, but he'd also believed it.

'Don't mock, dear boy. You know you need me.' Freddie had looked around as they turned the corner towards Parkway. 'Maybe your mother was right to install you in this part of the world – all these tumbledown mansions turned into rooming houses stuffed with Irish navvies. Oh – it gives me a frisson just to think of it.' A bellow of laughter.

Then, as they'd walked on towards the tube station: 'You know, you should look in on Regine. A Sunday tea party's boring for someone your age, but if you're serious about being a writer – you might meet one or two people who could help you later on, if you play your cards right. Regine's little salon isn't completely devoid of talent. And Regine herself has knocked about a bit. She was in Shanghai before the war, had a bit of a reputation. That's where I met her.' Freddie had stopped to light a cigarette. 'Want one?' Charles took it and Freddie bent towards him to light it, touching the boy's hand. 'You know – it took more than one man to change my name to Shanghai Lily.' He'd roared with laughter. 'Marlene Dietrich in *Shanghai Express*. They don't make films like that any more. Mind you, Regine's not *quite* in the Dietrich league, but she's very good-hearted.' They'd reached the knot of streets by the station. 'And now – I must love you and leave you, my dear. But I'll see you on Sunday. *Promise* you'll come.'

Charles had no idea how long it was before his mother called him down for dinner. They were eating in the kitchen at the moment, the only room with a floor. Furniture from other rooms had been relocated, so that you could hardly move without knocking into cupboards, stumbling against chairs, dislodging books, saucepans, toothpaste.

Charles couldn't bear the claustrophobia of their evening meals. Had it always been like this? Surely when he first got back from New York it hadn't been that bad?

'How are things at the hospital, dear?'

'Exactly what one would expect.' John Hallam examined the forkful of shepherd's pie he had scooped up. 'This tastes odd, Vivienne.'

'Madge added lentils to bulk it up a bit. You said pulses were good for us.'

Her husband masticated. His thin, bony face, always gloomy, seemed to lengthen further as he endured the food his wife had provided.

'Mr Tolliday said the health reforms are the most important for a hundred years.' Charles sort of knew this would annoy his father, but his form master's remark had genuinely surprised him. At home, few good words were spoken about the revolutionary new National Health Service.

'Did he! He, of course, doesn't have to work within the system. He's not been badgered and bullied by a foul-mouthed Welshman.'

'Mr Tolliday said Aneurin Bevan is the ablest man in the government.'

Vivienne caught her son's eye and her expression, half smile, half frown, was a plea not to provoke her husband and at the same time was meant to show she was really on Charles's side. 'It's bound to be difficult, darling, to begin with, and with so many shortages. But surely things will get better soon – I mean things are improving in any case.'

'You think so.'

Charles stood up to clear the table. 'Darling, I'll do that,' cried his mother, as if appalled at the thought of a man under-taking domestic work of any kind. But Charles gathered up the dirty plates and placed them in the sink. 'Don't leave them in the sink, darling.'

'There's no room anywhere else.'

'How long is this going to go on?' John Hallam spoke as if it were all Vivienne's fault. 'I really am going to have to speak to Lugg. The workmen seem to come and go as they please.' Lugg was the building contractor. 'Can't you be firmer with him?'

'I do try, but he always says there are shortages.'

'For God's sake! He's just off on another job.'

'So many government regulations. The pudding's in the fridge, Charles. Would you get it, now you're up, please?'

The fridge was old and huge with a wooden door. He took out the chocolate blancmange and found the right bowls. It was Madge's evening off. Charles liked Madge. She was only two or three years older than he was, and had taught him how to make Welsh rarebit and the right way to cook sausages. She'd have taught him other things as well, but his indifference to women blinded him to her melting glances and flirty smiles. Fortu-nately for Madge, Vivienne hadn't noticed either.

The sound of their spoons against the porcelain rang loudly. Afterwards his mother lit a cigarette. His father frowned. 'Vivienne, how often have I told you, smoking is *dangerous*. There's new research—'

But on this issue Vivienne was robust. 'Darling, that's ridiculous! It soothes my throat.'

Charles's father made an incoherent sound of exasperation and stood up. Perhaps wanting to placate him, Vivenne said brightly: 'Arthur Carnforth was here this afternoon, you know, he teaches at the school. He has a very high opinion of Charles, darling. I'm sure he can give him a lot of help.'

John Hallam scowled. 'What on earth was he doing here?'

Charles noticed the look that passed between his parents with a sudden lurch of dismay. Had Carnforth said something …

'Mr Carnforth doesn't know the first thing about my work. He's an art master, for Christ's sake!'

'Don't speak to your mother like that, Charles.'

Vivienne cast a nervous glance at her husband.

John Hallam glared. 'I know you never listen to a word I say, Vivienne, but I have never liked the man and it's a great pity you've taken up with him again – most unfortunate he turned up at the school. I'm astonished they'd employ him, quite honestly.'

'Why, Dad?'

But his father didn't answer. He got up from the table. 'Well, I've got work to do.'

'But John …' and Vivienne's dark eyes seemed larger than ever as her pleading gaze fixed on her husband. 'He's an old friend, that's all.'

'I know you ran around with that crowd before the war – you and Buckingham and Carnforth, the infernal triangle. But I thought things had settled down. I thought you'd finally seen through Buckingham … oh, I know you're upset because of what happened, but I thought … and then the moment he's – gone, Arthur Carnforth turns up again and he's even worse.'

Vivienne was whiter than ever. 'That's unfair,' she said in a low voice. She looked at Charles. 'You'll understand when you're older, darling.'

In the horrible silence, Charles thought: Dad wishes he hadn't spoken in front of me.

Then Vivienne said, as though nothing had happened: 'You'd like some coffee, dear?'

'Bring it up to the study, would you? I've some papers to look at – for the Glasgow conference next week. Oh … no, the ladder … I'll take it up myself.'

Charles stood up, trying to escape his swarming thoughts, he had to get away, be on his own. He climbed the ladder. Unable to concentrate on his maths he switched to Latin, but that was no better. Freddie's murder intruded all the time. And what had his father meant about Carnforth? 'The infernal triangle.'

He didn't like the way Carnforth had smiled at him either, seated like a toad in the dust-sheeted drawing room. Suppose the next time the art teacher went to the annexe things had been moved ... had the room been disarranged in the excitement of the moment with Harry Trevelyan? Everything about Carnforth was sickening. And Freddie had loathed him – Charles was sure about that. He could always tell what Freddie was feeling.

Not any more.

At nine o'clock he climbed down the ladder and looked in on his mother in the drawing room where she was listening to the news.

'I'm having trouble concentrating. I'm just going for a walk to get a bit of fresh air. Okay?'

'Don't be long, darling. You don't want your father to think you're slacking.'

There was an autumn chill in the air this evening. He thrust his hands in his pockets and walked to Primrose Hill, where he climbed the grassy slope towards the concrete bunkers left over from what had been anti-aircraft positions during the war. Now they were full of disgusting mess and at night couples came there, leaving cigarette packets, sweet papers and what he knew were spent condoms. But this evening the bunkers were deserted. He walked on, hardly knowing what he was looking for, and yet knowing all too well; but in the whole park there was no one. He followed the perimeter right the way round, passing the remotest corners. There was not much cover. He wandered stubbornly on for longer than he'd intended.

t e n

T HE HEATH WAS PEACEFUL under the mild, white sky,
but as Regine walked across the meadows along a familiar
path she was imagining its night-time transformation, when
darkness shrouded the encounters of strange men, and cloaked
crime and murder. It seemed hardly less unreal than the idea
that she was on her way to meet Eugene.

It was impossible. Eugene was dead.

He must have chosen the Heath because it was near where
she lived, to remind her of the threat he posed. She should have
insisted on meeting him in town. A bar or a restaurant in town
would have been safer. But how had he known where she lived?

After the telephone call … it was impossible. But his voice
was unmistakable.

Like everything else in Shanghai, their marriage was not to
be taken too seriously. They had fun, to begin with at least. And
later on, when he seemed to be mixed up in so many schemes,
they'd simply drifted apart, floating in different directions on
the oily currents of Shanghai's many worlds. For beyond the
cocktails and the dances and the picnics and the days at the
races, Shanghai *was* deadly serious.

In the dark undertow there were so many things she hadn't
known about, hadn't cared to know about. What looked like

froth on the surface had really been the scum surfacing from the invisible life in the depths, the predators ... the cruelties of a million hopeless lives, the warlords menacing the countryside, the charming British escorts who turned out to be counter-intelligence men ... and Eugene had been swept away by the currents, everyone said the Japanese were so cruel, he could never have survived ...

A mist was coming down and Cato had disappeared. She shouted and whistled, then called again, but her voice echoed eerily across the vacant fields and through the ragged copses. She reached a clearing, where the fog hung between trees deformed and bent in gnarled, preposterous shapes.

Then, out of the mist came a blurry figure, who dragged a reluctant Cato along by the collar. When Cato saw her, he began to leap frantically and bark and whine and as dog and man drew near she felt she might faint.

He smiled, the old, familiar, crooked smile: 'Roisin – darlin'! After all these years!'

She stared at him, her stomach hollowing out and cramping up at the same time, a horrible feeling: fear attacking your body when your brain was quite numb. It was him; exactly the same, but so painfully different. 'We were to meet up by Kenwood!' Her voice sounded squeaky and hoarse. The way he'd emerged from the trees like that had given her such a fright – and yet it was so like him, to make an arrangement and then do something completely different. He was never where you expected him to be.

Cato barked and leapt up against her, and this gave her time to steady herself, so that it seemed as if she only swayed because the dog had pushed against her. She hid her face by bending over the poodle. 'Bad boy, Cato. You are a *bad* boy, aren't you.'

'I always had a way with dogs – even those wretched curs

in Shanghai.' In the wood's dull twilight he seemed insubstantial. They walked towards the open meadow beyond the tunnel of trees. She was shaking, but tried to step steadily alongside Cato as he jumped and pulled at the leash. She felt as if the blood were draining from her body. God, he looked so much older ...

'Aren't you going to ask me how I came back from the dead?'

She laughed shakily. 'Are you back from the dead? I think you're a ghost. I think you've come to haunt me.'

He didn't laugh.

They came out into the open. 'Jesus, but it's quiet around here. Shall we walk down the hill? There's a café at the bottom.'

So they walked together like a normal couple down towards the row of shops and the houses. The mist swathed Regine in a veil of unreality. Yet she managed to hold a normal conversation, asking him what had happened, how he'd got away, how long he'd been back in England, what he was going to do now, her voice a little strained, but her shaking under control. No straight answers to her questions, of course; you never got a straight answer from him.

She kept glancing sideways surreptitiously, and the strange thing was he still had that jaunty walk of his, despite his bedraggled appearance. The pathos of it almost drove out her fear, replacing it with an awful sadness.

Everything about the café was perfunctory: battered chairs and tables, a few stale-looking cakes behind the glassed-in counter, a depressed-looking waitress.

She sat opposite Eugene. In the bleak electric light she saw his suit was shabby, his shirt collar frayed. His eyes were red-rimmed and his hair hadn't been cut for a while, so that it sprang in unruly waves from his scalp. His smile was the same as ever, but his teeth were stained and one was missing. And he'd been so proud of his teeth!

She had to try to take charge of the situation. 'This is rather a shock, you know. I was so certain you were dead.'

He smiled then. 'Don't sound so disappointed!'

That time in the club, he'd been smiling then too. In a dinner jacket – that's what he'd been wearing, the last time she'd seen him. They were at the club, but she wasn't even sure he was running it any more. They sat on the velvet banquette with the Chinese man and the girl in her cheongsam, with a gardenia in her oiled smooth hair. The man wore an expensive western suit. He smoked a cigar and when he opened his mouth his gold teeth gleamed. The Chinese girl said something, but it must have been the wrong thing, because her companion slapped her across the face. When she reeled back from the blow her smile was as fixed as ever.

Afterwards: It's lucky he doesn't like redheads, darling. He wouldn't be taking no for an answer, you know.

And if he had – liked redheads?

Oh … Teeth flashing laughter. You know you're always safe with me, darling.

He'd always been dapper, always … now …

'You look as if you've had a hard time,' she said.

She could see he was offended, still a dandy at heart. His hand moved along his chin, but he didn't answer her implied question. The tea urn hissed behind the counter. There was one other couple in the café.

'Have you come back for good?'

Eugene looked away as if into the distance. 'That's a rather stupid question, if you'll forgive me saying it. Do you think I could go back to Shanghai with all that's going on? Or had you not noticed there's a full-scale civil war?'

His irritation unnerved her again. She sipped her metallic tea and watched him wolf a Bath bun. 'How did you manage to get back home?'

He lit a cigarette. 'Home! This isn't home. To be sure I'll be back in Ireland as soon as I can. God, what a dingy hole London's become! Doesn't it make you weep?'

'It's all right.'

Another silence. Then he said: 'Of course, you've done well enough for yourself, or so I hear. I'm told you lucked out this time around – didn't pick another feckless devil like me.'

She was alert now. 'Who told you that?'

'You know I'd not dream of upsetting your apple cart.'

Cato sighed and heaved by Regine's feet.

Eugene was watching her, still smiling. 'That way you had – playing with your hair like that – that was always a sure sign something was by way of worrying you.'

'What are you doing now?'

'You're full of questions, Roisin. Like I said, I'm on my way back to Ireland, but there's a few things I have to sort out on the way.'

'I couldn't believe it was you on the phone.' Sweat gathered under her arms.

'Aw – did I upset you, Roisin?' He took a squashed packet of cigarettes from his pocket, fished one out. 'You still don't smoke?'

And now his mood seemed to change again. 'Sitting across from you – Holy Virgin, but it brings back Shanghai. I loved the old place.' He looked away into some invisible distance again and his face darkened. 'Of course it all changed when the Japs …' He didn't finish the sentence. 'You remember the racecourse! Holy Jesus, that was a scene!'

'You certainly loved the horses!' He couldn't keep away from the racetrack. One day he'd have banknotes coming out of every pocket, the next there'd be no money for food and she'd have to pawn the presents he'd given her the week before.

She watched his hands as he smoked. The nails were long

and dirty. The sides of his fingers were cracked and nicotine-stained. 'Shanghai was wonderful,' she agreed, going along with his mood.

'Not so good later on.'

'Are you really not going to tell me what happened to you, how you got away – how long you've been back in London?'

'It would be a long story – and a tedious one.' Pause. 'And cruel.'

He never told her what was going on – he'd be there, then gone for weeks at a time. But it was terrible to see him so brought down, it was embarrassing – she didn't know where to look, what to say and she wanted to be away from this place, this shabby café and this wreck of a man who was her legal husband. But her feeling of pity for him was a weakness, she mustn't feel sorry for him, he was too dangerous, a terrible threat. 'How did you know my phone number?' she asked.

'Oh, Roisin – the telephone directory, of course.'

She took the bull by the horns. 'You need money, I suppose.'

'Oh ...' and his gesture was magnanimity itself. 'That's awfully kind – as it happens I had a bit of bad luck with the horses yesterday, but I wouldn't want you to think – you believe me, don't you, darling, your secret is safe with me – but to be sure, there's no secret, is there? I'm sure you waited the full seven years.'

The silence opened as deep as a well.

'How much do you want?'

'Roisin, now, you're being very blunt.'

There was another silence. She was watching him. His gaze flitted to and fro. He fidgeted, picked a flake of tobacco off his lip.

'Something terrible happened,' she said. 'Freddie was killed.'

The white face stared across at her. He frowned. 'Killed?

How? Oh God, that's terrible, I was hoping – I was going to look him up.' He passed his hand across his face. 'Poor Freddie. Jesus ...' He picked a cigarette out of the packet on the table and she saw his hand was shaking a little. 'In the war, was it? Or an accident?'

She shook her head. 'He was murdered.'

'*Murdered*!' Eugene stared at her, drew deeply on his cigarette and blew out a plume of smoke. Again he looked away as if he saw not the corner of the café, but was gazing into some far-distant place – or the past. 'Freddie – Jesus.' There was another long silence.

Then suddenly he pushed his chair back. 'I must be going. But – I'll need to see you again, Roisin. There's things we have to talk about ...'

'What things?'

'Oh ... not bad things, sweetheart, nothing for you to be worrying yourself with. Suppose we meet here again, in this café, same time next week? What do you say? I'll ring you anyway.'

'No!' she cried, too hastily. 'Don't ring. You must have an address, I'll send you – what I can.'

He smiled. 'It's never a good idea to be sending money through the post. I'll be here, same day, same time, next week.'

The café door opened and shut. He'd gone, leaving her to pay. Well, it was only one and sixpence. She sat on. The other couple had looked up when Eugene left and now they looked at her. A self-assured, elegant woman in a fashionable jacket; she didn't belong in a place like this.

Eugene was dead. The more she saw him in her mind's eye walking slowly up the clearing with Cato straining away from him, the more he seemed like an apparition. It had been uncanny. He'd suddenly *appeared*. It was one of his jokes, coming out of the woods like that instead of waiting at

Kenwood. He'd always been a trickster, the joker in the pack ... and like so many of his jokes, it wasn't really funny.

Cato trotted faithfully beside her on the lead as she walked back across the darkening Heath and reached South End Green. 'How did he find us, Cato? Cato, what am I going to do?'

He hadn't frightened her in the old days, not at first anyway. And she wasn't frightened of him now, of course, that would be ridiculous ... and yet he'd changed, she couldn't put her finger on it, but he'd been different and not just because he was shabby and poor. And somehow he knew – how did he know? That hint – you waited the full seven years. But she hadn't. And he knew. Knew she was a bigamist.

Whatever happened, Neville mustn't find out.

She hurried up Downshire Hill. Neville was going to be late this evening and she'd arranged to go round to see Dinah; Alan was away on some outside broadcast. She needed to be on her own, to think, to work out what to do, but it would look odd to cancel. No one must guess. If only she could have talked to Freddie. Freddie would have known how to get out of this jam. There was no one else who could help. She could tell Cynthia, Cynthia was discreet, but she had troubles of her own.

There was no one. She would have to rely on herself.

They drank tea in front of the fire. 'Alan's worked so hard on the house,' said Dinah. And indeed the downstairs rooms were transformed. Cream paint had wiped out the rotting wallpaper with its Edwardian design of cabbage roses.

Neville and Regine had met the Wentworths at a private view at Noel's gallery. A friendship was established when the Milners helped the younger couple find the cottage they were now doing up. The Wentworths stood well to the left of Neville and perhaps of Regine, although she never knew where she stood politically. But Regine had taken to Dinah the moment she saw her. Dinah was so lively with her mop of black curls – rather like Cato's, in fact – and her rosy cheeks and friendly smile. She was ten years younger than Regine, of course, but that made her company all the more fun. Marriage to Neville had moved Regine into a middle-aged set, and her two closest friends, Cynthia and Dorothy, were both so serious. With Dinah she could talk clothes and novels and – desperately important, now Freddie had gone – gossip. Regine also shared a love of the cinema with the Wentworths – Alan had actually made documentary films in the war – and, as Neville was rather sniffy about films, Regine began regularly to make up a threesome with the younger couple on outings to the Academy in Oxford Street, and indeed to the Everyman, which was only five minutes away from the Wentworth cottage.

'Tell me about the Courtauld.'

'History of Art – you learn all about paintings – how to date them – which are the best ones – but I've only just started. Some of the other students are awfully nice.'

As Dinah described them, and her charismatic tutor, Anthony Blunt, Regine wasn't listening properly. Eugene coming up the glade, Eugene in the café, Eugene wanting money ... but perhaps he wouldn't show up next week, perhaps *she* wouldn't keep the appointment, perhaps he'd go back to Ireland. Regine always hoped for the best and knew from experience that – in spite of what everyone said – sometimes the best policy was to stick your head in the sand.

'Is she?' Dinah's question caught her by surprise.

'Sorry – I'm so sorry – my thoughts just wandered off for a moment. What were you asking me?'

'Alan said Cynthia brought Ernie Appleton to your party the other week. He was most intrigued.'

'I wanted to talk to you about Cynthia.'

'Alan says they talk about nothing else but the Board of Trade business at the Beeb. Appleton's all mixed up in that, isn't he. I don't really understand it, but – well, Alan thought it was very odd him coming with a ... she works in his department, doesn't she?'

'Dinah, you mustn't tell a soul about this, not even Alan, but she's going to have a baby.'

'A *baby*! You mean, she is – they are ...' Dinah looked horrified. 'What on earth is she going to do? And what is *he* going to do? He can't afford another scandal on top of all this ...'

'She's annoyed with me because I tried to persuade her to get rid of it. She was determined to go ahead right from the start. She was the last person I'd have expected. They've been having an affair for months. And now – Cynthia thinks he'll leave his wife now she's pregnant.'

'It'll ruin his career – if it isn't ruined already.'

'There was a picture in the paper of Appleton with his wife the other day. She looked rather frumpy and dismal; wearing one of those wartime hats.'

Regine couldn't help feeling that a woman owed it to herself to keep herself attractive after marriage. On the other hand, women had to stick together. It wasn't fair to steal another woman's husband ...

'Still, that's no excuse,' said Dinah briskly. 'And I haven't time to be sorry for Appleton. He's brought it on himself. But Cynthia ...'

'I've been trying to think how to help. What d'you think I can do?'

'I'm sure together we can think of a plan. She'll need money, won't she, and somewhere to stay. Let's go away and rack our brains and talk it over again at the weekend. Oh dear, doesn't sex complicate things. Sometimes I think my mother has the right idea. She likes you to think she's never enjoyed it at all. And she's shocked *I'm* not expecting yet. She thinks that's what sex is for. She used to say darkly "You can get a taste for it. You can *get to like it*", as if sex was an unpleasant sort of addiction. I suppose that's because women of her generation saw it as their main source of power. Something to withhold, to ration out. You'd weaken yourself if you enjoyed it too much. She told me, "I had to be very firm with your father." I'm afraid I'm not firm with Alan at all. Of course, I do want children, but I want something I can go back to afterwards, that's partly why the Courtauld's so important to me. It'd be so easy to sink into domestic servitude.' She blushed, looking through her cigarette smoke at Regine with a mixture of shyness and curiosity. 'But what about you – are you … can't you …?' She saw Regine's face close in. 'I'm sorry – I shouldn't have asked.'

'Neville isn't keen. He's over ten years older than me, you know. And I'm thirty-four, a bit past it, really.'

'Oh nonsense,' said Dinah.

But there was an awkward little silence.

eleven

MURIEL JORDAN'S EMPLOYER, Aynsley Denham, ran a small print works in the basement of his dilapidated house in the Gray's Inn Road. On this particular Friday she had extra letters to type, while Aynsley made urgent calls. Plagued by the ongoing paper shortage, he was desperate for the ream needed to print off an important leaflet. Everything had to be done before the weekend.

Muriel was afraid Hilary would get home before her with no meal ready, but she couldn't refuse to stay late. Aynsley was 'one of us', keeping the flame alive with the publication of leaflets and news-sheets under cover of the firm's less controversial products. And hers wasn't just a job, it was a calling. Hilary didn't like it, but it was a higher priority than her domestic chores.

By the time Denham left, it was nearly seven o'clock. She was often the last person to leave the office, but she never liked being there alone, although she was not an imaginative woman. The glare of unshaded lights couldn't dispel the eerie emptiness of the print room with its idle machines and the silence where there should have been clatter. In fact, her unease had more to do with the semi-clandestine nature of the enterprise than with a nervous disposition. It was also related to growing anxiety about its incipient failure, the dragging decline of a once glorious movement. But she must pull herself together. Depression was a cancer. There *would* be a new dawn.

She pulled on her mac and tied the belt tightly. After a last look round she switched off the lights and stood for a second in darkness. Only the dim twilight from the street beyond the basement windows illuminated the office and its looming cupboards.

She heard footsteps, saw a shadowy someone descending the area steps. The door rattled. Someone was in the corridor. 'Who is it?' Her voice sounded shrill. A figure emerged in the shadows beyond the room. Her hand shook as she switched the lights back on.

'Oh, it's you.'

Arthur Carnforth blinked in the unexpected glare. He seemed bewildered by her presence. 'I didn't think anyone would be here. I was surprised the door was unlocked. Aynsley gave me a key, you see.'

'I've been working late. What are you doing here?'

'He said there'd be some material.'

'Well, there isn't. We've had trouble with the paper people again. Everything's delayed.'

'Oh.' He frowned. He held his wide-brimmed black hat as if he didn't know what to do with it. 'That's not good enough.'

'Don't blame me.' Muriel had to remind herself not to feel nervous. Arthur could be unpredictable, but you had to be very calm with him. And basically he needed looking after. 'I'm not sure it's a good idea for you to come round here.' Her concern was as much for him as for the enterprise. 'You want to be careful, Arthur. You don't want to jeopardise your job, do you. You were lucky to get it. I daresay they're still keeping tabs on you, you know.'

He didn't answer at once, but continued to stand there,

looming in a way that was just short of threatening, and yet at the same time somehow nonplussed. After a while he said: 'Are they really that interested now? They think we're defeated, a spent force.'

'Don't talk like that. That's defeatism, not defeat. The Leader—'

Carnforth leaned against the table that ran the length of the room. 'Oh ... the Leader.' He looked around as if he thought the Leader might manifest from some neglected pile of old newsprint. 'O'Connell doesn't think much of the Leader. Not a patch on – the great one, he says. But I think what's needed is a more spiritual approach. That side of it's been neglected – the sense of vision, the spirit of self-sacrifice.'

'O'Connell's an adventurist. I don't like him. Who is he, anyway?' Muriel fiddled with her handbag. 'It's late, Arthur. Hilary'll be wondering where I am. I've got to lock up.'

Arthur didn't move. 'I'm worried. It's worse now than in the war. I feel I'm in a spiritual prison, a prison of the mind. And Buckingham – I'm not sure—'

Muriel interrupted him sharply. 'Buckingham was an evil man. Don't waste time thinking about him. He got what he deserved.'

Carnforth stirred, moved towards her. There was something alarming about the uncertainty of his bulk and she instinctively moved back. 'Vivienne was so upset,' he said.

Mention of the dancer irritated Muriel beyond endurance. She clicked her tongue against her teeth. 'Vivienne Hallam – now there is a lost cause if ever there was one. You're wasting your time. She's married.'

Carnforth looked shocked. 'Oh, I don't ... she needs spiritual comfort – I hope you're not suggesting – '

This was too much for Muriel. 'Oh, for heaven's sake, don't be so wet. Your trouble is, Arthur, that lunatic you met in the war – Battersby and the League of Christian Reformers – '

'He's a deeply spiritual man. And utterly misunderstood.'

'Battersby's in a mental asylum, Arthur. All that crackpot stuff sent him right round the bend.'

Carnforth frowned. 'Don't talk about that,' he muttered.

Muriel feared she'd gone too far. It was tactless to have mentioned the hospital. 'Cheer up, Arthur. Things aren't that bad. Triumph of the will. Remember – *"Wir kommen wieder".*'

They parted company at King's Cross, only five minutes' walk from Carnforth's flat. Muriel took the Northern line to Hampstead.

Their garden flat was in a side road off East Heath Road. The light was on, so Hilary must be home now. She called his name as she entered the passage. There was no reply, but she could hear voices. He wasn't alone.

At first she thought the two strangers in her front room might just possibly have come from the organisation, but both sprang smartly to their feet and introduced themselves: detectives.

Murray had expected a place like the Milners', but the Jordans' living room was spartan, furnished in modern light oak and devoid of pictures and books.

Muriel subsided in an easy chair with wooden arms. Her husband looked at her intently: a note of warning, but what about? Not Arthur, she hoped it wasn't Arthur ...

'Chief Inspector Plumer wants to know about Freddie Buckingham's will,' he said. 'I explained that so far as I'm concerned it's all in the past.'

Of course: the murder. Muriel said repressively: 'We didn't see eye to eye with Freddie. Our paths didn't cross.'

'Yet you were at a party with him the day he was murdered!'

Muriel flushed. 'Yes, well, it wasn't my idea.' The waspish look she cast at her husband was not lost on Murray.

'I met Buckingham through the Milners, Regine's an old friend of mine,' said Hilary. 'I'm a solicitor, I sorted out his will. But our offices were bombed right at the end of the war – a V2 – and by that time Muriel and I were married. I explained to Buckingham what had happened and I think there was an implicit understanding that he'd find another solicitor. We'd been quite friendly, well, in the war one let a lot of things go, but Muriel had made me see he was a rather unsavoury character.'

'Did he make another will?'

'No idea. You could ask Neville Milner. He might know. It's possible he died intestate, I suppose.'

'No will has been found,' said Plumer, 'but some items that certainly did exist are missing from Mr Buckingham's house. We can't discount the possibility the will has been taken as well.'

'If a will was stolen, it would be most likely in order to suppress it, wouldn't it?' said Hilary.

'That remains to be seen, sir.'

They'd hoped for useful information from this interview. Instead, they'd come up virtually against a brick wall. Murray knew you had to be prepared for all eventualities, take nothing for granted, rid your mind of expectations, but he felt intensely frustrated.

Muriel had taken out her knitting. The clicking needles irritated Murray, as though she wished purposely to draw attention to herself; to display her industriousness, perhaps, or the fact that they were wasting her time. 'You say you'd fallen out with Mr Buckingham?'

'I didn't say that,' she snapped, 'I said we hadn't much in common.'

Hilary Jordan looked a little uncomfortable. 'During the

war things got very lax, I suppose. One didn't notice so much at the time, but looking back – and Reggie invites all sorts of people to her little tea parties. For instance, on that particular Sunday that Labourite minister turned up, the one who's in trouble over the Sidney Stanley affair. Reggie herself is delightful, of course, but—'

'Regine can do no wrong as far as you're concerned.'

'Well, I go round on a Sunday from time to time for old times' sake as much as anything.' Jordan looked sheepish and uncomfortable.

'No one says you have to go, dear.'

'Which government minister is that?'

'Oh – what's-his-name – Appleton.'

His wife chimed in. 'That's absolutely typical of Regine. If she gets a government minister to one of her gatherings, it has to be a crooked one.'

'We don't know that,' protested Hilary mildly.

'Did *he* know Mr Buckingham?'

'I've no idea.'

'But *you* used to know him well? The dead man, that is,' persisted Plumer.

'I certainly didn't,' snapped Muriel.

'He fought in Italy, you know,' said Hilary, 'but he was very flamboyant. Always booming away doing his Oscar Wilde imitation and – well – I can only call it flaunting himself. I don't know how Reggie put up with him, quite honestly. They were a sort of self-indulgent, mutual admiration society. Though actually I suspect he sponged off her. She hinted he had serious money problems.'

'What about the original will?'

'What about it?'

'Did that seem to indicate money problems?'

Hilary frowned. 'It wouldn't necessarily, would it, even if he had them. I don't remember much about it now, but I think he left the bulk of everything to Charles Hallam.'

Murray found that interesting, but he wasn't letting on.

'Just for the record, sir, where were you on the evening he was killed?'

A strange expression passed across Muriel's face; almost, thought Murray, a whiff of panic, and it was she, not her husband, who replied, 'We were here all evening. A friend of ours came round to see us.'

'This friend would be able to corroborate that?'

'What?' Again Jordan looked startled.

'He would,' said Muriel.

'Perhaps you could give us his name, then?'

'His name's Arthur Carnforth,' said Muriel.

Murray wondered why she looked so anxious.

'Can you be exact about the time,' said Plumer, 'that is, when he arrived and when he left?'

The Jordans looked at each other. 'Quite late,' said Muriel, unhelpfully.

This Carnforth, thought Murray, must be someone they could rely on to cover up for them if necessary. Yet it was probably all irrelevant. It was most unlikely this couple had had anything to do with the murder. 'And Mr Carnforth's address?' he enquired carelessly.

'Number 20 Handel Mansions, Handel Street.'

At the knock on the door, Regine sprang to her feet. At this hour, past nine, it could only be – the police … Eugene …

If she pretended not to be there – but the light was on, he'd have seen the light. She steeled herself as she opened the door.

Hilary Jordan stood on the step.

'I'm sorry to disturb you so late, but – is Neville about?'

'He'll be home soon. He's having dinner with Noel.'

'The thing is – the police have just called round. Asking about Freddie – the murder, and all that.'

He refused a drink, so Regine had to make him a cup of tea. He followed her into the kitchen and they sat at the table. 'I expect it's just a routine visit,' she said. 'They don't seem to be getting anywhere, so they're delving into Freddie's background ... well, I suppose that's what it is. Or perhaps they think one of us did it, I mean, someone Freddie knew, but of course that's ridiculous.'

'Mind if I hang about for a bit? I want to have a word with Neville about it.'

'Of course, but ... surely ...' She paused, hoping he'd tell her more.

'They were asking about Freddie's will.' Hilary was obviously agitated.

'It's unpleasant, the way they question you, isn't it,' said Regine, hoping it would encourage him to say more.

Hilary cleared his throat. 'You know, I feel rotten – saying what I did about Freddie – that afternoon ...'

'I know you and Muriel didn't get on with him, but it's hardly your fault he was murdered.'

'Well ... it's a motive, isn't it. If the police got to hear ...'

Regine laughed. 'Oh, for goodness' sake, I can't even remember what you said. Disapproving of someone is hardly a motive!'

'The thing is, Muriel can be a bit ... fanatical.'

How unfair to blame his wife! But how like a man. He didn't have to marry her, after all.

'We've all got more serious since the end of the war,' said Hilary. 'Funny, isn't it, you'd have thought people would be more cheerful and instead – I often think of the Vale of Evesham, don't you, and how carefree we all were then. When we were absolutely losing the war.'

She smiled. 'Wasn't it wonderful!'

They'd met on the boat home from Shanghai and embarked on one of those insubstantial shipboard romances that flared up and died down like burning paper. She was on her way back to England, with a British passport, courtesy of her husband. It was, of course, odd that Eugene, so totally Irish, had a British passport, or, for that matter, that his name was Smith, but she didn't worry her head about that. The main thing was, he'd got her one too.

A friend of Hilary's found her a clerical job in a publishing firm. Then, when war broke out, Hilary told her they were looking for people with foreign languages. He'd put his solicitor's practice in mothballs and would be working somewhere in the country. His mother was German – he was bilingual. He could probably get her included. They were sent to the Vale of Evesham and became part of the 'Ears of Britain', mucking in with a polyglot group of refugees, Jewish exiles, Spanish communists, Austrian intellectuals and White Russians.

'Remember how horrified the local people were the first time they saw Sergei in his ankle-length fur coat and astrakhan hat, that very cold winter, 1940?' And Hilary glanced at her: 'Ever hear of him again?'

Regine shook her head. She tried never to think about Sergei. But now she couldn't help remembering and there was a lump in her throat as she thought what fun it had all been. They'd lived in a communal household at first, where you had to get water from the well. On washday they boiled up rainwater in a huge copper in the wash house, and the washing itself was done out of doors in a great big tub. Eventually the well ran dry and they had to split up, billeted on different villagers.

She remembered the thrill of skidding on her bike over

roads that had become an endless sheet of ice that freezing winter. They even skated on the fields, which was extraordinary. The ditches were piled high with enormous blocks of ice and the branches and twigs of the trees were coated in ice like giant icicles. And then the Siberian winter was followed by a scorching summer, which made the village, with thatched roofs and cottage gardens and orchards groaning with fruit, seem even more like a world lost in time, a hundred years behind London.

As she cycled to the night shift the moon shone on the silent glassy river and turned it to mercury, and the blossom-laden orchards glimmered in the moonlight. Then, when she biked home along the old Evesham road in the early morning the sun would be coming up and there'd be mist over the river, and the cows would stand peacefully under the heavy hanging trees.

Hilary must have been remembering too, for he said: 'The extraordinary thing was, it was the most peaceful place in the world, wasn't it, and yet we were in the middle of the war.'

'I was heartbroken when the whole outfit was moved to Reading and I went to the War Office in London,' said Regine. For that was when Sergei had left on some secret mission abroad.

The key turned in the lock. Neville was back. He came down the passage to the kitchen. 'Oh! Hilary.' He seemed put out.

'They were interviewed by the police,' said Regine.

'We've all had a visit from the police. It's their job. But why are you sitting in here? I need a drink. Noel Valentine can be so exhausting – on and on at me to invest in his bloody gallery.' He sat down and took out his pipe.

'Yes, but – well, Muriel got the wind up.'

The two men exchanged a look.

'That's absurd,' said Neville. 'It's nothing to do with her.'

'No … but it was difficult talking to the police; as you can imagine, Neville.'

'No I can't, actually. Her politics has nothing to do with Freddie getting murdered.'

'Freddie wasn't interested in politics,' said Regine.

They ignored her. 'Muriel's worried about Arthur, you see,' said Hilary.

'*Arthur*?' said Regine. 'Why should she be worried about him?'

Hilary leaned forward earnestly. 'You know, Neville, if I hadn't met you I wouldn't have met Arthur, and if I hadn't met Arthur I wouldn't have met Muriel.'

Neville made a rasping noise, halfway between a cough and a laugh. 'Don't blame me! Reggie introduced the two of us, come to that, so maybe your marriage is all her fault.'

'I'm not complaining about my marriage! I'm just saying it's a bit ironic, isn't it. You saw through it all and – and they didn't.'

Regine looked from one to the other. 'What on earth are you talking about?'

'The fact is, kitten, before the war Arthur and I were both rather starry-eyed about Oswald Mosley. It was just youthful indiscretion on my part. It didn't take me long to see through all the posing and claptrap. What a frightful man Mosley was – well, still is, of course, although he's a spent force now. Back then even Freddie fell slightly for the – the glamour of fascism, I suppose you could call it. 1937. He even dragged Vivienne along to one or two meetings, I seem to remember. I think they both rather loved the theatrical aspect of it all. In our defence, we weren't alone. Half of what Alan would term the British ruling class thought Hitler was wonderful. Now of course no one will ever take Nazism seriously again.'

'Don't be so sure about that,' said Hilary. 'Muriel does. And she's not a crackpot. Actually she's an idealist. That's the problem.' Without being asked, Hilary poured himself more tea.

'When I met her I didn't think – I mean, I know Arthur's mad, but … and to be absolutely frank, in many ways I agree with a lot of it. I'm a libertarian. I can't stand all this socialist regimentation, rules and regulations, I'm all for liberty and freedom. And Arthur was a persuasive speaker in those days.'

'Perhaps you should have been an anarchist,' said Neville drily.

Hilary took the remark seriously. 'Anarchism is quite similar in some ways. You know what they called the Nazis in Germany before the war: armed bohemia. Hitler wanted to be an artist. Goebbels was a novelist. Some anarchists embraced violence. And I'm not a pacifist. There's a place for violence in politics. But what I can't stand is all this stuff she's started to spout about Jewish conspiracies, niggers and Arabs – she seems to hate everyone who isn't Aryan. Perhaps that's why she fell for me, because I'm part German,' said Hilary, half joking, half bitter.

'I don't see what it has to do with the Freddie business,' said Neville.

'Muriel sees conspiracies round every corner. But then they are beleaguered.'

'They certainly are.' Neville's sharp gaze was trained on Hilary. 'I hadn't quite realised,' he said slowly, 'that Muriel was still … involved. Are you saying she still takes it seriously? Even Arthur—'

'Oh, Arthur's part of the problem. He's been behaving quite oddly lately. And all this business with the police worried Muriel. She told them Arthur was with us the evening – you know, when it happened. And now she's regretting it. She feels he's vulnerable, you know, because of what happened in the war.'

Neville removed his glasses and pressed his fingers against his eyes. He blinked, put the spectacles back on and said: 'And was he – with you that evening?'

'Yes. Why?'

'I met Freddie up here. It must have been very soon before he was murdered. He said he'd met Arthur earlier and they'd had a row.'

Hilary frowned. 'Arthur didn't say anything about that.'

'Exactly what time was Arthur with you? All through the evening, or—'

'Good God, Neville, you're not suggesting he had anything to do with it? I don't remember what time he arrived – after we got home from here, obviously.' He stared at Neville. 'I say, old chap, you having seen Freddie so soon before he died – doesn't that put you in an awkward position?'

'I don't see why,' said Neville huffily. 'Anyway, it's always best to be as frank as possible. You're a lawyer, you know that.'

'Oh – Muriel wouldn't hear of that. Absolute secrecy; that's the rule.'

The whole conversation was utterly mysterious to Regine. 'Surely Freddie's death hasn't got anything to do with any of our friends,' she said. 'It must have been a thief, a hold-up – it must have.'

'Well, let's hope so.'

They subsided into gloomy silence. After a while Neville said: 'It's hard to believe now, isn't it, how Arthur was so impressive ... then ...'

Hilary hauled himself to his feet. 'I must be off. Muriel will wonder where I've got to.'

In the hall Neville said: 'Tell Muriel not to panic. They won't be interested in Arthur. But can't you try and wean her off it all?'

Regine followed him into the drawing room.

'Gin?' Neville poured the drinks without waiting for an answer.

She watched him as he sat down in his usual chair by the

fire. 'What was all that about Arthur Carnforth and Muriel? Why did you never tell me about her? Freddie used to refer to Muriel as 'that fascist', but I never realised he meant it literally.'

'Well ... it's best to let sleeping dogs lie, don't you think.'

'And why are they worried about Arthur?'

'He was interned in the war. He was quite a prominent figure in the movement – well, not prominent, exactly, but he wrote stuff for them. He used another name, though.'

'You told me he was a conscientious objector!'

'I thought it was best. What was the point in dragging all that up? I felt sorry for him ... I don't know why, old loyalties, I suppose. I'd known him such a long time, before all the Mosley business. We were at school together, you know. And there's something about Arthur – he always seemed unable to look after himself. But in those days, well, I know you'll find this hard to believe, but there was something – attractive about him, compelling in a way. Anyway, in spite of everything I didn't cut him out of my life – I even visited him once or twice. Then he had a nervous breakdown and was in hospital for a while and after that they let him out.'

'But what has it got to do with Freddie?'

'It's a question of motive, isn't it. He hated Freddie's guts.'

'*Was* it an accident you met Freddie that evening, Neville?'

'*Yes.* I told you!' He hesitated.

Regine sat down again abruptly. Neville stared at her. After a while she said: 'Shouldn't you tell the police?'

'Arthur would never *kill* anyone. Anyway, it was the other way round. Freddie was threatening *him*. If only I could remember the time more exactly ... they said Freddie was killed about ten, it must have been nearly ten – he wouldn't have had time to go off and meet Arthur again ... no, it's just not feasible. Anyway, how would he have got hold of a gun?'

twelve

BLEAK, BATTERED TERRACES stretched away to the left of the Seven Sisters Road near Finsbury Park station, like wings of a prison advancing in grim parallel lines. Cobwebs of thin fog clung viscously all day, softening the edges of the buildings into further decay, muffling the ring of his feet on the pavement.

Four little boys dragged a cart made from an old crate up and down the road, shouting. They were childishly dressed, in worn flannel shorts, thick socks slipping towards the ankles with bare knobbly knees in between, yet they looked like little old men.

'Mister! Mister! Penny for the guy!' As he drew alongside them, he saw the 'guy' was actually a much younger child in the cart, trussed up, face red, eyes screwed shut, round mouth opened to emit a yell.

He chucked them a couple of pennies and the dwarfish creatures scrabbled on the pavement for the coins. Abandoned, the cart lurched towards the gutter. The infant guy howled.

He walked on until he came to the house. It was a risk, going to the house. Suppose someone else, not Kenneth, answered the door. But Kenneth was expecting him. He looked up at the blank façade. It was slightly less slummy than its neighbours; less peeling, broken stucco; neater curtains at the windows.

He knocked; waited. The door opened with a creak. Kenneth stood there, swelling muscularly out of his serge suit. 'You're late,' he said. And: 'Where are we going? Mum's inside. I don't want to—'

'Let's walk.'

'Wait a sec.'

When Kenneth reappeared he'd wound a muffler round his neck.

'It's not cold.'

'You're wearing gloves. But, fact is, I went back for – you know …'

They marched slowly along the main road, under the railway bridge and towards the park, but he steered Kenneth left and up the rise towards Stroud Green, talking all the while about the future, as if he had no idea what Kenneth had been up to. He discussed the outcome of a recent trial as they followed the road that wound off to the right and towards another railway bridge. Beyond that was the disused track, now overgrown and concealed by the trees that had sprung up during the war, a raised pathway, rural and secluded. He led the way and Kenneth followed him trustingly. Kenneth was not one to pay much attention to his surroundings.

He wasn't entirely sure why he'd brought Ken out here, he hadn't decided exactly what to do, but he liked to spring a surprise, he was annoyed with Ken for making such a mess of things and wanted to give him a fright. As they walked along, in silence now because he'd run out of things to say, he dwelt on the way Ken had cocked things up and his anger rose like bile in his throat. How he hated the lot of them. Ken was thick, an idiot, a stupid, fucking peasant.

After a while Kenneth, as if sensing hostility, seemed to get the pip. He did a sort of skip closer and touched his companion on the arm. 'About the money,' he said, more wheedling than threatening.

'All in good time, Kenneth. I'm grateful for what you've done.'

'You bleeding well should be, mate.'

His companion suppressed an acid swell of rage at the impertinence. Kenneth would regret that remark.

'It wasn't easy. I didn't get him first go off. He tried to scarper. It was a bloody great mess at the end.'

'I know it wasn't easy, Kenneth.' They walked on. 'You have got the gun, haven't you.'

'I told you. That's what I went back for.'

'Like I said, I need it. I've got a plan – to send the police scarpering off in the wrong direction. And I need your help again, Kenneth, if you're ready and willing.'

It was risky, but in fact, Kenneth drew the weapon out of an inner pocket and handed it over like a lamb. That was the trouble with these cosh boys and riff-raff: they were stupid. And Kenneth was so stupid he'd made a fatal mistake. In fact the whole idea of using a gun had been a mistake. But it was too late to worry about that.

He'd decided what to do now. Now he had the gun he had to get Kenneth unawares, seize a moment when he was off guard. But Kenneth *was* off guard. Kenneth had no suspicions, hadn't even asked why they were walking along this deserted path that no one knew about, hadn't even thought it was odd he was wearing gloves at this time of year – though in fact, it had turned colder.

He turned the revolver over in his hands. Thinking, thinking all the time. It had to be done quickly. He stopped, bent as if to pick something off his shoe, then as Kenneth halted, grabbed his arm, the revolver was against his temple before he knew what was happening; there was only his wide-eyed astonishment as the trigger was pulled. The report was loud, yet stifled in the dank air.

So Kenneth had helped him again, was part of the plan. It was almost impossible to drag the body to the ditch alongside the path, Kenneth weighed a ton, but he managed it, toppled it in and kicked dead leaves over it. With any luck Kenneth would be lying in that ditch for quite some time.

Only later that evening did it dawn on him – with a sickening lurch in the pit of his stomach – that eliminating Kenneth might have sent the law in the *right* direction after all.

thirteen

MURRAY TIMED HIS VISIT TO Downshire Hill carefully: 5.30 in the evening. Mrs Milner was likely to be at home, but her husband was not.

He hadn't counted on a visitor. That was stupid of him, he thought as he took in the scene: the warmth of the drawing room with its fire, sparks popping, the curtains drawn and cups of tea on the low table, and the boy languidly sprawled on the chaise longue.

When Charles saw the policeman he eased himself gracefully to his feet and said: 'I must be going ... Regine.'

'Must you? Do stay. The sergeant won't be here long – will you?'

Murray felt there was something forced and artificial about her smile and her manner, but he misinterpreted it, assuming her to be nervous at the thought of another grilling from the police, not that he intended to grill her. 'I just need to go over one or two things.'

'I should get along. My mother will wonder where I am.'

Regine followed Charles into the hall and Murray heard them talking about some French homework or something and the boy said: 'Until next week, then.'

'Do sit down.' Regine gestured at Neville's armchair and

took the chaise longue herself.

'I'm sorry to intrude on you again.'

She seemed to be miles away, looking into the fire; then sighed, sat up straighter and looked at him. 'Yes, it is only a few days ago, isn't it.' Now he felt her manner was slightly coquettish.

'We saw your friends, Mr and Mrs Jordan—'

'Yes! Hilary told us.'

'Mrs Jordan mentioned that there was someone at your afternoon party on the day your friend died, someone who wasn't on your list. It seemed odd you'd forgotten him. Ernest Appleton.'

Regine was playing with her necklace. Murray was mesmerised by the amber globules, the flashing emerald ring and red nails. 'I didn't forget. But you must see why I didn't want his name brought up.'

'Because he's a government minister? But that doesn't mean he's exempt from scrutiny. No one's above the law, Mrs Milner, especially in a case like this.'

'I didn't mean that. But he's in trouble already. You must have read it in the papers, these allegations about the Board of Trade. This man, Sidney Stanley – all these questions about corruption and bribery – Mr Appleton's a junior minister in that department. To then be linked to a sordid murder as well, even if accidentally as it were, would be so damaging.'

'No one need know. We certainly shan't mention it.'

'But you see there's more to it than that. He's married, of course, but he came to my Sunday with his mistress.'

Murray went red with embarrassment. A mistress! No one he knew talked like that. Coarse language about women, of course, but somehow the word mistress suggested rarefied, transgressive social worlds and it surprised him to hear a lady like Mrs Milner refer to such things.

'You're shocked,' she challenged him.

Murray felt the familiar tightening of resentment. She assumed he was just another narrow-minded, respectable, suburban policeman. And the truth was he was shocked. But: 'I'm just rather surprised,' he said, 'though perhaps I shouldn't be. I somehow thought this government was a bit different ...' Cynicism swelled, becoming part of his objectless resentment. 'But anyway, this is all strictly confidential. It won't go any further. There's no reason for his name to be mentioned in connection with the case.'

'But it so easily could get known,' she pleaded. 'If the police were to turn up at his house to question him about Freddie it would probably get into the press and destroy his career; and possibly his marriage.'

'I assure you that's not going to happen.'

'He didn't even *know* Freddie. Cynthia's an old friend of mine. She brought him. I was *flabbergasted*. I knew it was going on, but they've never appeared like that in public before.' She gazed at him. 'Please – you don't need to mention it to your inspector, do you? It's got nothing to do with – what happened to Freddie.'

'Probably not.' He offered her a cigarette.

'I don't smoke.'

He lit one for himself, watching her surreptitiously. She'd tied her blazing hair with a black ribbon, to reveal her creamy neck. There was a round, brown mole beneath her ear. He was startled when she asked: 'So what did you make of the Jordans?'

'We understood he was Mr Buckingham's lawyer, but that appears not to be the case,' he said cautiously.

Regine leaned forward. 'Muriel's a follower of Oswald Mosley. I had no idea – I only just found out.' Her hand pulled at her necklace again. 'Oh – I shouldn't have told you, should I – will she get into trouble? But to be honest I can't stand the woman. And what a spiteful cat to tell you about Cynthia's beau.'

'But they're friends of yours. How could you not know?'

'It was Hilary who was my friend. I met him during the war. He wasn't married then. Actually we had a shipboard romance. That's how we met. On a boat.'

She was teasing him, he knew, toying with him. He flushed, angry with himself, or perhaps with her. If only she wouldn't flirt. If only she wasn't so ... seductive.

He must pull himself together. 'Let's get back to Mr Buckingham. You're not suggesting, are you, that Mrs Jordan's political views had anything to do with all this?'

'No ...' Her mood seemed to change so quickly. Now she seemed pensive, anxious even. 'But Hilary, Hilary Jordan, came to see us right after you'd been there. He was in rather a state. Do you remember – my husband mentioned meeting Freddie on the night he died, when he went out to get cigarettes? Well, he didn't tell you that Freddie had earlier met someone we know called Arthur Carnforth, a friend of the Jordans. Freddie apparently told Neville that they'd had a tremendous row. And the Jordans were worried about him.'

'Why was that?'

'He's a Nazi. A crank, my husband said.'

She put her hand up to her hair and began twisting a curl that had fought free of the ribbon.

'But how does this connect with Mr Buckingham?'

'Well, only that he'd had a row with Freddie. And he hated Freddie's guts.'

'Why didn't your husband mention that?' He watched her closely. There was something febrile, strange about her, one minute cold, almost hostile, the next confiding, then again mischievous. He couldn't have known it was all to do with Charles; that she was furious with him for interrupting their tête-à-tête and at the same time thinking of how their hands had touched, hers and Charles's, and of how – so young – he was such a master of ambiguity.

Although Murray suspected nothing of this, an unconscious awareness caused him to say: 'Mr Buckingham took an interest in the boy – Charles Hallam – who was just here. Was there anything there shouldn't have been in their relationship? Might his parents have had cause to be concerned? Might they have – they saw no reason to intervene, to put a stop to it?'

'You don't have to interview Vivienne Hallam, do you?' She was anxious now. He wondered why.

'The people, your friends on that guest list. Who would be useful to talk to?'

'I still don't see why you have to talk to any of them, Sergeant Murray.'

'I know, but … it's background, partly, and, well, men he might have had relations with.'

'Freddie kept that side of his life very separate.'

Her coldness disheartened him. He leaned forward. 'I realise it's unpleasant,' he said, 'but we have to look at every angle. I know you want to protect him – avoid any scandal, unpleasant stories in the newspapers, but that aspect could be significant. The photographs you say are missing, for instance. Could they have incriminated anyone? Indecent photographs?'

'I don't know anything about them. Or if they even existed. My husband thought they did, that's all.'

'It couldn't be – forgive me for suggesting this – but is it possible your husband removed them – or anything incriminating – from Mr Buckingham's house?'

'Really! That's outrageous.' But she was blushing. There *was* something. She *had* taken something from Buckingham's house.

'In order to protect Mr Buckingham's reputation – or that of other people?' he insisted.

'If we'd taken them, we wouldn't have told you, would we,' she said with a triumphant smile.

She looked at her watch. He'd alienated her. 'I hope I haven't offended you. You do understand we have to ask all these questions.'

'I'm so tired of it all. It's all such a worry.' For a moment he thought she was close to tears.

'Is there anything else you'd like to tell me? Anything at all?'

She looked at him, a deep, serious look. Then her silence changed and her lips curved in the painted smile that tantalised him so unbearably. 'I don't think so. I've told you rather a lot, haven't I? I shouldn't really have said what I did about Arthur Carnforth. My husband would be furious.'

'Why?'

'He doesn't think it's any of your business. And he's – they were at school together, old school loyalties I suppose.'

'Do you know where the two of them met, Mr Buckingham and Mr Carnforth?'

'Somewhere in Camden Town, I think.'

'We made enquiries at public houses in the Hampstead area, but we didn't think of going as far as Camden Town. The pubs down there – we didn't think they'd be the sort of place Mr Buckingham ... Irish pubs, mostly.' Murray would have been shocked to hear Freddie joke with Charles about the erotic appeal of hulking great Irish labourers.

On the doorstep he said: 'Just one last thing—'

'Oh – you're impossible. There's always one more thing.' Her mood had lifted again. She laughed at him.

'I have to take a friend to a restaurant – it's a celebration meal, a special occasion – next week. I thought you might be able to suggest somewhere decent, somewhere in the West End perhaps.'

'A celebration ... well, there are some nice Italian restaurants in Soho. If you really wanted to make a splash you could try Quo Vadis. That is expensive, though. Is it for your girlfriend? Perhaps you want to take her somewhere special?' She was flirting again.

'No, no,' he lied, 'it's just – just a friend; a colleague, actually.'

'Bertorelli's perhaps – in Charlotte Street – that's nice. Or there's a dear little place called Fava's.'

'I'll remember those names.' It would look too lumpish to write them down. He lifted his hat and tried to memorise them as he strode away.

fourteen

MURRAY PARKED THE CAR beyond the bridge and the two detectives walked towards the disused railway through soft, drifting rain that came down like the twilight. The path was screened by the trees and bushes that grew up the bank, even though the leaves had begun to fall.

A huddle of uniformed police stood at the site. In the light from powerful torches and a photographer's lamp the figures looked blacker, faces whiter, sharply bisected by hat brims.

The pathologist said: 'Body must have been here at least a week, perhaps more. The weather's been quite damp, so – anyway, he's been shot in the head at close range, there's a burn mark ... nothing to identify him ...'

Whoever had hidden the body in the ditch had probably relied on its not being found for some time. Hardly anyone frequented the disused railway line or even knew about it. Boys larking around up there had only found the corpse because one of them had fallen off his bike and into the ditch. That must have been a shocking experience – put them off for some time from messing about in places where they shouldn't be, Plumer thought with satisfaction.

They stood round in the chilly autumn air for some time. When it was quite dark, they went back to the office.

* * * * *

A few days later, forensics came back with the news that the weapon was probably the same one that had killed Frederick Buckingham.

In Campbell Bunk the little knobbly-kneed boys were still playing and shouting up and down the pavement, but now with a football. Guy Fawkes Night had come and gone. They shrank back against the wall as the detectives passed, instinctively knowing themselves to be in the presence of the law.

'Campbell Bunk,' said Plumer. 'The worst bloody street in north London. More villains than you've had hot dinners.'

The detectives reached the house they were looking for. There was no bell. The knocker made a hollow sound and was so heavy it seemed as if it might smash the battered door. They waited.

Murray banged the knocker again. Eventually they heard slow footsteps scuffing nearer and a hoarse voice: 'All right, all right, I'm coming.'

The woman who opened the door wore men's old carpet slippers and was dressed in a faded flowered overall. Her hair hung lankly on either side of her face. It was hard to tell her age, because her cheeks had fallen in on her toothless gums.

'Yes?' She knew at once they were the Law. 'About my son, is it? Been in trouble again?'

That was, in the end, how they'd identified him: a uniformed sergeant had recognised the face, and then there'd been police records: fingerprints, previous. Kenneth Barker had form.

'Your son, Kenneth Barker? I'm afraid so. If we could just step inside for a moment ...'

The front room smelled stale, but was reasonably tidy and clean. Mrs Barker gestured them towards the broken-down sofa that lolled against one wall.

Plumer cleared his throat. 'I'm very sorry to have to tell you ...'

The woman showed curiously little emotion at the news of her son's untimely death. She sat motionless. Then: 'I'll make us a cup of tea,' she muttered. Plumer tried to demur, but she had shuffled off into some nether region before he could stop her. Murray dreaded the thought of dirty cups and sterilised milk, but she returned with a tin tray on which clean, though cracked, china and a metal teapot were arranged. The milk was sterilised. Fresh milk was one of the few luxuries Murray's mother insisted on.

'Ken was in with them Mosleyites, blackshirts, y'know. Real wrong-uns. Went off with one of them last time I saw him.'

'When was that, Mrs Barker?'

'Oh ... couple of weeks ago ... maybe longer.'

'Weren't you worried when he didn't return home?'

'Ken weren't living here. Or only off and on. 'E stayed over from time to time, but I never knew when I'd next see the lad.' Now a few tears oozed from her dark eyes.

'This was the address recorded at the time of his last conviction. For affray,' said Plumer prissily. 'Can you give us a current domicile?'

'He moved around a lot, see. This was 'is address, official like, but he didn't actually live 'ere, leastways not most of the time.'

'How did you know the man you saw him with was one of Mosley's lot?'

'I didn't, not really. It's just he's always knocking around with them lot. Trouble-makers.'

Plumer tried to extract further information about the dead man's associates, and especially a description of the man last seen with her son, but she wouldn't, or couldn't, be drawn. Murray met a lot of women like her in the course of his duties;

worn out by the war, by poverty, by her menfolk. She would only denounce the British Union of Fascists – or whatever they called themselves now – adding, 'Mind, I don't like the yids no more 'n anyone else, but you 'ave to put up with them when all's said and done, they never done me no 'arm – poor things, and those camps – and now it's the darkies coming over here. They're worse, they look dirty to me, saw one up the road the other day, black as yer 'at ...'

At least, reflected Murray, she'd soon be fitted with National Health Service dentures. The woman's flaccid fatalism filled him with a kind of horror. It was as if the slings and arrows of life had not only wrecked her sagging body, but deadened her soul as well.

'Ken wasn't a bad boy, y'know, just got in with a rotten lot.' She sat on the sofa with her feet apart, gazing into space. 'Hadn't seen much of 'im lately, but ... it's hard to believe ...'

Murray couldn't help feeling that Ken, whose reasonably, or at least intermittently, successful criminal career during the war he'd read up in the police records, could have provided his parent with a bit more in the way of worldly comforts, but he kept this thought, like many others, to himself. And anyway, perhaps she did have dentures, but badly fitting ones, or just didn't bother to put them in.

After twenty minutes, all they'd established was that a man had called for Ken, tallish, but she hadn't been able to see his face because he'd been wearing a hat with a rather wider than normal brim and had had his coat collar turned up 'almost as if he didn't want to be seen'.

'D'you mind if we just have a look at his room, Mrs Barker?' Plumer was as polite with her as he had been with the Milners, perhaps more so.

They didn't expect to find anything and the upstairs bedroom, clean and tidy, contained little of a personal nature:

no pictures, no magazines, no sports gear. Murray opened the drawers of the chest that stood against one wall and found only a few articles of clothing neatly folded. A string suspended across the recess by the fireplace held a jacket and a raincoat on wire hangers.

However, when Murray looked under the mattress he found a folded garment: a bloodstained shirt.

Plumer did not want to upset Mrs Barker unnecessarily, so he contrived to show her the shirt while concealing the bloodstains.

'Ken never wore a shirt like that. Stuck to white; or blue. Checks – never.'

'You don't mind if we take it away? It may help our enquiries.'

'Must've belonged to that friend of his. Stan.'

'Stan?'

'Pinelli. Nasty little Eye-tie.'

'That's very helpful, Mrs Barker.' And with that Chief Inspector Plumer explained the formalities for the release of the body; and that under new legislation she could claim a death grant to help pay for the burial. The two men took their leave. On the doorstep Plumer donned his hat, then raised it in leave-taking and said: 'If you think of anything else useful you could tell us, I urge you to contact us. We do want to bring your son's murderer to justice.'

Her look expressed the greatest cynicism on this score.

As they walked away down the street, Murray said: 'So he was in with Mosley's lot. That's what the conviction for affray was about then – one of those running battles in Dalston.'

'Mmm, but this looks more like an underworld business to me. The blackshirts don't usually go running round shooting each other.'

'I don't know about that, sir. They're always falling out,

splintering off into rival groups.'

Plumer frowned. 'I think we'll go easy on that. I don't want Special Branch poking their noses in. They try to be too bloody clever if you ask me. No need to complicate things by dragging politics into it. We'll get the blood analysed and see where that takes us. And what about Stanley Pinelli? I know that name.'

The policemen reached their car. 'She didn't seem too upset about her son,' commented Murray.

'Shock,' said Plumer tersely. And: 'I need a beer.'

Plumer regularly drank at a mock Tudor establishment by Hackney Marshes, near the police station where he'd served his time as a junior detective in the thirties. In both saloon and public bar useful contacts were still to be found. On this particular evening he encountered no familiar faces, but only the previous week he'd received information about the black market in weaponry from occupied Germany and the two detectives now returned to the subject.

'It was the same gun,' began Murray, 'the same German gun.'

'The hand of the underworld,' said Plumer.

'But in that case, why should the queer have been killed? He'd nothing to do with the underworld.'

'Ah – that's not quite true, is it? Remember – he was outside the law himself. Common or garden villainy, that's the most likely explanation.'

But the adrenalin was coursing through Murray. At last they had exciting information; a significant connection. 'This blackshirt business, sir. I saw Mrs Milner again. She said the Jordans are in with Mosley's lot. And the man they gave as an alibi – Carnforth, he's one of Mosley's lot too.'

'Mmm.' Plumer smoked and sipped his beer, deadpan as usual. Murray couldn't understand why he wasn't more excited.

Finally Plumer said: 'Whether Kenneth Barker ran around with a few clapped-out Mosleyites is beside the point. Mosley's a spent force. A yesterday's man.'

'They're still going round the East End making trouble.'

'I grant you that,' conceded Plumer, 'but it's not like last year. Hard to credit, really, you'd think everyone had had enough of the Nazis – yet they all came crawling out from under their stones when Mosley returned. But I still think the main point is Kenneth Barker was a villain. We need to see this Pinelli. I know some of them have Mosleyite connections. But that's a side issue. At bottom they're thugs.'

'Don't they hate queers, though? Couldn't it be that—'

'Could be, I suppose. But I still think it was some twisted little pervert or a cosh boy. I know we've turned nothing up so far. In the end someone'll come forward. At the end of the day someone always boasts or spills the beans to their mate. If we twist enough arms.'

'It didn't have to be a male prostitute, sir. It could have been someone Buckingham picked up who was a bit slow on the uptake, didn't twig what it was all about and then panicked or got in a rage.'

'We've been through all this. That sort of idiot wouldn't have had a weapon.'

'You're right, sir,' said Murray diplomatically, 'but don't you think what Mrs Milner told me could be important?'

'Could be. You have to ask yourself though, why did she come up with all that stuff? It may just be a red herring, something to put us off the scent.'

'Why should she do that?'

'We need to find out. The Milners acted suspiciously, going round to the house like that, whatever they say. But ... I still think it'll turn out to be some murderous little toerag who's gone mad with a revolver.'

fifteen

CHARLES HAD BEEN SMOKING in Upper School common room with Adam Mendelssohn and Oliver Vaughan. These three were already the stars of the sixth form, destined to become distinguished old boys who would bring glory to the school. Even more important in the short term, their parents were already public figures. Their blasé pose and iconoclastic views were therefore tolerated, although to risk smoking was pushing it a bit.

Oliver's talk of girls had irked Charles: saying that messing about with boys was just for kids and boasting about how he'd actually 'had' some woman. The way Adam had been going on about the atom bomb disturbed him too, yet he didn't know why he felt quite so irritable.

He felt more irritable still when he saw Harry Trevelyan hanging around in the corridor. Christ! It was the last straw. That scene in the art annexe seemed to have happened months ago, an incident he now for some reason found sickening. He eyed the despised ex-object of desire with exasperation.

'What is it, Trevelyan?'

Trevelyan gazed at him. To his horror Charles saw the boy's eyes were brimming with tears. A scene would be the last straw. 'Look, I can't talk now – you're not supposed to be up here anyway.'

'But when – when can I see you, Hallam?'

'I'm very busy at the moment.'

'But …'

'*What?*'

'We don't – I mean, I never see you any more.'

'I have a frightful lot of work to do now, Higher Certificate and all that.'

'But … please—'

'Look, I have to go now, old chap.' Then: '*Jesus.*' For Carnforth was looming towards them along the corridor. When he reached them he looked down at Trevelyan from his great height. 'What are you doing up here? I'm sure you're aware junior school pupils aren't allowed—'

'It's my fault – I told him to come and see me up here,' said Charles with self-conscious chivalry.

Carnforth's treacly eyes locked into his. There was a moment's silence in which they seemed suspended in some invisible web of calculation and surmise. Then Carnforth said: 'Well, get along now, Trevelyan. And don't come up here again.' He watched the boy scamper away along the corridor and turned to Charles. 'Come to the art room after school, would you? I need to have a word with you.'

'Is it about the backdrop, sir? It's almost finished, you know.'

'About four o'clock.'

Carnforth was seated at his desk. Charles dropped his school bag and sank onto the sofa, again remembering his encounter with Trevelyan on that very couch. A faint smile twitched his lips. If only Carnforth knew! The stain was quite noticeable. But his amusement faded. He felt unbearably tense. He was beginning to guess what Carnforth's game was. If he was right, it was unspeakable, obscene, but he had to be careful. He wasn't sure how far he dared go with Carnforth.

'Very kind of your mother to have everyone back after Mr Buckingham's funeral.'

Charles had thought it mad, in view of the state of the house, and he knew his father had thought so too. His father had been heroic in putting up with the guests who'd swarmed everywhere. The whole thing had been hateful and it was something else to hold against Carnforth that he'd mentioned now, weeks later, an event Charles wanted to forget.

'You must have been upset by his death.'

So Carnforth had only mentioned the funeral in order to get him to talk about Freddie, but he had no intention of discussing Freddie with this horrible man. Carnforth was staring at him. Charles looked away, his face stiff. 'Did you want to see me about the scenery? It's nearly finished, though it's been difficult to find time now, more and more prep this term, you see ...' The real reason was he no longer needed the art annexe for his trysts with Trevelyan.

'It was about your extracurricular activities.'

Charles hadn't expected that. 'Sir?'

'It's rather a poor idea to fraternise with boys in lower school. You want to stay away from that sort of thing.'

Charles hoped he looked puzzled, but he was beginning to feel alarmed. He looked at the floor.

'The paths of righteousness, Hallam. It is all too easy to stray from the paths of righteousness.'

The longer the silence lasted the less Charles knew what to say. He wasn't going to own up, but a denial might backfire. Then again, silence could be construed as guilt. The humiliation of being caught out by Carnforth of all people – but it was his own fault; he'd taken the risk, he'd done it on purpose, he'd tempted fate.

'And I didn't see you at chapel this morning. You've missed

chapel before, several times.'

But this was a bad move on Carnforth's part. 'Mr Tolliday gave me an exemption.' Charles felt sure Tolliday was a fellow atheist.

'I see,' said Carnforth. He paused. 'He doesn't object to your neglecting your spiritual life? I shall have to speak to him about that.'

The feeling of humiliation faded, because now Carnforth was being ridiculous. He was on the lowest rung of the hierarchy; as a part-time art teacher he had hardly more influence than the porters. Tolliday wouldn't dream of taking any notice of him. But Carnforth tried another approach.

'Your mother's been worried about you, you know, especially since Mr Buckingham died.'

Charles swallowed as he felt his face go hot right round to his ears. How dare Carnforth mention her! What did Carnforth know about what she felt about anything? The frightful thought that she might have discussed him with Carnforth almost choked him. But – it was impossible; she couldn't have betrayed him. The man had invented it.

Carnforth sighed. 'Your mother is a wonderful woman, you know, Hallam, a great artist. You wouldn't want to upset her, I know.'

Charles continued to look at the floor.

'A few words of advice. You may feel that because you're the most brilliant boy in your year, possibly in the school, you can get away with things other boys ... there's a rather lax atmosphere, I feel, at present. If only for your mother's sake, Hallam – or perhaps I may call you Charles as I'm getting to know you and your family better – try to steer a steady course. The temptation to sin is always very powerful.'

Charles could feel Carnforth staring at him. The silence was thick and sticky with what was unsaid. Finally: 'Your spiritual development, the spiritual development of all of you boys is important to me, you know. There is insufficient emphasis on that side of life, one feels, in the school at present.'

The silence was like glue. Charles was stuck in it.

'Prayer, Charles, it does help, believe me.'

Now Charles wanted to laugh. He bit his lip. Finally he said, hoping it sounded insolent: 'I'll remember that, sir.' He had to get away. He was about to stand up when Carnforth added:

'And it's a very great pity you spend so much time with a Jew.'

'*What?*'

'A vulgar boy – his father's some kind of theatrical impresario, I believe. You don't want to waste your time with that sort of riff-raff.'

Now Charles did stand up. He was too shaken to protest, but he made himself look Carnforth in the eye. 'Is that all, sir?'

He'd won; Carnforth looked slightly flummoxed. Then he rallied. 'Yes, that's all – for now. But remember what I said. You wouldn't want to let your mother down. If things went any further ...' The sentence hung unfinished in the air.

As if that were not enough, as he reached the door Carnforth spoke again. 'Remember me to your mother, won't you.' His voice was horrible: suddenly ingratiating, oily and sly.

Charles couldn't stop himself. He slammed the door. If things went any further! The threat was absurd, of course, and yet ... it had gone home. He was scared now. No one would take any notice of Carnforth, and yet ... he was rattled.

And those fat fingers all over his private life, his private thoughts, the slimy prick. The very thought of Trevelyan, of Freddie, of everything revolted him now. Carnforth knew somehow about Trevelyan ... the stain ... or was he spying on him ... but what he'd said about Adam ... that was unexpected, shocking ...

Oliver had waited for him by the back gate, so they could travel together. He took one look at Charles's face and said: 'What's the matter?'

Charles just shook his head. As they came out onto the main road he muttered: 'Carnforth is unspeakable.'

'But what did he say?'

'Nothing. He's so slimy. He's like a *slug*.' He strode along as if that would rid him of his rage. 'He's sucking up to my mother – I don't know why. He makes my flesh crawl.' But Carnforth was a fool. If he was after her, he should have tried to charm her son, instead of which ... 'He hinted about sex—'

'*What*? Is he queer?'

'I thought he might be, but now I don't. He knew about Trevelyan, though. The whole thing is ... Ugh! I don't want to think about it.'

'Well, you know what I think about that.' They reached the bus stop. Oliver looked at his friend. 'He's really got under your skin – I don't see why you're so angry. He's just a pathetic old beak.'

'He isn't. He's worse than pathetic. He said something horrible about Adam. He hates Jews.'

'Oh—' Oliver, taken completely by surprise, had no idea what to say. Jews weren't highly thought of in his own family, but some were all right, and it wasn't done to go round *talking* about it.

At Hampstead underground they took the tube. The train was unusually crowded. Charles hung on to a strap and swayed with the motion of the train. He felt as though the other passengers were staring at him, that his rage and revulsion were plain for all to see. He didn't understand it himself, but he felt close to tears. Carnforth's fingers poking into his private life; hinting at those private desires – that had sullied, had turned those dark, secret impulses, forbidden and therefore so compelling, into something nauseating, because Carnforth had torn off the skin, had exposed him.

He knew he had to calm himself down, so when he came out into the gritty dusk at Camden Town he walked very slowly up Parkway.

East 89th Street in the sun ... he was walking alongside Lally past the lofty apartment blocks and towards Central Park in the heavy sunlight; an American soldier whistling his way past; Lally's grown-up sister in her flowered dress and hat like a halo ...

He missed Lally. He felt even worse now.

He began to see what Carnforth's purpose might be. To cover it up with that slick veneer of religious hypocrisy ... when he was all the while trying to get his claws into his mother ... now that Freddie was out of the way ...

Two dark-clad men sat with his parents in the drawing room. Charles was startled to see his father home so early. It must be serious then.

'This is my son, Charles,' said his father. 'Charles – Detective Chief Inspector Plumer and Detective Sergeant Murray.'

As he sat down, for some reason a memory flashed up of the time Freddie had brought Regine. Freddie's last visit. He'd see Regine tomorrow. He'd definitely visit her again. He'd talk to her about Freddie. She'd understand.

s i x t e e n

I N THE BEDROOM HE SAID: 'Am I supposed to undress you?'
Regine turned her back to him. 'Perhaps you could undo
the buttons. They're very fiddly.'

Charles let fall his own clothes with easy grace. She thought
of a snake casting its skin, but that must be slower than the
boy's quick yet fluid movements.

She'd known this was going to happen the minute she'd
opened the door.

There he was, suddenly, on the doorstep again, and again
the langour of his youth, *écrasé* with melancholy and the
burden of being admired, entranced her. The time before –
when the policeman had interrupted them – how infuriating
that had been, she'd wanted to scream with impatience – it was
Freddie he'd wanted to talk about, but he'd kept up his blasé
attitude. For a moment she'd thought the mask was going to
slip, his hand with the cigarette was shaking. And then their
hands had touched when she was looking at him and he hadn't
moved his away, but it might have been accidental, you
couldn't tell what he was thinking.

Today there was something about him – something hard
and desperate.

'Freddie said you should always try everything once ...'

Managing to be both oblique and crudely direct, hardly flatter-ing, clumsy – but she so desperately wanted him –

Sergei had helped her get over the crippling shame instilled at the convent, but there remained a sense of defiance in lying back on the deep blue eiderdown, which, she knew, set off her white skin. But when he lay down beside her the contrast dis-mayed her; between his body, the bloom on his skin and his thighs that were like soft marble, and hers, *usé*, with a red mark where her girdle had been.

He put his hand to her head. 'It's such an incredible colour, your hair. Freddie always said you were like a Titian.'

So Freddie was in the room with them, then.

'Freddie liked to think of people as works of art.'

She brought her lips to his. He was not aroused. His mouth, even his skin, were soft, like a girl's. She'd thought he might have started shaving, but his face felt childishly smooth. His whole body was in a way girlish, slender, pale, almost hairless, and there was no sense of raw, male desire. She put his hand on her breast and moved her own down his body. His eyes were shut as they kissed, kissed and gradually as she worked her hand his cock began to swell, but she knew it was going to be diffi-cult. She laboured. It wasn't really getting anywhere until she thought of turning over. That was when he made a stifled sound and moved his body over hers. Finally it began to be all right and her flood of hungry longing came like a sob as he was sud-denly piston-like and got the rhythm of it and the creaking of the bed and his silent intensity … she thought of the rocking horse in her childhood going back and forward, back and forward …

It was over too quickly for her and he fell back beside her, his eyes shut, silently cast away. After a little while she leaned up on one elbow and looked at him, brushing aside the dark hair that fell over his face. He opened his eyes and smiled.

'You're beautiful,' he said, but he could have been admiring a painting, a Titian indeed ... and he was a thousand miles away, in some place where she couldn't reach him, her longing for him unsatisfied. She wanted to ask him why, but it was better not to ask questions.

He lay on his back and looked at the ceiling. 'The detectives came to see us yesterday.'

She gazed at him, besotted and also disappointed in him for not having satisfied her, yet then again tender, imagining how she would show him, teach him the ways ... How could she be so mad about a sixteen-year-old boy? Why was he so unhappy? She searched desperately for the right words, the key to unlock him.

'What did they say?'

'Oh ...' And suddenly he sat up and rolled out of the bed. He had his back to her as he pulled on his clothes. 'They asked my father a lot about Freddie. Trying to insinuate they didn't get on. I think it rather upset my mother. And then she began to say things about Freddie, things that weren't really true. I mean she was criticising him ... it was all ...' He sat down suddenly on the little chair near the dressing table and put his head in his hands. He was sobbing.

'Oh *sweetie* ...' She pulled on her robe and stood awkwardly, close to him. She put a hand on his shoulder.

He swallowed, stopped crying, sniffed, wiped his face with his shirtsleeve. He looked up at her. 'I'm sorry. I must be going.'

'You can't go like this. I'll – I'll make you a cup of tea.'

He sat there, drooping. Suddenly he was little more than a child. The transformation was shocking. Their intimacy was ebbing away, had never existed.

In the hall he couldn't look at her. A sheet of glass had slipped between them. His pallor was like cream cheese. His blazer didn't fit well.

Suddenly he said: 'How well do you know Arthur Carn-forth?'

'*Arthur?*'

'He teaches at my school. But you knew that, didn't you. Part time. And he … for some reason he's decided to take an interest in me. Or perhaps it's my mother. You've known him for a long time, haven't you?'

'He used to be my husband's friend. I hardly know him at all. And we never see him.'

'He and Freddie were friends too, once, a long time ago. But they quarrelled. Freddie told me Arthur was evil in some way.'

'Evil?' It was a strong word. But then, as everyone knew, fascism was evil. Which made Muriel's belief quite sinister.

'I must go,' said Charles rather desperately. 'I don't want any tea.' He wrenched open the front door as if he couldn't wait to get away from her.

Cato, who had been sleeping, woke and came eagerly to greet her. 'Cato, leave me alone.' She pushed him away, went into the library and shut the door. He barked shrilly in the corridor. Now she was crying too.

Father and son faced each other at the kitchen table. John Hallam helped himself to carrots and pushed the dish towards Charles. There was cod, and vegetable marrow in white sauce, which Charles hated. 'It's like eating deliquescent slugs,' he said; the squishy texture nauseated him. On the other hand he liked the word 'deliquescent'.

'Eat it and be grateful,' said his father. 'Displaced persons are starving all over Europe.' Then: 'Why is your mother always out these days?' The attempt at jocularity sounded close to despair. Charles couldn't think of anything to say.

'How're you getting along at school?'

'Okay.'

'Okay! Must you use these Americanisms all the time? Okay! I haven't a clue! I couldn't care less! I can't stand all that slang – why can't you speak the King's English.'

'Sorry, Dad. It's just what everyone says.' Charles knew it wasn't really about 'okay'. He ate, hardly noticing the food. The afternoon had left him with a feeling almost of nausea, it was all mixed up with Carnforth and Freddie ...

'Is she bored? There's not much for her to do now, apart from supervising the building works ... though I suppose that's pretty much a full-time job and I'm not sure her mind's really on it.'

Charles thought it was unfair to leave it all to his mother.

John Hallam's knife rang against his plate. 'When I was out in the desert I used to think there'd be nothing better than all of us being at home together again – just think, we were in three different continents. And it seemed then – well, if one could just get through to the end of the war things would resolve them-selves, things would get better, a fresh start.' He lapsed into silence. He put his knife and fork together neatly.

Charles did not want to have to pity his father, but his forlorn expression was unbearable. He did not know what to say. ... New York. He wished he were back there. The longing was so strong it became a physical pain. He remembered the sunny surface across which he'd skated; feelings shut away in a box 'not wanted for the duration of the voyage' – the label on one of Mrs Denton-Bradshaw's trunks. 'Everything was differ-ent in the war,' was all he could think of to say.

'It certainly was,' agreed his father grimly.

Charles collected the two lonely plates and placed them on the draining board. Madge had left an apple pie for pudding.

'Still, one must look on the bright side.' John Hallam pushed his bowl away, the apple pie only half eaten. He looked out of the window at the derelict garden. 'I saw an old chap today – well, he wasn't that old, forty-five, looked more like seventy – stomach cancer – so far gone, far too late to do anything. I suppose people like him, the great unwashed, they had a rough deal before the war – now the pendulum's swung the other way – ' He was talking to himself rather than to Charles.

They heard the key turn in the lock; the front door opened.

'I'm sorry I'm late, dear. I went to the movies with Regine Milner.' There was a glittery feeling about her. '*The Fallen Idol*. It was *marvellous*. The boy acted so beautifully.'

'You seem very friendly with the Milners these days.' John Hallam pushed his chair back. 'I have work to do.'

In Madge's absence Charles cleared away the dishes. All the time he was thinking about his mother's lie. She couldn't have been at the movies with Regine, because Regine had been in bed with him.

He opened the French windows that gave onto the ledge beside the canal and leaned against the lintel. His mother went out onto the ledge itself and lit a cigarette. Its red coal glowed intermittently in the dark.

'The evenings are drawing in,' she said.

It was difficult to see, but he was almost sure tears glittered in her eyes. Something was even more wrong than usual.

'How was school today?' She threw it out casually.

He shrugged. 'Fine.'

'You know – I was thinking about Freddie this morning. You must miss him; he was always so fond of you.'

It was so much more complicated than that. He said nothing, merely continued to stare down at the treacly water.

'Did you ever think he was – too fond of you?'

'How could he be *too* fond of me?' Charles managed to sound puzzled. 'He was like an uncle to me,' he added, hoping that would shut her up.

His mother turned to look at him. 'Yes ... of course ...' Her voice trailed off.

Charles shut his eyes for a second. He wanted to get away before this all became even more difficult, but remained rooted to the spot.

'I saw Mr Carnforth the other day. He seemed a little worried that you – that things at school – you might be finding it all a bit difficult this year. Now that you're studying for the Higher School Certificate.' She said it as if in quotations, as if it were an incomprehensible foreign phrase.

'Really?' Charles managed a drawl. 'Where on earth did you see Carnforth?'

'*Mr* Carnforth, darling! We just ran into each other.'

'It's always odd, isn't it, coincidences like that,' said Charles dreamily. 'One always feels it was *meant*, somehow.'

'I invited him to dinner next week. Wednesday, you won't forget, will you.'

'Doesn't matter if I do, I'm always here, aren't I.' This time he couldn't prevent some of the antagonism coming through.

'Oh, darling, you don't mind, do you. I thought it might be rather helpful for you.'

'I've told you before, he's an *art* teacher. How on earth could he help me with my work?'

'I just thought ... your father's so busy and preoccupied ... and there are things you could talk over ... problems ...'

A chilly breeze licked the surface of the canal. The over-grown bushes on the far side rustled and sighed. 'It's cold. I'm going in,' said Charles.

She followed him upstairs. By the drawing-room door she turned: 'Stay and talk to me, Charles. Tell me what you've been doing.' She sat down on her sofa and switched on the wireless.

'I had tea with Regine.' He eyed his mother, wondering, as if from a great distance, how she would react. Her eyes opened wide. She didn't say anything.

'Look, Mama, I've got loads of prep to do. I must get on.'

'You're not angry with me, Charles?' Her timid smile was unbearable, a knife in his heart.

'Of course not. Why should I be?'

'I only thought—'

'I've got *loads* of prep to do, Mama ...' He turned away and climbed the rickety ladder to the upper floors.

In his room it was impossible to settle. He had to talk to someone: Oliver, it could only be Oliver. He couldn't use the telephone, it was in his father's study, so he crept down the ladder again, past the drawing-room door – closed, for once, he could hear the Home Service droning away – and out up the hill to the phone box on the corner.

'I did it.'

'You did? *Really*? I didn't think you would!' He could hear the laughter in Oliver's voice. 'Did it work?'

'Not really.'

'But you did *do* it.'

'Yes.'

'You're not fibbing. You did fuck her?'

'*Yes*.'

Oliver's laugh exploded down the line. 'You've pipped me to the post and you sound as if you didn't even bloody enjoy it!'

'I didn't *not* enjoy it exactly.'

'Well, go on. Tell me the details!'

But Charles didn't want to talk about it and went on the offensive. 'I thought you said *you'd* had a woman!'

'That was a tart. That only half counts. You stuffed a real woman – an *older woman*.'

Charles leaned his forehead against the grimy glass of the kiosk. 'My mother was home late today. She's – I think she's seeing Carnforth.'

There was silence at the other end. Then: 'Have you gone completely raving mad?'

It was impossible to explain. He felt very tired. 'Never mind,' he said, 'I'll tell you tomorrow.'

'My father says he'll take us to Twickenham on Saturday, to see the rugby.'

seventeen

MURRAY THOUGHT THEY'D BE looking for Stan Pinelli the day after they'd found the bloodstained shirt in Kenneth Barker's bedroom, but Plumer said they should wait until the blood analysis came back and in the meantime Murray was sent off to tie up some work on another case. When the analysis came, it was inconclusive. The blood belonged to group O, which was Frederick Buckingham's; but a third of the population belonged to that group and it was also the same as Ken Barker's.

'Surely we have to interview Pinelli, sir?' Murray couldn't understand why Plumer was dragging his feet.

'Yes, yes, we'll go. Find out where he's living. But after that I want you to pay another visit to – ' and he reeled off a string of names.

'But we've talked to them already.'

'Well, have another go. It's arm-twisting time.'

It took a while to track Pinelli down, but eventually Murray found out he was staying with his sister in a dilapidated terrace off Vallance Road in Bethnal Green. Luckily Stan was in, so they invited him down to the station.

* * * * *

Murray felt at home in the interviewing room. The twenty-year-old who faced them seemed equally inured to the dirty walls, the battered furniture and the smell of stale tobacco smoke, metal and a distant memory of disinfectant.

'Kenneth Barker – he was a mate of yours, wasn't he.' It wasn't a question. They knew Stanley Pinelli and Kenneth Barker had been at school together – or more accurately had truanted together – had been to Borstal together and had more recently been caught red-handed burgling a pawnbroker's shop in Poplar. God knows how they'd avoided another spell inside; some bleeding-heart magistrate no doubt.

The young man nodded in answer to Plumer's statement. His white-as-junket face, a gaunt face, with features too large – bony nose, full lips, soulful eyes – was handsome in its own way. His quiff of black hair had disintegrated into long, greasy strands.

'Your friend Kenneth Barker's been murdered,' Plumer said with a deliberately nasty smile. 'What can you tell us about that?'

'Dunno nothing about it,' muttered Pinelli. His eyes swivelled off towards the floor and he chewed the side of his mouth.

'Must have upset you,' commented Plumer quietly. 'Friends all your life and now he's had his head shot off.'

'I'd like a smoke.'

'Of course, Stan.' Plumer offered him the packet. The young man's hands were shaking as he extracted the cigarette and lit it.

The fear interested Murray. 'You know who killed him, don't you.'

'*No.*'

'Tell us what you do know. You must know something about it. Ken told you everything, I expect, he hadn't any secrets from you.'

Stan was slumped low in his chair, chin on chest, and maintained a sullen silence.

'Come on,' said Murray, growing impatient and thinking a little more menace wouldn't come amiss. 'We're not accusing you of murdering your mate. But we want to know who did. Look – your best mate's been shot. You're not going to let them get away with it, are you?'

Stan's eyelids flickered. He was genuinely scared, Murray was sure of it. If they shouted at him at bit … but the guv'nor wouldn't hear of that. He played by the book. He was always quiet, formal, polite even.

'Kenneth Barker was one of Mosley's lads. Are you a black-shirt too?'

Stan shook his head.

'Last January you were arrested and cautioned after a fight in Ridley Road market.'

'It was just a rumble with the Jew boys, weren' it,' muttered Stan.

'But you say you're not one of Mosley's lot.'

'Nah.'

'But Barker was.'

Stan acknowledged this with a minimal shrug.

Plumer intervened. 'What we're interested in is who murdered Ken. Who d'you know who's got a weapon?'

Stan sat up, eyes wide. 'I don't know nothing about it.'

At this point Plumer, his expression sphinx-like, produced the shirt. 'What do you know about the shirt? How did it come to be covered with blood and in Barker's bedroom?'

Stan, whiter than ever, denied all knowledge of the shirt.

'Ken's mother thought it was yours.'

A spasm of fury distorted the bony face for a moment and Murray hoped Stan wouldn't be paying the old woman a visit, but Stanley recovered himself and produced a sullen mutter: 'I lent it 'im, didn't I.'

'That doesn't account for the blood.'

'He cut himself shaving or something.'

This was bordering on the insolent. Murray felt like landing him one on that big conk of a nose of his.

'When did you last see Barker?'

Stan launched into a long-winded tale of evenings spent drinking and afternoons at the snooker table. 'Hard to see where you get the money from when you're not working,' Murray commented sarcastically.

But it was Plumer who leaned forward and said: 'I suggest you consider seriously the danger you yourself may be in. I believe you know more than you're telling us. Whatever Kenneth did, he ended up as the victim of a cold-blooded, deliberate murder. There must be a reason for that.'

But Stan insisted he knew nothing. His memory was a blank page. They'd nothing on him. He hadn't even been arrested. There was no alternative but to let him go.

Afterwards Murray said: 'We could have pushed him harder on the blackshirt angle. And what about the Milners' friends, sir? You thought they were important to begin with.'

Plumer's glance flickered away. 'Go easy on all that, son.'

'But I told you what Mrs Milner said about this man, Arthur Carnforth. A fascist, she said. And Ken Barker was mixed up with them, too.'

Plumer shook his head. 'Go round the East End – talk to the people we know.'

Noel Valentine's gallery was unlike any place Murray had seen. The paintings on the white walls were not wispily romantic canvases by John Piper or the tougher realism of a Paul Nash, but alienating abstracts from New York and Europe. Murray thought the pictures were a joke, but he liked the white walls and black sofa; very clean and modern.

Murray hadn't been expecting Valentine to be quite so short or so bald, but as he shook Noel's plump hand, he found himself responding to the dealer's smile. The bright eyes were full of curiosity. For once here was someone who actually seemed to be looking forward to an interview with the police.

Behind its modernist frontage the house was unchanged from Georgian times. Noel Valentine led Murray up narrow stairs to the small, cluttered first-floor rooms. A young woman was typing in one; the other, Noel's office, was one of the untidiest Murray had seen. The two men were only able to sit down after Noel had removed stacks of papers, books and art journals and catalogues from chairs to floor, after which he placed himself behind his desk and looked at Murray. 'How can I help you? It's about Freddie, I assume. Poor old Freddie – he was so full of vitality, it's almost impossible to think of him as dead. Marvellous character. And completely infuriating and irritating. Hardly surprising someone bumped him off in the end.'

'Why do you say that?' To Murray, the jokey manner was slightly suspect. He wasn't accustomed to people who talked like that. And although he had no reason to suppose that Valentine's gallery was anything other than above board, he cynically wondered about the possibilities for fraud behind a front such as this smart little operation.

'Freddie liked to throw a spanner into other people's works. Then he'd step back and watch the explosion.'

'Can you give me an example?'

Noel stood up, accidentally kicking over a pile of books. He moved round the various obstacles to reach the door, where he shouted at the typist to bring them coffee. 'She's temporary. My real secretary, Dinah Wentworth, she's gone off to the Courtauld. Unfortunately. This girl's hopeless.' He sat down again.

'Give you an example? I don't know if I can, off-hand. He'd introduce people and see how they got on. Of course sometimes he didn't like the result. Sometimes he'd be jealous if two of his great friends got on too well. He couldn't resist doing it, he'd get carried away and afterwards regret it. Say, if a man and a woman who'd met each other through him started an affair, or something like that. Then he'd have sort of lost control, wouldn't he. Or for instance, I know for a fact he didn't like the way Arthur Carnforth was worming his way into the Hallam household. He thought he was trying to get them to stop Freddie seeing the boy.'

'Arthur Carnforth? You mean the fascist?'

'The very same. I see you know all about him. A rather gruesome character in my opinion. I mean to say, sticking up for Hitler these days is just a bit beyond the pale, *non*? But then he's crazy. They put him in a bin during the war. Neville actually suggested I might have a look at some of his daubs. He *actually* wanted me to do an exhibition! Christ! Have you *seen* them! They're worse than Hitler's own efforts. He wrote stuff for the Mosleyites before the war, under another name, I think. Freddie couldn't stand him, "I'd like to murder Carnforth" he used to say.'

The hopeless girl brought them cups of coffee.

'I'm very interested in what you say about Mr Carnforth. But can you tell me more about the party, the Sunday Mr Buckingham died?'

'One can turn up any time after three, and most of the guests have usually drifted away by about seven o'clock or half past. I got there at four. I know that, because I'd been expecting a transatlantic telephone call at 3.30. We spoke for quite a while and when it was finished I checked the time, to see if it was too early to pop over to Reggie's. I knew Alan Wentworth would probably be there and he was. We had a chat about a programme we've been working on together, on the air next week: "Surrealism, aftermath or new dawn?". I remember Freddie talking to Ian Roxburgh. He's a dark horse. Spent the war in the Far East and still seems to have a lot of contacts there. Business interests.' Noel paused. 'Perhaps I shouldn't say this, but – well, he approached me about some Chinese art works. It's not my area, but I do rather wonder how he got hold of them. According to Reggie he'd become very friendly with Freddie. And then there was Vivienne Evanskaya – Freddie finally managed to get her along. Poor old Reggie. She'd wanted it so much, and now ... mind you, Reggie's not one to give up. Never say die, that's Reggie. What a woman! No lack of enterprise there!'

Murray frowned. He didn't like to hear Regine spoken of in that way.

Noel went blithely on. 'Freddie was also fluttering around Vivienne's son, of course, the one who looks as if he ought to be Jean Cocteau's muse. What a dirty old bastard Freddie was, really. But I expect the boy can look after himself. No flies on him, as the Americans say. Been round the block a few times already, I should think. The American way with language, don't you love it? They're so much less constipated than the British.'

'Thank you very much, Mr Valentine. You've been very helpful.'

'Have I? I can't see how anything I've said gets you nearer to finding out who killed poor old Freddie. It's all gossip, really, well, not gossip exactly, just the natural friction of social intercourse. Friendship networks are full of rivalries and minor hatreds, aren't they. In fact, when you think about it, friendship is a very odd human activity indeed. Do animals have friendships? Perhaps the primates do, some of them. Or are human friendships merely part of the struggle for survival, necessary in an economic social order such as orang-utans and chimps don't have?'

* * * * *

Murray travelled straight from St James to Swiss Cottage and as he came out of the tube station, his mind was less on the interview he hoped shortly to be having with Dorothy Redfern, and more on Noel Valentine's throwaway characterisation of Regine Milner as somehow a bit too racy. She was certainly flirtatious. She'd passed on bits of information too, but possibly it was all to put him off the scent. Perhaps the Milners had some guilty secret, were more involved in all this than they'd let on. And after all, she was nothing, really, but a silly, shallow, middle-class hostess. She'd probably married Milner for money, he decided bitterly. God knows the man wasn't much to look at.

And he wished he'd never taken Irene to that Italian restaurant Regine had recommended – Bertorelli's. Irene had hated it, she hated oily foreign food, she said.

Regine had dazzled him. That was the only word for it. He must pull himself together.

Dorothy Redfern watched Terence Cole play at the small sandpit on legs, which stood in a corner of the consulting room. The six-year-old made the miniature dolls fight, hitting one repeatedly with a second, then forcing it into the sand. 'He's dead now.' He turned to look at Dorothy. He laughed. Then he threw one of the dolls on the floor. He stamped on it; it broke. He laughed again.

Dorothy watched and waited. Most of her time in the consulting room was spent in watchful silence. After her previous session with Terence, she'd said to a colleague in the coffee room, 'Terence Cole wants to kill his father.' For Dorothy took it for granted that all toddlers were thwarted murderers in the seething cauldron of love, hate and incest that was the family.

Mrs Cole looked up listlessly as Dorothy led Terence into the waiting room.

'Have you been a good boy today?'

'He's not here to be good, Mrs Cole. He's here to understand his feelings.'

Dorothy watched the departing mother and child, Terence banging about in his usual defiant way, never holding hands, clearly not 'with' his mother, who in turn ignored her son, even when he attempted to stand on one of the plant pots in the lobby, nearly bringing it crashing to the ground. Dorothy knew the woman was depressed, and the social worker had told her about the silent father who never mentioned what he'd seen at the battle of Arnhem.

All these silences, after the war. Everything back in its box, like the toys at the end of the session.

As Dorothy turned to go back to her room, the reception-ist made a face and jerked her head surreptitiously in the direc-tion of a man seated near the waiting-room door. 'He wants to see you. He's a policeman.' She spoke in an undertone, as though the information were vaguely indecent.

The young man stood up as she came up to him. He was about thirty, eager, yet guarded. He apologised for intruding on her working time, but he needed to talk to her in connection with the investigation into the death of Frederick Buckingham.

'I have about a quarter of an hour before my next appoint-ment.' She led him back to her consulting room. He looked round with interest and sat down in the seat near the window towards which she gestured and which was placed at an angle to her own. Here she interviewed parents and older patients; the toys and sandpit were nearer the door. 'How can I help you?'

'It's about the death of Freddie Buckingham. The afternoon of the night he was murdered, Mr Buckingham had been at a party you also attended.'

Dorothy watched him.

'We're asking all the guests if they had any idea what he was planning to do after he left. We've been told he left on his own, but did he mention anything, say anything that might give us a clue?'

Dorothy stared silently in front of her. She had tried several times since Regine had warned her the police might want to talk to her, to remember what had happened during the party. It was distressing to find one had forgotten so much. 'It's difficult at a party, isn't it. You talk to one person and then another, I can remember more about what I talked about than what other people were doing and saying. I hardly spoke to Freddie anyway. I didn't know him well. A group was gathered round him, I was on the edge of it at one point ... quite a few of us had been to the opera, to see Schwarzkopf, you know. But after that I wasn't with him at all.' She was trying to visualise the shifting human kaleidoscope of that afternoon. 'I'm not very fond of parties, they always seem to be the same. The only time – well, I was talking to Reggie, and Freddie came up to us. I had a feeling he wanted to get her on his own, so I went to talk to someone else.'

'And how did he seem?'

'Oh, Freddie's always the same. Very well defended.'

Murray frowned. 'I beg your pardon?'

Dorothy smiled. 'Defended. That's a term we psycho-analysts use. What I mean is, Freddie's flamboyant manner was a mask, psychological armour, it defended him from real inti-macy with other people and it prevented other people from *really* getting to know him. It was a kind of false persona, a false self. At one level it worked because it was amusing and people liked him, but men like him pay a price in terms of inner lone-liness.'

'You mean he wasn't very happy?'

'I don't think he'd have seen it like that.'

'But he didn't have any enemies?'

'I'm sure he had enemies! When I say people liked him, I meant at this sort of superficial, party level. But theatrical circles are full of rivalries and hatreds, or so I'm told. And Freddie could be quite spiteful too, at times. I've heard him tell some really very cruel anecdotes – merely amusing to him, I'm sure, part of his performance, but yes, I'm sure he had enemies.' At once she regretted her words, because she could see that the detective had latched on to them, and she did not actually know of anyone who might have harboured murderous thoughts towards the dead photographer. Quickly she added: 'But by that I don't mean that anyone was seriously out to kill him. I should have thought that would be most unlikely. The fact is, I really know very little about him. He was Reggie's friend, not mine. In fact she was quite seduced by him. Of course, as a homosexual, his relations with women were defective. Homosexuals are full of hatred – there's a lot of killing there, somewhere.'

'*Killing*?'

'Oh, not literally. But homosexual men have never got over unconsciously wanting to kill the father and have sole rights over the mother. The result is their actual relations with real women are based on a fantasy.'

These ideas were too outlandish for Murray to grapple with, but unable to resist an opportunity of talking about Regine, he said: 'Mrs Milner was very upset – his death was a great blow.'

'It's very inconvenient for her. He attracted people she wanted to meet to her Sundays. Her social life will suffer.'

Murray protested. 'But she was genuinely distraught.'

Dorothy smiled enigmatically. 'Reggie is one of those women who doesn't really *believe* in homosexuality. They think that their sexual attraction is such that it is capable of converting even the most confirmed invert.'

Murray stared at her. He longed to ask more, but her strange

notions were making him feel quite angry. She used impossible
language and her remarks about Mrs Milner were gratuitously
offensive.

Noticing his reaction to her words, she added: 'I shouldn't
have said that. Don't misunderstand me. Regine Milner's my
friend and of course she's enormously upset. It was a terrible
thing to happen.'

'But you're saying someone might have wanted to kill him.
Do you have any idea who?'

'I'm not really saying that, Sergeant Murray. I'm simply
stating the obvious, that men like that attract hostility for a
variety of reasons.'

'Well, we know Mr Buckingham did, don't we,' said Murray
crossly.

'I suppose it's all very frustrating, the investigation, I mean,'
said Dorothy, observing him closely. 'It isn't the obvious solution, then, that Freddie Buckingham was murdered by a thief or
someone he'd encountered casually for sex?'

'We haven't ruled it out.'

'Have you talked to Vivienne Hallam? She knew him very
well, though I think they didn't see so much of each other any
more. People say she used to be absolutely devoted to him.
When I say that men like Freddie invite hostility, I didn't mean
they don't arouse devotion too. That's destructive too, of course,
to lavish love on an individual who is incapable of returning it.
That sort of love can turn to hatred in the end.'

Murray uncrossed and recrossed his legs as he struggled
with a half-formed idea. 'As a psychologist, Dr Redfern—'

'I'm not a psychologist,' said Dorothy repressively. 'I'm a
psychiatrist, that is to say I am medically trained; and I am also
a trained psychoanalyst.'

Murray apologised, but he had no idea what the differences
were. 'You observe people, behaviour, you help people with ...

people who have problems with their nerves. I was hoping you'd be able to give us some insights into who might have had a motive – in this case.' He petered out rather at the end, as he saw her almost satirical expression, amused and sceptical, yet at the same time somehow disapproving.

'I already have, haven't I?' she said enigmatically.

The telephone rang. 'That means my next patient has arrived, I'm afraid.'

He was dismissed.

Murray walked back towards the tube. He hadn't taken to Dorothy. She reminded him somehow of the way the clergy talked, taking themselves so very seriously as if they were preaching to you from a higher plane. He puzzled over what she'd said, but he couldn't make head or tail of it. She'd almost hinted that the ballet dancer had hated the queer. When love turns to hate – that could certainly be a motive. But it was ridiculous to think of the famous dancer gunning him down on the Heath. And then there were Noel Valentine's remarks about Carnforth ... and Carnforth and Kenneth Barker were both with the blackshirts ...

eighteen

REGINE, ARRIVING LATE, looked round the crowded Army and Navy Stores restaurant and saw Cynthia already seated in a corner. Waitresses in olive green frocks with white parlourmaids' aprons and caps hurried between the tables.

Regine relinquished her new coat – purchased with Mrs Havelock's coupons: nigger brown velour trimmed with black astrakhan at the collar, cuffs and pockets – to the manageress and sat down beside her friend.

'I'm sorry I'm late. What's happened?' For Cynthia's phone calls had been urgent.

Cynthia was marble calm.

Evesham – that red bicycle – how Cynthia wobbled along the track to the sheds where they worked ... you turned off the old Evesham road ... lost happiness never returns ... who had said that ... Cynthia had been so kind, so soothing then, when Sergei went away ...

'Ernie's all caught up in this Sidney Stanley affair at the ministry. It's all over the papers now, every day, it never stops.'

Scandal was needed more than ever when life was so drab. It was drama, excitement, the sleazy comedy of human frailty, and, best of all, the spectacle of the powerful being caught with their trousers down. It was a glorious respite from the dull anxiety of life in Austerity Britain, where day after day the news lurched from the atom bomb to black-market petrol, from the diminishing meat ration to the communist menace, between gigantic horror and petty controls, all equally beyond one's power to change.

'He's wined and dined ministers, arranged deals, promised American loans, God knows what else. And now they're saying there've been all sorts of irregularities within the department, that Stanley's been involved in bribery, it's something to do with paper allocations for some football pools firm.' As she spoke Cynthia was becoming less calm. 'Ernie's completely innocent, of course, he had nothing to do with that, but the awful thing is he's somehow got involved. I think Ernie may have been foolish, he accepted meals from this – this *spiv*, and then – well, he somehow let slip that we were going away for the weekend. He should never have mentioned it – I suppose he was worried, preoccupied, he's so overworked, you know, but – well anyway, Stanley recommended a hotel outside Exeter, very quiet, out of the way, on Dartmoor, actually, it was lovely, but when we got there, we discovered it had all been paid for. By Sidney Stanley. Can you imagine! There's proof, it's all recorded. It could come out in the press at any moment – any day. And now there's this special tribunal, to look into the whole thing, headed by some judge – Lynskey – Ernie's terrified they'll turn up the hotel bill – but he didn't know *anything* about it, he didn't *want* Stanley to pay for it – '

Regine was appalled, yet thrilled, as the words tumbled out. So they'd even been away together! If only Freddie were here to gossip with.

'He's usually so cautious.' And for a moment Cynthia looked happy. Perhaps she thought the huge risk was proof of love. Perhaps it was. But Cynthia's smile faded. She leaned forward, lowering her quiet, melodious voice still further: 'And now Ernie's being blackmailed.'

The steely waitress hovered. Cynthia opted for fish pie.

Regine said: 'Oh, Cynthia – don't have that. It'll be snoek or whalemeat. I'm going to have a nut cutlet. Much safer.'

'The letter came last week,' said Cynthia slowly. 'Ernie was to send money to a post office box address. Cash.'

'Did he?'

'I said he should go to the police, but he felt it was best to pay, he said he wanted to protect me, didn't want my name dragged through the mud.'

Nor his, thought Regine cynically. 'If it came out that you were his mistress it'd mean the end of his career, wouldn't it.'

Cynthia said in a low voice: 'Now with this other scandal it may come out anyway and it will all seem doubly, triply bad – that he took a bribe to entertain his *mistress*.'

'D'you think ... could it have been Stanley himself? Could he be the blackmailer?'

Cynthia frowned: 'I don't know ... blackmail is a different sort of thing, isn't it, from being a con man, spiv, whatever he is. But you know, it's not just us.'

'You mean *other people* are being blackmailed?'

'No, no, I mean it isn't just about our personal situation. Ernie's devastated because of what it'll do to the government. You know how the Tories are always going on and on about bureaucracy and controls, how they say that's what socialism is, all petty rules and regulations, that Labour's all about priggish puritans wanting to spoil everyone's fun. Of course it's nonsense, but if they're shown to be taking what amounts to bribes, and breaking the rules the Board of Trade was specifically set up to protect – that's what the department's about, you see, to ensure fair play in a time of shortages – but now it'll look as though it's one rule for ordinary folk, while people like him can break the rules with impunity. Only he didn't mean to break the rules. He didn't even realise he was breaking the rules. You do see? It's not just a case of misconduct or foolishness; it's everything he's built his life on.'

Regine couldn't help feeling that the minister had been at the very least naive – the mounting government scandals seemed due to thoughtless, silly accidents or gullible politicians, rather than deliberate wrongdoing or malice. But that was irrelevant now. 'You have to go to the police,' she said.

'Ernie won't hear of it.'

'I could talk to the detective, the younger one, you know, who's investigating the – the Freddie business. He really is quite kind and sympathetic.'

'No! Regine – don't do that. Don't tell anyone. Please! What earthly good would that do? It'd only make matters worse.'

Regine did not see how matters could be much worse for the adulterous couple, especially for Cynthia. 'Just informally. He might have some idea of something you could do, some way of approaching the situation.'

Cynthia shook her head. 'I'd much rather you didn't.'

Regine tried to look on the bright side. 'Perhaps from your point of view it could even be better this way. If it weren't for his career Ernie could leave his wife and have a fresh start.'

Cynthia pressed her lips together. Her marble calm was cracking and Regine was afraid she was going to cry. 'He doesn't *want* a fresh start. The Labour Party means everything to him!'

Regine put out a hand, touched Cynthia's arm. 'Have you told him about the baby yet?'

Cynthia flinched away from her friend's touch. 'I haven't seen much of him since all this blew up. I have to pick the right moment, and he's so worried—'

'It's four months now. It'll begin to show soon.' Sixteen weeks; now it really was too late to do anything about it; but Cynthia was determined anyway. 'Cynthia – I'm so sorry. But however worried he is you *have* to tell him. And it would be much better if he did go to the police about the letters. It's separate from whatever's happening at his ministry. It might even *help*,' Regine added, 'because it shows someone's determined to damage him, that he has enemies. And if he knows about your condition he'll have to make a choice.'

Cynthia shook her head. 'That's just what I don't want. I don't want him to have to choose.'

Regine said: 'Whatever you decide, I'll help you.' But she felt completely impotent. Cynthia would need money, but how would she ever be able to persuade Neville to stump up any cash? He hadn't inherited Lydia's fortune in order to support fallen women.

The waitress set down their plates of food. Regine poked her cutlet. She hadn't meant to, but she blurted it out: 'Eugene has turned up.'

Cynthia looked completely blank. 'Eugene?'

'You know – my Shanghai husband.'

For a moment astonishment displaced Cynthia's anxiety. 'But he's *dead*!'

'He isn't. He's come back. And the awful thing is – ' And the frightful confession of bigamy tumbled out.

Cynthia's faint frown was puzzled rather than disapproving. 'I don't understand. Why didn't you wait just those few extra months?'

Even now, Regine hadn't quite told the truth. It had been more than six months. She should have waited a whole year more. 'I don't know,' she said. 'He wasn't actually reported missing, but it didn't seem to matter then – you know, in the war, we were all a bit more impulsive, don't you think?' (But not Cynthia, not then.) 'Of course I thought he was dead. He was a – an adventurer, Cynthia, and the Japs had taken over, and he was always sailing close to the wind, he'd have done something stupid, got himself killed – you don't know what he was like. And also, well, I wasn't sure Neville would come up to scratch to begin with – there was that woman at the War Office who was after him too, don't you remember, so when he did propose ...'

Cynthia smiled. 'You're impatient, Reggie. You don't like waiting for things.' She added: 'I don't mean you're greedy. I think you always think things will slip away, so you grab ...'

Regine felt her face hot, thinking of Charles; greedy there, too, seizing the moment, another painful mistake ... 'I've met Eugene once. I thought that might be the end of it, but he insisted on seeing me again – it's as if it's a game to him – he thinks it's amusing. At the same time there's something desperate about him.'

'Don't you think you ought to take legal advice?'

'Hilary Jordan's our solicitor. I can hardly confide in him!'

'You could go to someone else.'

'Perhaps he'll go back to Ireland soon. He says he's going to. And he hasn't threatened to tell Neville or anything, it's just that ... he scares me. He's so shabby now, on his uppers, you know.'

Cynthia wiped her lips with her napkin. 'Yes. Shabbiness would scare you, wouldn't it, Reggie.'

n i n e t e e n

THE HEATH, STILL WOUNDED and scarred with trenches and mounds and barbed wire, was fading, greens dying into browns and greys. Cato whirled ahead of her. She walked through the silver birch glade towards the ponds. She wasn't due at the café yet.

Then, as he'd done before, Eugene appeared suddenly from among the trees. The moment before the path had been empty, but now he stood there. He smiled. The collar of his old linen jacket was turned up and met the edge of his hat with its wide brim, and he'd wound a scarf round his neck on this chilly day. He must be cold – a down-and-out without a coat. How did he know she'd be here? He must have been following her, tracking her, spying on her. She was terrified he'd come to the house.

He fell into step beside her. Cato came gambolling towards them, barking and waggling his bottom and with a grin on his slavering mouth. 'I told you I had a way with dogs. He remembers me, see.'

'When are you going back to Ireland?' She'd blurted it out without meaning to.

'That's not very friendly, now, is it, Roisin? Will you be so pleased to see the back of me then?'

Her headscarf was loose. As she walked along she pulled it

tighter and redid the knot under her chin. 'Is everything all right? You look tired.'

He smiled his crooked, boyish smile. 'To be honest I'm in a spot of trouble. But then I'm no stranger to trouble.' He spoke lightly enough. 'And it's good of you to be concerned.'

They crossed over a stream and up the hill, then down a slope and up again until they rounded a corner and Kenwood House came into view, neglected, grey and bleakly shuttered.

As they paced along he talked about the old days, and he was as he'd been then, trying to spin a yarn, to seduce an audience, any audience, into laughter. How carefree he'd been as he worked the foreign concession. The world was his friend ... he and Freddie had in a way been two of a kind. She'd liked men like that, the risky ones. Only now it didn't work any more. There was no spring in his walk, no fun to be had, only a shifty con man in an uncertain, jittery mood.

'What happened to you in the war?'

'It's a long story. I'll not bore you with that.' The smile was gone. His expression hardened. He put his hand on her elbow as they passed beyond the house and into another muddy meadow. 'The thing is, darling, I'm a bit short of money.'

She said hurriedly: 'I brought ten pounds, I know it's not an enormous amount, but I don't want Neville to notice. You understand, don't you.'

'I wouldn't want your husband to think I'm a sponger, I was never a sponger, was I now, darling. I wouldn't want him to think I *existed*.' He held her arm tighter. 'I wonder sometimes if I do.' It seemed to amuse him. 'Do you believe I exist, my love?'

She tried to laugh off his strange mood. 'Oh, Eugene—'

The smile was gone. He stopped and pulled her round roughly to face him. 'I don't want your charity, Regine, thank you kindly all the same. It's the necklace I want, the jade necklace I gave you.'

'Necklace?' Her heart beat frantically. She managed to pull away from him.

'You know what I'm talking about. I told you it was valuable. When you left, I told you to leave it behind – you'd be safely back in England and I'd need it more than you. It was my insurance policy.'

She shook her head. 'But I *did* leave it. I left it in Shanghai.'

Coiled like a cold green snake in Freddie's dressing-table drawer …

'Now, Roisin, you won't lie to me, will you.'

She swallowed. 'I'm not lying.' And then to have found it in the house in Markham Square.

They were in an overgrown, bosky copse. The brambles coiled above and round them and dense rhododendron bushes crowded in. She was alone with him, no one for miles around. Even Cato had disappeared.

'But you see when I went round to the flat it wasn't there.'

'You didn't find it? Oh God – that's extraordinary – someone must have stolen it – that houseboy we had. He was light-fingered.'

'No, no, that won't do, Roisin.'

Fear sent her on the offensive. 'If it was so valuable, you shouldn't have left it with me. It should have been in the bank—'

'Oh – ' He laughed bitterly. She had made him angrier. 'They'd have smelled a rat as soon as look at it.'

'I didn't take it with me,' she said obstinately. And that at least was true. It wasn't there. She hadn't decided whether to leave it or not, it was so beautiful, but when she opened the box it was empty, and she was afraid to tell him. Freddie knew about it, but it hadn't occurred to her then that … 'You don't think Freddie could have – he was still living in the flat …'

'You didn't *tell* Freddie about it, did you? Now, that would have been a stupid thing to do.'

Of course she'd told Freddie. She'd trusted Freddie. She'd said goodbye to Freddie before she'd discovered the jade had gone. She'd been in a hurry to catch the boat and maybe she hadn't looked properly, or the houseboy or …

'You're not holding out on me, Roisin. You wouldn't do that now, would you. Because you see I did ask Freddie at the time and he swore he hadn't seen any necklace and he thought you'd taken it with you.'

Freddie had lied too. Perhaps he'd been frightened of Eugene. Eugene was becoming unpredictable, already by then there was more of his temper, less of his laughs …

'Well, I didn't.'

She turned back. 'Let's get out of here. It's so gloomy. There's hardly any light. And I don't know where Cato's got to.'

She was afraid he'd do something, try to stop her, hurt her even. But he shrugged and they soon came out onto open ground again. When they reached the place where the paths diverged she gestured to the right. 'I'm going home now,' she said. Cato rushed towards them from the undergrowth and snuffled joyfully round Eugene. She made a grab for him, and managed to snap on the lead at the first attempt. He shook his head, pranced and whined, but she jerked him to heel.

Eugene called after her: 'Think about it, darling. I have to have that necklace somehow or other. I'll ring you in a day or two.'

When she reached home, she sat over the fire as the light ebbed beyond the window, and she was still there when Phil arrived, banging his bike in the hallway. 'Anyone home?'

'I'm in here.'

'Oh!' Startled to find her in the dark, he switched on the light, which glared cruelly down.

'I think I must have fallen asleep,' she lied.

'Are you all right?'

'Of course. I went for such a long walk with Cato, I'm feeling a bit tired.'

'I'll get you a cup of tea.'

She knew it was mad, but she had to see Charles. The Wednesday after that Wednesday he hadn't turned up. She'd frightened him away. He was regretting the whole thing. But she had to see him. And this way she'd kill two birds with one stone. She'd renew her efforts to make friends with Vivienne.

Behind the scaffolding, the house was still full of dust and rubble, everything exposed. The workmen were on the roof now.

Charles himself opened the door. There was an awkward moment. They stared at each other.

'My mother isn't here. She's out.'

'You didn't come to see me last week!' Regine could have bitten the words back as soon as she'd spoken; too flirtatious and at the same time reproachful, begging, the woman rejected.

His glance flickered away. 'Do come in anyway.'

'Oh no, I don't want to disturb you.'

'Come in,' he insisted. He ushered her into the dust-sheeted drawing room. 'God knows where she is. With Mr Carnforth, probably. Can I get you a cup of tea?'

'No thank you, I won't stay. I just came to see your mother.'

'She and Carnforth are trying to get me interested in religion now.' He attempted a laugh, but he sounded a bit desperate, she thought. 'If only Freddie was still here – he'd have told Carnforth where to get off.'

Puzzled and disturbed, she could think of nothing to say. It was all so peculiar.

They heard the key in the lock and the front door opened.

'Oh Christ,' muttered the boy.

Vivienne looked paler than ever. She undid her dark red coat to reveal a formal woollen dress with diamond clips at the neck, also maroon – a terrible colour, though it suited her pallor.

Freddie had always been so critical of one's clothes. He'd always known exactly what was right and what wasn't, what worked and what didn't.

Regine stood up. 'I was just leaving. I came round to see … how you were … well, I was going to ask you – I was hoping you'll come next Sunday … I think lots of people will be there who knew Freddie. I cancelled the one at the beginning of November, so this one will be rather special, I hope.'

'Would you like some tea?' said Vivienne in a chilly voice.

'No thank you. I must go – it's getting late.' She couldn't understand why Vivienne was so hostile. 'It must be so difficult living in all this dust,' she said. 'Wouldn't you be better off staying in a hotel while all this is going on?' Oh, but that was the wrong thing to say too. Vivienne looked colder than ever.

'John wouldn't hear of that. It's costing a fortune already. And someone has to be here to see what they're doing. Anyway, he doesn't really notice. He's out all day – and you don't seem to mind either, Charles, do you.'

'It's quite fun, actually. Look – I'm going upstairs if you'll excuse me.'

The door banged. Vivienne lit a cigarette.

'He's such a nice boy. He has beautiful manners.' Regine hoped this would soften Vivienne.

'He's too old for his age.' Vivienne puffed greedily. 'He came to see you, didn't he. I suppose he talked about Freddie.'

Regine swallowed. 'Not really,' she lied, 'I helped him a bit with his French. Does he talk to you a lot about Freddie, then? You were close to Freddie …'

Vivienne's face was rigid. 'Oh, Charles never talks to me.

And I didn't see nearly so much of Freddie – not since the war – '

⚬ That hadn't been the impression Freddie gave. Perhaps his effort to get Vivienne to her Sunday had been more to regain the dancer's friendship than to please her, the hostess, his other best girl. 'I really must go,' she said.

As she walked back up Regent's Park Road she heard footsteps thudding behind her. When Charles caught up with her, he was out of breath. 'Look – I'm sorry if I was rude. I – I need to talk to you – about Freddie.'

'Well, you can come and see me tomorrow.'

'Okay, I will.'

Vivienne sat on the sofa and smoked. Then she lit another cigarette and paced up and down. Two, three cigarettes. She'd heard Charles leave the house. She inhaled voraciously and took the cigarette out of her mouth between finger and thumb, like a navvy, her gestures quite lacking the elegance an onlooker might have expected.

The front door banged again. She called Charles's name, but he didn't answer and she heard the creaking sound the ladder made as he climbed it.

How dare that woman come here. During the war she hadn't noticed ... Freddie was called up and she was always dancing ... oh, those wonderful times ... *Giselle* ... her great role ... but after the war it all fell apart and she wasn't dancing any more ... that dreadful evening at Sadler's Wells; nearly two years ago. It had turned very cold. It wasn't even warm inside the theatre, although the golden glow embraced you after the freezing chill outside. They had a box. How she'd longed to be on the stage, to be anywhere but in the box ... the audience could see her, they'd pity her ... in the interval she wouldn't mingle with Freddie and Charles in the bar and the foyer and now in retrospect she imagined amid the greetings and smiles – effusive, almost frantic, as if every member of the audience were desperate to enjoy things again after the long years of war ... and the smell of mothballs, they'd all got their evening dress out again ... and the knowing looks of Freddie's friends as they looked Charles over. Worst of all, Freddie must have told everyone she was there, for at the end of the interval the audience gradually realised where she was, standing and turning as one in her direction and there was applause that Freddie must have somehow organised, and she'd hated it, shrinking away at the back of the box ... and all the while it had been Regine this, Regine that. And John didn't like her seeing Freddie anyway.

Arthur was right. Freddie had used her. He'd only had eyes for Charles – she realised that now – but how could she have been so blind, not to have noticed – to have made herself not notice, because ...

But if only it had all been different – as it was in the beginning, in the old days, before Freddie went to Shanghai, before Charles was born, when they were all really young.

Nothing had been the same, ever again. He'd gone off to China, chasing that stupid young dancer ... and then he'd had the gall to bring the redhead round to visit ... that day he'd brought the Milner woman round ... that was the day she'd realised she *hated* Freddie ... she'd only agreed to go to that wretched party because Freddie nagged and nagged her ... and now Regine bloody Milner had got her claws into Charles. She ground her cigarette out in the ashtray.

She climbed the ladder in her high heels, unafraid, turning her knees out and springing sure-footedly from rung to rung. Fury revived her dancer's energy, when usually these days she was so tired and lethargic.

She knocked on her son's door, but pushed it open before he'd answered. He looked up from his books.

'I don't want you to go round to the Milners' again. She's a very unsuitable person for you to be ... visiting.'

The two marble masks looked at each other, but their eyes didn't meet. 'I wasn't going to, Mama.' Charles was at his most languid. 'But she did help me with my French.'

Charles on the doorstep said: 'Can we go for a walk? I need some fresh air.'

So he didn't want to come in. But she couldn't insist. She fetched her new coat. 'We'll walk up towards Jack Straw's Castle. There's a garden along here I want to show you. Freddie used to take me there.'

Now he was here he was awkward and silent. Perhaps Freddie's name would get him talking.

They turned off the main road and she briefly held his arm as they scrambled down the path, she in her high heels, to the rusty gate and the wrought-iron spiral staircase. 'Anna Pavlova the dancer lived here once. I don't know if Freddie ever visited her here. He used to sort of imply he knew her.'

Charles still wasn't talking.

At the top of the steps he followed her under a stone pergola and out onto a long colonnade. In places the stone balustrade was broken, as were some of the trellises that supported spindly, overshot climbing roses, still blooming here and there, pink, yellow and white, their shoots reaching out into thin air over a wild, overgrown garden that spread out far below. The colonnade turned a right angle, then another, a pergola at every corner, until it ended in a cul-de-sac where the stone coping had gone altogether, replaced by some flimsy wooden palings, sagging outwards. They looked down on another part of the garden at a cracked, dried-out ornamental pond. Grass grew between flagstones.

They were alone. The place was deserted. Charles stared moodily out into the grey, distant blur, spotted with rusty red roofs, of London's northern suburbs.

'Freddie and I used to come here,' she repeated. Suddenly she was overwhelmed with sadness.

'They're never going to find out who killed him, are they,' said the boy.

'I don't know. Do you mind? Is that important to you? It won't bring him back.'

'Do you mind if I smoke?' He leaned against the wall that cut off the colonnade at the end. He looked very beautiful, and older again. 'I think my mother is having an affair with Arthur Carnforth.'

A cold wave of astonishment hit her. 'An affair? What makes you think—?'

Of all things, she hadn't thought *that*. There was something about Arthur that repelled her physically. When pressed, Neville would insist on Arthur's alleged former charisma. He would insist also that Arthur wasn't queer, but to Regine his bachelor status cast a subtle doubt over his amours, even his morals; perhaps he was one of those men who preferred prostitutes, or just a loner, or afraid of marriage.

'That's very unlikely. I'm sure Vivienne wouldn't – wouldn't …' She couldn't think of a good way to put it.

'Unlikely? Because he's such a reptile? But you see, she said she'd been to the cinema with you, but it was the afternoon – it was the Wednesday before last and you were … I was at your place – with you.'

How bereft he was, beneath the blasé surface. She longed to put her arms round him.

Charles's face twisted into a sneer. It was the first time she'd seen him look so unpleasant. 'And he's always trying it on with this God stuff. It's sickening. I don't believe in God, do you?

And he's turned her against Freddie – and they're always trying to find out if Freddie – ' He didn't finish the sentence.

'Led you astray?' she said boldly.

He looked away.

'And did he?'

Charles inhaled, then blew out a plume of smoke. 'I'm not sure what that means,' he said.

twenty

PLUMER ON MONDAY MORNING was in a good humour. He had attended some social function with his superiors at the weekend. Murray wondered if a promotion was on the way, and how he would feel not to be working with the inspector any longer. It raised the question of his own promotion.

Plumer again said, in no uncertain terms, that the whole Mosley blackshirt element in the Buckingham case was a distraction, but Murray was determined not to let it drop completely. He arranged to meet his Special Branch mate, Detective Sergeant James McGovern, in a café on the Whitechapel Road.

When Murray arrived, McGovern was seated in front of a large white mug of tea. His mousy hair, pale face and indeterminate features helped him pass unnoticed in the places he frequented as part of his job. For he was the Special Branch intellectual. His job was to know what made them tick: the BUF, the Reds, the IRA. He spent his days reading leaflets, communiqués and theoretical works and his evenings sitting in the back rows of political meetings in draughty halls and in shabby rooms above pubs. He followed noisy demonstrations and was a silent participant at party conferences. It was a lonely job. His Special Branch colleagues treated him as a slightly quaint boffin. And the more his morbid fascination with the ideas of extremists grew, the more isolated he became. So Paul Murray's interest was balm.

'Arthur Carnforth,' he began, 'used to be known as Peter Janeway. He wrote for fringe magazines before the war, he was one of their intellectuals. He was interned in the war and went a bit bonkers. He went all religious and became involved with a group who believed Hitler was a manifestation of the divine spirit. Hitler – the divine spirit! Can you beat it! They tried to link Christianity to their movement. It became an obsession with Carnforth and caused a lot of problems with other internees. He became depressed, tried to commit suicide and spent the rest of the war in a mental hospital.'

Murray swilled his tea round in its thick, white mug. 'Just how significant are these people now?'

'It all blew up again last year. The Jewish terrorists in Palestine, the Stern Gang, Irgun, the King David's Hotel affair, our boys getting killed, that stoked-up support for Mosley. It's fizzling out again now, though.'

Murray found it hard to believe that after the war and Hitler anyone would want to be a fascist.

'Well, they're completely irrelevant,' said McGovern, 'but the hard core – I suppose it's *because* they've been defeated – they cling more desperately to what they believe. Some people can never admit they were wrong. And then again, in a way they haven't been defeated. Not really. The poison goes underground, but it never disappears completely. Since I started this job I read this drivel all the time, you know. I can tell you, in this job – these crackpot little groups, they're unimportant, they're ludicrous, and you become completely cynical, you think, what are we doing, chasing around after a few lunatics. But at the same time it's your life, you live it and breathe it and it begins to get a hold, these people are ruthless, they want to take over the world, some of them still think they will come to power in the end and so you begin to think so too. You know what they say: "*Wir kommen wieder*", we shall return. And sometimes I think they will – in a different form, possibly.'

'What about Ken Barker?'

'They're always falling out, splintering, they feud all the time. Still – it doesn't usually come to murder. Your boss could be right. It could have more to do with the underworld.'

'Would he have known Carnforth?'

McGovern shrugged again. 'Might have. Hard to say. Probably not. I told you, Carnforth fancied himself as one of the brains of the movement. Those at the top pretend they don't know what's going on further down, they wash their hands of the violence. But there aren't many of them, so, yes, they could have met.'

'The same weapon was used in both murders,' persisted Murray. 'It must have something to do with these people. But the guv'nor doesn't want to know. He's adamant. We're not to follow it up. He doesn't know I'm talking to you.'

McGovern raised an eyebrow. 'That's interesting. Why not?'

'Search me. The top brass isn't keen.'

'Really? I wonder why not. Well, I shan't mention it. And I don't mind you picking my brains. Oh, and by the way, the other one you asked about, Neville Milner, there's nothing on him. There's no record of him ever being a paid-up Mosleyite. He did visit Carnforth from time to time in the asylum. And it occurred to me, I wonder if he helped him get a job afterwards. I'm surprised at St Christopher's employing Carnforth. It's a top school, how did he get a job there with his record? Someone must have recommended him, given him a reference. Of course, schools were desperately short-staffed just after the war, but all the same …'

'You mean Milner might have lied to the school, to help an old friend.'

McGovern shrugged. 'Possibly. And he might still be a secret sympathiser for all I know. But there's nothing to suggest that.'

Murray had hoped for something damning, but after all what difference did it make? Regine Milner, comfortably married to a man who was obviously well off, what did she care about her husband's politics?

'There's a Mosley meeting up in Hampstead this evening,' said McGovern, hopefully. 'Want to come with me?'

'Okay. I'm going to pay Carnforth a visit this afternoon. I'll go round there about five – or six – and meet you afterwards.'

Arthur Carnforth lived in a small mansion block in Handel Street, near Coram's Fields. This part of Bloomsbury was sunk in seedy decay. A few yards to the south was a large bomb site. Beyond it, mean shops crouched alongside rotting Georgian terraces now doing service as rooming houses and dingy hotels, or worse.

The sooty block must have been built to house the deserving poor at the end of the last century. Murray thought it an odd place for one of the Milners' friends to live; if, that is, Carnforth could count as a friend of the Milners. He stepped inside the hallway and faced concrete stairs rising into the gloom. As he climbed he heard dim cries and muffled voices from behind the doors he passed; families in overcrowded flats, but lucky at least to have a flat. Number fifteen was on the top floor.

Arriving at the top landing, he paused to catch his breath before pressing the bell. Almost at once the door opened and a tall, fleshy man dressed in black stared at the detective.

Murray identified himself and Carnforth stood aside reluctantly. The hallway of the flat was the size of a cupboard, but led into a largish, low-ceilinged room lit by two table lamps. It was dark outside, the two windows were uncurtained and Murray watched his own reflection and Carnforth's in the panes, apparitions against the night sky.

Murray looked round at the Spartan furnishings: a modern-looking recliner covered in cracked black leatherette, a bentwood dining chair and an ancient, overstuffed armchair, a desk against the window and some open bookshelves. There were no pictures on the walls, apart from a photograph of Vivienne Hallam, seemingly torn from a magazine, pinned to one wall. A door led to a kitchenette. Murray glimpsed a sink and a Vantona water heater.

'What do you want? Why are you here?' Carnforth reminded Murray of a cleric in some dimly remembered film, played perhaps by Alastair Sim, but behind Carnforth's agitation, Murray sensed a kind of ruthless obstinacy.

'I think you know why. As part of the investigation into the murder of Frederick Buckingham. You knew him, didn't you.'

Carnforth stared suspiciously. 'I used to know him. Our paths haven't crossed for many years.'

'I'm surprised to hear that, sir, because we've been told you met him on the night he was killed.'

'Who told you that?'

'You were seen.' It was a lie. He would have to find out the name of the pub where they were supposed to have met and try to find someone who remembered seeing the two men – and it was weeks ago now. Until he had a witness it was only gossip and hearsay, and he had to be careful. Plumer knew nothing about this visit. If Carnforth made a complaint ...

'You deny meeting Buckingham that night, then?'

'I don't even know what night you're talking about. But it doesn't matter, because I haven't seen him for years.'

'It was the first Sunday in October.'

'Ah ... I spent that evening with friends, Mr and Mrs

Jordan. They'd been to the Milners'.'

'So you remember that very clearly. Is there some reason that evening sticks in your mind? Something out of the ordinary happened? You ran into Buckingham perhaps.'

'I didn't. I never saw him.'

'Do you mind if we sit down for a moment?'

Carnforth didn't move.

'I shan't keep you long. I just have a few questions.'

Slowly Carnforth lowered himself onto the recliner. Murray swung the bentwood chair round and straddled it, American-style. There was something about Carnforth that he found alarming and at the same time you wanted to bully him. He somehow invited persecution.

'You're not denying you knew Kenneth Barker?'

Carnforth shook his head. 'I don't know what you're talking about. Who is Kenneth Barker?'

'He's a member of your organisation. Or was. He's been murdered – like Freddie Buckingham. I'm surprised you didn't know that. It made quite a splash in the papers.'

'I don't read newspapers.'

'But you are a member of Oswald Mosley's Union Movement. All the blackshirts must have been talking about it.'

Carnforth said nothing.

'You're not denying that?'

'Denying what?'

'That you're a member of Mosley's Movement.' Murray's patience was already wearing thin. The man's silent obstinacy provoked him, as perhaps it was meant to.

'What business is it of yours?'

'In a murder inquiry, you understand we have to follow up all sorts of different bits of information. In this case, your former friend's murder is linked with Barker's. Barker was a blackshirt. Therefore—'

'False logic, my good man,' said Carnforth, as if on surer ground.

'You admit you used to know Mr Buckingham. You quarrelled with him, then? You fell out? You parted company.'

'Buckingham was an objectionable character, an immoral man.'

'More immoral than the fascists? Worse than Hitler? Did he murder Jews?'

Carnforth stood up and Murray sensed that he'd got under his skin.

'If you read some of what I've written you'd see how woefully misinformed you are. All the propaganda about death camps came from Churchill and his henchmen.'

'That's very interesting, Mr Carnforth.'

'One day the truth will come out.'

'I'm more interested in why you accuse the late Mr Buckingham of immorality.'

Carnforth had sat down again. He ignored the question.

'It wasn't only Jews in the concentration camps, was it,' continued Murray. 'There were gypsies, queers, the mentally retarded. Perhaps someone murdered Buckingham as a kind of rough justice for his sexual tendencies.'

'That's preposterous.' Carnforth seemed genuinely indignant. 'What happened on the Heath ... Freddie Buckingham had a penchant for picking up rough characters. He liked to flirt with danger.'

'You knew that, did you? Although you say you've had nothing to do with him for years? How do you know he hasn't changed, that he's not a reformed character?'

'Everyone knew,' said Carnforth stonily.

'Who is everyone, sir? Everyone in the homosexual underworld? Perhaps you were familiar with that world? Perhaps you had more in common with him than you like to admit?'

'How dare you!' Carnforth stood up again. A tongue of straight, greasy hair had come loose. He swept it back with the rest. 'Get out!'

Murray cursed himself for going too far. He stepped away from the chair – getting up from his straddled posture was clumsy – and put up a hand in a placating gesture. 'I'm sorry if I've offended you, sir. But we have to explore every avenue. So what you're saying is one of these rough characters killed Buckingham. Someone like Kenneth Barker, for example.'

'I want you to leave. You've insulted me. I know nothing about any of this. I'm an artist and a writer. It's the thinkers of this world that change things, not grubby little detectives. I've had enough of being hounded by the secret police – that's what this country is becoming, a socialist police state.'

That was rich, thought Murray, coming from a bleeding blackshirt. He'd messed up the interview, but he wasn't quite ready to leave yet.

'A writer and artist, sir; that's interesting. And I see you have a photo of Vivienne Evanskaya. You're fond of the ballet?'

Carnforth was still staring at his tormentor, threatening and at the same time indecisive. He turned to look at the image pinned to the wall. 'I'm interested in beauty,' he said, 'we live in such ugly times. There was a time when life was beautiful. Ballet is about perfection, symmetry, order, discipline – she was a dedicated dancer.'

'Mr Buckingham admired her too?'

Carnforth turned with a flash of venom. 'He destroyed her,' he said.

As Murray and McGovern made their way through the gritty darkness to the school where Mosley's meeting was to take place, McGovern explained that Mosley had wanted the town hall, and the Tory council had been all set to let it go ahead, until there was so much local pressure they were forced to take a vote. By a narrow margin Mosley had been barred.

In the winding streets around the school policemen stood half-concealed in the shadows. Outside the main gate an agitator on a soapbox harangued a muttering crowd. It had grown cold again after another mild spell and breath smoked from the man's mouth.

'Commie,' said McGovern, speaking in an important undertone; and: 'There may be infiltrators.'

'*We're* the infiltrators, aren't we.'

'No. We're fascists, mind you remember that.'

People were milling around outside in the asphalt yard, waiting to get into the meeting. They looked perfectly normal, men and women you might see any day in the street, a crowd with the ordinary, shabby appearance almost everyone had these days. Ordinary: except for the look of tense exhilaration on every face.

'Better get inside.' They moved forward with the queue. It was a ticket-only event. McGovern didn't let on how he'd got their tickets. Inside, all the seats were already taken, so they stood at the back of the hall. A couple of huge men in demob suits stood by the door. Blue smoke loitered above the heads of the crowd; the buzz of voices wove up and down; heads turned. The platform and walls were hung with red flags with a lightning symbol in black and white.

Someone called out. The audience rose. Murray could hardly see the tall figure in black, for he was surrounded, but women stretched out to touch him. The waves of excitement – the cheering – to Murray it was dreamlike, extraordinary. He felt he was drowning in the roars of cheering. A woman near him had tears pouring down her cheeks.

Murray craned his head, trying to see the leader as he

approached the stage. As he did so he noticed a figure near the front to his left. He looked away; he didn't want Carnforth to see him. He nudged McGovern and jerked his head in Carnforth's direction.

Carnforth seemed to be with someone. 'D'you recognise his friend?'

'Not sure,' muttered McGovern, 'but I'll try to get a good look at him later. You too. You have to remember their faces. That's very important.'

The hectoring oratory rolled over Murray, the raised arm, the plummy vowels, the hysterical braying; the once-dazzling leader shouted about the great anti-communist crusade, the spearhead of righteousness against the red, dark heart of Bolshevism.

Afterwards, there was a sense of anti-climax. The phalanxes of fascists shuffled out of the hall. The muscled thugs hung about outside the school gates, spoiling for a fight, but the soapbox communist had disappeared.

twenty-one

THE HEATH WAS HIBERNATING, misty, sodden meadows leading to a distant grey blur of leafless branches. Regine's normal routine was to work on her translation in the morning, shop for food at lunchtime and walk Cato on the Heath in the afternoon. After that she might visit Dinah or meet Neville and other friends in town. To roam across the Heath was often the best part of her day, or had been. Even after Freddie's death the Heath had been a solace. Whatever the horror of his murder, she felt close to him there – until now in haunting the Heath Eugene's presence poisoned it. It was no longer a question of a rendezvous at the café. Every time she and Cato set out there was the dread of meeting him. He'd taken to loitering around her favourite walks. He walked towards her up the paths; he appeared from the woods; he waited by the ponds; he slipped insidiously out from the birches, a lopsided figure approaching with his soft smile and his Irish voice and his battered clothes.

She remembered now. That's how he'd always been. The smile, the soft cajolement, the sidling suggestion ... now you'll do this for me, won't you, darling, and if there was any resistance the smile would only become more insistent and the hand on her elbow would tighten and he'd still speak so quietly, and anyway it was never anything unpleasant or awkward, just an evening spent with a Chinese 'businessman' or it might be: look after the Germans, the Strausses, will you, darling, I have to be away for a little while, you know, show them a good time ... and then he'd disappear altogether and she wouldn't see him for weeks on end, after which he'd turn up with a piece of jewellery or a length of silk – and making love was never a big part of it all ... he'd always been soft spoken, but you always ended up doing as he told you, because there was always a vague threat behind the smiles. It wouldn't be his fault if something unpleasant happened; it was always: the Strausses could make life unpleasant, you know, I need to keep on the right side of them; or: Mr Cheng has friends in high places, has links with the Green Gang I shouldn't be surprised ...

Now he kept saying he was going to Dublin, but he didn't go. Instead he lay in wait for her on the Heath.

They walked along beside the ponds. 'Is there any news of the necklace? Have you heard from the lawyer fellow? What can Freddie have done with it, d'you know? Are you positive you didn't find it, darling, when you left Shanghai? It was a dirty trick of Freddie if he pinched it, wasn't it now – but then it would still be in his keeping or so you'd have thought.'

It was indeed a dirty trick. It had shocked Regine that Freddie must have taken it – unless perhaps it had somehow got misplaced and he'd found it after she left. In that case, though, why had he never returned it to her, instead of keeping it all those years? It cast a new and unpleasant light on Freddie and his friendship with her. He hadn't 'adored' her enough to return the necklace. He must have believed it belonged to her. It certainly didn't belong to Freddie.

'Why do you want the necklace so much? Is it really that valuable?' She spoke in a neutral tone and gazed ahead of her, keeping an eye out for Cato who was twisting and twirling with another dog, revelling in the chilly wind.

'Oh yes, it is valuable,' smiled Eugene. 'It's worth a fortune I should say. It might be a bit tricky selling it – in case it was recognised. It was taken from a museum, you see. But then again, unless it was one of the top auction houses or an important jade specialist, anyone else would probably turn a blind eye.'

Murray believed Mrs Milner might well have more useful information. On several occasions he almost picked up the telephone to dial her number, but at the last minute resisted the impulse. He'd resolved to steer clear of her. When Plumer had talked about romancing, he hadn't meant you were to get involved yourself. It was a cardinal error to get involved with a witness or a suspect. It almost always got you into trouble.

When she telephoned him, it was another matter.

'You see, something's happened and I need your advice ...'

She suggested they meet at Lyons Corner House, the one by Tottenham Court Road tube station. She had some shopping to do in the West End and it would be a convenient place for tea.

In Murray's scheme of things a Lyons Corner House was where he really should have taken Irene, who would have enjoyed it much more than Bertorelli's. The Corner House was a place for special occasions. To meet Mrs Milner there seemed all wrong, as if their relationship was on some special footing. He protested feebly, but she couldn't see what the problem was and of course he gave in.

In the brasserie the geometric-patterned carpet and assembly line rows of tables fanned out in the golden glow from up-lit columns. He sat woodenly, waiting, while all around him families, couples, mothers and daughters, fidgeting children tried to relax, exhausted or exhilarated after their shopping. Voices consolidated into a continuous roar, almost drowning the three-piece women's band, which was playing popular dance tunes.

'I'm sorry I kept you waiting, Sergeant Murray.'

He looked up and she was there, glowing out of her dark coat as she unwrapped her mauve scarf.

He stood up and pulled back one of the solid chairs for her. 'You were lucky to catch me yesterday evening when you rang,' he said. 'I was about to leave the office – we'd been working late.'

'I'm so glad I did.' She slipped her coat off her shoulders, set down her parcels on a spare chair and seated herself opposite him. 'It's so kind of you to see me. I'm sure you're very busy.'

'How are you? You're looking very well, if I may say so.' As soon as he'd said it, he felt he was blushing. He could not help looking at her intently and it seemed as if, like a flower opening automatically at the approach of a bee, she smiled expansively, a look of responding admiration on her face.

The nippie appeared beside the table with a peremptory 'Yes?'

'Shall we have tea and fruit cake?'

'Just tea for me, please.'

He lit a cigarette to steady his nerves. 'What did you want to discuss with me?'

'Well … there are several things. To do with Freddie … I'm not sure how, but …' She paused, as if marshalling her thoughts. 'Well, in the first place it's about blackmail. I don't know if there's a connection with Freddie's death, but I wanted to ask your advice anyway.'

So Appleton was being blackmailed! It wasn't perhaps surprising, in the circumstances, but if Plumer was being leaned on not to upset people in the public eye, he was going to hate this. It probably had nothing to do with the Buckingham case, but …

'You mustn't think badly of my friend,' said Regine softly. 'Cynthia's absolutely the opposite of everything this sounds like, she's the most moral person in the world. It's because of that, in a way, that's she's got herself into this frightful jam. I know she shouldn't have got involved with a married man, but you really mustn't judge her, will you.'

Paul Murray couldn't take his eyes off Regine. 'I'm not judging either of them. It's not my place to judge. But the only advice I have is what any policeman would say: that in a case of blackmail you must go to the police.'

'I suppose someone at the hotel they stayed in recognised him.'

'But you say that was months ago and the letter only came recently.'

'Yes, that's true. That is rather odd. But you've had experience of this sort of thing. You must know what sort of person – what blackmailers are like.'

'As a matter of fact I've never dealt with a case of blackmail. Did Mr Appleton keep the letter?'

'I don't know. I don't think so.'

'So there's no evidence. No handwriting, no typing, no postmark.'

The waitress clanked the tea things down on the table as though she had a massive grudge against the world in general and Murray and Regine in particular. Regine lifted the metal teapot. 'Strong? Weak?' She smiled. 'This isn't really the normal police interview, is it!'

Murray would have liked to make a gallant remark, along the lines of: I wish it could happen every day – something like that. But it would sound ridiculous. He said: 'Strong, please.' He stubbed out his cigarette and cut his slice of cake into fingers.

'You see now, don't you,' she said, 'why I didn't mention Appleton to you at first. I wasn't trying to be obstructive. I wanted to protect my guests, that's all. I'd never met him before that afternoon. I still don't know what on earth made Cynthia bring him – or at least, why he agreed to come. It can't have anything to do with Freddie. Can it? The blackmail, I mean? But I wanted to talk to you about it anyway. I hoped you might have some kind of idea about how Cynthia can get out of this mess.'

Murray didn't answer; hardly heard the question. His wooden silence was due to the abrupt recognition that he'd fallen in love. It was already too late. He shouldn't have met her, least of all like this. But even if he hadn't he'd already lost his heart.

'But what will happen if she persuades him to go to the police?'

'What? Oh … sorry … what were you saying?' He desperately tried to gather his thoughts. He gulped some tea, which went down the wrong way and made him choke.

'Are you all right?'

'Yes, yes.' Embarrassed by his uncouth behaviour, he tried to pull himself together, and grabbing a lifeline to get him away from the rapids, said: 'I'm afraid I don't know. Well – there would have to be an investigation, so it would all be out in the open. That's presumably the last thing the minister wants.'

It had nothing to do with the Buckingham case, of course. His imagination let rip as he dared to hope that perhaps it was just Mrs Milner's excuse to see him again. No – that was ridiculous.

And yet there just might be a possible connection with the murder. Plumer had linked Buckingham and blackmail – an occupational hazard for queers, he'd said. 'We had thought of blackmail in Mr Buckingham's case,' he said. 'Men like your friend are particularly vulnerable to blackmail, but there was no reason to suppose Mr Buckingham was being blackmailed, was there? Did he ever mention it? And even if he was it's hard to see the connection with this other thing.'

'I'd have known if he was being blackmailed,' said Regine

firmly. 'He was always short of money, of course, but I don't think ...'

All around them the sound of plates, voices, the music from the band as she stared silently into the distance. 'There's something else,' she said, 'something I need your advice about.'

She leaned towards him. She didn't even mean to do it, but it was always as if she was making an offering of herself, her smile seemed to promise something very intimate and special; nothing so vulgar as a sexual proposition, something more akin to understanding, sympathy, rapport. 'If I tell you – you must promise not to breathe a word – it has to be a secret – oh dear, it's all so difficult ...' And she looked away, her lashes veiled the expression in her eyes, but he knew she was even more nervous than he was.

'Of course I won't tell anyone. I'd never betray a confidence.'

'Not even if a crime's involved ... Paul?' She was trying to make a joke of it, but he knew she was deadly serious. 'The thing is, you see, I'm in rather a jam and I need your advice.'

'Yes?'

'I don't know where to start, it's all so—'

'Just take your time, Mrs Milner—'

'Please call me Regine.'

She smiled at him. It was almost too much. He swallowed. 'Well – Regine, just take it slowly.'

'I don't know where to start,' she murmured. Her fingers were playing with her curls. 'Well—' and she took a deep breath with a rueful, self-mocking smile, 'I was married before, to a man in Shanghai, before the war. It was very ... lighthearted. He was a bit of a scamp. He always had lots of irons in the fire, he gambled, he had all sorts of things on the go. When I left, in 1938 – things were getting difficult – he stayed behind.' Regine paused.

'He was going to follow you back to Europe later?'

Regine laughed, frowning at the same time. 'Do you know, I really don't think we even discussed it. I think I thought ... perhaps we were separating ... it sounds rather implausible now, but we just didn't discuss it. We were both Catholics, in theory anyway, so divorce would have been difficult. I'm lapsed and he was too, but the idea of divorce ... anyway,' and she sat up straighter, 'I never heard of him again.'

'He was reported missing, presumed dead?'

'Actually ... no, not officially. I just never heard. But I was so sure. I was sure he couldn't have survived the Japs, you know. And – well, I knew one's supposed to wait seven years before re-marrying, but I'm afraid I didn't wait quite that long. I thought it didn't matter because Eugene must be dead.'

He smiled at the way she'd put it: 'one's supposed to', as though it were a matter of the done thing, good manners, when actually it wasn't a case of 'supposed': it was the law. But all he said was: 'That's very understandable.'

She paused. 'Only he isn't dead. He's come back.' She looked at him, smiling at her own stupidity, and a wave of protectiveness swept through him. 'So my current marriage isn't valid, is it.' When she flushed she was lovelier than ever.

'He's come back – you mean he's here, in London?'

She nodded, and bit her lip, like a little girl caught doing something wrong.

'And he wants to resume the relationship – is that it?'

'Oh no, that's not it at all. But I don't know what to do. You see, he's blackmailing me – well, not exactly, but that's what it amounts to.'

'You've given him money?'

She nodded.

'It's the same as with your friend. You should have gone to the police.'

She laughed then. 'Well, this is what I'm doing now, isn't it, here with you. At first I thought he'd just go away. He kept saying he was going back to Ireland. But now he's behaving more and more strangely.'

'In what way?'

'At first I was sorry for him. But quite soon he began to frighten me. He hasn't exactly threatened me or anything, not in so many words, but there's something more and more disturbing about him.'

'Have you told your husband?' he asked, knowing perfectly well what the answer would be.

'Oh no!' She looked horrified. 'I couldn't possibly do that.'

'I think you may have to. You should report this formally to the police, that you're being blackmailed. And you should consult a lawyer. And you must tell your husband too. Surely he'll stand by you, won't he?'

'I don't want to tell anyone. I don't want anyone to know. My husband – Neville – he's such a stickler for convention, he'd be – I don't know what he'd say. He'd be absolutely beside himself. Horrified. It would be such a scandal.'

He watched her. 'You set great store by your marriage,' he said casually, dreading her answer.

'Neville's been very good to me. I'd be letting him down so badly.'

He extracted a grain of comfort from her reply – it suggested gratitude, yes, but something less than passionate commitment.

He began to think the unthinkable – but of course to marry a divorced woman, or, worse, a bigamous one, would do him no good in the Force.

'I understand,' he said. But he wasn't sure he did. He hadn't yet taken it in. He tried to think straight. 'It must have been a great shock – him turning up like that.' It sounded stupid, out loud. Of course it had been a shock! 'Look – whatever the legal situation, whatever the rights and wrongs of it, he's no right to threaten you. I'll – I'll try to find out how you'd stand, legally speaking. Or – would you like me to speak to him directly? Frighten him off – would that work, do you think?'

'I don't know.' Regine looked at him. She shook her head. 'I don't think so. I'll – let's see what happens. In any case I'm not going on the Heath any more, for the time being. I don't think he'll come to the house.'

Murray wondered why she was so sure of that, but he didn't want to frighten her. He watched her surreptitiously, from behind the smoke from his cigarette. She was looking dreamily away from him. There was a small dance floor in front of the band. A young man moved his partner slickly round to the thin strains of the string trio and Regine was watching the couple. He wondered what she was thinking about: about her husband, perhaps, come back from the dead; or perhaps she was thinking of Buckingham. Her friendship with the queer was incomprehensible. Perhaps, and this brought a pang of jealousy, she'd been hopelessly in love with the dead man. And yet in spite of his doubting thoughts he experienced a curious, light-headed feeling, almost a sense of euphoria. He watched her face: the eyes like green grapes, the red lips, the radiant skin. She felt his gaze and turned to smile at him. Her long fingers with the red nails and green ring twisted her amber necklace. Unexpectedly she stood up. Startled, he was scrambling to his feet as well. 'Must you leave? I—'

She interrupted him. 'Let's dance.'

'I'm not much of a dancer, I'm afraid.'

'Oh, I'm sure that's too modest. I haven't danced for ages. My husband isn't a dancing man. Come on.' She moved in the direction of the floor and of course he followed her.

twenty-two

REGINE HAD HOPED Paul Murray might have reassured her on the subject of bigamy. She'd hoped he'd say that a few months, even a year, wouldn't be taken seriously by the courts, if you were 99 per cent certain your first husband was dead. But Paul Murray had looked rather grim. It was sweet of him to have offered to act more or less as her bodyguard, but that wouldn't solve anything.

In an attempt to avoid Eugene she no longer walked on the Heath, but as a result she dreaded a knock on the door, looked up and down the road each time she left the house, in case Eugene was lurking nearby. If she didn't do something soon, he would come to the house eventually, of that she was sure.

If Neville found out about Eugene he'd turn her out of the house. She had to be prepared. She had no money of her own. She had to somehow try to become more independent.

She invited the Wentworths for supper. After they'd eaten, Neville and Alan retreated to the library, leaving the women to gossip on their own.

'The hare was lovely,' said Dinah. They'd all praised the hare; it had been a great success. 'Where did you get it?'

'Mr Graves has rather a soft spot for me,' said Regine, as if it were inexplicable, when in fact she flattered him outrageously, so that every time she walked into the shop he beamed with pleasure and grew six inches in height. 'He sometimes saves little things for me. He told me a friend of his caught the hare on the Heath, but I don't believe *that*. I've never seen a hare on the Heath, have you? How lovely it would be if there were! Cato would love chasing them! Not that he ever catches anything. He can't even catch a mouse, let alone a squirrel.'

But Regine didn't want to talk about rationing and the high street butcher, or Cato's shortcomings as a mouser. There was Cynthia's situation to consider, and, obliquely, her own.

'There's been a new development – Appleton's being blackmailed.'

'*Blackmailed*! Do the police know?'

'Appleton refused to go to the police. I told the sergeant on Freddie's case, but he wasn't very helpful.'

'You do mean blackmailed about Cynthia?'

'Yes. They went away together,' she said. 'Cynthia thinks someone at the hotel must have recognised him, but why wait until now? And I keep thinking – you see, I was the only person who knew about the affair, Cynthia said I wasn't to tell anyone, not a soul, but then somehow I did tell Freddie—'

'You *can't* mean *he* would have blackmailed anyone – anyway he couldn't because he's dead.'

'No, of course not.' Regine remembered the afternoon Cynthia had confided in her that she was in love with Ernie Appleton – it was months ago, last April, May ... a cold day, she'd had to light a fire and they'd sat there and talked and talked. Later, after Cynthia had left, Freddie had arrived and Regine and Freddie had gossiped until Neville came home and the conversation had turned to museum politics and the awful philistines who were running the country. 'I *swore* him to secrecy, but I'm just afraid he might have told someone else.'

'But who?'

'I don't know. But Freddie used to take photographs of his friends and Neville said some of them were rather risqué. Actually he photographed me in a sort of glamour pose, but that was just a bit of fun, it wasn't indecent, just me in a corset and suspenders, stockings, one leg on a chair. Neville loved it. But Neville says some of the photos of his men friends were a bit more than that.'

'I thought all that sort of thing only went on in Soho.'

'Oh, it wasn't for money. But those photos are missing. Someone has them, and so perhaps the same person ...'

Dinah said: 'Does that mean someone Freddie knew? Someone you know – or we know?'

It was an unpleasant thought. 'The police don't seem to have considered blackmail.'

'Alan says queers often get blackmailed and they can't go to the police because it's against the law.'

Their conversation moved by means of an unspoken connection – the only half-acknowledged, darkly secret homosexual current – to Dinah's life at the Courtauld. Her enthusiasm was so obvious that Regine felt envious.

'What happens when you have children?'

'I don't see why married women shouldn't work. After all, it was women who kept everything going during the war,' said Dinah defiantly. Perhaps there'd been arguments with Alan. Regine's own unspoken agreement with Neville was that, children or no children, her translations should be only a rather ladylike, amateurish occupation, but that would have to change. She had an appointment with Edith Blake at Crispin Drownes tomorrow. She'd talk to her about it. Edith Blake was said to be an old-fashioned feminist. It might be fashionable to say women were only too pleased to be back in the home now the war was over, but Edith had decidedly different views, and wasn't afraid of being jeered at as a frumpy spinster and worse.

The men joined them again. 'We've been talking about the Courtauld,' said Regine.

Alan's handsome face flushed. 'Oh, Dinah talks about nothing else these days.'

'I'm jealous. I'm thinking of becoming a career woman too.'

'Oh, but it suits you down to the ground, being a lady of leisure, a wonderful salon hostess.'

'Alan! She's *not* a lady of leisure,' cried Dinah. 'And you know, since the war, you men can't keep us in purdah any longer.'

He laughed. 'More's the pity. Though actually, if you're serious, Reggie, there might be something at the Beeb I suppose. Why don't we meet for lunch? We can talk about it in more detail then. When are you next in town?'

'Tomorrow as it happens. I have an appointment at my publishers.'

'You can meet me for lunch then.'

When they were alone, Neville turned on her, a glint in his eye. 'I hope you're not thinking seriously of getting a job. I think Dinah's having a bad influence on you. If Alan's got any sense he'll get her pregnant. That'll put a stop to all that nonsense about careers. Only then it'll give him more time for adultery I suppose. You were flirting with him again, weren't you! I don't believe all that talk about lunch, let alone a job. He's not interested in finding you work. A hotel room somewhere, that's what Alan has in mind for you, isn't it? I thought the spanking I gave you last time would have taught you a lesson. But I think you're going to need another good thrashing.'

But suddenly the accumulation of fear and anxiety, all her confused emotions and everything since Freddie had died, fused into a single gesture of revolt. She jerked herself away from him. 'Oh, for God's sake *stop it*,' she cried. 'Just leave me alone.'

She wasn't going to play his games any more.

* * * * *

The offices of Crispin Drownes, publishers, spread through the whole of a Georgian terraced house off Bloomsbury Square. A repressive receptionist whose outdated black pompadour towered above her marble forehead presided behind a battered mahogany counter. She directed Regine upwards to Edith Blake's sanctum and as Regine climbed the staircase, with its dangerously tattered carpet waiting to trip you up, what struck her was the dust. The narrow stairs were lined with shelves filled with slowly disintegrating books that seemed not to have been touched for decades. The terrace had escaped bombs, but not the fallout from nearby explosions. The chalky smell from the miasma of plaster grime still lingered three years later, mingled with two centuries of London soot and human detritus, from men, mostly men in Victorian black, and a few women in bombazine dresses and bonnets like bats, treading the stairs year after year, leaving flakes of human skin, human hair, brushing the walls with their greasy clothes, endless, ant-heap human activity all in the pursuit of the production of thousands and thousands of forgotten books.

Edith Blake was waiting for her on the landing, dauntingly tall, with thick grey hair swept back in waves from her face, like an Eton crop that surprisingly turned into a bun at the back. She wore a tweed suit, its belted Norfolk jacket incongruous with the longish pleated skirt, whose length bore no relation to the New Look, the whole ensemble left over, surely, from a grouse-shooting expedition in the thirties.

As Regine approached her, ready to take the outstretched hand, she felt more as though the appropriate move would be genuflection. A sense of awe, almost dread, echoed her long ago emotions in the presence of the Mother Superior. She had no idea how full of confidence she appeared to the older woman.

Edith Blake's office was a wood-panelled nineteenth-century sanctum, one corner consecrated to the chair that had belonged to the firm's most famous Victorian author. 'Mr Drownes senior is away today,' explained Edith, but everyone knew that she was the power behind the throne. Paid a pittance by the family firm, hers nevertheless was the achievement of the reputation that was rebuilding since the war.

'So – how are the Dark Ages progressing?'

'Slowly, I'm afraid – well, about another seventy pages to go.' There would be no vulgar mention of deadlines here, she knew, but the book weighed on her.

'Well done – it certainly is long.'

'I'll try to finish it by the end of the month; definitely before Christmas.' She was trying to think of a suitable approach to the topic of proper employment. No tactful way of begging for a job had occurred to her on the bus journey into town, but as it turned out she need not have worried.

'That wasn't what I wanted to talk to you about.' Edith Blake wore a signet ring on the little finger of her right hand and turned it as she spoke. Regine, trying to peer unobtrusively, thought it was engraved with a family crest. 'We need to expand and invigorate our foreign list. Now that things are beginning to get back to normal, the war memoirs and the personal accounts of fighting with the Yugoslav partisans and so on need to be augmented by some serious foreign literature. News is beginning to trickle out of new French philosophers: the Existentialist movement, I don't know if you've heard of it?'

'Of course. Jean Paul Sartre, Camus ...'

'Exactly. But I'm not suggesting more translations for you. We need someone here to develop the whole area of continental literature, but that's not really it either. We need someone to expand the publicity side and we think you, with your contacts and your ...' Edith hesitated, then continued, 'You're so good at getting on with people. You'd be our public face. Things will be different soon. It will be a different world. We won't be able just to rely on our readers coming to us. We'll need to promote ourselves. It will be an age of advertisement.'

Regine recognised this as unexpectedly forward-looking of Edith, and it was a wonderful idea. She mentioned one or two ideas about how it could be done.

'I was sure you're just the person we're looking for, Mrs Milner.'

Regine had never imagined it would be this easy. She hardly listened as Edith Blake ran through the details. The salary wasn't enormous, but it would do for now.

'It's midday,' said Edith. 'Time for a sherry, I think.' She produced a bottle and three glasses from a cupboard, along with a battered tin of dusty biscuits. 'I'll just call William in to share the good news.'

'Delighted to have you with us, Mrs Milner.' William Drownes shook her hand and blushed slightly. He was untidy and carelessly dressed, the grey pullover he wore under his tweed jacket was unravelling at the edge, his corduroy trousers were crumpled and going bald at the knee.

A toast was drunk, then Edith said: 'We thought you might care to join us for lunch at Rules.'

Regine silently cursed, but she'd agreed to have lunch with Alan Wentworth and couldn't back out now.

When she arrived at the Soho restaurant, Alan was already seated at a table at the back.

'I've got a new job! With Crispin Drownes.' She'd known at once she had to grab the chance with both hands. Of course, she should have said: I must discuss it with my husband. But Neville would be displeased, so it would be better to present him with a fait accompli.

'Well – we must drink to your new publishing career.' There

was already an opened bottle of wine on the table. He poured her a glass. 'There's my excuse for inviting you to lunch gone down the drain. Though if you change your mind – foreign broadcasts might be more exciting than the staid world of publishing.'

As they scanned the menu Alan said: 'Any news about Buckingham's murder?'

'News?'

'Are the police nearer to catching anyone? The whole thing seems to have stalled.'

'Don't let's talk about it, Alan. It's too upsetting. Let's talk about something cheerful.'

Over the spaghetti, Alan heaped praise on her talents as a hostess, dwelt on her charm, her beauty, so that, at first flattered, Regine began to fear the inevitable, unwelcome conclusion. Sure enough: 'You really are the most alluring woman. I'd love to take you to bed.'

She laughed – it was so blatant. Ironically, Neville had been right, after all. Alan misunderstood her reaction. He didn't pick up on the anger beneath her smile, and when she said, still smiling, 'Alan, please! I couldn't possibly,' he persisted.

'Regine, you're a woman of the world. A little dalliance never harmed anyone.'

'You forget Dinah's my friend. That sort of thing just isn't done.'

'Dinah's all taken up with the Courtauld. Got a huge crush on her tutor, Anthony Blunt. I might as well not exist, quite frankly.'

'Don't be absurd, Alan.' How tiresome it all was. Sadly, she wasn't even surprised. She was quite familiar with husbands whose wives didn't understand them, weren't interested in sex, had a serious illness, or were recovering from childbirth. Appleton had probably bamboozled Cynthia with all the same clichés.

Alan took her hand across the table. 'I won't take no for an answer.' He tried to look deep into her eyes, yet her intuition told her that this was his way of retreating. She kept the smile on her face, but withdrew her hand. 'What a flatterer you are, Alan.'

And for this she'd passed up a lunch at Rules with the regal Edith Blake and the bashful William Drownes! Life was so unfair.

She walked along Oxford Street through the crowds of shoppers and office workers as they hurried back from their lunch hour through the grey November air. She had the strangest feeling she was being followed, turned back several times to see if he was behind her and again in the station she looked along the platform, but it wasn't crowded at this time of day and Eugene wasn't there.

It was the same again when she came out of the tube and walked down the hill. He wasn't there, but she kept looking over her shoulder and thinking she heard his soft, mocking laugh.

twenty-three

MURRAY WAS ON HIS WAY to join McGovern, who was shadowing a Mosley march at Ridley Road market.

He couldn't get Regine and the Corner House tea dance out of his mind. Perhaps she was a woman of easy virtue, no better than she should be, but if she was – why could he not somehow take advantage? No one need ever know. The memory of her body, lightly pressed to his – there should have been a decorous narrow space between them, but she'd moved closer ... But he reined himself in. There was nothing loose or light about her. That afternoon in the Lyons brasserie they'd lingered on. He'd talked about himself and she'd encouraged him, her face intense with interest as he'd poured out his hopes and ambitions. I think you're so brave, Sergeant Murray ... Paul ... it must be a frightfully difficult job ... I don't know how you do it. It was just her beauty and her friendliness that drove men mad and made them jealous because they couldn't reach her. And that tale of her marriage – by rights she'd broken the law, but ... she needed his help. He felt so protective towards her. He could not possibly betray her. Neither, though, could he think of how to help her. She could be in real trouble.

As he approached the market he heard shouts. Half a dozen youths exploded out of a side road and hurled themselves onto a passing bus as it slowed on the bend of the road. Blood ran down the face of the one in front.

Three uniformed policemen pelted out into the main road after them, stopped short, looked around, then waited for a moment before disappearing back in the direction of the noise. Murray followed.

A crowd was dispersing, a defiant band of fascists marching away as stallholders disconsolately kicked squashed fruit and broken packing cases into the gutter. As Murray stood on the corner, standing back in a doorway so as not to be seen, but looking out for McGovern, he caught sight of a familiar figure: Stanley Pinelli was loping along talking to another man. Murray recognised the face he'd been told to remember. It was the man who'd been with Carnforth at the Mosley meeting.

Murray and McGovern had agreed that if they missed each other in Ridley Road they'd meet up at their usual café in Whitechapel, so Murray followed the two men. Pinelli looked gangling and awkward beside his companion, who wore a hat and a raincoat and moved lightly with a springy walk. The two men were going in the direction of Dalston Junction.

They turned left into Kingsland Road. On this grey day there was a sullen atmosphere along the battered street, its surviving buildings cracked and grimy, the squalid shops with their listless display of a few miserable wares, seemingly indifferent to customers. The men and women who trudged along the pavement looked dwarfish and shrunken in their shabby clothes. And yet there was something about the dull London streets that went to Murray's heart. They'd stuck together all through the war, he and they, and now they were glued together in something like a long enduring marriage, which might not have been a love match in the first place, but which over the years had become so familiar that it was impossible to imagine life without it.

It was a long walk. There were enough pedestrians for Murray not to have to worry too much about being noticed by the two he was tracking, and although by the time they reached Shoreditch he was footsore, he was glad they hadn't taken a bus, for then he'd have had difficulty in remaining unseen by Pinelli.

He followed them down Commercial Street past Spitalfields market. They turned left again along the Whitechapel Road, trudging on and on until finally Pinelli split off to the right and his companion disappeared into the great forbidding Rowton House near the hospital. And as Murray walked back towards the café to meet McGovern he noticed how new buildings were going up on some of the bomb sites. In the end, he thought, Hitler had done the East End a favour, by destroying the old slums so that new, modern housing estates could take their place. A new, better London would rise in the end from the devastation.

'Good lad,' said McGovern. 'You took your time. I'd almost given up waiting, but I'm glad you got here.'

'I saw a mate of Kenneth Barker's: Stanley Pinelli. We think he might be involved indirectly with the Buckingham murder. We had him in for questioning, but we didn't get anywhere. He denied he was one of Mosley's lot – but then there he was this afternoon.'

'Och – ' McGovern's grunt was as dismissive as it was contemptuous. 'These wee lads can't resist a bit of a fight. They're too daft, some of them, to understand what it's all about.'

'He was with another man, who went into that big men's hostel – but he didn't look like a tramp or a down-and-out. But you know what – it was the bloke Carnforth was with at that meeting.' Murray paused. 'Pinelli could be the key to it all in a way. But Plumer doesn't like the blackshirt angle. He doesn't like it at all.'

McGovern stared at his friend. 'Have you wondered why that might be?' He looked round the café, quiet in mid-afternoon. The proprietor, a grim-looking man in an apron, was reading the *Daily Sketch* behind the counter. Two solitary customers, who looked as if they might have come from Rowton House, sat at their separate tables and stared into space.

'What d'you mean?'

McGovern believed he was always better informed than others; his job had nurtured a belief that conspiracies were everywhere and that a complicated explanation was always to be chosen over a simple one. 'Mosley still has plenty of fans in high places,' McGovern said.

'You think Plumer's being leant on?'

'Think about it, laddie. Why's he dragging his feet? He's not exactly pulling all the stops out in this investigation, is he. I'd say he has a dilemma. Here's the press clamouring for a crackdown on gun violence, but he isn't following up the most obvious lead. And, you know, those fights up the Ridley Road – it's nae the blackshirts get done, it's the Jews are ending up in the courts.'

'At first Plumer did think that Buckingham's murder and Barker's were connected. It seemed so obvious because of the gun. But now he's insisting they're just two messy random episodes in the ongoing war of London's underworld. He won't have it there's a connection.'

McGovern laughed contemptuously. 'Of course there's a connection; the gun, apart from anything else.'

'It could have been anyone, he says, any of his underworld mates, that is, who shot Buckingham, then later got in an argument with Barker and shot him too. He won't budge,' said Murray.

McGovern leaned forward. 'We're well aware of the links between Mosley's lot and the Soho gangs. Last June the blackshirts tried to march through Brighton but there was a big anti-fascist counterattack and they were routed. So Mosley's lot hired some underworld thugs to get their own back. There was another fight in Romford when the 43 Group tried to disrupt a meeting. Mosley's lot pelted them with potatoes stuck with razor blades. There's Jews and gentiles in the underworld too, you know. Bud Flanagan from the *Crazy Gang* and Jack Spot – they give money to the 43 Group and then their rivals side with the other lot. Ken Barker was very small fry, but – well, just let's say the links are there. If you could sell it to Plumer on the grounds that Barker was involved in these gangs – you don't have to mention the blackshirts.'

Murray shook his head. 'I don't know. I honestly don't think Plumer is in with Mosley's lot. I just don't think so.'

McGovern looked more knowing than ever. 'But if he's being *influenced* by someone from higher up—'

'Are you saying there are senior coppers who support Mosley?'

'Come on now, Paul, you know there are bent coppers.'

'Well, bent's one thing, this is different. Politics – you could even say it's treason.'

'The war's over now, laddie.'

'If you're right, then how am I going to get him to do anything more about Carnforth?'

'You could use Pinelli – on the grounds he's just a crook. Think up some yarn – say you've got more on him. Or use that woman you're sweet on – the one who was friends with the pansy – tell Plumer she's given you more information about Carnforth. Say they're threatening to complain because nothing's being done to solve their friend's murder.'

'I'm not sweet on her ...' Murray swallowed. 'I need some more tea,' he said. 'How about you?'

He brought the white mugs back to the table and said:

'That's something else I need your help with. She told me something ...'

McGovern heard the story of bigamy in silence. The corner of his mouth twitched. 'I hope you know what you're getting into,' he commented finally.

'I'm not getting into anything,' protested Murray.

'You know best, laddie. But if you're going to help her, maybe she should help you.' He drank off the rest of his tea and stood up. 'And I'll see if I can dig anything up on this Shanghai husband of hers. Not that it's likely.'

twenty-four

WHEN MURRAY GOT BACK TO HQ, Plumer was waiting for him. 'You're bloody late. What happened to you? There's been a development. The chief's heard from Buckingham's family. There's a will, but they're challenging it. We're going round to see the executor. He's one of the Milner woman's pals. And you know who the other executor is? It's Tommy Warwick. Warwick's the lawyer who acted for Ken Barker last time he was up in court.'

Which was interesting, Murray thought, because Tommy Warwick was bent as hell. That, at least, was the general police view.

Ian Roxburgh's office was hidden away in a turning off Cheapside. Like many Victorian buildings, this had a gothic façade like a church, as if to give a veneer of high-mindedness to the sordid workings of commerce. The frontage was now grimed with dirt, its ornamental brickwork broken in places.

The two policemen trudged up the lino-covered stairs to the third floor. An inconspicuous card, pinned beside a glass-panelled door, stated: Captain Ian Roxburgh – Import Export. They knocked and Roxburgh himself opened the door.

'We're detectives, Captain Roxburgh, looking into the death of Mr Frederick Buckingham.'

Roxburgh's smile was as clipped as his moustache. 'Come in.' He stood aside for them, but although his manner was pleasant enough, Murray could tell he wasn't pleased to see them. Then again, who, after all, ever welcomed a visit from the police?

In Murray's view this visit should have been made weeks ago. Now that McGovern had planted the seed of suspicion, Plumer's lethargy appeared to Murray no longer inexplicable, but downright sinister.

He looked round Roxburgh's office. The room was furnished with battered metal filing cabinets and a large desk with splintered corners, its top marked with ink stains. The only wall decoration was a pre-war railway poster, torn at the edges, advertising holidays in Skegness with an image of an impossibly rotund and cherubic man skipping across the sands. The place seemed surprisingly shabby and impermanent for an allegedly successful businessman.

Plumer wasted no time. 'We understand you're one of the late Mr Buckingham's executors.'

Roxburgh nodded. 'Yes, that is the case.'

'And the other is Thomas Warwick of Warwick and Partners.'

'Yes.'

'And it seems the Buckingham family is challenging the will.'

'I believe so, Chief Inspector.' The way he enunciated Plumer's title made him sound insolent rather than deferential.

'It would be helpful to know the provisions of the will.'

'What's the form, Chief Inspector? Am I obliged to? Aren't these matters confidential? As his executor, I'm not sure—'

'This is a murder investigation. I'm sure you'll understand

that the provisions of the will may have a bearing on a possible motive.'

'Freddie was up to his eyes in debt. He'd been living on capital for years and it had pretty much all gone. There'll be nothing. The sale of the house will cover some of what he owes. His photographic archive may be worth a bit – he bequeathed that to the ballet company, but I think it may have to be sold as well – the lawyer's dealing with that side of things.'

'Mr Milner told us part of the photographic archive you mention is missing,' said Murray.

'I don't think so. His ballet photographs are all at the house.'

'These were pornographic photographs.'

Roxburgh raised his eyebrows. 'Really? I know nothing about this. Some portraits of friends, perhaps. And Neville Milner showed me a glamour photo Freddie had done of his wife, but that's hardly pornography. Of course one gathers Mrs Milner had a bit of a reputation out in Shanghai – in the nicest possible way. And that was a long time ago, before the war. Mind you, she's wasted on that dry stick Neville – well, not dry, since he drinks such a lot. Please don't misunderstand me. I like Regine. I suppose her husband might have been worried in case a slightly saucy picture of his wife got into the papers. But anyway, they had nothing to do with poor Freddie's untimely end. On the contrary, Regine was tremendous friends with Freddie. They had one of those friendships, you know, that men like Buckingham go in for.'

Murray was tense with hostility and suspicion. Probably all the talk about Regine Milner was some kind of smokescreen, intended to put them off the scent – but of what? 'Mr Milner told us he'd been under the impression he was the executor. It seems odd that Mr Buckingham hadn't informed him of the change. Anything you can tell us about that?'

Roxburgh's disdainful smile and dismissive shrug seemed calculated to annoy Murray. 'All I know is, he asked me to be his executor. I only know the Milners through him.'

'How long had you known Mr Buckingham?'

'Oh ... a few months, I suppose.'

'So you hadn't known him for any length of time? And yet he made you his executor. That was a bit odd, wasn't it, to make a virtual stranger his executor?'

Again the slightly patronising smile to rile Murray; everything about Roxburgh was controlled – his movements, his facial expressions, his tailoring, his starched white shirt and regimental tie – and all equally got up Murray's nose. 'I wouldn't say we were virtual strangers. We met through mutual friends and found we had quite a lot in common, struck up a rapport, you know.'

Murray wondered if that meant Roxburgh was one of *them* – a pansy. He didn't look it, but then nor had the dead man.

'What sort of interests?' enquired Plumer stonily.

'The fact we'd both been in the Far East created a bond,' said Roxburgh smoothly. He hesitated, then: 'I understand your surprise. I was surprised myself when he asked me to be his executor.' Roxburgh paused. 'The truth is, I don't think he wanted Neville Milner to know what a frightful mess he was in, financially that is. He was ashamed of the whole thing. Of course now this has happened the Milners will find out everything in any case.'

They waited for Roxburgh to say more, but he smoked silently, looking at them with that irritatingly know-all expression.

'Were there changes to the provisions of the will as well?' Plumer's pale, flat face was expressionless.

'I have no idea. He said something about having wanted to leave something to his friend Mrs Hallam, the dancer, or to her son, but there was some difficulty about that. I don't know what it was. I got the feeling her husband disliked him.'

'Oh? Did you have any occasion to observe them together?'

'I met them altogether just the once.'

'What sort of occasion was that?'

'We met at a restaurant. Buckingham took me to meet them. It wasn't a great success. Hallam didn't seem to be a very sociable sort of chap – or else he wasn't in a sociable mood.'

'Why did he dislike the dead man? Have you any idea?'

'Prejudice? Jealousy?' Roxburgh shrugged, Captain Roxburgh, the worldly man about town, looking down on the two plods with their common assumptions and painful absence of sophistication. Murray didn't even try to quell his dislike.

'Was he at the Milners' afternoon event on the day of the murder?'

Roxburgh frowned. 'Oh, I don't think so. I'd never seen *her* there before either, his wife, the ballerina. And I tell you who else was there, very unexpected, a government minister. The Board of Trade chappie. But surely the Milners will have talked to you about all this.' He moved some papers around on his desk. He looked at his watch. 'I have an engagement this evening, so ...'

'You say Mr Buckingham was up to his eyes in debt. Was there any suggestion of blackmail at all?'

'Not that I know of.'

'Where were you on the evening Mr Buckingham died?'

Roxburgh took it in his stride. 'When was it? Remind me of the date.' He leafed through a diary on the desk. 'I had dinner at my club with a friend. He could vouch for me, I suppose, if necessary. Would you like his name and address?'

'That would be helpful, sir. It's only a formality, you understand.' Plumer paused. 'You still haven't told us who stands to benefit from Mr Buckingham's will. Accepting what you say about his financial position, but if there was any money, who would it go to?' Plumer's strong suit in interrogations was his blank neutrality. He seldom displayed emotion. But Roxburgh's calm was a match for him. He rose to his feet. 'It would go to me – but I assure you that's entirely hypothetical. There won't be a bean.'

'Thank you for your help, sir,' said Plumer with deadly politeness. Then as he reached the door he turned and looked back at Roxburgh. 'And what exactly do you import and export, sir?'

'Tea.'

The detectives found a quiet pub in a side street off High Holborn.

'He wasn't being straight with us,' said Plumer.

To Murray's way of thinking, the interview had been a kind of slippery mirror in which they'd seen only themselves. Roxburgh *had* given them some information, but Murray had the feeling he'd been tantalising them. There was something concealed, glimpsed round the edge of a curtain as it were; something there in the room that they couldn't see. 'I thought he was a pretty shifty sort of bloke,' he said, 'and he didn't bother to conceal how much he looked down on us.'

Plumer looked sideways at the younger man. 'I imagine his manner is much the same with everyone,' he said mildly, 'and, you know, Murray, I've said this before, you don't want to take everything so personal. They're not out to get us; we're out to get them, so no wonder they come across a bit dodgy at times. They often are dodgy, of course, but that's another question. You're a smart young man, Paul, don't let that chip on your shoulder get in the way. And don't let winning ways and red hair cloud your judgement. Acting friendly is one thing, but don't overdo it.'

Murray knew that on the rare occasions Plumer addressed him by his first name, kindness was motivating him. And he had no defence where Regine Milner was concerned. But he couldn't resist a dig at Roxburgh. 'He seemed to be half suggesting that the Milners might have pinched the photos themselves. And isn't it possible the motive for Buckingham's death might have been to get hold of his photographs? In order to blackmail the men who appeared in them? After all, we know now that Appleton's been targeted.'

'Appleton spent a weekend away with his bit on the side, Mrs Milner's friend. That was back in the spring. Anyone from the hotel could have recognised him. It's odd to have waited till now, but perhaps with the current scandal it seemed the right moment to strike. Anyway,' he added, 'as I said, we don't even know these photographs exist.'

'Milner thought they did. And the fact he told us they were missing means it's very unlikely he took them himself.'

Plumer shrugged. 'Not necessarily. Anyway Milner could have made the whole thing up. It could be some sort of red herring. Of course Buckingham's address book was missing too … but an address book would only be of use to someone who knew the individuals and could marry up the photos.'

Plumer ground out his spent fag and with a fresh one between his lips, said: 'We'll look a little further into Captain Roxburgh. A tea importer – I think that's just a front. What bona fide tea importer works out of a cupboard like that? With not even a secretary? And I don't like those men who go on using their wartime titles – Colonel this, Major that. He wasn't in the regular army. *And* he was only a captain.'

That evening Murray took Irene to the flicks. She chose *Another Shore*, because it starred Robert Beatty. Murray had to admit the actor was good-looking, but the plot was a facetious frolic, full of Irish whimsy and stereotype. He was bored stiff. It was as much as he could do to sit through it, but Irene was enraptured and shed tears of laughter. Murray thought about Regine Milner, although he tried and tried to get her out of his mind and concentrate on the feeble little film.

On the walk home Irene irritated him with her chatter about the film, interrupting his daydreams. He snapped at her. She usually respected his moods. She was a good girl, of course, and pretty, but – she was so practical and sensible. *She* didn't need protecting, she didn't gaze at him in admiration, although she deferred to him, and all she talked about was saving up and getting married.

'What's the matter, Paul? You're so moody lately. Don't you love me any more?'

'Don't be ridiculous.' But on her doorstep he turned on his heel. Usually they had a kiss and a cuddle on the sofa in her parents' sitting room. Now he left her in tears and marched along the road with rage in his heart because she wasn't Regine Milner.

twenty-five

R EGINE DRESSED AS CAREFULLY as ever for her December Sunday, the first since Freddie's death. One had to keep up appearances, even if the effect desired was a slightly unconventional one. Yet the very phrase 'keeping up appearances' had developed a sinister undertone, as if she were performing an act. Appearances might change; she might be a different person underneath. She might not be at all the person she pretended to be.

And of course, she wasn't. Wasn't *really* – at least legally – Mrs Neville Milner. She was a bigamist. She was a fraud. She was Mrs Eugene Smith – and probably not even that, for the name Eugene Smith was likely another fiction.

She'd lied to herself as well, pretending the first few times that she was just doing Eugene a kindness, that he'd had a hard time, that she somehow owed him something, that she should return all the favours he'd done her long ago – the passport, the place on the ship out of Shanghai – and in her turn help him to get away to Ireland.

Only he hadn't gone to Ireland. He wanted more and more – as anyone could have told her he would.

It was sinister and uncanny, the way he'd guessed, the way he *knew* she had it. There it had been, so slyly and seductively coiled in the box among Freddie's cuff links. She hadn't meant to take it. She'd just picked it up for a moment, to pass the beads through her fingers like a rosary. Then somehow it had slipped into her bag.

After all, it was hers. Only it wasn't. She thought back to those last hectic days in Shanghai and that evening, the last time she'd seen him. And it was true – he'd mentioned the necklace; he'd told her to leave it behind.

On the whole she'd planned to ignore that instruction. Yet if it was so valuable, why hadn't Eugene been there to make sure it was still in the flat? Something had happened – he'd had to go away, another of his business trips ... But the decision, to take or leave the necklace, didn't arise, because when she came to pack, she couldn't find it. It wasn't there. She'd been in a hurry then, hadn't time to make a proper search.

Freddie could have found it after she'd left. Yet she had to admit he might have taken it at the first opportunity. She'd shown it to him. He might have understood, which she didn't then, how valuable it was. She'd been so careless of things in those days, so heedless. You couldn't blame Freddie – if that's what he'd done.

Yet it seemed like a betrayal. At the very least it was a deception, a cheap ploy. He'd exploited her thoughtless naivety.

Now that she'd made the terrible mistake of quarrelling with Neville, of breaking the unspoken pact, the *arrangement* – his illusion that she shared his fantasy – the necklace had become important. She'd been a fool to alienate him like that, at the very time she needed him most. He was still angry and *hurt*. He sulked. She knew she should have abased herself. She should have been a clever wife and created a situation in which he could punish her, take his belt to her arse so he could get his erection. Somehow she couldn't. She'd stopped pretending. She'd destroyed the illusion, that she was asking for it, and it

couldn't be recreated. She'd rejected his fantasy; and if the marriage that after all wasn't a marriage had really been based on
that – her whole future was thrown into question.

If only Freddie had been there. He'd have known what to
do; except that her trust in Freddie had also gone. It hadn't sunk
in, when she first found the jade, but he'd deceived her. Whatever had happened in the flat in Shanghai, he'd had the necklace all along and he'd never told her. He'd kept it. He'd
effectively lied to her.

As she chose her old bottle-green dress – lengthened with
navy blue insets in the skirt to make it more New Look – and fas-
tened her amber and coral and ivory necklaces (but not the jade,
of course not the jade) round her neck, she was not looking
forward to her Sunday afternoon. On this damp, dingy December day she almost hoped no one would come.

She found Ian Roxburgh in the library with Neville. They
looked up, startled, from their contemplation of a barrel-shaped
vase, which stood on the desk. With its dull, pearly, undeco-
rated grey glaze it looked far more modern than Neville's other
Chinese ornaments with their multicoloured flowers and
figures, but she had a feeling it was much older.

'Isn't that someone at the door?' said Neville.

As she left the room, he was saying to Roxburgh, 'The
museum couldn't possibly … and I couldn't really afford …'

Phil had opened the door to Charles. 'Oh, it's you. How
lovely,' she cried with false brightness. 'Is your mother with
you? Is she coming too?'

'I want to talk to you—'

Another knock on the door interrupted him. He followed
Phil into the dining room.

This time it was Noel with a young woman in tow, the kind

of girl Regine thought of as arty tarty, in narrow black slacks and black polo neck sweater, to which her bleached hair and scarlet lipstick made a striking contrast. The Wentworths were close behind. The afternoon was under way. If anything, more guests than usual traipsed up the path, but Regine sensed something was wrong with the atmosphere – or perhaps it was just with her. She felt febrile and jittery. It wouldn't do for a hostess to be depressed or anxious, but as usual her guests were too preoccupied with themselves, their projects and their social triumphs, to notice anything wrong with Regine.

'I'm Jeannette,' said Noel's new girlfriend. 'Why do people give these boring parties? Have you been dragged along too? Isn't it awful, they're all talking shop, I might as well not be here.'

'Let me get you a drink, that'll make you feel better,' said Regine, stifling her fury, and led the girl into the dining room, where Charles, leaning against the sideboard, looked a bit squiffy already, thoroughly debauched in fact. He was deep in conversation with Phil and ignored the two women.

Regine was feeling so tense that she considered retreating to the bedroom to lie down for a few minutes, but as she came into the hall she almost bumped into Ian Roxburgh. His smile was foxier than ever. 'Come into the library,' he said.

Neville had left and the vase wasn't there either.

'You know, Regine, if your husband plays his cards right, he could be of enormous benefit to the museum. With my contacts I could put him in the way of some wonderful pieces. He's a cautious man, isn't he, but I thought you could persuade him … you see, now the war's over and things are getting back to normal, the museum will be able to increase their acquisitions once again. Of course money's in short supply, but I'm in a position to offer exceptionally favourable terms.' He smoothed the crisp frill of his moustache. 'There's something else. It's about Freddie. I was wondering if you'd like to come over to the house sometime, to choose something to remember him by. He had so many lovely little objects ... perhaps Mrs Hallam would like to come too as she was another great friend of his.'

'That's very kind.' But Regine could hardly keep her bitter resentment from bursting out: that this stranger should have such rights, when she was excluded.

'There were also one or two things I need to discuss with you about Freddie's will. Perhaps it might be a better idea if we meet at my office? Why don't I take you to lunch? Neville says you're at home on your own in the day. You must get lonely. And you really are the loveliest woman I've met since I've been back in London.'

'Oh, nonsense, Ian.'

'Do say you'll have lunch. We've so much to talk about – you know, about Freddie.'

Curiosity won out. 'That would be lovely.'

In the dining room arty-tarty Jeannette had sidled up to Charles and was trying to flirt with him. Moving towards the window, Roxburgh said in a low voice, 'Boys like that – you can see why Freddie raved about his beauty, but in a few years' time he'll have over-ripened, like a rotten peach.'

'What an extraordinary thing to say.'

'Debauchery always shows in the end.'

In the drawing room Edith Blake was talking to Neville, another cause for alarm. God knows what Neville might say to her soon-to-be employer. When she reached her husband's elbow he was questioning the older woman about a memoir of the concentration camps, one of the first, but when Regine came alongside, he changed the subject. 'So you've seduced my wife into working for you. I hope you're not going to give her a hard time. I hope you're not a strict disciplinarian.' Edith bridled slightly. 'And what am I going to do without her? I need her here at home.'

'Don't be ridiculous, Neville.'

'But who's going to look after Cato?'

'I've sorted all that out with Phil, darling.'

'Cato must be a dog?' suggested Edith in a strained tone of voice, but the expression on her face changed as she looked beyond Regine's shoulder.

It was Vivienne. Edith's manner changed too, as she gripped the dancer's hand and gushed: 'It is such a privilege to meet you, Mrs Evanskaya, I've long been a devoted admirer.'

Vivienne was paler than ever. 'I'm Mrs Hallam now,' she said faintly. She walked up to Regine. 'Is Charles here?'

'Yes … he's somewhere about.'

'I must talk to you. Where can we go? In the garden?'

'It's raining.'

'No it isn't. It's stopped.'

They stood outside. Rain dripped from the bushes and the trees. Vivienne looked quite ill.

'The police called round to see us again. They asked John all these questions. As if they thought he was jealous of Freddie. And the thing is … John *was* terribly jealous, you know, because I wouldn't give up dancing. Even after Charles. Ballet dancers don't have children, he said. He was right! I was the only one! The company travelled a lot. I wasn't always in London. I think John even thought for a time that Charles might not be his. Of course that wasn't true. It was just his jealousy. Jealousy's such a terrible thing.'

'I'm sure they don't suspect John!'

Vivienne was smoking frantically. 'No, but – he was always jealous of Freddie, you know. But never mind about that. That's not what I've come about. It's – ' She paused, then burst out: 'I don't want you seeing Charles any more. There've been so many unhealthy influences – Arthur says – Arthur's been a tower of strength. But he … he told me some things about

Freddie I hadn't realised. He's made me understand what Freddie was really like.'

'Oh, Vivienne, we all know what Freddie was like.' Regine tried to speak lightly, but the woman seemed unhinged. Was everyone going mad? Freddie's death had blown everything apart.

The dancer frowned. 'You encouraged Freddie, didn't you. You brought out the worst in him. So far as you were concerned all his excesses were just some kind of frivolous amusement.'

'That's rather unfair, isn't it? You were close to him too.'

'I might have been once. And anyway Arthur told me things. He showed me ... He said it was his duty. I had to know.'

'Know what? What did he show you?' Charles himself spoke from behind them. He must have stepped silently across the grass. 'What are you doing out here in the wet and cold? I'm leaving, if you don't mind, Regine. I'm sorry not to stay longer, but we're reading a Jacobean play at school and I have to prepare one of the parts.' He looked a bit drunk. 'It's about a woman who plots to be rid of her husband so she can marry her lover. She has this hideous servant, de Flores. De Flores agrees to poison the husband, because he's mad about her. But he only commits the murder so he can make her sleep with him in return; a kind of blackmail. The irony is, she ends up infatuated with him, in spite of his having killed her husband and more or less raped her.' His gaze moved between them.

His pale face ... a rotten peach ... but peaches weren't white ... would he decay ... Freddie's fingers bruising the flesh, his body crushing the marble limbs ...

'One doesn't talk about such things,' cried Vivienne. 'And it sounds most unsuitable for a school play. I shall speak to Arthur!'

'I don't think that'll get you very far.' There was a sneer in his voice.

'Do stay a bit longer, Charles.' But he wasn't listening, he was staring at his mother.

Cato bounded from the house barking hysterically. He must somehow have escaped from the prison of the boxroom. Released into the garden, he leapt on his hind legs ecstatically, trying to embrace Vivienne, who recoiled with a shriek, stumbling backwards and lurching into her son who only just managed to remain upright himself.

Regine dragged Cato away by his collar. 'Bad dog! Bad boy!' She jostled him upstairs, pushed him back into the boxroom and slammed the door. His furious barks echoed through the house, then he began to whine and cry, which was even worse.

To get away from it she ran back downstairs and out into the garden, but the Hallams had gone. She dashed out into the road, but there was no sign of them.

She had had nothing to drink all afternoon, and so was unusually aware of how drunk her guests had become. In the drawing room Jeannette was weaving up to Noel.

'You're drunk.'

'If you weren't so bloody boring—'

'What d'you think you were doing, cradle-snatching – the boy's fifteen!'

Regine had never seen Noel lose his temper. He surely couldn't be in love with this horrible girl.

'What am I supposed to do, then, when—'

'You stupid bitch!' Noel slapped her in the face and grabbed her arm. The door banged behind them as he frog-marched her down the path.

Edith and Dorothy looked on, startled, from the sofa.

'God!' said Alan. 'Oh well, that'll teach him to pick up girls in Soho drinking clubs.'

Regine longed for nothing so much as to follow Noel's example and flee her own party. What on earth must Edith

Blake think of it all! She escaped into the garden again.

She was standing forlornly in the damp dusk when Alan emerged. 'I'm off,' he said. He hesitated. 'Look, Reggie, I don't want to be officious or anything, but does Neville know what he's doing?'

'What d'you mean?'

'Before Noel lost his temper and flounced off with his tart he seemed to be quite exercised about that friend of yours, Ian Roxburgh. Something about him touting various works of art around. Noel said with things like that you really do need to be absolutely clear about provenance. He says a lot of things have gone on – still are going on – and people are getting away with a lot. But Neville should be very careful. He works for the museum after all, he's not just any old collector who could have the wool pulled over his eyes by someone like Roxburgh. Noel says he doesn't trust Roxburgh, thinks he sails very close to the wind. If the museum gets to hear about it – well, I just hope Neville doesn't do anything stupid.'

Regine and Phil washed up in the kitchen.

'Until today, I was thinking your Sundays needed some new blood,' said Phil, 'but now—' He didn't finish the sentence, but raised his eyebrows and pushed his glasses up his nose, leaving a drip of washing-up water on his face. 'That frightful woman Noel brought along!'

'I'm afraid Edith was offended.'

'I shouldn't worry about that. I think Vivienne made up for everything so far as she was concerned. But I'm sorry about Cato. I was sure I'd shut the door. When I went to get him for his walk afterwards he was in the most terrible sulk.'

'He was very naughty. I hope you refused to speak to him.'

'You know, a funny thing happened on the Heath. There

was a bloke hanging about just the other side of the road down there and when Cato saw him he went potty – jumping up, all over him. It was as if he *knew* him or something.'

'What did he look like?'

'Oh … well, it was dark, I couldn't see too clearly, but … odd, wasn't it.'

She leant against the draining board for a moment, but all she said was: 'Oh, you know Cato, one friendly pat and he's anyone's.'

Vivienne paid off the taxi. Its metal for-hire flag went up with a clink. Charles watched the cab accelerate away and disappear round the curve of the wet road smeared with reflections of light. He looked up at the house, which was in darkness.

'Is Dad out, then?'

'He didn't say he was going out. He's probably in his study. I expect you'll want something to eat, won't you, darling?'

'I'm not hungry.' There had been foreign chocolate biscuits at Regine's and he'd eaten too many. He felt if anything slightly sick, but that was perhaps from drinking three cocktails. Or from thinking about Carnforth all the time.

Vivienne switched on the hall light, which dangled, unshaded, from the high ceiling. From upstairs came John's voice: 'Is that you?' Charles climbed the ladder to the first floor. Father and son met on the landing.

'Is your mother downstairs?'

Charles nodded. The next flight of stairs was intact. He began slowly to plod up to his own room, but he was listening to the voices below. He could hear clearly, for sound carried up through the void at the centre of the half-restored house.

'Where have you been?'

'At Regine's.'

'What – all day?'

'I went to church first.'

'To church! With Carnforth I suppose.'

Charles's heart raced. He was sweating. He stopped halfway up the stairs to his room, then crept back down to the landing where he sat on the bottom-but-one step.

'He's trying to help.'

'*Help*? What with?'

'Freddie's death opened my eyes to so many things ... I'd never realised, I was a fool—'

'You were besotted with Freddie.'

Charles gripped the banister.

'You were in love with him for years. You couldn't accept that he'd never ... you, a beautiful woman in love with a man who—'

'Shsh, don't shout, *please*, John, the boy—'

His father lowered his voice, but Charles could still just hear.

'And now this Arthur Carnforth. He's got some sort of hold over you, hasn't he.'

'John, you don't understand. You mustn't be jealous. It's nothing like that.'

'I don't know what's the matter with you. I've given you everything you asked for – this house—'

'This house! You don't even notice I'm here. It's like living in a morgue, this airless house, all on my own—'

'*On your own*! I'm here, your son's here.'

'Don't shout. Don't shout – *please*—' Vivienne was crying again.

'Stop snivelling, Vivienne. You're hysterical.'

But Vivienne's sobs increased.

Though he didn't realise it, Charles's hand was clamped across his mouth as if to stifle a silent scream.

'I might as well be on my own ... and I blame myself so much. We stood by and let it happen. How *could* I not have known? But that was why – it was because I thought Freddie could do no wrong. But *you* should have known and instead you just did nothing. You didn't even notice. You notice *nothing* about your son.'

A door slammed. The silence was suffocating. Charles didn't know how long he'd sat on the stairs when he heard movements. His father was climbing the ladder. Charles leapt up the stairs to his own room and shut the door. He had just time to sit down at his desk, before his father came into the room without knocking.

He looked tired and spent as he sat down on the bed. 'Your mother's a bit upset,' he said.

Charles sat rigidly in his chair. He stared at the desk.

'You know ...' His father hesitated. 'Ever since you came back from America ... I feel we've grown apart. Your mother feels we haven't ... I haven't taken enough notice of you. But you seem to be getting along all right at school ... I know I've been preoccupied. It's not been easy working at the hospital – there are so many shortages. And then there's the chaos of reconstruction. But she feels you've been neglected.' John Hallam was seated with his legs apart, his hands clasped between them as he stared at the floor.

'Everything's fine, Dad.'

'Perhaps we didn't take enough account of what a big change it would be for you – coming back here after years in America.'

'It's okay. I'm all right.' But there was a tight feeling in Charles's throat.

'Do you miss New York? Your mother's right, I suppose. We never talked about it much. We were so pleased to have you back.'

Charles swallowed. Yes, he wanted to shout. I wish I was back there all the time. The trees spurting green at the end of the street in the spring against the blue sky; the church nestling in the arm of the lofty skyscrapers; the housekeeper, Nell, and sitting with her and Lally in the kitchen eating cookies ... the tomb-like somnolence of the drawing room on a summer day, boring and at the same time soothing, and the ice cream they ate at the end of almost every meal ... oh, Lally ... there was a lump in his throat, but he mustn't, *mustn't* blub.

'Your mother – ' Charles's father unclasped and clasped his hands. 'The murder – of course it was unsettling – a terrible thing to happen. You must have been upset.' The words came out stiffly self-conscious.

Charles sat dumb.

'Someone's given your mother the idea – I mean I ... to be honest, I never hit it off with Buckingham, I don't care for that kind of man, but he never ... did he ever – well – ' and at the end it came out in a rush ' – try to seduce you.'

Charles looked up. He looked his father straight in the eye. 'No, Dad, never.'

'Ah ... I didn't think ... I'm glad to hear it.'

'But if you want to know, I do miss New York. I hate it here, I wish I'd never come back, I wish I could've stayed there for ever.'

The silence rolled back over them in a smothering wave.

twenty-six

MURRAY SAID NOTHING to Plumer about Ridley Road. McGovern's theory, that someone was leaning on Plumer, was alarming. He had to think of an excuse for bringing Pinelli in for questioning again without mentioning the blackshirt angle. And there *was* an obvious solution, he realised: Pinelli had killed Buckingham *and* Ken Barker. Okay, Barker was his mate, but thieves fall out, and so on.

The problem remained that with Plumer present questioning would be useless if Pinelli's connection to the Mosleyites couldn't be raised. But now Plumer was to be sent up to Yorkshire to talk to Buckingham's family. Normally Murray would have accompanied him, but this time Plumer was taking a colleague who knew all about forged wills and fraud.

To start with Pinelli took refuge, as before, in slightly cocky stonewalling.

'You ain't got nothing on me.'

Murray did not actually believe Pinelli had murdered anyone, but he said: 'Chief Inspector Plumer thinks you shot that queer on the Heath and if you didn't, he doesn't care, he's going to nail you for it anyway.'

Startled out of his confidence, Pinelli sat up. 'I never! He can't do that!'

'Tell us about your mates in the Union Movement, Stanley. It's not just a question of fights up the Ridley Road, is it. Who was the man you left the march with last week?'

'I just met him, didn't I.'

'But who is he? You walked all the way back to Whitechapel with him. You seemed to have a lot to talk about.'

A startled look from the prune-like eyes with their long lashes.

'Did Kenny know him?'

'Give us a cigarette?'

Murray passed him the packet. He said: 'Ken Barker was murdered, Stan, you know that, don't you. That must have upset you. An old friend – somebody blew a hole in his head and dumped the body in a ditch. That's not right, is it. Don't you want that person brought to book, the bloke who murdered Ken? Or perhaps you know who it was already.'

Stan drew on his cigarette. The hand that held it was shaking.

'Worried they might come after you too?'

Stan fidgeted about in his chair.

'You see, Stan, Chief Inspector Plumer isn't here today. If he was, you'd be in dead trouble. He wants you fitted up for these murders. He said I should do whatever it takes. He wants a confession. Now as it happens, *I* don't think it *was* you. But I think you know something about it. You know something about someone called Carnforth, for instance, don't you? A friend of the man you left Ridley Road with.'

Stan shook his head. 'That name don't mean nothing.'

Frustrated, Murray grasped for another key. 'But you've been to Handel Street.'

Stan's eyelids flickered. He looked down.

Murray waited. He tried again. 'Let's go back to what Ken Barker was doing in the days before he was killed. I want to know why there was blood on that shirt of yours he borrowed. You know all about it, don't you, and the more you refuse to talk, the more it's going to look as if you did it, Stan. Is it that you don't want to grass Ken up? But he's dead, it can't do him any harm now. It might seem disloyal, I understand that, but he'd want you to tell the truth now, wouldn't he. He wouldn't want you to go down for what he did.'

Murray almost invoked the idea of Ken looking down from heaven or up from hell and begging Stan to come clean. But that would destroy the atmosphere, reduce everything to farce. As it was, he had to bite his lip in order not to smile. He'd obviously guessed right, however. Some kind of thieves' honour had been holding Stan back.

'D'you think so?' His expression changed to one almost of trustfulness.

'Yes. I'm sure of it. He'd want you to come clean, to save yourself.'

'It was a while back. Ken said he had a big job, he'd be well paid, he'd be in the big time. Someone important give him the job. He was supposed to do it on his own, but he said I could come in on it, he needed my help. He didn't say exactly what it was, but he showed me – he had a gun. I was scared, to be honest, I mean we never done nothing like that – shooters, firearms. But he just wanted my help afterwards, he said. I was to meet up with him at King's Cross and when I did Ken had the keys to this house – in Chelsea, he said it was – so we go over there. It wasn't to look like a robbery, he said, and there was only certain things we was to take. Some boxes, mainly from the back of the house.'

They'd nicked a few bits of silver and some loose cash as well, but Stan had no intention of mentioning that.

'What was in the boxes?'

'He said they was dirty pictures or something. We 'ad a look. Disgusting they was.'

'What then? What did you do with them?'

'We was to take them round to some geezer in King's Cross.'

'Handel Mansions, Handel Street. That was it, wasn't it.'

'Yeah, it was some old flats. I wasn't to come in, he was supposed to be on his own.'

'So you went to this flat with Barker, but you didn't go in.'

'Yeah, well not exactly. Ken wanted me there. He was nervous.'

'He was frightened of the man who lived there?'

Stan frowned. 'Not exactly. Dunno. But he said he was supposed to be alone, but I was to come up.'

'What happened then.'

'Well, I went up with him, but I stayed on the turn of the stairs. I could see the bloke, but he couldn't see me. He answered the door and soon as I saw him – I knew him.'

'You'd met him? On marches? With Mosley's lot?'

'Yeah – sort of. There was smaller meetings – I went along once or twice. Load of rubbish, I didn't understand half of it. He spoke at one of them. He was a preachy sort of bird.'

'Arthur Carnforth.'

'That's not the name – when I heard him speak it was … Peter James, Jameson, something like that.'

Murray remembered the pseudonym from before the war. He wondered why Carnforth still used it. 'Peter Janeway,' he said.

Stan nodded.

'And when you'd previously been to the house in Chelsea – are you saying you really didn't know how Barker had acquired this set of house keys? You didn't know the owner of the house had been murdered?'

'No, no, I never.'

'You want to be careful, Pinelli. You've just admitted to what amounts to being an accessory after a murder.'

Stan's mouth opened. He shook his head. Murray couldn't believe he was so stupid he didn't know the score. 'You know, too, don't you, that when a murder is committed and more than one perpetrator is involved, all those present may be charged with murder.'

'I wasn't on Hampstead Heath!'

So he did know! Murray smiled and leant forward. 'How did you know this had anything to do with Hampstead Heath? I think perhaps you were there, Stanley, and that's very good news, because as you know, your friend Kenneth is no longer with us and so we can't charge him, but now you're saying you were part of a murder team, so we'll be able to charge you and there'll be a trial. We need a trial, Stan, because those people up in Hampstead don't take it kindly when someone gets murdered on their back lawn. They want to see someone brought to book, they want to see justice done. And as far as they're concerned, that means a conviction for murder, followed in short order by a hanging.'

Stan was snivelling now. 'No! Don't get me wrong. I only met him afterwards. Honest. In Chelsea.'

Murray believed him, but it wouldn't do to show it. 'But then Kenny was shot. And you must be frightened you're going to be next. That Arthur Carnforth will be coming after you. You're frightened of him, aren't you.'

Stan nodded. He stared at the floor. Murray thought he was going to say something, but instead he was violently sick.

Murray couldn't arrest Stan. Plumer knew nothing about the interview and wasn't going to like it when he heard about Stan's confession. Murray was unsure how to persuade his boss they had to take Carnforth in.

If the photographs were still in Carnforth's flat ...

He was afraid Stan would just disappear, lie low, so he ended up by giving him money. He also threatened him that if he didn't stay in touch he'd be the number one murder suspect.

When he got to the office next morning, there was a buzz of talk about a big vice squad raid. Inspector Victor Ramsgate of the vice squad had visited Rodney Ellington-Smith, well-known author of books of essays and *belles lettres* and a highly regarded review column in the *Sunday Times*.

Murray knew how it went. The victim had reported the threats to the police. Ramsgate had visited the charming period mews house in Knightsbridge. The result had been not only the arrest of the writer himself, but further raids on friends of his, whose names had been found in an address book and diary.

Murray guessed that from Ramsgate's point of view it was all a great success. He decided to liaise with Ramsgate. If Buckingham's photos were only in Carnforth's flat ...

He would have to see to that shortly.

twenty-seven

O N HER WAY INTO TOWN to see Edith Blake and then
have lunch with Ian Roxburgh, Regine stopped off in
Kentish Town to visit Mrs Havelock, who'd caught flu from Phil.
She passed half-bombed terraces where the remaining houses
were in a state of near-collapse. She wondered why everyone
still looked so poor, when, according to Neville, they were
getting so much money from the government. Of course Dinah
and Alan saw it differently.

She found the shrunken Georgian cottage in Leighton
Road, its windows curtained with dingy net. Mrs Havelock was
wrapped in an old dressing gown and she'd bound up her head
in a flannel scarf.

'Oh my goodness, ma'am, you shouldn't have.' Her voice
was croaky, her eyes red. 'I've caught something shocking.' A
bluish gaslight hissed in the corridor that was the hall. That
must account for the strange smell. It was probably quite dangerous. 'I brought you a few things.' Regine pulled the paper
bags of fruit and the cough mixture and pills from the chemist
out of her basket. 'I just wanted to make sure you're all right.
Have you seen the doctor?'

'Oh, no, Mrs Milner – I'm not on the panel, nothing like
that.' She was seized with a violent fit of coughing.

'But that's all changed now – you just have to register with a doctor. Everybody can.'

'I know. There was a leaflet and I heard on the radio, but I haven't had time.'

'We'll sort it all out for you. I'll get the forms.' Neville had grudgingly done the paperwork for both of them, while protesting he intended to stay with his private Harley Street doctor.

At Crispin Drownes, Edith was extremely cordial and pleased to receive the French history translation ahead of time. Regine was invited to take coffee with Edith and Drownes senior. To meet Jonathan Drownes himself was, she knew, the confirmation of her appointment and an honour in itself. She would commence work after Christmas. William Drownes escorted her to the door and shook her hand warmly. 'We're looking forward to your joining us, Mrs Milner.'

By the time she left Bloomsbury Square the morning mist was thickening into fog. The traffic had slowed, and lights only partly pierced the gloom.

It took Regine some time to find Roxburgh's office. The viscous fog had crept into the tiled hall and clung to the walls. She climbed the linoleum-covered stairs, surprised by the dinginess, and knocked at his door.

Roxburgh was cordial, but the room could have come straight out of an American film about some seedy detective. And who was Ian Roxburgh, anyway?

Across the desk, he swivelled his office chair, watching Regine all the time. 'You found it all right? The fog seems to be getting worse.'

'You wanted to see me about Freddie's will?' She loosened her coat, although the office was far from warm.

He opened his desk drawer, still looking intently at her. For a second she had the strangest sensation, as if he were about to whip out a revolver. 'Probate will take months, of course.' He drew a sheet of paper from the drawer. 'In the end I didn't bring anything with me, but I've drawn up a list of little things I thought you might like. You'll be familiar with them, won't you.'

'He didn't actually leave me anything, then? It doesn't seem right, somehow, if he didn't intend it.' It was odd, because Freddie used to joke about what he'd leave her: the Regency desk and the Venetian mirror – not that it *mattered*, she didn't care that much about the things in themselves, although they were lovely, of course, it was just hurtful that he hadn't left her anything at all. In fact, it was downright odd.

'Did Freddie ever tell you how we met?' His sly, knowing smile unnerved her. 'You see, when I was in the Far East at the end of the war, I naturally – you can imagine in my line of business – came across a wide range of individuals.'

'I've never quite understood exactly what your line of business was, Ian, in the war, that is.'

'Especially out there – Shanghai was a magnet for any and every dubious character. Always had been – as you must have realised yourself. I was put in there to sort things out – along with others, of course. I met a chap in the Philippines, this was just after the end of the war. He was a crook if ever there was one – managed to get away from Shanghai with a couple of other notorious characters. I was in touch with British intelligence. They were keen to get hold of him too. An Irish nationalist – hated the British. He'd lain low in occupied Shanghai all through the war. He got by, working for the Germans or the Japs – ran a nightclub, something similar to what he'd been doing before the war. Much more dangerous of course. But to all intents and purposes, or at least so far as many of his pre-war friends were concerned, he simply disappeared. No doubt most of his old acquaintances – those that weren't scattered to the four winds, that is – assumed he was dead; if they thought about him at all. At the end he had a couple of narrow escapes – that's how he came to be in the Philippines. He was on his uppers, but he still had a few contacts – he still knew people who knew how to get hold of all sorts of items. He was helpful to me, put me in touch with some lucrative sources, so in return I helped him in getting away. He was desperate to get back to Ireland.'

Regine looked blankly at her own hands and twisted the emerald ring. 'What are you saying, Ian?' Although she knew very well.

'You didn't know your husband was involved with the Germans in Shanghai? Before the war, that is?'

'Eugene never talked about politics – or Ireland. He knew some Germans, the Strausses, but then he knew everyone ...' She tried to remember Hans and Lotte. She'd quite liked them ... was he saying they were *Nazis* ... 'I don't think Eugene was a traitor.'

'Not a traitor, an Irish patriot in his eyes, my dear. As you know, Ireland was neutral in the war. Many of the Irish fought with the Allies, but there were also nationalists who hoped Germany would win. Anyway, when I met him things were at a low ebb for him and I was able to help him. He talked a lot about Freddie. He was very bitter about him. I wonder how much you know – or knew – about what was going on under your nose out there. Did you know pre-war Shanghai was the absolute epicentre of intelligence and espionage in the Far East? And there were a lot of people like Freddie who passed bits and pieces of information to the British. To put it bluntly, Freddie informed on your husband. He told British intelligence your husband was involved with the Shanghai Nazis. Your husband at least was convinced of that. He told me a lot about Freddie, so I made it my business to look Freddie up when I came home.

He confirmed the story. He had been involved in intelligence. He wasn't too pleased when I turned up with the news that Eugene was still alive. Like you, he assumed he'd died in the war, when the Japs invaded. Mind you, neither of us expected to see him again over here, where he risked being arrested for treason. Not very likely, perhaps, but anyway we thought he'd go straight back to Ireland.'

'This is all rather a shock.' Regine stood up and took a few steps up and down the crowded, untidy office. 'I had no idea Freddie was mixed up in anything like that. But why does it matter now?'

'Freddie was worried for you, Regine. A dead husband turns up out of the blue – a crook and a traitor into the bargain – he wanted to protect you from that. That's why he changed his executor. He didn't want Neville to know.'

It sounded implausible. 'But why should Neville have found out?' She didn't trust Roxburgh. She sat down again.

'I can help you, Regine. He's been in touch with you, hasn't he. He's frightened. He's a desperate man – he thinks some of his former associates are after him. Perhaps they are, though I'd have thought it's more likely they're rotting in jails in Manila or Hong Kong, or at the bottom of the South China Sea, but he's afraid. He's afraid the British will catch up with him as well. He needs money. After all, we know there are plenty of ex-Nazis floating around the place, don't we. He also seems to think we all owe him money. He doesn't seem very grateful for the help I gave him.'

Regine looked past Roxburgh out of the window. Beyond it the air had turned thick white and solid.

'I don't want to frighten you, Regine, but I'm afraid he's becoming a little unhinged. His nerves are shot to pieces. He's at the end of his tether. And you know yourself, he was always a bit of a wild card, wasn't he, a bit unpredictable.'

All the time Roxburgh was speaking, he was looking at Regine, a knowing, sardonic, insistent gaze.

'Can we get back to Freddie's will? I don't see what this has to do with Freddie.'

'What your husband had told me about Freddie – well, I made sure I got in touch with him when I got back to London. You see, there was this yarn about the jade necklace. Eugene claimed he'd got it from some gangster, it was supposed to have been stolen from a museum or … God knows. Valuable, anyway, very, very valuable. He insisted Freddie had stolen it. And Freddie *did* have it. He showed it to me. And his photographs. I saw those as well.'

Regine hated the way Roxburgh's pale blue eyes bored into her, full of meaning. He went on: 'Only now the necklace isn't there. Nor are the photographs.' His smile never wavered as he scrutinised her. 'And you and Neville were round there like a shot, weren't you, the minute you heard Freddie was dead. So …'

Regine sat very still, but her thoughts raced. Finally she said: 'How dare you suggest we stole anything from Markham Square.'

Roxburgh stood up. He walked round the desk and stood behind her. His hands were on her shoulders. 'Of course, my dear, I apologise. Insulting of me even to suggest it. And I wouldn't dream of mentioning anything to Neville either – about our friend from Shanghai. Only – ' and he bent down and she felt the prick of his moustache against her neck, 'I think I deserve a little gratitude, don't you, for my reticence.' He held her tightly from behind. She tried to break free. He held her more tightly for a moment, and then let her go. She stood up, untidy, flustered, cornered.

He walked over to the window. 'The fog's getting worse. If we're going to have lunch I think we ought to get going.'

When they reached the street the fog was a pale pall out of which figures emerged eerily from a foot away, a sudden shock as they wafted forward out of the ectoplasm. Traffic was sparse and moved slowly, headlights barely piercing the murk. The dim, leaden light muffled sound as well as sight. The air tasted acrid and her throat began to feel sore.

Roxburgh took her arm. 'I think the restaurant's this way.'

'Perhaps we'd better try to flag down a taxi – and perhaps just get home, for now,' suggested Regine.

But there were no taxis that they could see.

'Oh, I can find my way,' said Roxburgh smoothly. He held her closely, but there was nothing reassuring about his grip.

As they walked along the pavement the slabs gradually disappeared. The suffocating fog crept closer still. She could see barely a foot ahead. A white wall rolled towards them. They were alone in this suffocating, silent world. Sound, too, was deadened; no traffic, no footsteps. She stretched her free arm sideways groping for a wall or something solid to hold on to, and when she found it she edged her way along it. Roxburgh lit a match, but the feeble glow did nothing to disperse the miasma.

The wall fell away. Now they were unanchored, adrift in a blanket so thick it was like moving through veils. Roxburgh too seemed to have lost all sense of direction. He stopped. She was on the edge of panic.

'There's no point in turning round,' he said. 'We'll just have to walk on. We'll get to somewhere eventually.'

Their footsteps echoed dully ... or perhaps what she heard were the footsteps of another being lost in the fog.

They edged forward in the white blindness and after a while the sound of their footsteps changed in timbre. A darker whiteness; she slipped, tottered and almost fell. He gripped her arm so tightly it hurt. 'Easy does it.' The smell of the fog had a metallic edge to it now.

He stopped and lit another match. He stepped forward, stretched out his hand, gasped and lurched back against her. 'A carcass, I banged up against a damn great side of beef. We're in Smithfield meat market, slipping on entrails and guts and blood.'

Carcasses! It was macabre, and yet half comical too.

He turned and caught her closely. His moustache scraped her lips. His hand thrust inside her coat, his fingers pinched her nipple, his leg was thrust between hers.

'I'm going to have you, you know.'

'For God's sake, Ian, are you mad!'

But her anger seemed only to amuse him. He laughed. 'Not the most romantic location. You were right. We should have got a taxi. Me and you in the back of a taxi.' His hand roamed down her body.

She wasn't going to scream or fight. What use would screaming be in this empty world? She said between gritted teeth: 'Let me go, Ian.'

He moved back, still holding her arm. 'No, you're right. This isn't the time or the place.' He obviously found it amusing. 'Although in the fog – the last man and woman in the world …'

'How are we going to get out of here?'

'I can get my bearings now, I can work out which way to go. We'll walk this way. The underground station is at the end of the street.'

She had no choice but to stick to his side.

In the trackless palls of swirling solid air they walked with slow uncertain steps, like, she thought, a bizarre, blind couple suddenly struck by age and infirmity, going God knows where.

'The trains will be running.'

She wasn't sure of that, but at last they reached a turning and the dim glow of the Aldersgate station sign.

She could see his face now in the brackish light of the

underground foyer. He smiled. 'You see, I brought you safely
through the fog. But I'm afraid we'll have to postpone our little
luncheon to another day. I'll ring you. In the meantime – ' and
he looked her up and down as though she were as much a piece
of meat as the carcasses in Smithfield, 'you'll think about what
we've talked about, won't you. And I'll be thinking about our
next meeting. I'm sure we'll both enjoy it. But I wouldn't
mention it to Neville if I were you – well, I'm sure you wouldn't
dream of that. You wouldn't want Neville to discover he's a
bigamist – or is Neville just an adulterer? Is it only you that's
committed bigamy?' And before she could answer he bent
towards her, his mouth bruising hers, the moustache scraping
her lips, his body tight against her.

Throughout a journey punctuated by long delays, what most
puzzled Regine was how Roxburgh had known she and Neville
had been round to Freddie's house the day after the murder.

As soon as she reached home she telephoned Paul Murray.

twenty-eight

MURRAY COULD TELL Plumer hadn't enjoyed Yorkshire, although the guv'nor's pale, closed-in face was as flat and inexpressive as ever, and all he said to Murray was: 'Bloody waste of time.' So it was risky to come clean about the interview with Pinelli, but Murray knew he had to, although it meant risking Plumer's displeasure or even, worse, some kind of permanent rift.

Plumer looked paler than ever. 'Who told you to bring Mosley's lot into it?'

'Pinelli was seen with a friend of Carnforth's and Carnforth and this third man attended a rally where Mosley spoke. And Pinelli admits to passing stolen goods to Carnforth, goods stolen from Buckingham's house in Chelsea. He also admits to going to the house with Barker, who had the keys.'

'I told you to leave all that alone. And you argue from that, that Carnforth had something to do with the murder. Pure speculation, Murray. It's no concern of ours whether Carnforth is a blackshirt or not. It may explain how he could have known Ken Barker, but that's all.'

'Several witnesses have told us Carnforth hated Buckingham, sir.'

'He's hardly the sort of man who'd hire a killer.'

'Not hire, sir, but given they knew each other ...' Murray knew he'd gone much too far, he'd exceeded his authority. To have interviewed Pinelli like that was tantamount to mutiny. Suppose he was disciplined – demoted – even lost his job – his mother would be devastated ...

Plumer coughed horribly, a long, bubbling, hacking cough that seemed to surge up from the bottom of his lungs and nearly sent his cigarette hurtling from his mouth. The paroxysm over, he stubbed the cigarette out and lit another. 'Very well. We'll interview Carnforth,' he said, 'but as a potential witness. And in my office, not the interviewing room.'

Carnforth looked round suspiciously as he entered Plumer's sanctum, like a bull being coaxed into a pen. His raincoat caught on a chair as he passed. He pulled at it clumsily, embarrassed.

'Where would you like me to sit?' As if all the chairs were too small.

Cigarettes were lit. Carnforth didn't smoke. He sat with his large hands clasped in front of him, holding the rather unusual black tweed cap he'd pulled off in the entrance hall. That must have been how he'd looked at school, Murray thought: awkward, shy, unattractive.

'As you know, we're investigating the murder of Mr Frederick Buckingham and there were just a few points we think you might help us clear up.'

Carnforth pulled at the peak of his cap. He smiled anxiously, revealing teeth too large for his mouth, just as his hands were too large for his arms.

'You know of course that the deceased was a photographer, primarily of the ballet. But we have reason to suppose that he also took photographs of a more intimate nature, photographs of his friends. Were you aware of that?'

'I hadn't been on friendly terms with him for many years. I know nothing about his activities.'

'I think the existence of these photographs was well known.'

'But why should I know about them?' Carnforth's expression bordered on the truculent, yet laced with pained innocence.

'The thing is,' said Murray pleasantly, 'we have a witness who claims to have illegally entered Mr Buckingham's Chelsea house after the murder. This witness has told us that he and his companion were under instructions to remove the photographs and that they later gave them to you.'

Carnforth stared at them, more bovine than ever. 'I don't know what you mean.'

'We have a reliable witness who tells us that is what happened.'

'But – how can that be? That's impossible.'

Murray pounced: 'Impossible? Why? Impossible because he's dead? Right? Kenneth Barker's dead. Murdered; like your friend Freddie Buckingham.'

'He was no friend of mine.'

Murray watched his victim, who was huddled into his black coat, the picture of angry misery. 'Kenneth Barker came round to your flat, didn't he, Mr Carnforth? The cat's out of the bag. The late Kenneth Barker delivered the photographs or negatives, or both, to you at your flat. That's what happened, isn't it. They were pornographic photos of Buckingham's friends. I can see it's embarrassing – you're not only the receiver of stolen goods, but the goods are dirty pictures. What did you want them for? Blackmail? Or did you find them titillating?'

Carnforth went very red. 'How dare you suggest I wanted anything to do with such filth.' He kept his voice low, but he moved about in his seat.

'Well, we'll see about that, won't we, when we search your flat.'

'They're not there. I – you're making this up.'

'But our witness isn't Kenneth Barker, Mr Carnforth. Of course that would be impossible. Like Mr Buckingham, he's been murdered. But unfortunately for you, he had a friend with him. This friend tells us he went with Barker to your flat and gave the photographs to someone who looked like you.'

Carnforth shook his head in apparent bewilderment.

'After they'd been stolen from the dead man's house.'

Carnforth passed his hand across his face.

'How did you know Barker? It was through the blackshirts, wasn't it.'

Carnforth stared at them. 'Why are you tormenting me like this? What has this to do with Freddie Buckingham's death?'

As if it wasn't plain as a bloody pikestaff; Carnforth's mulishness irritated Murray.

'Steady on, Murray.' Plumer had let the interrogation continue so far, but now he interrupted. 'That's a little strong, isn't it, sir? Tormenting you? We're only trying to get things straight. We just want to hear from you what actually happened. We're not suggesting Barker stole the photographs for you.'

Carnforth shook his head to and fro like a cow trying to ward off bluebottles. There was a heavy silence before Carnforth spoke again: 'It's bad enough what we went through in the war. All this talk about concentration camps. They put *us* in concentration camps. *We* were the ones who were persecuted. Persecuted for our beliefs. Interned without trial. And now you're persecuting me again.'

'Mr Carnforth,' said Plumer, 'if you don't answer these perfectly reasonable questions, we shall have to arrest you and question you under caution. You don't seem to realise how serious this is.'

Murray glanced sideways at his boss. He seemed to have changed tack.

'We can obtain a warrant to search your flat and if the photographs are there, then you will be charged with receiving stolen goods,' continued Plumer, his grey face as expressionless as ever. 'At the very least. This all happened within twenty-four hours of Mr Buckingham's murder. That suggests to me that you knew that the murder was planned before it took place. Otherwise, how would Barker and his mate have known to come straight round to you?'

'No, no, that's not it at all!'

'Who murdered Mr Buckingham?'

'I don't know.' Carnforth was slumped in his chair now, as though his outburst had exhausted him.

'Did you murder him?'

Carnforth shook his head.

'What was your opinion of the dead man?'

'He was evil, he was a wicked man. He preyed on others. He corrupted Charles Hallam, for example, and probably many others.'

'How do you know that?' asked Plumer.

Murray chipped in. 'You teach at St Christopher's – you know the boy's parents. Did you tell them of your suspicions? Mrs Hallam was a close friend of the dead man, I believe.'

Carnforth moved around in his chair. 'She had nothing to do with this. She's a wonderful woman. I met her again after many years. When I got the job at the school – Neville Milner told me her son was a pupil there. We met to discuss Charles's work ... and then ... I met someone who knew Freddie – I realised what had been going on between him and the boy.'

Carnforth paused and smiled; a strange smile, which Murray couldn't read. 'Freddie Buckingham caused untold harm to that boy. He's an insolent boy. Whenever he sees me he looks at me with that contemptuous smile on his face, that way he has, of making you feel you're an ant he's just about to step on – except that he can't be bothered, you're not important enough. His mother thinks the world of him, of course. I felt it was my duty to tell her and when I heard—' He stopped, then started again. 'There were always rumours about Freddie's other photographs. Neville used to laugh about it. And then when there was – when they – I thought if Vivienne saw she'd have to believe me. She'd see what Freddie was really like.' Carnforth was sweating. There was something rank and raw about him, Murray felt, his emotions too exposed, so that he seemed defenceless, abject, and yet repulsive.

Even Plumer lost his deadpan expression. 'You showed his mother an indecent photograph of her son? You thought she'd be grateful?' said Plumer. 'So you're saying Mr Buckingham was murdered for his photographs? Did you arrange his murder?'

'No. No!' Carnforth shook his head. 'I was shocked he was dead – it was a shock,' he said. 'But I can't say I was sorry. He was a revolting man, an evil influence, he did Vivienne untold harm.'

'Do you know who killed him?'

'One of the people he preyed on, I suppose.'

'You haven't told us how it came about that Barker brought you the photographic negatives. What you've just told us doesn't tally with the fact that Barker came round to your flat so very soon afterwards – the following day, wasn't it – so you must have had the idea about the photographs days if not weeks earlier, mustn't you. You must have known that Buckingham's death had been planned. And you must therefore have known who murdered him.' Plumer spoke icily now.

Carnforth shook his head.

'I suggest you do know who it was,' insisted Plumer.

Carnforth sighed deeply. The silence continued for what

seemed a long time, but the hands on Murray's watch had only ticked round for a minute before Carnforth said: 'I've told you all I know. I admit Kenneth Barker came round with the photographs. I'd told – he must have known I wanted them. But I only wanted the one – he took the rest away again. I haven't got them and I don't know where they are.'

Murray couldn't understand why Plumer hadn't gone on the offensive about the political angle. He said: 'You met Barker in the blackshirts, a disreputable and violent organisation spreading treasonable views you presumably agree with. Your dedication to such an organisation, which wanted this country to be defeated by the Nazis, a view for which you were rightfully detained, must make us suspicious of your motives and your truthfulness.'

Plumer ground his cigarette out violently. Murray knew he'd said the wrong thing. But why not mention it? It was surely relevant.

Carnforth drew himself up. 'The beliefs upheld by Oswald Mosley have been completely distorted and misrepresented. He is a man of peace, not violence. Ours is not a violent creed. Our members have been provoked time after time. Our enemies have been the violent ones. And just because our views have been defeated, for the time being, that doesn't mean – don't you understand that you can believe something ever more strongly the more you're persecuted and scorned. Like Jesus Christ on the cross – he was scorned, he was ridiculed, he was murdered—'

Plumer interrupted him. 'Your political views do not concern us, sir. For the time being you are free to go, but we will need to see you again.'

Carnforth stood up. 'Can I go now, then?'

'Yes.'

Murray could not believe the interview had ended so abruptly. 'Why didn't we arrest him, sir? He must be involved –

the photographs are damning. We should search his flat. We can't just let him off the hook like that!'

Plumer looked at the floor for a while, always smoking, smoking. Finally he said: 'This is strictly between us, but – there's someone higher up who wants him left alone.'

The thought of a Nazi in the force – in a powerful position – horrified Murray. But worse than that was that Plumer had given in to pressure. Murray knew some coppers were corrupt – and everyone bent the rules a little, but he'd always believed Plumer was fundamentally straight. And now –

'You can't do that!' It didn't come out as he'd intended, but instead of tearing him off a strip, Plumer simply said:

'We'll do what we have to do. Pinelli's statement isn't that strong and we haven't any evidence that Carnforth got Barker to shoot Buckingham. He doesn't seem the type to do a thing like that. Order someone's execution – that takes us back to the underworld, professional criminals. It's possible he shot them both himself. The first murder was certainly amateurish enough. But there isn't a shred of evidence. It's pure supposition. The man's insane, I grant you that, but just because he's got a screw loose doesn't mean he killed anyone.'

'What about the photographs?' Murray was so angry that in standing up he almost knocked over the chair he'd been sitting on. He was flinging himself out of the door when Plumer said: 'There is another angle. We might be able to get at it another way. If you just wait a moment instead of charging off in a temper—'

'I'm sorry, sir, but—'

'The vice squad's investigating an allegation of blackmail. Ramsgate's arrested a whole ring of queers and perverts. He's more interested in locking them up than in the blackmail itself. But I'm going over to have a look at the photographs – copies that several of the men were sent – and from what he told me, and who these men are, theatrical circles and all that, I'm willing to bet that they'll be the Buckingham photographs.'

Murray couldn't see what difference it made.

'Look, Paul,' said Plumer patiently, 'Ramsgate's not interested in the blackmailer, but the demands were sent in typewritten envelopes apparently – not very smart – and he's agreed to share information. I told him it may link in with our case. It may even be connected with the fact that Appleton has been blackmailed. In the meantime you could pay the Hallams another visit. See if the boy's mother was shown a photograph. It seems implausible to me, but I grant you Carnforth's a very strange man.'

'But you're saying we can't touch him. So what does evidence matter?'

'It's not as cut and dried as all that. If there was a watertight case, then maybe … but at the moment, there ain't.'

'I'll phone Mrs Hallam then,' said Murray. He went back to his desk, still too angry to think straight, and searched furiously among the litter of papers for the Hallams' number. But at the moment he was about to dial the number, there was an incoming call from Regine Milner.

twenty-nine

H E WENT TO DOWNSHIRE HILL the next day after lunch. They sat in the cosy room with the warm red walls. The fire glowed.

She was perhaps not exactly beautiful, but her skin was so luminous. Her eyes were so green. His drawn-in breath was like stepping into an icy sea. Was that what they meant when they said it took your breath away?

Murray was mesmerised by her proximity, her colour, the faint scent when she leant towards him, but he listened carefully to what she told him about her meeting with Roxburgh.

'So Captain Roxburgh suggested your first husband, Eugene Smith, possibly murdered Mr Buckingham?'

'Yes, but I told Eugene about the murder the first time I saw him. He seemed horrified, upset.'

'But he's threatening you. And the suggestion is he wanted revenge because Buckingham had informed on him. In fact he had two motives for killing Buckingham: that, and this jade necklace.'

'Ian wants the necklace too.'

'Is Smith in touch with Mosley's lot over here? Has he ever mentioned anything about them? Does he know Arthur Carnforth?'

She shook her head.

'Do you know when he arrived in this country?'

'Ian didn't say. I remember the day Eugene rang me, because it was the day of Freddie's funeral. But actually – the last time I saw Freddie, he said something about wanting to talk to me about something … someone … we were going to meet the following day, but of course he was dead by then. Perhaps he'd just met Eugene. Perhaps he wanted to warn me …'

'And now your husband – ex-husband – is threatening you. And you're frightened of him. And Roxburgh also believes you have this necklace.'

Regine nodded. 'I think they may be working together – or against each other. Paul – I am frightened. I know it's cowardly of me. And there's no one I can talk to, who can help me, except you. I've talked to my friend, to Cynthia, but she's in trouble too … and …'

She leaned towards him. She didn't even mean to do it, but it was as if she were making an offering of herself, her glance seemed to promise something intimate and special, not a vulgar sexual proposition, never that, but something more akin to sympathy, rapport, even innocence.

'You mustn't worry, Mrs Milner. I'll do everything I can to help.'

He felt certain there was, there must be, a link with Arthur Carnforth. Whoever paid Barker to shoot Freddie knew Carnforth as a fellow Nazi, knew Carnforth had his own particular interest in the photographs, or learned about them *from* Carnforth and then whatever the motive for the murder, blackmail became an opportunity …

Or perhaps Carnforth and the man from Shanghai had combined to murder Buckingham. They both hated him. Then again, Roxburgh wanted the necklace … could Roxburgh be the blackmailer?

'This could mean we'll be able to solve Mr Buckingham's murder.'

It didn't please her as much as he'd expected. She looked even more upset. 'But you know I said you weren't to tell *anyone* about Eugene. It mustn't come out! You promised!'

'Of course I understand ... I understand what an awkward situation you find yourself in. You did the right thing by telling me, and of course I wouldn't dream of doing anything to compromise you.'

'Eugene's given me a sort of final ultimatum. He's in a hurry to get back to Ireland. He needs money badly. He really believes I have the necklace, he's become so insistent. He's given me one last chance to return it. Otherwise he'll come to the house, come here. And that would be – awful. He says if I don't give him the necklace he'll make me pay. He'll ruin me for life.'

'Where are you supposed to meet him?'

'At the Euston Hotel. He'll be getting the train to Ireland. That's his idea – that I'll give him the necklace and then he'll leave me alone, leave the country.'

'I think you should meet him. I'll be there. I'll see you don't come to any harm.'

It was risky. Could he arrest the man? For demanding money with menaces? And how would Plumer react? Murray knew he was acting far too much on his own initiative. He must have gone mad to be risking his career for this woman.

But he accepted a second cup of coffee. And now she encouraged him to talk about himself, her face intense with interest as he poured out his hopes and ambitions. And – I think you're so brave, Sergeant Murray ... Paul ... it must be a frightfully difficult job ... I don't know how you do it ...

When she smiled she was irresistible. The dark red lips; what would it be like to kiss them?

* * * * *

'Where have you been, Murray?' Plumer's flat, pale face was as expressionless as ever, but Murray knew trouble was brewing because the guv'nor had stopped smoking for a moment and was sucking an indigestion tablet instead. And Ramsgate was seated on the edge of Plumer's desk.

'Mrs Milner phoned me. She had some new information. It puts things in a new light—'

'Never mind Mrs Milner for the moment. My visit to Buckingham's family doesn't seem to have helped. They rang the superintendent this morning. They're convinced the will is a forgery. They claim to have found an earlier will. So they're still contesting. That's their privilege, of course. But it puts even more pressure on us to solve the case. The super's furious. He feels we should have taken more notice of the family to begin with instead of listening to the Milner woman saying they weren't interested.'

'About Mrs Milner, sir—'

'Listen to me, Murray. Ramsgate and I have been looking at the photograph that was sent to Mr Rodney Ellington-Smith, who confirms that it was taken by Buckingham. Pinelli admits he and Barker stole the photos, so we've got him where we want him. The two of them murdered Buckingham in order to get hold of these photographs and now Pinelli's started to make use of them.'

Murray remembered the way he himself had threatened Pinelli, but he'd never believed for a moment that Plumer would actually try to nail the boy. 'D'you think he's bright enough for that, sir?'

Plumer ignored the question. 'We'll have to question Ian Roxburgh about the will again. He told us there's no money, so I don't understand its importance, but we'll have to at least go through the motions.'

'That's just it, sir. Mrs Milner told me—'

'I said I didn't want to hear any more about the woman.'

Vic Ramsgate sat back on the edge of Plumer's desk, a cocky smile on his fat, red face. Murray knew Ramsgate and Plumer didn't get on. Having to work with him would have been enough in itself to put Plumer in a bad mood, quite apart from the bollocking he'd apparently had from the superintendent.

'The dead man was probably blackmailing his mates himself.' Ramsgate seemed pleased with the idea. 'That's the sort of thing men like that do. Spiteful, vicious, no sense of loyalty, just like women.'

'He could hardly do that from the grave,' said Plumer drily.

'With respect, sir, please hear me out. According to Mrs Milner Buckingham did have something to leave.'

Having heard Murray out, Plumer merely said: 'Inspector Ramsgate has kindly shared valuable information with us and we've both wasted time here waiting for you. So Mrs Milner turns out to be a bigamist! I knew that woman was no better than she should be. And it sounds to me as though she's trying to use you to get her out of the hole she's dug for herself, by spinning some yarn about a necklace and trying to drag Roxburgh into it. Her marital difficulties have nothing to do with us. If she broke the law then she'll have to face the music. It has no bearing on this case.'

'Yes, sir. She is being blackmailed though, sir.'

'Tell her to report it then.'

'Well, she did, she reported it to me—'

'To the local force, Murray, you fathead. You've really let yourself get far too involved with that woman. She's strung you along with all sorts of information that's led nowhere. If she now thinks we're going to get her off the hook by – what – arresting this man she alleges is blackmailing her? – she's got another think coming.'

Murray stood red-faced, silent. It was humiliating enough to be reprimanded in front of Ramsgate, who was smiling broadly. Worse was the unfairness of it all; as if it hadn't been Plumer who'd *told* him to cultivate Regine. Worst of all, though, was that Murray realised only now, too late, that he'd done what he promised he wouldn't do; he'd told his superiors that Regine was a bigamist.

thirty

'THERE YOU ARE, Charles.'

Something must have happened. His father was never at home when Charles returned from school.

'Let's sit down in here, old chap.' He pushed open the drawing-room door. The room was empty.

'Where's mother?'

'That's what I wanted to talk to you about.' John Hallam sat down and gestured to Charles to do the same. He cleared his throat. 'The fact is – you know she hasn't been well lately. It's, well, it's what they call a nervous breakdown. I suppose it's partly my fault, I've been preoccupied ...' He left the sentence unfinished, as he encountered the blank unresponsive gaze of his son. How difficult the boy was, an enigma. Perhaps Vivienne had been right, they shouldn't have sent him away ... too late now ... 'She's gone for a rest cure, in a nursing home, it's not for long, just a few weeks, to build her up again – you know she wasn't eating properly.'

The lump in Charles's throat was as unexpected as it was unwelcome. His jaw trembled with the effort of holding back the sudden urge to sob. He looked down, blinking. He couldn't speak.

'We'll give her a few days to settle in and we'll drive down at the weekend if I can get hold of some petrol. Otherwise there is a train.'

The lump subsided and Charles leant against the back of the sofa. As the dustsheet shifted it gave off a dank smell of plaster. It was a mental home, a lunatic asylum, that's what his father was talking about, he knew it was. 'Mr Carnforth will be upset.' His voice came out strangely squeaky and high.

John Hallam looked at him. What an extraordinary thing to say. And yet – perhaps the boy knew more than one realised. 'That's been part of the problem, you see. You're old enough to understand these things. She got in with all those long-haired friends of Freddie's. I'm glad you mentioned Mr Carnforth, the man's a crackpot. I shall speak to the school.'

'You should, you should tell them. You should tell them Mr Carnforth supports Oswald Mosley.'

'How do you know that?'

'He spoke to me about Mendelssohn. He said he was a dirty Jew and I shouldn't have anything to do with him.'

John Hallam sat stiffly, staring ahead. Things were even worse than he'd realised. How *could* Vivienne have consorted with such a man. 'I can't understand why your mother became so … it's beyond me. But I'm glad you told me this. I shall certainly talk to the headmaster. It's disgraceful.'

In the corridors, on his way to the detested gym, in the dingy basement dining room, whenever Charles was not in a classroom he was on the alert for a sighting of Carnforth. Not that Carnforth was often to be seen in main school. His duties as art master were light, for the subject was compulsory only for the first two years, and so he spent most of his time in the art annexe, developing his photographs or painting; not, as Charles had once imagined, weaving a web to ensnare little boys, but lying in wait and plotting, plotting to have Vivienne all to himself, to seize her, to take her away from them. And Freddie must somehow have got in the way of the plan and so he'd had to be eliminated.

That it must have been Arthur Carnforth who'd murdered Freddie had come to Charles in a blinding flash of inspiration. The idea had such economy; it explained everything. He began to devote to it all the single-minded energy that had previously been divided between school work and his pursuit of men in the secret meeting grounds he'd begun to discover in pockets of Camden Town, down towards the railway terminals and even as far south as Leicester Square and Piccadilly Circus.

Twice he'd followed Carnforth home to his flat in Handel Street, had waited and waited as it grew dark until he'd heard a taxi draw up in the street and watched his mother step airily into the cavernous flats where Carnforth had his lair. On both occasions his mother had re-emerged shortly afterwards, accompanied now by the art master, and they'd walked away westwards. Charles had followed them, keeping a careful distance. They had walked some way until eventually they came to a curious church set between two other buildings. He could not follow them in there. In his gnawing, torturing curiosity he imagined their discussion with the priest – about marriage? divorce? Perhaps Carnforth was trying to brainwash her into becoming a nun. Crazy thoughts buzzed like wasps through his brain.

At home no one spoke, but the air was thick with it – or rather, the opposite. The vast, empty, half-renovated rooms were as if abandoned before having even been lived in; airless; the three of them living in a vacuum. Life deprived of oxygen shrivelled up in the great, gaunt house.

Perhaps it was a good thing his father had had her locked up. At least she was beyond the reach of Carnforth now. But it was all Carnforth's fault – and if Carnforth was a murderer, who might he murder next?

At the end of afternoon school, Charles took the back way round the playing fields to Carnforth's isolated hideout. Although he knew he'd be alone with a murderer, he wasn't frightened of Carnforth. He knocked, then opened the door without waiting for a reply.

Carnforth was emerging from the darkroom.

'Oh, Hallam ... Charles.' Carnforth seemed stymied. 'I didn't expect you,' he blurted, stating the obvious. 'But – but as it happens, I'm glad you're here.' He hesitated, then stumbled on. 'It's always good when boys feel they can drop in unannounced. Sit down – sit down.' Carnforth dropped heavily in the chair by his desk, but Charles remained standing, leaning against the door jamb.

'I was hoping to speak to you, because I telephoned, but I was told your mother had gone away. Is she on holiday? She mentioned nothing to me. We were supposed to meet.'

Charles had expected to feel triumphant, had expected to gloat inwardly. But he was too frightened, now, not of Carnforth, but by the thought that his mother might never come home, might be locked away for ever, that he barely registered the art master's desperation. He spoke the words he'd prepared quite mechanically.

'I'm afraid she's ill, sir. She's in a nursing home for a week or two.'

Carnforth stared blankly at Charles. 'A nursing home?' He stared at the floor. Then he gathered himself together with a deep sigh. 'Is she allowed visitors? You must tell me where she is. I must go and see her.'

'That's why I came to see you, sir. As soon as she's able to have visitors, she asked me to arrange for you to go there. My father isn't keen – he doesn't want her over-excited, but I'm sure

I can fix something up for you.'

'That's very good of you, Charles.'

Charles walked away from the art annexe towards the goods entrance and the anonymity of the main road. It had been easier than he'd expected. Carnforth was a fool. But now there would have to be a plan. He'd thought of going to the police. But that would be no good. He hadn't any proof of anything. And the police were useless anyway. He would just have to take matters into his own hands.

thirty-one

MURRAY MET JAMES MCGOVERN in a pub near King's Cross.

'The man you saw with Pinelli at the demonstration, and who we both saw with Carnforth at the Mosley rally: I've found out a bit about him. He's known as Patrick O'Connell now. He showed up earlier in the year, in the summer sometime. He was in a lot of trouble in the Far East. He was an Irish patriot – if that's what you call it; very anti-British, pro-Nazi. He went under another name out there – or several. So it looks as if he is the husband of the scarlet woman of Hampstead.'

'You were right about Plumer, you know. He admitted it – there's someone higher up who wants Carnforth left alone.'

'I told you so. Someone who doesn't want Mosley annoyed.'

'He wants to arrest and charge Pinelli.'

'Pinelli's not the murderer, though, is he?'

'He hasn't got the brains for blackmail, I can tell you that much. I doubt if he can even read and write properly. And the boss knows it really. That's why we haven't been round there already.'

'Would Carnforth not fit the bill if you were able to touch him?'

'He has an alibi, although if he paid Barker to do it the alibi isn't relevant. But I'm coming round to the view he did it himself. Then possibly Barker found out and had to be got rid of too. Because I don't think the alibi means much. The couple, they're blackshirts too, they'd stick by him.'

'You can't just assume that.'

'I admit he's not the only one with a motive. A lot of people hated the dead man.' Murray stretched towards the Player's packet on the table, then withdrew his hand again. 'And Ian Roxburgh, the executor – he's threatened Mrs Milner too.' He repeated what Regine had told him. 'The guv'nor's decided she's led me astray. He's simply not interested in Mrs Milner's husband. I don't think he even believes her story. I think he thinks she's making it all up because she's in a jam.'

Murray's hand crept forward again, and this time he did extract a cigarette. Smoking helped you think, after all. 'The dead man has left him everything. Roxburgh says there's nothing but debts, but if this necklace exists and is valuable then—'

'Do you believe Mrs Milner? She hasn't got it?'

'No – I'm sure she hasn't. She'd have told me.'

'Perhaps we should go and talk to Ian Roxburgh.'

'We're not supposed to be working on this together. Plumer's angry enough with me already.'

'He can't do much, can he, because of what you know – what he told you.'

The friends emerged into the bleak wastes of the Gray's Inn Road and passed the Royal Free Hospital on their way up to King's Cross.

At Bank station Murray saw the *Evening News* headline: MINISTER RESIGNS. He paid for a copy and glanced at it as they walked along Cheapside towards the side street where Roxburgh had his office. So Ernie Appleton had bitten the dust. He wondered if it would make a difference to the Buckingham case.

'It's half past four. He may have left.'

'How much time does he spend here anyway? He's not a bona fide businessman, is he?'

But when Murray knocked on the glass-panelled door, there was a noise from within and Roxburgh opened it.

'We've a few more questions. Mind if we come in?'

'I'm in rather a hurry.'

Roxburgh was clearing out. Papers were scattered on the floor. Filing cabinet drawers hung open. Half-packed cardboard boxes stood on the desk and on a chair.

'Mrs Milner says you've been threatening her.' As he spoke Murray moved round the office and behind the desk, by the old-fashioned typewriter that hadn't yet been packed. He examined the few abandoned files and letters. He picked up a sheet of paper, wound it between the rollers and typed a few words.

'I think there's been a misunderstanding. Mrs Milner's rather prone to exaggeration – like so many women. Women tend to be rather emotional, don't they.'

'She says you and her former husband—'

'Her legal husband, you mean, I think.'

Murray was still typing as he talked. 'Eugene Smith, also known as Patrick O'Connell. She says you and he have been demanding the return of some jewellery she doesn't have. You also told us Buckingham had no money, only debts. But if this necklace exists, that changes the picture, doesn't it? Then there's the question of the naughty photographs he took. A number of men have been blackmailed. The vice squad is close to arresting the blackmailer.'

This was a lie; indeed, it was the opposite of the truth, since Ramsgate was concerned only with arresting victims; but Roxburgh wasn't to know that. His pale blue gaze wavered.

'And now we find you're leaving,' chipped in McGovern.

'Bit of a coincidence, eh?'

'Not at all.'

'I hope you're not planning to leave London, Captain Roxburgh. We'd rather you didn't go too far for the moment, because we will need to talk to you again.'

Roxburgh raised an eyebrow. 'You forget I'm Buckingham's executor. I'm hardly in a position to leave permanently. But I have family in South Africa and a relative of mine has died.'

'*South Africa*! That's a long way away. Have you and O'Connell agreed to divide the spoils, then? He'll get the necklace and you keep the photographs?'

'You shouldn't believe everything Mrs Milner tells you. As I said. And I know nothing about any photographs. If you're really interested in solving the Buckingham business then I suggest you talk to O'Connell. But it doesn't seem as if you *are* very interested. You certainly haven't made much progress.'

After he'd parted from McGovern at King's Cross, Murray went to a telephone kiosk and dialled the Hampstead number. A man's voice answered. Murray silently cursed, but to his relief it was not Neville Milner, but the lodger.

Regine was out. At once Murray imagined her walking on the Heath – but it was too late, getting dark. She was in danger and he couldn't reach her. He started to walk back to the centre of town. He crossed Russell Square and passed the length of the British Museum. He was in that state of mind when frustration and anxiety combine to create a mood of indescribable tension, an almost physical irritation as of the skin burning with eczema, a dreadful discomfort. He couldn't stand it. He had to see her. He would go up and wait outside her house. No, he would telephone again. No – because if she still wasn't there he'd just feel more frustrated.

He stopped at Tottenham Court Road. There was the Corner House. There he'd met her. Now he had no idea where she was. There was nothing he could do. He was not going to see her this evening unless he hung about outside her house and that was too servile, too desperate.

He turned and walked back in the direction of Russell Square and King's Cross, through the yellow pools of light that splashed the prevailing darkness of the acid streets, past the flow of anonymous strangers to which he was so accustomed, bought a ticket and ran down the escalator. There was nothing for it but to go home.

In south London the lights seemed dimmer than ever, the buildings more decayed, the pedestrians more weary and the rows upon regimented rows of terraces more lonesome and endless. As he walked from the station he was gnawed by the conviction that something – everything – the case, Regine, his future – was almost within his grasp, yet tantalisingly beyond it.

thirty-two

MURRAY WALKED UNDER the great arch in front of the station and towards the station itself, looking cautiously around as he did so. He had arrived early on purpose. Inside the main station he saw a queue forming for the boat train to Holyhead and thence to Dun Laoghaire and Dublin. He stepped back into the cover of an archway, and scanned the patient line of passengers, but there was no sign of O'Connell. The hands of the huge clock pointed to five to five. He slipped along among the travellers scurrying to and fro and met McGovern, as arranged, by the bookstall.

'I told the guv'nor he's a member of the IRA,' said McGovern, grinning, 'which he might be.'

'She's meeting him in the Euston Hotel,' said Murray. 'I'd better walk over there.'

'I'll wait outside and follow him when he leaves.'

Murray walked casually into the hotel foyer. The faded dun-coloured wallpaper and shabby green-and-pink patterned carpet had seen better days. The woman at the reception desk glanced at him, but he turned aside towards the bar. It was only five o'clock, but perhaps the hotel had a different licence, for there were quite a few drinkers standing at the counter and they didn't look like hotel guests. Several of the tables were occupied as well. Murray took up a position at the bar and ordered a half pint. He'd purchased a newspaper at the kiosk and from behind it he glanced round the panelled lounge. No sign of Regine.

For a grim moment doubt assailed him. She wasn't coming. It was all some kind of hoax or fantasy or …

She stood in the doorway in a black astrakhan coat and long, red gloves. She looked round the room, then set off across the bar to a table half hidden by a heavy curtain at the nearby window. The man already seated there was the man who'd been with Pinelli and whom Murray had followed to Whitechapel. He couldn't see whether the man's clothes were new or old, well cared for or unkempt, but there was something about the set of his shoulders, his too-long hair and what he could see of his expression in the dim lighting from the electric candelabras suspended high up in the ceiling, that made him look somehow defeated rather than menacing. But then he leaned forward as he spoke to Regine and as she recoiled slightly, Murray had a different impression. O'Connell had a nearly empty glass of beer in front of him and the smoke rose from his cigarette as he spoke intensely to Regine.

When O'Connell approached the bar Murray shielded his face behind his paper. O'Connell stood quite close to him, but showed no sign of being aware of his presence – and why should he, thought Murray – as he ordered an orange squash and a double whisky.

O'Connell carried the drinks to the table. The conversation with Regine continued. O'Connell leaned forward; Regine sat upright, and spoke hardly at all.

Then she opened her bag. So perhaps there was a necklace after all. She drew out an envelope, which she passed across the table. O'Connell didn't look inside it, just thrust it in his pocket.

Murray wondered if he dared attempt to get closer. There was an unoccupied table to the near side of the curtain, which was drawn back from the lofty window with a tie, so that its thickness would have provided a minimum of cover if he moved there, but it was too risky, he decided. O'Connell might notice.

Time passed slowly. Regine stood up. O'Connell stayed seated. Regine passed across the lounge. She didn't look at Murray, but he knew she'd seen him. He glanced back at O'Connell, but O'Connell wasn't watching his wife. He was digging in his pocket for the envelope. It was safe to follow Regine out into the foyer as they'd arranged. Murray just hoped McGovern wouldn't miss O'Connell when he left the bar.

It was another foggy evening. Murray looked back as he caught up with Regine in Euston Square, to make sure O'Connell hadn't followed her out, but figures were indistinct in the mist.

'Thank you for being there.' Regine looked pale. 'I saw you in the bar, of course. It was dreadful,' she said. 'He was angry. I brought him some money, but he only wants the necklace. He's so sure I have it. It's a delusion. I've never had it. He says he's giving me one last chance. And then he started on about how Freddie might have had it and Neville and I might have taken it when we went round to Markham Square. He knew we went there. But how did he know? So I asked him. He knew he'd slipped up then, he was angry, but he didn't pretend or anything. He came right out with it. He said he was watching the house. And – I can't remember exactly the words he used – but the way he said it, it was obvious he knew Freddie had been murdered. I mean *then*, the morning after, before it was in the papers or anything.'

'Why does he go on meeting you like this? You say he's desperate to get away to Ireland. If that's the case, and if he's so sure you have this necklace you'd think he'd have come to your house, or staged a burglary while you were out.'

'I think he does it to torment me.'

'Perhaps he's afraid of the dog.'

'Oh no!' She smiled sadly. 'Cato adores him. He's played with him on the Heath. That wouldn't be a deterrent at all.'

Perhaps he was in league with Roxburgh; waiting perhaps for some of the proceeds of the blackmail. And Roxburgh was leaving the country in order to double-cross him ...

They had to stop by the kerb as the traffic fled by. She looked right and left. 'Look – I'm so late. Neville will wonder where I am – I'll have to get a taxi.'

'But – ' He couldn't conceal his dismay. 'I need to talk to you – to know what he said – is he leaving tonight?'

She flagged down a cab and opened the door. 'Ride up with me to Hampstead. That way we can talk.'

Disappointed – he'd planned another intimate rendezvous in a bar somewhere – but without hesitation, he climbed in behind her. They sat together in the black leather cell and the confined space itself created a curious intimacy. He closed the glass partition between themselves and the driver and asked in a low voice: 'What else did he say?'

'He said he had a gun, I don't know if that's true, I didn't see it – he threatened me – he went on and on about the neck-lace.'

'He'd hardly bring out a gun in the middle of a busy bar.'

'He was in such a strange mood I wouldn't have put it past him. What was so unnerving was his mood seemed to fluctuate, so one minute he was threatening me and then he started rambling on about Freddie and Shanghai.' She leaned back in the cab and glanced sideways at Murray. 'Do you think perhaps he might be ill? There was something feverish about him. He asked if I'd seen Ian Roxburgh – yes, I think he must be ill. The way he was talking was as if everything's against him, everyone. He seemed angry with Ian Roxburgh as well, he said he'd double-crossed him too, but, you know, the whole world was against him. He was clear about one thing, though. He said he's giving me one more chance. He was angry because he'd had to put off catching the boat train because of me. He's going tomorrow, but if I don't produce the necklace ...' She shut her eyes for a moment. 'It's like a bad dream,' she murmured, 'there are times I still don't even believe it.'

'You're to meet him again, then?'

She nodded. 'On the Heath this time. In the morning.'

That would be more dangerous: few people about, great empty spaces and not much cover. He swore silently.

'I'll be there,' he said.

'Promise? I'm frightened. But – wouldn't it be better not to go at all?'

'Perhaps ... but why is he so certain you have this necklace?'

Regine didn't answer. She was playing with her gloves, massaging the soft suede against her hands, pulling the fingers, then smoothing the backs of her gloved hands again.

Unable to resist, he placed his hand on hers. 'You are telling me the truth? There isn't something else – anything – anything I need to know?'

She looked up at him with such a naked, defenceless gaze that, without intending to, he bent forward and kissed her. To his astonishment the pressure of lips became, shockingly, more, her hot open mouth sending an electric jolt to his groin. He bent further, pressed closer ...

The taxi drew to a halt. Flustered, she put her gloved hands to her face. 'I'll pay – no please, I wouldn't dream of letting you – ' and she was on the pavement before he could stop her, only leaning back in through the open door to say: 'He'll be under the beech trees. At eleven.'

He told the cabbie to drive back to Euston and lay back against the padded seat, stunned.

thirty-three

CHARLES WALKED ROUND to the art annexe. When Carnforth saw him a strange smile crossed his features. 'Hallam – Charles! This is a surprise. How is your mother?'

Charles knew Carnforth was in his power now. 'Good news. She's much better. She's coming home much sooner than expected, today in fact. She wants to see you, but it's rather difficult as you can imagine. The idea is I take you to meet her – she hasn't thought of exactly where yet, but I can meet you at Hampstead station on Saturday. My father's on call at the hospital. We'll have sorted something out by then.'

It sounded utterly implausible, but Charles was counting on Carnforth's desperation, and it worked. 'Thank you. Thank you, Charles. That's good of you. I'm so grateful. I've been worried.'

Charles smiled.

With Vivienne away, work on the house ground to a halt. Lugg and his men dispersed to other jobs. The dust settled. The house was colder than ever.

But now Charles was no longer brought down by the paralysing depression of living in the ruin. His father was at the hospital. Madge had the half day off. No one saw him leave the house.

He arrived at Hampstead underground station ten minutes early and waited just inside. He kept looking at his watch, but it was only five minutes before the lift doors clanked open and Carnforth shambled towards him, his shoulders hunched into his black coat as if to minimise his height, but still Charles had to brace himself against the overpowering bulk of the man.

'So glad you could make it, sir.'

'Of course I could – make it, as you say.'

Charles led him out of the station and up Heath Street. He'd tried to prepare some topics of conversation to get them through the walk to the rendezvous, but had no need of them, for Carnforth was eager to talk, stammering his way through a series of futile attempts to get Charles to engage on the subject of religion. 'I've been praying for your mother, you know. I know you haven't yet experienced the power of prayer, but I do assure you ...'

Charles wasn't even listening. It was unbelievable what tripe people talked and he also found it astonishing how people lied all the time, even when they must know everyone knew they were lying. But perhaps they believed their own lies. All this stuff about God was lies. Carnforth just spouted on about it to make himself feel good. It was pure self-importance.

Carnforth walked rather slowly. Charles sauntered along at his side, controlling his impatience, noticing the worn edges of Carnforth's coat, his heavy black shoes, like a policeman's, and, today, his ridiculous homburg hat, shiny and going green with age at the edge.

What on earth had his mother – but he couldn't bear to think of Vivienne and this ... hulk, who increasingly reminded him of the convict in the film of *Great Expectations*. Yes, something of the convict clung to him. And Regine's lodger, Phil, knew Carnforth had been locked up in the war. Charles was vague on the details, but he'd definitely been in prison. The Nazis hated everyone who wasn't like them. Yet the curious thing was Carnforth didn't seem like that. He seemed ponderous and slow and in a way quite gentle. Only when he'd started to spout on about Adam Mendelssohn had his words become violent. Then Charles had glimpsed another side of the man. That, he now thought, was the moment when the idea of Carnforth the murderer had first crossed his mind. But he wasn't frightened.

They had reached the main road now. 'Where are we going?' Carnforth moved his unwieldy head to and fro.

'It's not far. Just along here.'

Charles had no difficulty finding the path Regine had shown him that day. He led Carnforth down the mud track towards the rusted staircase. 'There's a garden,' he said. 'My mother used to come here when Anna Pavlova lived at the house.' This was pure invention, but he liked it. 'This is where she wanted to meet you.'

It had been a stroke of genius on his part. The place was deserted. No one ever came here. The walkways looked even more neglected than he remembered in the still grisaille of the wintry air. The roses had withered. Yellowed leaves lay scattered along the paving. In the gardens below, flower beds were tangled and overgrown beneath bare, blackened trees. They walked along the balcony as it turned and twisted above the overgrown lawns and terraces.

'A melancholy place, isn't it, sir,' commented Charles. He wasn't sure what he was going to say when they came to the wall at the end. But he knew what he wanted to do. Now he *was* feeling nervous.

'What time was Vivienne to be here? Is she late, do you think? Do you think she had trouble getting away?'

'Oh, she'll be along soon,' said Charles carelessly, but he was shivering with tension.

They reached the dead end. Charles leaned against the last column, near where the coping had broken and been replaced by wooden palings. 'Look, sir,' he said, 'even when it's misty like this, and dusk's coming down, the view is amazing.'

Carnforth looked. He gazed northwards, hands in pockets, suddenly an unexpectedly commanding figure, a captain at the prow of his ship. He turned and said:

'There's something I wanted to say to you, Charles. I know you were angry with me. I know you believe you were fond of Freddie Buckingham. But what he did to you was unforgivable. And I couldn't bear the way he influenced Vivienne, she couldn't see how everything he did was tainted and false and … and artificial. There was a time before the war when she even thought she was in love with him. He came between us – her and me – he turned her against me, you know. I never forgave him for that.'

'You shouldn't have shown my mother the photograph of … of me.'

'I had to prove to her what he was really like.'

'So you *did* show her the photograph.'

'I had to show her what he'd done to you.'

'Freddie didn't *do* anything to me,' said Charles between gritted teeth. 'It's just the way I am. I did it to myself.'

And then it hit him – the implication of what had just been said. 'How did you get hold of the photograph?' The icy certainty of it was appalling. But it was also liberating. His instinct had been right all along.

Carnforth slowly turned his head. 'She's late, isn't she? Is she coming? What can have happened?' Carnforth peered along the shadowy terrace.

Charles had planned what to say next: it's a joke, she's still in the mental home, you'll never see her again. But he would play Carnforth along for a little while yet. 'She may have found it difficult to get away,' he said vaguely, 'but I'm sure she'll be here soon.' He brought out his cigarettes and lit one. The sense of triumph was ebbing away, because he'd remembered the photos. Everything between his mother and himself was poisoned now for ever. 'You really shouldn't have shown her that photo of me and Freddie,' he repeated. 'That was a rotten thing to do.'

Carnforth stood to his full height. He suddenly advanced across the restricted space and Charles felt real, searing fear of this man, a murderer after all. But Carnforth stopped a few paces from him.

'Don't you see, Charles, how he sinned against you. Someone had to do something. Freddie had to be stopped – and you need help too – don't reject the help I can give you – spiritual help – '

Charles started to shake, but he said coolly: 'I'm sorry, sir, what did you say?'

'He had to be stopped, Charles. It had to be stopped.'

So he'd confessed.

The inhaled smoke steadied Charles's nerves. 'I suppose you killed Freddie because you were jealous. That's why you killed him.'

It was spoken so calmly that Carnforth took a few seconds to take in the meaning of the words. He stared at Charles. 'I – killed Freddie? You think that?'

Charles stared at him. His smile was insistent, relentless. 'Who else could have done it?'

Carnforth's face reddened. 'Does *she* believe that – are they trying to poison her mind against me? Are they?'

He took another step towards Charles. His bewilderment and distress seemed to be turning to rage. 'She isn't coming, is she? This is all some sort of ... joke. Is that what it is? You think it's funny, telling me she's meeting me here? Did you think this up?'

'Keep away from me! Don't touch me, murderer!' shrieked Charles. 'Of course she's not coming. She loathes you, she always loathed you!' And driven by a frenzy of loathing he lurched forward and pushed the great bulk of the man away.

Caught off guard, Carnforth staggered back against the wooden rail. There was a frozen moment when he seemed to realise it was giving away and flailed, grasped at the air, grasped at Charles, but Charles leapt backwards in a paroxysm of infantile glee at having got the better of him. With wonderful exhilaration he saw Carnforth topple away out of sight towards the terraces below, the fall forcing from him an eerie howl before he smashed onto the stone.

Silence folded back in on itself. Charles was shaking. His cigarette had fallen to the ground. He stared at it. After a while he bent very slowly, like an old man, and tried to pick it up, but his fingers were shaking too much. He stood up and stamped it out instead. He walked along the colonnade and when he came to the first corner, where the stone of the balcony was more secure, he leant over, but what lay beneath was obscured by bushes. He walked on until he came to a flight of steps leading down to the garden. He stood for a while at the top, then descended slowly and walked back towards the pond. Carnforth lay, horribly huddled and twisted on his side, one eye staring at the sky as a pool of blood seeped from under his head.

Just one little push and Carnforth's great bulk was crumpled and broken. But now the exhilaration was gone, wiped out by an overpowering weariness.

Charles's innards cramped. He gagged, turned away and was sick into the bushes. He gasped, still bent over, then breathing deeply, he stood upright, walked slowly back up the steps again and returned to the dead end of the colonnade.

It would be clear what had happened. An accident – or suicide perhaps. The wooden palings just weren't safe. No one would ever know the truth.

He'd forgotten about the cigarette stub he'd stamped into the ground. He walked slowly away in the gathering dusk. When he reached the main road he crossed onto the Heath. He trudged through the wooded landscape. At the crossing of two paths a man was loitering. He asked Charles for a light. They stood together for a few moments and then together they sought a hiding place in the undergrowth.

thirty-four

'WHERE THE HELL HAVE you been?' Murray almost collided with Plumer as he plunged along the corridor to his superior's office. 'We've got Roxburgh. His plane was delayed by fog. It was almost accidental – someone from customs and excise recognised him and – I'll tell you later. He's in the interview room. I'm going to see him now. You'd better come too.'

How could this all have happened so soon? Murray let himself be hurried downstairs in a state of stupefied bewilderment.

The way in which suspects comported themselves under questioning always interested Murray. It was an indicator of truth or falsehood if you knew how to interpret small movements, glances and nervous tics, a point made by Hans Gross in his *Criminal Investigation*, the detectives' bible.

Ian Roxburgh was one of those whom Murray would have expected to give a performance of fake upper-class hauteur. But Roxburgh seemed relaxed and was not on his high horse at all. He asked politely if he might smoke.

'I'm sorry I was rather brusque when you called round, Sergeant Murray,' he said. 'And I know I gave the wrong impression – as you've realised now, my flight was today, or ought to have been.' He offered them a smile of conscious ruefulness. 'But I can explain the items found in my luggage.'

This was yet more puzzling to Murray.

'That's a matter for my colleagues,' said Plumer, 'we're not interested in that. If you were smuggling art objects or anything else, that will be dealt with. We want to know about your relationship with Frederick Buckingham. I have just returned from seeing his family in Yorkshire. You know they're contesting the will. They have produced a different will and question the validity of the later one, of which you are the executor. I'd be interested to know how it came about that Buckingham made this later will. If he did. I want to know exactly what happened.'

'Well – I suppose I'd better come clean,' said Roxburgh. 'The fact is, I found myself in an awkward position,' he said almost coyly. 'The man known as Patrick O'Connell. Well, the fact is, he tried to blackmail me.'

'What was your relationship with this man? When did you meet him?'

'I met him in Manila, late 1945. He was in a bad state. He was called Eugene Smith then, by the way, but let's stick to O'Connell. He'd escaped from Shanghai on a boat with some other crooked pal. Their idea was to deal in cigarettes, medicines … I don't know the details of it, but his friend had lit out back for Shanghai with the money and O'Connell was left stranded. The Americans wanted to arrest him, they didn't believe he was an Irish citizen at first, they thought he was a British quisling – which wasn't surprising as he had a British passport, illegally acquired, no doubt. Anyway, I managed to sort it out for him. In return he put me in the way of useful contacts. Along the way he told me about Freddie Buckingham. He was very bitter about him, said Buckingham had informed on him and so forth, but that I should contrive to get to know him when I got to London, because he moved in wealthy artistic circles – he'd know all sorts of people who'd be interested in what I had to sell.

'So I looked Freddie up when I arrived in London – I told him I'd met O'Connell. That rattled him. He didn't trust me at first, understandably, but oddly enough Freddie and I got on like a house on fire. But he was, well, he was vulnerable, wasn't he, and I soon found out his major weak spot – he was just mad about the Hallam boy. So – well, I could see ways of benefiting from the situation. One sort of knew about these photos he'd taken of his friends, and I began to think how one could make use of them, if only one could get hold of them. I tried to think of ways – I thought the friendlier we became – let's say I thought there'd be ways round it. I was convinced I'd be able to persuade him to let me have a look at them, and then – but then he was murdered! That upset me. And it made me very nervous. But at the same time – there was my opportunity.' Roxburgh passed his finger to and fro across his moustache.

'You forged the will,' said Murray. It was a shot in the dark.

Plumer said in his uninterested voice: 'And where does O'Connell fit in? You were in this together, weren't you.'

'No, you're wrong there,' said Roxburgh pleasantly, but he looked uneasy. 'It was a bit of a shock, him reappearing like that, so suddenly. I never thought he'd make it back to Europe. I thought he'd blow his money on gambling and drink or that someone would kill him; or both. But now here he was – and he began to be rather annoying. He began to suggest that some of my activities weren't quite pukka – which is far from being the case, by the way, your colleague who arrested me has got completely the wrong end of the stick – but he was very insistent; a little unhinged, I thought. Men like that make me nervous, and I got even more nervous when I found out the first thing he did when he got to London was link up with the blackshirts. I thought the best thing to do was to pretend to play along with him. I even told him about the photographs, pointed out how useful they could be. And he got in touch with Buckingham. This was not long before Buckingham was murdered.'

'Why didn't you go to the police at once?' said Murray. 'Buckingham's death would have been avoided, O'Connell wouldn't have terrorised Mrs Milner – whatever O'Connell did or was trying to do, you were involved, weren't you. You knew O'Connell planned to murder Buckingham, or have him murdered.'

Roxburgh shook his head. 'No, no, you're quite mistaken. You've got it all wrong. I guessed who was behind it, though, that crazy mad dog, O'Connell.'

'Conspiracy to murder is a serious matter,' said Plumer. 'You are already under investigation for other crimes; it might help your case if you were to be a little franker with us than you have been so far.' He spoke with as much emotion as if he'd been reciting some minor by-law. Yet the utter lack of drama with which he spoke was effective, dampening down the tension, lulling Roxburgh into a false sense of security. 'You were party to this man O'Connell's plans, that's what you're saying, isn't it.'

It was the opposite of what Roxburgh had said, but he hesitated.

'Tell us the truth, Captain Roxburgh,' encouraged Plumer.

'I only pretended to go along with the blackmail scheme,' said Roxburgh, 'and I didn't know about Buckingham. O'Connell just said something about giving him a fright – I think it was meant to look like a queer thing – a proposition that went wrong, just to get Freddie out of the way for a couple of hours so someone could go over and get the photos.'

'So you must have been pretty frightened when Buckingham ended up dead.'

Roxburgh lit another cigarette. 'I thought the stupid little bastard had cocked things up,' he said in a low voice. 'I was *devastated*. And then I began to think that – that he was meant to die all along ... but once it had happened there was no point in not ...'

'In not benefiting,' said Murray.

'And what did you think when Kenneth Barker was killed?' asked Plumer.

Roxburgh swallowed, coughed, looked into the coal of his cigarette as though it held the answer. 'I don't know anything about that,' he said.

'And you do benefit,' commented Plumer in his dry, neutral way. 'Not only do you get the dead man's estate, but with O'Connell you demanded money with menaces from various individuals, including – yes? – a government minister, whose wrongdoing you have heard about from Freddie Buckingham or his friends.'

'I had nothing to do with Mr Buckingham's murder. I am absolutely innocent on that score.'

Murray pulled the sheet of typed paper from his pocket. 'I was surprised you didn't ask me why I took a typewriter sample when I was in your office. Or did you think you'd be out of the country by the time we matched it to the envelopes sent to the blackmail victims?'

'Didn't it occur to you, Captain, that the family was bound to contest the will? It was a hare-brained scheme, wasn't it,' said Plumer.

Murray silently agreed with that assessment. Yet it didn't surprise him. Most of the crooks and conmen he'd encountered were in one way or another stupid. Sometimes they had too much imagination and too little sense. They thought their daydreams had become reality when they were only on the drawing board. Often they deceived themselves almost as much as they deceived other people and most of the more ambitious had delusions of grandeur.

Later, in a pub near the office, Plumer said: 'No one told

you to meet up with Mrs Milner – in fact the whole of your afternoon's activities require explanation.'

But Murray knew he was no longer in hot water. Plumer wasn't angry any more. In fact he was grateful to Murray, who'd diverted attention from Carnforth and changed the direction of enquiries.

'We'll get Pinelli as an accessory, burglary and so on. That'll put him out of circulation for a while.'

'What about O'Connell and Mrs Milner, sir? I do believe she is in danger from him. She says he's armed, and she's agreed to meet him again tomorrow. On the Heath.'

'On the Heath. That's bad. It might be a better idea to go down to Whitechapel and arrest him now.'

But Eugene Smith, alias Patrick O'Connell, wasn't to be found in Rowton House. The overseer, a grim NCO type, had seen him come in, but hadn't seen him leave.

In spite of the rows of small windows in the long, forbidding façade there was a magnificence in the sooted brick, the ogee turrets and the grandiose portico, although whether this was to celebrate the generosity of the donor, Lord Rowton, or to overawe the inmates was impossible to tell. The detectives walked round to the back of the building. There was a back exit, but it was locked. There was also a fire escape.

'It will have to be the Heath then,' said Plumer grimly.

Murray, wearing a dun-coloured raincoat to make himself, he hoped, less conspicuous, followed Regine at a safe distance onto the Heath. She had told him of O'Connell's habit of appearing where she least expected him and that made it even trickier. Murray felt exposed. There was no cover until they reached the trees.

Murray's supporting officers would have to be stationed well away from the beech trees. And they'd just have to hope that O'Connell turned up as expected and didn't waylay Regine en route.

They'd discussed whether she should have the dog with her. That might lull O'Connell's suspicions, but Regine had said the animal was too unpredictable and it would only complicate things.

In the end, Murray had taken one of the revolvers himself. He shouldn't have done that, but he couldn't rely on armed support in the exposed wastes of the Heath.

The whole thing was crazy. They should never have let her meet the man out here. Her life was in danger and they couldn't protect her.

There was no sign of O'Connell among the beech trees. Regine stopped, looked round, paced to and fro. Murray couldn't see his men. He'd told them to take up a position behind him in the undergrowth some yards from the beeches. He himself was standing shielded by overgrown brambles. Too far away.

Suddenly O'Connell was there. Murray hadn't seen him walking up the hill. He'd appeared out of nowhere, as Regine had said he would.

Murray had to act at once. O'Connell had his back to him. He crept forward. O'Connell was speaking to Regine, in a low voice at first, but then it began to rise. Murray took another step forward, but his foot cracked on a twig. O'Connell whirled round, looked wildly from side to side and then started to run. Murray pulled out his weapon. O'Connell was running and stumbling away down the hill, Regine left rudderless, white-faced, staggering against a tree trunk. 'Run – run the other way!' shouted Murray as he passed her and plunged after O'Connell.

Where were the others? But now Murray saw them break out from where they'd been hiding further back and to the right. He was in front of them and as he gathered speed O'Connell stopped, took aim and fired. The shot went wide and the

Irishman started running again, but he must have hurt his foot when he stumbled, for he'd slowed down and was limping. Murray sprinted down the hill, shouting at him to stop. He was gaining on him fast, but O'Connell was taking aim again. Murray fired first. O'Connell stumbled again and fell. His weapon shot out of his hand.

Now Murray had him at his mercy. He heard his men pelting down the hill behind him. O'Connell looked up at him, cringing. His expression was a mixture of malice and fear. 'You'll not be kicking a man when he's down.' His tone was almost wheedling. He winced as he moved. 'I think my ankle's broken. You can arrest me now. I'll come quietly. I don't have much choice.' Now there was a faint, lopsided grin on his face. 'I know when I'm beaten,' he said.

Murray shot him in the head.

Murray's officers backed up his story. The suspect had fired first. Murray's life had been threatened.

He'd walked back up the hill. Regine was still leaning against the tree where he'd left her.

'What happened? What happened?'

'He tried to shoot me. I had to return fire.' He put his arm round her and slowly they walked back the way they'd come, but when they reached Downshire Hill, she moved out of the circle of his arm.

'You killed him, didn't you.' She put her hand to her mouth. 'Oh God – I …' She didn't finish the sentence, but just stood staring. Finally she said: 'I need to be on my own. The shock …' She turned and walked slowly away up the road.

He started after her. 'Wait – please – Regine – '

She didn't turn, but made a gesture with her hand, as if pushing him away.

* * * * *

He telephoned her the next day to ask her when they could meet. He wanted to take her out to dinner, but she said it would be better if they just met for a drink and suggested a quiet, exclusive pub near St James's Square. It was near Noel Valentine's art gallery, she said.

He brought their drinks to the table where she was seated. Beer cost a packet here ... he'd never be able to keep her in the manner to which she was accustomed ...

'Thank you.' She smiled through the scrap of mesh veil that fell from the ridiculous little hat perched on her glowing curls.

He took her hand. 'You'll have read the official version in the papers,' he began.

She moved her hand away to loosen her astrakhan coat. 'Official version? Isn't – wasn't that what really happened?'

'Yes, of course, but – well – my boss wasn't pleased. He naturally wanted an arrest, a trial, a conviction. He feels a bit cheated. He feels a case is never properly closed until he's had the satisfaction of having it fully tested in the courts and reported in the press.'

Regine sipped her sherry. 'I'm so grateful for all you've done. It's such a tremendous relief – and yet I can't quite believe he's actually dead. You can't possibly know how terribly anxious I've been. But that wasn't quite what I expected.'

He slid closer to her. He wanted to put his arm round her. 'You do realise he had Buckingham murdered and then killed the man who did it?'

She nodded slowly.

'I had to do it,' he murmured, 'just think what a trial would have meant for you.'

It had been a result, but not the way Plumer had wanted. No gratifying headlines; no impressive appearance in the witness box. The execution of a suspect who'd resisted arrest was theoretically justifiable – just about – because he'd threatened the life of an officer and had fired the first shot; nevertheless a Chicago-style shoot-out between police and gangsters on Hampstead Heath was hardly the right sort of publicity. And even given the provocation, even given the fact that it could be passed off as accidental, it didn't look good for a copper to shoot a suspect. Plumer, instead of being wreathed in glory, had been quietly reprimanded. Plumer in turn blamed Murray for botching the arrest. Murray's promotion, already overdue, was doubtful. A tearful Irene had asked if that meant they couldn't afford to get married now. From Murray's point of view this was the only mitigating factor; he couldn't bear the thought of marrying the girl.

'I'm glad it ended the way it did for your sake,' he said and looked at Regine hungrily. She simply sat, expressionless, lost in thought. He went on: 'It looks bad, of course. My guv'nor's furious with me. It's got him in trouble with the high-ups. Me too – it certainly won't help my promotion.'

'I'm so sorry,' she said dully. Then she made an effort to rouse herself. 'But – why? You caught him. You solved the case.'

'Yes, but it's not how it should have been done. We won't get the credit in the way we should if there'd been a trial. In fact, it's rather the opposite: trigger-happy police mow down defenceless suspect.'

'It didn't come across like that in the papers.'

'Not in the papers you read, perhaps,' he said.

Murray wanted desperately to spell out to Regine what he'd done. Why didn't she understand? Couldn't she see the sacrifice he'd made, the risk he'd taken? 'You know, if it hadn't been for you – we were convinced it was Arthur Carnforth who'd killed your friend. If it hadn't been for you, we might not have stumbled on the truth.'

Regine seemed to make a great effort to pay attention. 'I should have come to you sooner,' she said, 'but I thought – hoped – he'd go away. He'd changed so much ... he wasn't like that before ... or perhaps he was really, all along ... disconcerting how different people can be from what you thought.'

'Disconcerting's hardly the word.' He hesitated. 'Am I different from what you thought at first?'

She looked at him, faintly surprised. Oh God – and he began to dread her answer. Because *she* was different now. She'd retreated. He began to realise that she'd never understand just what he'd done for her.

He'd shot O'Connell deliberately, in cold blood. For her: he'd saved her from the publicity of the trial. There'd be no femme fatale appearance of the bigamous wife in the witness box. The respectable civil servant's bogus marriage wouldn't be splashed across the pages of the *Daily Graphic* and the *News of the World*, Regine revealed as the wife of a blackmailing murderer.

Instead of spelling it out to her, he said abruptly: 'I'm thinking of leaving the force and going abroad.'

Regine's eyes widened at this stark announcement. But if he'd hoped she'd look distressed, even beg him not to go, he was bitterly disappointed.

'I might join the Hong Kong police,' he said. 'Everyone's travelled except me. I'm sick of London. I was stuck here all through the war. I want to see the world.'

'Why Hong Kong?'

'I don't know, really. Perhaps it was because of the way you talked about China. You made it sound very exotic. And it sounds as if there's a lot of crime to be solved out there.'

'Hong Kong would be much more staid and British than Shanghai,' she said.

He caught her hand again. The final throw: 'It would be so

wonderful – I know I can hardly expect to hope that … you are the most beautiful woman I've ever met … and I think you care a little for me too …'

He'd gone bright red; he knew he had. He stammered into silence.

She looked down for a long time. If only the silence could last for ever. So long as the silence lasted he still had hope.

At last she squeezed his hand, removed hers, smiled her sad, sweet, alluring smile. 'Oh Paul, if only I could, but you know it's impossible.'

And now the silence was horrible. At last he managed: 'I'll think of you when I'm out there.' Moments later he was watching her pull her astrakhan coat around her and he followed her with his gaze as she stepped elegantly across the lounge bar and disappeared into the night.

A week later a gardener from the big house found Carnforth's body.

It seemed to have been dark all day and what little light there was thickened into dusk as Plumer and Murray stumbled up the flight of steps to examine the spot from which, the pathologist pointed out, the dead man must have fallen. The temporary wooden palings had clearly broken away, but whether the death was accident, suicide or murder was impossible to say.

Murray stooped and picked at the remains of what might have been a cigarette stub. But the rain and damp had softened it and it disintegrated between his fingers. He brushed the fragments from his fingers and thought no more about it.

They retrieved the key to Carnforth's flat from his pockets. They drove to Handel Street and began their search.

They found an undated, unfinished letter to Vivienne.

They were not to know that it had been written before Charles had arranged the rendezvous at the garden. It ended with the words: 'I pray to Our Lord continually for strength, but I am finding life difficult without you. Please believe that what I did was only to protect you and Charles, but—'

It broke off at that point. For Plumer, though, it was evidence enough. Clearly their one-time chief suspect had topped himself.

thirty-five

REGINE WALKED UP TO THE Wentworth cottage. Alan answered the door. He greeted her cheerily. He'd long ago forgotten his failure to seduce her over lunch. 'You're looking wonderful as usual.' He helped her off with her coat. 'I'm meeting Noel for a pint, you women'll have the house to yourselves without the presence of the clodhopper male of the species.'

Dinah said: 'Cynthia's not here yet. She didn't want to come, but I made her. We simply have to talk about future arrangements. Oh, but there's the bell. That'll be her.'

Cynthia as yet had put on little weight, was still svelte and cool in her blue dress and grey coat. Dinah had made sandwiches, but Cynthia would only have a cup of coffee. She lit a cigarette. Regine found her friend's self-possession actually more worrying than a grim despair or hysterical anxiety.

Cynthia spoke levelly. 'Even before he resigned, Ernie and I had decided the only thing is for me to leave the department. As an unmarried woman I shan't be entitled to the benefits that – but of course if I were married, I'd have had to resign from the civil service anyway, pregnant or not. They are supposed to allow you to stay on if you're married now; the law was changed last year, but there's a lot of hostility. Life would be impossible.'

'What will you do?' Regine twisted her emerald ring. 'For money, I mean.' Perhaps she could persuade Neville to let her have a hundred pounds ... fifty at least ... if all else failed, her allowance ... the £20 she'd got for the French history ... She'd be earning a full-time salary after Christmas, but it wasn't a huge amount ...

'That's what we have to talk about,' said Dinah. 'I've got a plan. My parents have a cottage – it's on the little bit of land that goes with the house and it's empty. It could be made quite comfortable.'

'I thought your mother was so conservative,' said Regine, struggling with surprise and shameful resentment that Dinah had been so much more helpful to Cynthia than she had herself.

'Mother's changed, rather. Last Christmas – things were a bit difficult between Alan and me for a while – Alan was in a state because that friend of his was in such trouble – anyway, in the end I did talk to Mother, not about Alan, not directly, but I think she's more come round to my point of view about one or two things. I mean, she was brought up to think that men ruled the roost. I suppose that's at the bottom of her attitude to sex. That was your one little bit of power, if you could withhold that, turn it into a reward. It's horrid, really. But she's really pleased I'm at the Courtauld. She's all for education for women. It was Dad who was so against it. Anyway – the point is, she'd love to have you stay. As a matter of fact she'd love to have a baby to help look after. And it might stop her nagging me about grand-children for a while.'

'I can't accept charity, Dinah,' said Cynthia. To Regine, she seemed too composed. There was a steely obstinacy, but under-neath the brittle calm Regine was afraid she was close to break-ing point.

'It's not charity. We talked about that, you know we did.'

'Dinah,' said Cynthia in her cool, calm voice – how it must have soothed the minister – 'your father's a prominent barrister, famous even. Think of the publicity, if the truth got out. It would be so embarrassing.'

Dinah was determined. 'Nonsense. He's *agreed.* When the time comes you can go to the hospital in Southampton. After-wards you'll have time to think out what you want to do.'

'I'm going to keep the child.'

'Yes, well …'

'Ernie says with things as they are we can't really see much of each other at the moment. With the tribunal and all that there's no time for anything else. Afterwards … things may be different. But for now he can't afford to risk yet another scandal, so …'

Regine said angrily: 'But he's resigned now, anyway. And does he really think the hotel bill stuff won't come out? How'll he explain that? Will he at least be able to get his wife to pretend she was with him? He'd have to tell *her* the truth in that case.'

'He has told her – about us.' Cynthia still betrayed no emotion. 'He says she's forgiven him. But of course she wants him to give me up.'

Regine wondered if it would be better to be brutal. Someone had to make Cynthia see the truth. But it was blunt Dinah who said: 'It sounds as if he is. Giving you up.'

Cynthia flashed her a glance. But she said serenely: 'We'll see.' She looked at Regine. 'And when are you starting your new job?'

'In the New Year – and I don't think I'll have time to organ-ise my Sundays once I'm working full time.'

'Give up your Sundays!' said Dinah. 'Everyone will be so disappointed.'

'One can't go on doing the same thing for ever. Anyway, I think my Sundays have really had their day.'

She and Cynthia left together. 'Come back to Downshire Hill with me, for a bit, I don't like you going back to that flat all on your own now that—'

Cynthia smiled. 'Well, I am on my own. And I will be on my own. Perhaps in a way I always have been.'

Neville had come home early. 'Is that you, kitten?'

She'd braced herself for the talk they had to have. She needed a drink first – and it might be better if Neville was slightly squiffy. 'Neville, there's something we have to talk about.'

Neville sat in his chair by the fire, sucked his pipe, poured himself another glass of wine. He listened intently, as if she were explaining some difficult, abstract concept in a foreign language. She even confessed the lies about her family before stuttering to a halt. But she could not bring herself to broach the subject of sex.

Neville said: 'I know I'm not demonstrative, kitten, but I'd miss you a lot, you know, in fact I really don't know what I'd do without you.'

She'd expected disbelief and anger. His sadness was worse.

'Is it children? I always thought you agreed with me about the absurdity of reproducing oneself, but you might persuade me to change my mind about that.'

She shook her head.

'Is your life not fulfilling enough? Idle housewife syndrome? But you'll have your new publishing job in January.'

Freddie's death had started all this. She saw that now. Freddie had filled a void in her life so successfully she hadn't even noticed the void was there. Freddie had *distracted* her.

'I knew all along about your family, you know,' added Neville. 'You didn't ever imagine Freddie could keep a juicy little secret like that to himself, did you?'

That was what finally made her cry. Neville put an arm round her, kindly, fraternally, and passed her his large, snow-white handkerchief. 'Don't let's do anything hasty,' he said. 'Let's just let things settle down. It's all been so upsetting. You're really not yourself at the moment, kitten.'

thirty-six

FOR THE LAST TIME Charles trudged across the playing field and turned the key in the lock of the art annexe. It was risky, but he had to find the photo. Mr Tolliday and the headmaster had made a search of the annexe in an effort to find some clue as to Carnforth's disappearance. Later they'd searched a second time in the hope of finding an explanation for his suicide. The police had searched the place too, but if the photographs were there, they'd all missed them.

Charles assessed the scene. On a number of occasions, when painting the scenery, he'd nosed about. The only thing of interest he'd ever found was an ancient snapshot of his mother, which must have been taken before the war, before he was born most probably. Charles had wondered why Carnforth had kept it there instead of wherever he lived, but then it occurred to him that he might have made, or wanted to make, a copy from the print in the darkroom.

He'd found the photo when he'd noticed that a corner of the linoleum covering the concrete floor was detached and when he'd lifted it up, there was the photo. So now he looked in the same spot.

Freddie's photo of the two of them lay there, along with the snap of his mother. Charles lifted both prints between his fingers. He looked at the photo Freddie had taken. It was the only one he had of Freddie. But he hesitated only for a moment and then took both prints into the darkroom, put a match to them and held them over the butler sink until the flames nearly singed his fingers. He relit the scraps that had failed to burn the first time and then broke up the ash until it was small and powdery, turned on the tap and brushed the fragments down the plughole. He rinsed his hands under the running water and dried them on the towel Carnforth always kept there.

He switched out the lights, locked the door and walked away towards the goods entrance. He had thought the playing field was deserted, but then he heard the soft thud of footsteps coming up behind him. He swung round to see Harry Trevelyan trotting along behind.

'What are you doing here?'

Trevelyan was a little out of breath, but he smiled his endearing freckly smile – though the freckles were but a memory, since Charles couldn't see them in the dark.

'I might ask the same of you, Hallam. What were you doing in Carnforth's art annexe?' Something about the kid had subtly changed.

'I was looking for something that belonged to me. He'd taken something of mine and I needed it back, that's all.' He carried on walking, irritated by the younger boy's presence.

'It was awful, him dying like that, wasn't it.' Harry kept up with him easily; he'd grown too.

'Yes.'

'Perhaps you didn't mind too much, though.'

Charles ignored the remark.

Trevelyan did a little hop to get slightly ahead of Charles, then turned round and trotted backwards, facing him for a moment. 'I know what happened.'

'What happened about what?'

'I followed you. I followed you – more than once. After you chucked me.'

'What are you talking about? Anyway, I didn't chuck you. It was just that Carnforth smelt a rat.'

'I saw you and him walk up to Hampstead Heath that day and go into that garden.'

'Have you gone mad or something?' Despite himself, Charles tried to grab the boy, who skipped out of range.

'I shan't tell anyone. You needn't worry.'

'I don't think it's a good idea to threaten me, Trevelyan, in fact it's rather absurd.' Charles hoped his drawl sounded unconcerned.

'I'm not threatening you. It's just our secret, isn't it, you and me.'

'Get lost, Trevelyan.' They were near the goods entrance now. Charles stopped in his tracks. He turned to face Trevelyan full on. 'Get away from me. Just go. You're talking utter balls. You're talking through your hat. If you ever come near me again, I'll – I'll get you expelled if it's the last thing I do. Go away.'

Trevelyan didn't give ground. 'I'm not fibbing. I do know what happened. But I wouldn't ever tell anyone. I just want you to know that I know.' He laughed, an unnatural, high-pitched sound. 'It'll be our secret.'

'Bugger off. Or I'll kill you.' Charles feinted a lunge towards the boy and grinned in the darkness. That had frightened the boy. He could tell. *He really believes I'd do it. He knows I've killed one man already.*

Now the boy did scamper away. Charles walked on slowly. His thoughts were churning as he opened and shut the goods entrance gate. He took the key to the art annexe from his pocket, wiped it carefully with his handkerchief and, looking round to make sure the coast was clear, chucked it down a drain as he passed it. No one saw him. Trevelyan had vanished. The road was shrouded in fog.

epilogue

H EAT PULVERISED THE CAMPO. The sun's glare bleached the paving stones and flaking walls. The tall houses leaned stiflingly inwards so that the square felt like a roofless room. Regine was weighed down by the heat as were the pale cat, stretched out on the cobbles, and the two old ladies on a bench beneath the single withered tree.

When two men entered the square, their footsteps shattered the somnolence. Their voices ripped the motionless air. They bore down on the café where Regine was idling away the afternoon.

It was only the movement he made as he sank into the plastic chair that aroused a long-forgotten memory, for his long dark curls and lean, tanned face bore little resemblance to how he'd once been. If she'd passed him in one of the *calle* or in some square crowded with tourists she wouldn't have recognised him, looking like so many others in his hippie flares, collarless shirt and bead necklaces, but that careless, lazy movement and those heavy-lidded eyes …

She stared at him so hard that he looked up. She saw, from the expression that flickered across his face, that he at least half-recognised her too, but his gaze shied away again, as if he'd decided the encounter wouldn't be worth the effort.

She, though, as always, automatically smiled, reaching out and offering her warmth. 'It is – isn't it – Charles Hallam?'

He half-rose from his seat in a gesture of politeness. '*Regine*. Christ! What an amazing – How are you? What are you doing here?'

'I'm waiting for my daughter – she went off to try and find a little hat shop we'd seen. She's probably lost by now – impossible to find your way around Venice, isn't it, we're always getting lost.'

'Well – ' and he smiled at his friend, 'you work it out eventually – it does have a logic of its own. Took me six months though.'

His friend said something in Italian.

'Sorry – this is Renato.'

Regine didn't entirely like the look of Renato. His weaselly face was not improved by a straggly little beard and his straight blond hair was even longer than Charles's, giving him that rather awful Jesus Christ look so many young men went for now – Pre-Raphaelites on the cheap.

'I'm living here at the moment.'

'Here? In Venice? I thought you were teaching at Oxford.'

'Oh, I chucked that up ages ago. Oxford was so bloody stuffy. I couldn't stand it any longer.'

'Is that why you didn't write another book? Everyone thought your first was so good.'

'Of course – you married my publisher. How is William?'

'We're not together any more.' No need to tell the whole story. 'These days, well, recently I met an old flame. He's back at the hotel. The heat of the day's too much for him. He likes his siesta.'

Charles was obviously not very interested. But she knew why she'd had to say it – to show him she wasn't a woman on her own, that she still had a man.

An awkwardness came between them. After the silence had lasted too long, Charles said: 'I meant to write another book, but writing's such a chore. And anyway I don't have time to write out here – it's wall-to-wall politics in Italy, so much going on.'

Renato pulled at the whiskers round his lips and frowned. Charles spoke to him in Italian. She prided herself on at least understanding Italian, even if she hardly spoke it, but she couldn't catch the words. Charles's hand was on the other man's thigh. 'Italian politics – shit, man, it's something else, isn't it. *Lotta Continua* – the Red Brigades – '

Regine smiled, but it seemed … *wrong*, somehow, for a man his age – what would he be now – getting on for forty? – to behave like some student revolutionary.

The waiter sauntered out from the cavern of the café and Charles looked up at him, ordering *due birre*, flirting with the boy before turning back to Regine. 'Anyway, how *are* you? You're looking wonderful.'

She smiled harder, but she knew that her hair was now brighter than it had ever been, too bright, thanks to henna, while her skin had faded to dry, freckly middle age.

'I'm well – I'm just here on holiday with my daughter and my … friend.' Which was true, yet not quite one hundred per cent of the truth.

There was another little silence. To break it, she said: 'So you're actually living here. I envy you. Venice is so beautiful.' Such a cliché, but what could you say about Venice that hadn't been said a thousand times?

He smiled, but it was an empty smile. There was dead space between them. The vacuum of the afternoon. The cat was giving herself a dust bath, rolling over and back again on the uneven pavement.

Then suddenly Charles spoke. 'Freddie always used to say he'd take me to Venice one day.'